WHEN
SHADOWS
FALL

WHEN SHADOWS FALL

BOOK THREE OF THE DARK SUN DAWN TRILOGY

Stephen Zimmer

SEVENTH STAR PRESS

Cover art: Bonnie Wasson
Cover art in this book copyright © 2019 Bonnie Wasson & Seventh Star
Press, LLC.

Editor: Holly Phillippe
Published by Seventh Star Press, LLC.

ISBN Number 978-1-948042-90-1

Seventh Star Press
www.seventhstarpress.com
info@seventhstarpress.com

Publisher's Note:
When Shadows Fall is a work of fiction. All names, characters, and places
are the product of the author's imagination, used in fictitious manner.
Any resemblances to actual persons, places, locales, events, etc. are purely
coincidental.

Printed in the United States of America

First Edition

ACKNOWLEDGEMENTS

My love and gratitude to my beloved Holly Phillippe, a warrior herself who walks at my side during this unusual journey I have taken. I deeply appreciate her work on this novel in the capacity of being an editor and helping me to see the kinds of things that sometimes you cannot see as the creator of a literary work.

I am honored and thankful to have Bonnie Wasson as the cover artist for the first editions of the Dark Sun Dawn Trilogy. She captures the spirit of Rayden Valkyrie in her art and truly makes magic visually.

I want to thank my mother and father. Though they are departed from this world in a physical sense, I carry both of them in my heart always. Their love, encouragement, and support is felt in my heart every day, and I know that they would both love this novel and the trilogy..

Finally, I would like to thank my dear readers, without whom I could not be an author and take the road that I have taken. Your faith, support, and enthusiasm helps me to endure the trials involved during the writer's journey. It is my wish that you always find something to inspire and uplift you within the pages of my work. Onward and Upward!

DEDICATION

To the One Whose Light will reign forevermore.

To my mother and father, for guiding and preparing me in a world where shadows yet dwell.

To my beloved Holly, who stands with me steadfast against the shadows.

To my sister, who shows that the love of family can bring about the fall of shadows.

CHAPTER 1

Summoning to the ravens' feast, screams hailed the rippling lightning, booming thunder shaking the air under the glow of a blood-red moon.

Then, shadows began raining downward, falling upon the land within a growing maw of darkness.

Sweat beading across her brow and heart beating fast, Rayden opened her eyes. Within the gloom, the scene of a pair of figures strolling among flowering trees met her gaze. The details of the fresco difficult to make out within the dim ambience, the sight of the wall and images painted upon it testified to an end of the prolonged nightmare.

Faint rolls of thunder sounded in the distance, marking the end of the fading storm that had battered the Imperial City throughout the long night.

Rolling onto her back and taking a few deep, cleansing breaths of air into her lungs, Rayden thought about the previous day.

Memories of her first experiences within the Imperial City flowed through her mind, the recollections vivid and striking.

***

An ox-pulled cart trundled along the stone-surfaced roadway, the wheels rolling within grooves carved through the passage of high volumes of traffic, across an abundance of years.

An older man walked just ahead of the cart, a narrow wood staff in his right hand. A younger man, with facial features echoing those of the older, tended to the cart and oxen.

Off in the distance, the rumble of thunder sounded, signaling the storm now encroaching upon the outskirts of the city. Before much longer, the black clouds would be draped over the city. An assault of wind, rain, and lightning loomed nigh.

At the moment, sunlight still beamed down through silken blue skies. Breezes had begun to pick up, the tendrils of air carrying hints of the rain that would soon be falling.

Just ahead, a gateway into the Imperial City loomed. Two grand arches stood open beneath a high architrave covered with inscriptions. Atop the architrave, a robed figure of gold stood.

Staring unblinking, facing the north, the man depicted had a proud, defiant bearing. A wreath of laurel curling about his head, the gleaming figure maintained an unwavering, silent vigil.

Posed with arms raised high, the left hand grasping a spear and the right open, the man had the air of a warrior and conqueror.

After the ox cart had rolled past them, Polybius remarked, "The Imperator himself greets us to his great city."

"I wish that he would be here to greet us himself," Crassor replied in a low, gruff voice. "Then we could bring all of this to an end much sooner."

"Best keep such thoughts quiet," Polybius countered. "We will soon be among a host of ears and whispering tongues."

"I am Alettani," Doros declared with a smirk, referencing the northern tribe that had allied with the Teverens.

Crassor glowered at Polybius and Doros. "I know. We all have our guises. I just needed to get that off my tongue in the last few moments we have to speak our minds."

"When we are alone, we can speak our minds a little more openly," Polybius said, glancing toward Crassor with a hint of concern on his face. "For now, it is time to perform our roles."

"You need not worry," Crassor grumbled in reply to him.

Drawing closer to the gates, a realization came over Rayden. She had seen the man represented by the golden sculpture before, in the midst of a dream where she had witnessed an army marching through crowded streets during a triumphal procession.

Keeping the recognition to herself, Rayden turned her attention to the city's great walls.

Rayden eyed the robust square towers flanking the double-arch gateway. With small, arched windows set high and a crenellated top, the protruding towers protected the prominent entrance well enough.

Any force reaching the thick, iron-banded gates would be exposed to projectiles and missiles from both sides and above.

A few helmed Teveren guards stood watch about the entrance. Most had the disinterested air of soldiers assigned to a dull and unwanted task; save for a young-looking one who had a more focused expression while engaging those entering or leaving.

Thunder rolled again off to the south, heralding the incoming storm.

"It looks like we reached the city just in time," Polybius announced to the guard in an amiable manner. "That storm looks like it will be a rough one."

"What is your business in the Imperial City?" the guard asked Polybius, ignoring his comments.

"I have undertaken great risk to come here, to make arrangements for my trade concerns affected by all the upheaval in the north," Polybius replied to the guard.

"Peronnius and Marus will have the barbarians crushed to bits soon enough," the soldier responded, eyeing Rayden, Doros, and Crassor. "Who comes with you? They look much like the barbarians we are facing."

"The big one is my personal slave," Polybius replied. "The other two are friends of mine, from the Alettani, loyal allies of the Teveren Empire. They agreed to escort me here and help me to avoid any scouting or foraging parties of the enemy. I can assure you that both took great risk to help a Teveren wine merchant."

The guard stared at Rayden and Doros for several long moments. Finally, he turned his eyes back to Polybius.

"Proceed and may your business in the Imperial City go well."

"Thank you," Polybius replied, nodding to the guard.

Starting forward, Polybius crossed through the gates with the others following behind.

Beyond the gateway, Rayden slowed her pace, taking in her first unobstructed sights from close proximity of the Imperial City; a city like none that she had ever set her eyes upon, in all her life.

"It is a sight to behold," Polybius commented, looking toward Rayden. "I still remember the first time that I set foot into this city."

"It is like gods built all of this!" Doros exclaimed in a tone of awe, looking all around her.

"No, it is what men and women can do if they have the will for it," Rayden commented, her eyes shining with amazement. "Minds set to greater purpose are capable of wonders."

Another wave of thunder broke out, this time sounding louder and nearer.

"Best we get moving to where we can secure a suitable place to reside," Polybius stated, walking forward.

"I have no desire to be out here when that storm breaks," Rayden agreed, walking along Polybius' side, with Crassor and Doros following close behind.

Rayden gazed down a broad, stone-paved street flanked with a grand colonnade on each side. Placed along the center at even intervals, plinths and columns, fashioned of marble or stone, supported a variety of detailed statuary.

Depicting majestic and heroic-looking figures, the statues had been created in a variety of different materials, whether bronze, stone, marble, or, in the case of a couple of them, gold.

About midway down the broad thoroughfare, a mythical beast spouted a continuous stream of water from its open maw. The water tumbled down in a sparkling cascade, plunging into a broad pool encompassing the statue's base.

Intermingled with the majority Teverens, people from a wide range of lands strolled along the stone-inlaid street. By their distinctive dress, adornments, and ethnicity, Rayden recognized several individuals who had come from the Mystic Kingdom. Others within the polyglot crowds hailed from lands under Kartajen control, Griaca, places farther to the north, eastern lands, and even a few unfamiliar to her.

Many languages reached her ears. The scents of exotic perfumes, burning wood, and flowers mixed with the noxious aromas of body odor, animal dung, urine, and other less pleasant sources.

Looking up, Rayden could make out several prominent hills in the distance, the rises crowned with grand temples or majestic-looking edifices that she judged to be palaces.

"Is the whole city like this?" Rayden asked Polybius.

"No, it is just that we entered near an area of higher status," Polybius replied. "We have more than enough in coins to provide for our comforts while we are in the city."

Beyond the end of the street, they walked along the edge

of a sprawling park. Flowering trees provided shade throughout lush expanses of grass, interspersed with fountains and small ponds brimming with glittering, crystal clear waters.

Leisure and opulence intertwined in a flowing, harmonious atmosphere, enjoyed by a wide array of Teveren citizens.

Once they had walked past the park, Polybius guided them onto a narrow street with a hard-packed dirt surface. Tall structures loomed on both sides, casting the street in a cool shade that Rayden welcomed after traveling in direct sunlight since morning.

Tilting her head upward, Rayden counted four levels on the structures flanking the street.

A tall, burly man with a shaved head and broad face covered in thick gray stubble stood attentive at the entrance to a doorway. He wore a knee-length tunic tied about the waist with a leather belt, with sandals on his feet.

Though past his physical prime, the man's brawny limbs and wide shoulders gave an unmistakable hint that he possessed more than enough strength to be regarded in a serious manner.

After telling the others to wait for him, Polybius walked straight up to the doorman and spoke with him for a few moments. The doorman then turned and took him inside.

"I wonder what he is up to," Doros said, eyeing the people walking past them in the street.

"A matter of our accommodations, I think," Crassor replied.

"A guarded door?" Doros asked.

"Means that these are not dwelling places for those of low means," Crassor answered her.

While listening to her companions, Rayden continued to watch the crowds.

Slaves bearing a curtained litter, a man carrying an armload of wood planks, an older man cradling a wax tablet, and a young woman in a long, plain tunic, carrying a small jar, were but a few of the distinctive sights within the steady flow of humankind.

Resembling a bright flock of birds, a cluster of women shuffled by wearing finer, colorful attire, shawls covering their heads and worn atop a tunic-like garment descending to the ankles. Rayden caught a staunch whiff of flowery perfumes and oils from the nearest of them.

With all of their faces painted thoroughly in various hues of makeup, and shining pieces of jewelry adorning their necks, arms, and ears, there could be little mistaking the higher-level status of the women.

A quartet of stout-looking slaves trudged by a few moments later, manning poles that supported a chair where a well-dressed man of about forty years sat with a haughty expression etched upon his face. Casting a few glances about, he caught Rayden's eyes for a moment.

While his countenance remained unchanged, his eyes began churning with a desirous luster, but the slaves carried him onward before he made any unwanted overtures.

When Polybius finally emerged from the doorway, he called Rayden and the others over to him.

"The gods have us in their favor today," he announced when they neared. "An assistant to a member of the Imperial Council was caught knee-deep in graft. The scoundrel and those with him were expelled from their apartments, leaving an opening for us to take, including furnishings! Come, let us go inside and I will show you our quarters."

Keeping a stern expression, the doorman stepped aside to allow the group entrance.

The doorway led into a narrow hall that culminated at the base of a flight of wooden steps. Set in the corner where they turned to go up the staircase, a large vessel stood.

Rayden wrinkled her nose at the pungent stench of urine coming from inside it.

After climbing two flights of steps, Polybius took the others down a short walkway, proceeding to a wooden door where came to a stop. Fitting a key into a lock, he opened the door.

"Second floor apartments would be a little more lavish, however, this will serve our purposes well-enough, and still leave us plenty to use in the city," Polybius announced to the others, grinning wide.

"Far better than staying at any inn or tavern," Rayden replied, a smile rising on her own face.

A copper oil lamp burning inside, presumably lit when the doorman showed Polybius the available space, illuminated a square area with a curtain draped across the back and openings leading into rooms on either side. A black and white mosaic floor, consisting of alternating diamond-shaped tiles, lay beneath their feet.

In the room to the right, a table, chair, a couple of wooden stools, and a small rectangular chest had been arranged in an order suitable for conducting business. On the table, a few sheets of blank parchment, a vessel of ink, and a feather quill rested.

"I have not written in quite some time," Polybius remarked, eyeing the writing implements. "I may have to put all of this to use."

"Something I have long wanted to learn," Rayden commented, a little melancholic. "To put the words I speak into symbols that others can understand ... it is like a kind of magic."

"When all of this is over, I would be glad to show you how to do it," Polybius told her, smiling.

"To be able to store the words that we speak," Rayden stated, eyeing the blank parchments. "It is an incredible knowledge."

"Yes, it truly is," Polybius replied.

"My belly has more interest in the other room," Crassor remarked, striding away.

The room to the left had been set up as a kitchen and eating area. A round wooden table with several stools situated around its circumference occupied a large portion of the floor.

Wooden planks on the wall to the right within the kitchen space had been fitted with extending nails, from which pitchers, pans, canvas bags for holding food, ladles, and other cooking implements had been hung. Aligned with a small, shuttered window set higher up the same wall, a square brazier made of solid bronze squatted on the floor.

"One visit to the market and we have everything we need here to make our own feast," Polybius commented, looking over the assorted items.

Past the large curtain serving as the back of the entry area, a short hallway contained doorways to three rooms; one set at the far end, and one to each side.

All three rooms had beds of low wooden frames set with feather-stuffed mattresses. Topped with coverings of softer linen and provided with feather-stuffed cushions, the beds offered invitations to comfort and a restful sleep.

"Should we decide through dice, the picking of straws, or will two of us share a room?" Polybius asked the others, when they had finished viewing the last room.

Rayden pressed the fingers of her right hand into the smooth, pliant surface of a bed cushion. She could barely imagine how pleasant it would feel to lay her head against it for an entire night.

"You can take the rooms," Rayden stated to the other three. "It is good enough for me to have shelter and a place to call our own for a little while."

"No, you have given far enough of yourself Rayden," Crassor replied in a firm voice. "I will not argue this. You, Polybius, and Doros take the beds, but I want my own mattress."

"It is unacceptable to me for you not to have a room to call your own," Doros added, eyeing Rayden from where she had been crouching and taking a closer assessment of a bed.

"I insist that you take a room as well," Polybius added. "The rest of us are in unanimous agreement."

Rayden grinned. "Enough of this uprising. I will accept a room."

"A mattress on the ground in the front area will be like the bed of a king for me," Crassor stated. "A straw-stuffed pallet will be fine and will cost little."

"A much more comfortable one will not cost too much for concern," Polybius told Crassor. "I will speak with the doorman on the matter and have it taken care of."

Rayden chose the room at the end of the hall.

In addition to the bed, the room contained a small stool, a large bowl for collecting bodily waste, a timber chest, and a small window to the outside. The walls had been decorated in beautiful scenery, the frescoes making use of a vivid array of colors that could not truly be appreciated in the dimmer ambience.

Opening the shutters on the window, Rayden peered outward. A spectacular view of the city lay before her eyes. Rolling overhead and pushing onward, the dark skies that she and her companions had espied in the distance now covered the city.

The sharp line of demarcation between the bright, sunlit region farther away and the advancing shadow-filled territory under menacing storm clouds created a surreal atmosphere to behold. The stark contrast captivated Rayden and held her attention for several lingering moments.

Watching the forefront of the dark cloud mass creeping across the city, she could see the color leaching from everything beneath as it fell into shadow. Growing louder and carrying an edge of defiance, thunder rumbled across the skies within the dark formations.

Off in the distance, Rayden could see the walls and towers warding the northern boundary of the city. Over to the right, the greatest of the hills within the walls had been crowned with the Imperator's sprawling palace complex.

A broad, multi-level facade exhibiting arcades and galleries hinted of opulence on a scale that Rayden found difficult to comprehend. Around and beneath the prominent structure, an array of other buildings and walled enclosures stood, several of them impressive edifices in their own rights.

Not far from the throng of palace buildings rose a majestic temple, the lofty building's front portico supported on towering columns of white marble.

Somewhere within the palace dwelled the man they had come to overthrow; a man whose likeness had been rendered in the golden statue presiding over the gate they had arrived through.

Pulling away from the striking outer view at last, Rayden rejoined her companions at the front of their quarters. After a little deliberation, they agreed to put their thoughts to eating and resting up.

With the storm looming even closer, none of them voiced any pressing inclination to explore the city. The growls of thunder served to dissuade any temptations.

Polybius and Crassor left the apartments to address the need for another mattress and scrounge up a few things for everyone to eat. Staying back in the apartments, Rayden and Doros rested for a little longer, content to try the beds in their rooms.

Polybius and Crassor returned with pouches full of bread, olives, figs, and goat-milk cheese. Crassor carried a roasted chicken wrapped in cloth. The tantalizing scent of the cooked meat caused Rayden's mouth to water.

All of the victuals had been procured from an inn located close by. A small amphora of wine that Polybius also purchased at the inn served to slake their thirst, though Rayden found it to be much more watered down than she liked.

Rain began falling by the time a mattress had been secured for Crassor. Similar in type to the ones found in the bedframes within the other rooms, the porters set the mattress down on the floor a few paces inside the entrance at Polybius' instructions.

Not long after the porters had left, the storm that had been building throughout the day broke out in full force across the city.

Beneath the churning underbelly of the black cloud mass covering the skies, wind and rain lashed the city without respite. Splitting into brilliant rivulets spanning from sky to ground, jagged bolts of lightning lanced downward all over the area.

Deafening booms of thunder shook the air like the war cries of a furious god. Massive waves of lightning rippled through the clouds, illuminating the vast city below.

Howling in fury, surging gusts of wind battered the plaster-coated brick wall of the tenement, eliciting creaks and groans throughout the timber elements of its inner skeleton. Filling Rayden's ears between the periodic eruptions of thunder, the robust air currents whipped the pelting rain in towering sheets against the tenement.

Chancing a few glimpses from time to time through the window of her room, Rayden could not recall witnessing a more violent storm. Paying for each view of the storm with a harsh face-full of the frigid rain, she could not refrain from looking upon it.

Rayden and the others had come to the city to seek answers and gain all possible insights that would be of use to the approaching northern horde.

With the storm yet raging outside, Rayden undid the high laces of her sandals and set them to the side. Preparing to get some rest, she took off her knee-length primary tunic, leaving the creme-colored woolen undertunic beneath on.

Slipping under the coverings on the bed, a sigh escaped her lips as she lay her head upon the soft cushion. Sinking into its embrace, Rayden stretched her legs out, settling on the mattress.

Fatigue had accumulated to the point that her eyelids grew heavy before she had a chance to examine the frescoes surrounding her on the walls. Amid the cacophony of blasting thunder, flaring lightning, roaring wind, and thrashing rain, Rayden's eyes fluttered shut and remained closed, deep into the night.

Only then did dreams of a blood moon and falling shadows come to her.

***

Dense masses of fog ebbed and dispersed in the morning light, revealing the city they had cloaked and pronouncing the arrival of a new day.

Dawn brought along clear blue skies and a brilliant sunrise, making it difficult to think that a massive storm had pounded the city without any letup just the night before. Gazing toward the palatial structures on the hilltop to the north and east, Rayden harbored a nagging eagerness to begin exploring the massive city.

A light repast of bread, cheese, and some olives, accompanied with a cup of wine, sufficed to placate her appetite. Dressed and with her sandals laced up snug, Rayden stood in the entrance area and waited for the others to join her.

Growing impatient, Rayden rounded up the others, not wanting to waste any more time in setting out from the tenement. Doros, Crassor, and Polybius gave her no resistance. All of her companions displayed great enthusiasm toward the day's imminent foray.

Having gained a solid rest despite the raging storm and later nightmares that had caused her to awaken earlier than she needed to, Rayden had a bounce to her step when they set foot into the streets.

Assuming the guise of a Teveren citizen of means, Polybius

took the lead of the quartet. Crassor, posing as his personal slave, strode just behind him.

Rayden and Doros walked together, keeping close to the other two so that they would not be separated within the dense pedestrian traffic.

They had not gone far when Polybius took advantage of a ground-level shop to get a hair trim and shave. Using only a blade and water, the barber removed the stubble-formed shadow that had manifested on his face. A short trim and combing forward of Polybius' hair completed a look common among Teveren males.

"I look a little more suitable for presenting myself to those of means," he remarked, when he had emerged from the shop.

The extensive rainfall and a constant stream of footsteps had muddied the unpaved, narrower streets that they trod upon. Holding a few slicker spots, the softened ground proved more treacherous in some places, especially within stretches of inclines or declines along the meandering streets.

Divots, pockets, and wheel tracks in the ground had collected water from the storm, including a few puddles large enough to engulf a foot. Rayden heard more than one loud curse erupt as people unwittingly stepped into the puddles and splashed those near them within the congested environs.

Rayden and Doros kept their footing well-enough on the dampened surfacing. Polybius slipped once on the slick muck, though Crassor's quick reflexes kept him from falling to the ground and splattering his clothing in the mud.

Eyeing the open-faced establishments on the ground level, Rayden heard the telltale metallic strikes of a hammer coming from inside a coppersmith's workshop. In front of another shop stood tables covered in baskets and canvas sacks filled with various kinds of nuts and dried fruit.

Shop after shop contained the wares of skillful artisans, foodstuffs, fabrics, and all other manner of goods. Before long,

Rayden began to doubt that a person could fail to find anything they wanted among the extensive array of offering from the various artisans and merchants.

Entering an area of even taller buildings, Rayden counted as many as six or seven levels on some of the towering edifices they passed. The sight of a massive pile of wood and rubble, where one of the high buildings had collapsed in a heap, lowered her confidence in the vitality of the lofty structures.

The winding streets often proved far too narrow for the great volume of traffic now moving through them. Shopkeepers placing stands or stalls in front of their establishments created choke points in many places, drawing forward movement to a standstill.

The inconvenience sparked higher levels of irritation among those striving to get through. Those on litters or accompanied by multiple slaves forced their way through, showing no regard for those in the way.

Needing no urging from their masters or mistresses, the slaves unceremoniously shoved the people in their path aside in the manner of a routine act. A few of the jostled pedestrians took offense and protested, but it did nothing to deter the slaves from advancing through the street.

Bearing up a front pole segment, supporting a cushioned chair with a heavy-set, well-dressed man seated upon it, a brawny, thick-bearded slave approached from behind. Looking Griacan in origin, the large man made the mistake of giving Rayden a hard shove with his shoulder.

"Out of the way now, woman!" the slave exclaimed in a barking tone.

Had he not spoken in such a manner, Rayden might have let the incident pass.

His boorish attitude compelled a response.

With a short, quick sweep of her left leg, Rayden tripped the slave up, sending the chair and its rotund occupant toppling to the ground in a disheveled heap.

Without changing expression, Rayden continued onward.

Looking back to the commotion and then over to Rayden, Polybius asked her, "What happened?"

Rayden shrugged. "One of the bearers lost his balance, I think."

"Lost his wits, you mean," Doros commented with a smirk. "I heard."

Rayden grinned and shrugged again. Behind them, the portly man from the chair, his fine clothes now smeared all over in mud, had begun hurling a stream of curses at his bearers.

"Let us try not attracting too much attention," Crassor remarked, looking unamused at the fracas.

Rayden glanced at the frowning man and laughed. "I think that is one of the first times I have heard you counsel caution."

After a moment, a grin broke across Crassor's somber face and he shook his head. "Maybe I have spent too much time around you."

"I am afraid we will have to remain together for a little while longer," Rayden responded in a lighthearted manner.

"Not a bad tiding," Crassor replied, his expression and tone filled with sincerity.

"Since it is so, we should drink tonight," Rayden suggested. "We can find out what this city really has to offer."

"After we take care of some business," Polybius said.

"Yes, afterward, of course," Rayden replied, fixing her gaze on him. "You forget, Polybius, even when I drink, I do not lower my guard."

***

Rayden and her companions passed the better part of the day walking about the city.

Before midday they partook of some wine and a light meal consisting of fish, olives, figs, and some cheese.

In the early part of the afternoon, Polybius took them into a long, open space surfaced with tiled stone and lined with colonnades. Containing several exquisite pieces of statuary atop splendid columns and a couple of magnificent fountains, the place held a large crowd of people.

Predominantly men, they milled about in pairs or small groups, engaged in a variety of conversations.

Bordering the huge space and elevated high above the multitude were the facades of several temples and other grand buildings.

Two particularly impressive edifices beckoned from the far end of the vast space. Both multi-level structures harboring a series of arcades supported on columns of white marble, each had a wide flight of steps leading up to their entrances.

Staring at the gleaming white buildings, Rayden asked Polybius, "What takes place there?"

"Places of judgment for disputes and crimes in the city," Polybius answered. "Many come just to watch the deliberations."

A large number of those strolling about the area looked toward Rayden and Doros with heightened curiosity. Polybius exchanged pleasantries with many of those they passed by, leading to a few halts for extended conversations.

Each time the men that Polybius spoke with expressed interest in his pursuits and the nature of his companions. Polybius' tale of being a wine merchant from the north, traveling through dangerous territory with friends who belonged to the tribes allied to the Teveren Empire, appeared to spark keen interest in the others.

After the fourth lengthy interaction, Rayden began to get restless. There seemed to be no purpose to the exchanges other than mere casual conversation.

By the time they left the area, Polybius looked to be in a buoyant mood. Finding his uplifted demeanor perplexing, Rayden drew close to him.

"What is being done here?" Rayden asked him in a low voice, wondering why they had spent so much time talking when they could have been getting a look at other parts of the city.

"By tomorrow, I will have gained us an invitation to dinner in the home of someone with influence and power here," Polybius declared. "It will give you a chance to get closer to the power that underlies this city. Perhaps you can make use of what you learn."

Understanding Polybius' purpose at once, a smile crossed Rayden's face. "I would find that very useful."

"I assure you, it will be," Polybius replied.

CHAPTER 2

After another night of solid rest, Rayden and the others headed into the city after the early morning fog lifted. Patches of clouds drifting in a slow procession overhead, a few of them light gray, no threats of rain loomed imminent.

Walking along the same streets as the day prior, Rayden found herself recognizing a few places. A skilled potter of earthenware vessels marked the end of one street, while a wood carver displaying a wide array of figurines served as the centerpiece of the next.

A seller of perfumes that were contained in beautiful little vials in the shapes of humans and various creatures heralded a crossing where they had found the tavern to take a light, midday meal.

Among the merchants and artisans that they passed, Rayden slowed to a halt when she espied the workshop of a ropemaker. She admonished herself for not seeing it the day before.

"Give me just a few moments here!" Rayden called ahead to Polybius and Crassor, her voice loud enough to carry over the bustling traffic.

Both men turned back to follow Rayden and Doros.

Rayden and her companions shouldered their way through the crowd, making their way to the forefront of the ropemaker's shop. A short, stocky man in a light brown tunic greeted them as Rayden set her eyes on the hempen lengths coiled upon the tables.

"As strong as you will find in all the Imperial City," he proclaimed with a proud air. "I use the strongest hemp in the land for my ropes, whether you are constructing a building, going to sea, or working any other task where you need strong, dependable rope."

"I am in need of a dependable rope, and a good length of it too," Rayden stated. "For the hauling of significant weight up or down a fair height."

"For construction then," the man replied, nodding with a knowing expression.

Without delay, he walked over toward a table with several larger coils on it. Abruptly, he kicked at something behind the table.

"Get out of here, you bastards!" he yelled at the unseen offenders. Looking back up to Rayden, he composed himself swiftly.

An edge of irritation clung to his voice as he stated, "The damnable rats. The city is infested with the vermin these days."

"Where they go, disease often follows," Rayden told him.

"A fear many have," the ropemaker replied. "But you kill one and ten more take its place. I have never seen this many before."

"Maybe Teverens should bring more cats into the city," Rayden said. "I have seen a few scampering about the temples in the city."

"They have free reign of the temples, and they do not stink like the weasels so many keep, but I fear they are vastly outnumbered too," the ropemaker replied. He then shook his head, "But you did not come to me to speak of cats, rats, and the reek of weasels. Let me help you find a suitable rope."

The ropemaker showed Rayden a few coils until she settled upon one propitious for climbing that had the kind of length she sought.

She then turned aside to Polybius.

"I know little of Teveren prices for rope," Rayden told him. "You know what is more reasonable." Nodding, Polybius turned to the ropemaker and conducted the transaction. After a little haggling, the two men agreed on a price. Lifting his coin pouch, Polybius counted out the agreed upon price and placed the payment in the ropemaker's hands.

Bidding the ropemaker well, Rayden took up the new coil of rope and continued onward. A little farther down, she had Polybius buy a hide pack large enough to hold the rope in.

"What is the for?" Doros asked her when they proceeded onward.

"A means out of the city, on my terms, when the need arises," Rayden answered her, shouldering the hide pack.

Drawing nearer to the great hill where the Imperial palace buildings were located, Rayden took immediate interest in what looked to be a fortress adjacent to the rise, just to the south of it. From a higher vantage on the hilly streets they walked along, she gained a solid view of the apparent stronghold.

A long stretch of the city walls formed the front of the fortress, with three walls beyond warding its outer boundaries. Small square towers at even intervals ran along the three outer walls, and one prominent gate on the eastern wall allowed entry from outside of the city.

A broad gateway gave access from the shared city wall to the stronghold's interior. The tops of many elongated buildings, most of them grouped into concise quadrants, could be seen beyond the walls. An expanse of clear ground occupied the southeast portion of the fortress.

"A large fortress, attached to the city?" Doros queried.

"Teveren legions are not quartered in the city, but a legion dedicated to the Imperator resides there," Polybius commented. "The Imperial Guard assists with many functions, serving to protect the Imperial Council, magistrates, and others of higher position, though you will not see them in armor, helms, or carrying weapons openly when they are conducting many of their duties."

"That fortress looks like it can hold more than one legion within it," Rayden said, assessing the magnitude of the space.

"I am sure that it does," Polybius replied. "But it has not been used to quarter anything more than the Imperator's legion, the Imperial Guard."

"It is set in a good position to help defend the Imperator's palace buildings and the large temple on the hill," Rayden observed.

"Then we need to learn what we can about it," Crassor stated.

"It is why we are here, inside the city," Rayden replied. "To learn as much as we can about everything."

"Should we continue onward and see more of the city now?" Polybius asked, looking toward Rayden.

"I want to keep my eyes on this place for a little while longer," Rayden said, eyeing the fortress.

"It is an ideal time for me to seek an invitation for all of us, to attend a feast tonight in the home of someone influential," Polybius told her.

"Seek the invitation," Rayden replied. "Doros and I can find our way back to our quarters. You need not worry about us."

"Then let us gather again, at the tenement, just after midday," Polybius responded. "That should give me plenty of time to gain us an invitation."

"We will see you then," Rayden responded.

Polybius and Crassor took leave of Doros and Rayden.

Rayden thought back to the crowded open space with the

prominent temples and buildings situated around its perimeter that they had visited the previous day.Polybius was far more suited for that kind of atmosphere, and she had little doubt that he would succeed in his aims.

After Polybius and Crassor had walked away, Rayden and Doros returned their attention to the fortress and the steady flow of activity taking place around it.

Gleaning everything that she could, Rayden knew that what she learned would be of value when the time came for the tribes of the north to take the Imperial City.

***

Polybius had a beaming smile on his face when he stepped through the front door of their quarters.

"I am pleased to tell you that I have secured an invitation for us this evening, to the home of a most prominent Teveren," Polybius announced.

Rayden could sense that Polybius viewed the invitation as a tremendous opportunity. She knew that she would get her first chance to interact with the higher ranks of Teveren society.

Yet she had no idea what to expect, or even how to behave, at such a function.

"I trust in your judgement," Rayden said, showing little change in expression.

"What is wrong?" Polybius asked her.

"Doros and I do not know the ways of Teverens," she replied.

"When we are inside the home of our host, only I am expected to know Teveren habits and customs," Polybius stated. "I have explained your foreign nature. They will have great interest in you, but all you and Doros have to do is watch and follow the rest of us."

Polybius' words reassured her.

Rayden did not wish to make an unintentional infraction

that would see them incurring trouble so soon after arriving in the city. She could not do anything to jeopardize the chance to scout the city and its defenses.

At the same time, they needed to take some chances to get into a position where some of the deeper workings at the heights of Teveren society could be uncovered. Something of tremendous power, dark and ancient, lurked beneath the surface and Rayden had to learn everything about it that she could.

Looking back at Polybius, she smiled, knowing the coming evening would be a strange mixture of discomfort and luxuriousness. "At least our bellies will be full."

"They will be more than full," Polybius replied. "A Teveren feast given by a host of great status is like nothing I have ever experienced, but the tales of them are clear enough. Your wine cups will be kept full, and you will be served more food than you could ever hope to consume, often of kinds you can barely imagine."

To Rayden, it sounded like an extraordinary experience, but she would have to maintain wariness in the midst of such an indulgent atmosphere. In a carefree environment where copious amounts of wine flowed, much could be discovered and revealed.

***

Late in the afternoon, a contingent of stout male slaves appeared at the entrance to the tenement. Bearing three litters among them, the men set them on the ground and waited for Polybius, Rayden, and Doros to approach.

Crassor followed a pace behind the others, acting the part of Polybius' slave. The scowl on his face spoke loud and unmistakable about his feelings on the matter.

One of the slaves gestured for Rayden to use the middle of the three litters.

Rayden eased into the litter compartment. Ample

cushioning within and a reclined posture should have enabled great comfort, but the idea of being carried forth by people held in bondage made her uneasy and cheerless.

Like Crassor, her face could not hide her dislike, but she cooperated with the process.

Two of the slaves carrying her litter had the appearance of northerners and could easily have been men from the Gessa tribe. Likely warriors taken captive in skirmishes involving the southernmost tribes bordering the Teverens, they now endured a life of forced servitude.

Both of the men eyed Rayden close, and she could sense their curiosity toward her. She wished that she could speak with them; to let the men know her true purpose and give them hope.

Yet she could not whisper a single word, having to adhere to her own role as an Alettani friend in the company of Polybius.

Pulling the curtains back on all sides, Rayden eschewed the veiling canopy and afforded herself a full view of the surroundings.

The late afternoon sun casting long shadows, many of the narrow stretches running between tenements five stories and higher rebuffed the golden orb's rays entirely. Dusk would be arriving soon, but a fair amount of pedestrian traffic still persisted along the meandering route.

Brimming with curiosity, stares and glances directed at Rayden, Doros, and Polybius rose in abundance from the passersby. Most of the looks focused upon her and Doros, and Rayden did not doubt that many of the lingering gazes found the sight of the two foreign women traveling in a litter strange.

The litter jostled and wobbled as the group proceeded through the streets, but for the most part Rayden traveled in comfort. Spared the inconveniences of the pedestrians, the small column of slaves and litters kept a steady pace, the forefront being headed by a pair of tall, muscular slaves.

Having pulled their temporary stands and stalls back

inside for the night, the ground-level shopkeepers and artisans no longer encroached upon the street, lessening the congestion. The servants escorting the litters had no need to muscle their way through the people.

Most pedestrians stepped aside with mild prompting. Rayden only heard a few instances of raised voices on the part of the two slaves at the forefront.

In the litter just ahead of Rayden, Polybius looked back. Catching her eye, he grinned wide.

Rayden returned the smile and chuckled to herself. She could tell that Polybius derived great amusement from the arrangement, in taking the part of a Teveren noble of higher rank in the company of two important guests on the way to a grand feast.

Taking a glance at Doros following in the litter behind, Rayden elicited a smile from her friend. Thinking about the moment at hand, Rayden laughed, finding the whole idea of riding in a litter an absurdity.

While the slaves bearing the litters looked robust, Rayden and Doros were likely in better physical condition than the entire lot of them. She certainly had no need for assistance to make her way along the streets.

Still, she found herself in a quandary.

Everything centered upon the appearance of high status, and Rayden abhorred ostentatious displays. She would much rather have been walking alongside Crassor at the side of Polybius' litter, but she knew that such an act would be deeply frowned upon by their hosts.

Once more, Rayden battened her discomfort back down and reminded herself that a role had to be performed for a short time. Soon enough, she would be able to return to her natural state; a warrior and woman who shunned the things that ensnared the hearts and minds of so many others, commoner and noble alike.

Navigating through a few more streets and proceeding up a modest incline, the group arrived at the forefront of a two-level edifice. No tenement, the outside of the building had the air of a small fortress.

A couple of small windows on the second level were the only openings within the facade beyond a tall set of wooden double doors at the street level.

Looking attentive and somber, a pair of strong-looking servants stood in front of the door. Both carried cudgels, and Rayden had no doubt that the two would not hesitate to use them on drunks, beggars, or other rovers of the streets at night.

`Nearby, a few empty litters rested on the ground. A large group of plain-clad individuals, most likely other slaves, milled about the unoccupied litters. Whispering among each other, they eyed the newcomers with great interest.

Rayden and Doros proceeded to disembark from their litters without any assistance, drawing surprised expressions from more than one slave. Polybius waited until a slave brought him a short stool to descend from his litter, while a couple of others stepped forward to lend their help to him.

"Remember, you are Alettani, and not expected to know the customs here, so feel at ease," Polybius exclaimed in a voice loud enough for the onlooking slaves to hear. "But this is the manner in which a Teveren exits a litter."

Finding great amusement in the lofty, pompous air that Polybius projected, Rayden stifled the grin threatening to burst upon her face. She could not deny that he played his role wonderfully, balancing haughtiness and formality without a trace of it being an act.

Crassor had to remain behind on the street with many of the other slaves, but Rayden and Doros continued toward the ground level doors with Polybius.

A slave walking ahead of them made use of a doorknocker,

in the form of a bronze eagle head grasping a ring in its beak. The thud of the metal against the thick wood echoed in the street.

A narrow-faced, middle-aged man with a sharp gaze and dutiful air greeted them at the doors to the residence.

Nodding to Polybius, Rayden, and Doros, he greeted them in a polite, formal manner. "Polybius of Trasterro, we have been expecting you. Welcome to the house of Sulpinnio Onnidaccus! You and your guests from our esteemed Alettani allies may follow me."

The servant guided them across an elaborate mosaic floor. Colorful inlaid tiles had been arranged to create a scene of the hunt, depicting a cluster of spear-carrying men pursuing a large boar.

After traversing a short hallway, Rayden found herself within a large, square atrium. Far above, daylight streamed through a square opening aligned over a pool strewn with flower petals on the ground level.

A few stools had been set close to the pool. The servant guided Rayden and her companions over to them and indicated that they sit.

At the emergence of the new arrivals, a number of house servants came forward. Holding pitchers and cloths, they set about washing the feet of Polybius, Rayden, and Doros.

Taking her cue from Polybius, she remained upright on the stool and allowed a young female slave to undo the laces on her sandals.

Rayden found the process awkward, but she had to perform her role and accepted the treatment without complaint. The young woman handled Rayden's feet with a gentle touch, pouring perfumed water over them and using a soft linen cloth to wipe them dry.

Once finished, the slave took her sandals away and the guests were guided onward. Beyond a large curtain on the other side of the atrium, they crossed through another mosaic-surfaced space that looked like a much more lavish version of the room with the writing implements back at their own quarters.

A stack of blank parchments, several scrolls, and multiple ink vials rested upon the surface of a beautiful table crafted from a dark wood. Rayden imagined that business of great importance to many in the Teveren world was conducted at that table on a daily basis.

A spear and a rectangular shield displayed on a wall drew Rayden's eyes. Both had been cleaned and the metallic elements of both shined in the lamplight, but her eyes did not miss the array of nicks and indentations testifying that both of the items had been used in combat.

The writing room opened into a lush garden. A couple of statues, one cast in bronze and the other carved of marble, had been placed within the foliage. Both depicted voluptuous women, whose loose folds of clothing looked to be on the verge of slipping down at any moment.

The bronze figure had a hand extended toward the sky, as if inviting the sun's rays to grace the thriving growth surrounding her.

The marble figure exhibited a coy grin, as if hinting at an abundance of spectacles that she had observed from her vantage in the garden.

The scents of many kinds of flowers blended into a wondrous cornucopia, greeting Rayden the moment that she stepped into the open air. The soft, elegant notes of a stringed instrument played lightly drifted along the light tendrils of air, caressing the leaves and flowers.

The house servant took them to the right, where a spacious dining chamber looked out upon the garden. Within the large room, two long couches had been placed well apart and parallel to each other, with another spanning between them at one end.

In the midst of the couches stood a few round tables, their legs short and tops set low to the ground. Placed within arm's reach of the guests, the tables held an assortment of small platters filled with delectable food items.

Blue cushions on the three long couches marked the spaces for those attending the feast.

All eyes within the chamber turned toward the newcomers at their entrance. The house slave proceeded to announce them in a loud voice.

"I present to you Polybius of Trasterro, a wine merchant, and his two companions, Rayden and Doros of the Alettani, tribal allies of the Teveren Empire."

A portly figure with a bulbous nose and broad face reclining at the center couch gestured to Polybius. "Welcome to my home! I am honored to have you, and those with you, dine with us tonight."

"The honor is mine, Sulpinnio," Polybius replied with an air of formality, bowing his head toward their host. "Your invitation was most generous, and you have my gratitude."

The slave then guided Polybius, Rayden, and Doros to their places on one of the parallel couches.

Rayden emulated the other guests, reclining with an elbow resting upon the cushion she had been provided with. Servants approached Rayden, Doros, and Polybius, washed their hands in rose-scented water, and then dried them with soft linen cloths.

Outside, twilight had finally arrived, draping the garden in a violet hue. Gentle breezes drifted into the chamber, bringing a soothing, cool touch as they brushed across the faces, shoulders, and arms of the guests.

Gazing around the chamber, Rayden eyed the detailed frescoes covering the walls. The images depicted in vivid colors included a grand temple, an azure lake, and rolling, forested hills beneath blue skies accented with patches of white clouds.

Finding a bowl of olives on one of the low tables before her, Rayden picked one up and popped it into her mouth. Around her, conversations resumed among the other guests, though more than one cast furtive glances in her direction.

Gauging from their looks, Rayden imagined that none of the Teverens had ever dined with a northerner before. Then again, she had never experienced a feast with a Teveren.

"Polybius of Trasterro, from the land that gives the Imperial City the finest of wines, know that I have the bounty of Trasterro here in abundance tonight," their rotund host proclaimed in a boastful air, drawing Rayden's attention. "We shall indulge in these wines this very night! I am not concerned about getting more! We shall prevail against the barbarian invasion soon enough! Bring in some more wine!"

Sulpinnio's comments were met with lively exclamations from the other guests.

Carrying silver drinking vessels filled to the rims with wine, a few more servants entered the chamber and approached the guests.

Taking a sip from the cup given to her, Rayden found the taste of the burgundy wine within exquisite. Bursting with flavor that had a sweet, berry edge, the liquid passed smooth down her throat.

Murmurs of approval came from others as they sampled their own cups.

"Polybius, you are fortunate that you made it safely to the Imperial City," Sulpinnio stated. "We shall crush the barbarians, but they have swarmed throughout the north."

"We had to abandon our estates with little warning," Polybius stated. "A harrowing flight ensued, and it is by the will of the gods that I am here with you tonight."

His voice rising and coursing with anger, Sulpinnio exclaimed, "Such an unnecessary thing! To have such abundant vineyards left to the mercy of such curs!"

The other conversations ebbed. Rayden could sense the rapt interest from the other guests in Polybius, Doros, and herself.

"Yet I am here, thanks to those who embraced friendship with our divine Imperator," Polybius responded, giving Sulpinnio a warm smile. He then gestured toward Rayden and Doros. "Two of whom are with us tonight."

"Alettani, and also the Sarrimena, I am told," a woman situated across from Rayden stated. "Tribes of the north, but wiser in their choices."

Rayden found the woman's elaborate hairstyle, featuring layers of tight curls ascending into a high, tapering point, a fascinating display to behold from a close vantage. Fathoming that it had taken a very long time to fix the woman's hair in that fashion, she had pity for the slaves that undoubtedly had been given the painstaking task.

"Yes, they are the ones who will be coming along with Marus, to join with Peronnius in crushing the barbarian scum," Polybius replied to the woman.

"Yet are you not barbarians, too? A different tribe perhaps, but still barbarians, yes?" the woman asked, shifting her gaze toward Rayden and Doros.

Gathering her thoughts, Rayden answered the woman in an amicable tone, "We are, but we seek to learn Teveren ways and grow in our friendship with your people. We do not wish to take the path the other tribes have taken"

"It is said that the Alettani are most wonderful horsemen," an older man across from Rayden stated. He then added, with a grin, "Or, I might say, horsewomen too."

Looking impressed with his own wit, he laughed and glanced around, prompting a round of laughter from the other guests. Rayden laughed along with the rest of them, finding her humor in the narcissistic man's buffoonish air.

"We are well-skilled on horseback," Rayden answered the man, keeping her tone amiable and relaxed. "A horse has a mind of its own, and we have to be disciplined to guide them well in battle."

"Know we are grateful for the Alettani and for your protection of Teveren citizens such as Polybius," a lean man reclined a few places from Rayden chimed in. "The news that has come in from the north is just awful to hear. These northern barbarians are nothing more than savages, raping, burning, and killing their way through our lands."

"It will all be over soon enough," Rayden replied to him, maintaining her composure. She could only hope that Doros managed to do the same in the face of such provocative comments.

"We will need to begin capturing a few of the miscreants, or they will run out of fodder for the games," Sulpinnio declared, his comments provoking laughter from most of the others. Looking around the chamber, he grinned wide. "I may have some games of my own waiting for all of you, after we have partaken of tonight's feast."

The woman across from Rayden clapped her hands with delight. "Transgressions to be punished?"

Sulpinnio nodded to her.

Looking to Rayden and Doros, the woman said in a jubilant manner, "You will have a chance to see how order is kept in a proper Teveren household."

Rayden did not miss the cold look embedded in the eyes of the woman, nor the anticipation intertwined with it.

"Now that I have tempted one appetite, allow me to provide for another," Sulpinnio stated. Clapping his hands, he raised his voice higher, declaring, "Let tonight's feasting begin!"

Tranquil music given life through the plucking of strings and breath channeled through reed or wood continued drifting through the air. A cluster of servants bearing a large platter approached with the first wave of the feast. Gasps of surprise and acclamation greeted the sight of a massive fish spanning the length of the platter.

A throng of oysters had been arrayed on either side of the dark-scaled fish to simulate the parting of waters.

"A Black Maero," the lean male guest exclaimed.

"Acquired at great cost," Sulpinnio replied. "It is not a common thing to pull from the waters of the Daragen Sea."

"I have long wished to discover what a Black Maero tastes like," the woman across from Rayden said, watching the servants prepare to cut into the fish and serve it to the guests. "You have exceeded yourself, Sulpinnio."

"It will not be easy to surpass this, I can say that," Sulpinnio replied with a laugh.

Eating mainly with her fingers, Rayden made use of a small knife and a couple different types of spoons, the utensils provided for her by one of the servants. A female servant with a pitcher of water went among the guests, pouring the liquid over their hands and drying them off when requested.

Tipping their shells to access the delectable contents within, Rayden consumed several oysters, the little portions of meat gliding smooth down her throat and into her belly.

She found the fish to her liking. Draped with a sauce that contained a sweet edge, the tender meat had a smooth texture, proving effortless to chew.

After the large fish had been reduced to scattered bits of bone, scales, and other remnants tossed upon the mosaic floor, a new platter holding roast peacock was brought in. Spread around the base of the peacock, a plethora of small roasted birds had been posed to look nestled in snug against the prominent centerpiece.

The woman with the lofty hairstyle clapped excitedly in response. "A Hen and Chicks! What a pleasant surprise!"

Sulpinnio nodded to her. "The chicks in this preparation are thrushes ... each one of them selected with care by my Master of the Kitchen."

Abounding with flavor, both the thrushes and peacock had been roasted with an assortment of herbs and spices. Fingers becoming slick and greasy, Rayden indulged in the juicy morsels of bird meat.

The guests, both male and female, belched frequently, while casually tossing bones and other small bits to the floor.

More than once, one of the other diners excused themselves, departing the chamber for a short time before coming back. After returning, they continued to eat at the same pace as before.

Catching Rayden watching one of the guests settling back in after being absent for a brief period, Polybius spoke up.

"One must purge at times to create room in the stomach to enjoy everything served in a feast this grand," he said to her.

Nodding to him, she kept her disgust from showing on her face; finding the idea of vomiting just to eat more both repulsive and illogical.

Not about to purge like the others, Rayden had begun to slow down by the time a spit-roasted stag with an impressive display of antlers was carried in.

A pair of servants dressed to look like Teveren soldiers used short swords to carve ample pieces of the roasted meat for the guests. The meat would have tasted good enough by itself, but the combination of herbs and spices added to it made for a succulent taste on the tongue, one that caused Rayden to close her eyes and savor more than a few bites.

A few servants then entered the chamber and layered the floor with sawdust, before others came in bearing platters piled with and abundance cakes and fruit. Though on the brink of gorged, Rayden partook of a little cake drenched in honey. Afterward, she helped herself to a peach, knowing that the round, luscious fruit had come a long way from the east to reach the small platter resting on the low table before her.

Close by, Doros devoured a couple of apples.

"It has been some time since I enjoyed one of these," Doros remarked, wiping juices off her face using the back of her hand.

Rayden smiled and held up the half-eaten peach in her own hand. "It has been awhile since I picked up one of these."

"You will not want for anything at one of my feasts," Sulpinnio stated, looking to them. "My feasts bring together the abundance and variety of the Teveren Empire!"

"For that we are indeed grateful," the older male guest across from Rayden commented.

"Even the wine served late in the feast is not watered more, not in the slightest," the woman with the tall hairstyle proclaimed.

Rayden could not dispute the woman. After a few fills of her cup, the wine within had continued to remain strong; to the degree that she had to be careful, lest she lose hold of her wits.

Groans, belches, and drowsy expressions on the part of the other guests accompanied the gradual winding down of the feast. Rayden held her hands out and accepted another pour of water over them, the servant drying her skin with a soft linen cloth afterward.

At long last, Sulpinnio called for everyone's attention.

"I have most wonderful entertainment prepared for you tonight," Sulpinnio stated, looking around at the faces of his guests. "No recitations of poetry, demonstration of acrobatics, or anything of a common nature ... what I, Sulpinnio Onnidaccus, will provide for you is something much more thrilling and rarer in nature... and it is sure to cause the blood in your veins to race!"

The gleam in Sulpinnio's eyes and the faint tremor of excited anticipation within his voice invoked a deep unease within Rayden.

***

"Come along with me and let us enjoy our own games!" Sulpinnio proclaimed, smiling broad. "Who needs the arena when you are a guest of Sulpinnio Onnidaccus? Ready yourselves for an exhilarating spectacle!"

It took a few moments for Sulpinnio to rouse his bulk from the low couch, but once the master of the house had gotten to his feet, he shuffled across the mosaic floor and entered the garden. Though sluggish, the other guests rose up from their own places and followed after him.

Polybius nodded to Rayden and Doros. The three of them got to their feet and added their number to the other guests in the outflow from the dining chamber. Behind them, a wave of servants streamed in and began attending to the many cleanup tasks pending from the extended feast.

Light, crisp breezes rustled the leaves of the trees and swept through the beds of flowers and other foliage. Rayden would have found the atmosphere pleasant were it not for the figure walking with a purposeful stride at the lead of the group.

Her unease continued to swell.

On the far side of the garden, a waist-high, square wall of stone encased a pool of water. Large enough that the guests could array themselves around its perimeter, Rayden, Polybius and Doros had no difficulty finding space to view the proceedings.

Rayden caught movements in the water the moment that she set her eyes upon the moon-glistened surface. Sleek and sinewy forms roved beneath the surface, but a paucity of available light prevented her from seeing what manner of fish or creature moved within the waters.

Looking around at the other guests, she beheld the glow of eagerness and excitement on their faces. Talking amongst each other, they kept eyeing the shimmering water.

It stood clear to Rayden that some of them knew what lurked within.

Many heads began turning and smiles spread on a couple of the women's faces. Rayden looked in the direction that Sulpinnio's guests were all gazing in.

Half-dragging a lanky man of about middle age, a couple of robust male slaves trudged toward the pool. Behind them, two more male slaves walked with blazing torches held high in hand.

At the rear of the little procession strode a man in a long, flowing tunic. His head shaved bare, the round-faced man wore a silver medallion suspended from a necklace of leather cording.

Gagged with a strip of cloth, the man in the clutches of the slaves wore nothing more than a tattered, soiled loincloth. His body bore the marks of many severe lashings, with a few of the marks looking recently inflicted. Eyes shining with fright, he struggled to no avail against the two brawny figures holding onto him.

The approaching group came to a stop at the edge of the pool, and the slaves holding the man looked toward Sulpinnio. Folding his hands together in front of him, the robed figure with them had a placid expression.

"Have our Alettani guests take a better look at my pets," Sulpinnio proclaimed, glancing toward Rayden and Doros. "You should have a glance yourself, Polybius."

The slaves bearing the torches stepped forward and held the flames out over the water, casting increased light into the pool.

Many elongated, narrow shapes could be seen swimming within the water. Several of the serpentine forms were easily the length of Rayden's height.

The light appeared to rouse the creatures, speeding their movement and bringing a few along the surface, casting ripples in their wake.

Looking from the water to the man held at its edge, Rayden

had little doubt of what was about to transpire. She had witnessed a ritual involving pools far to the east, in the caverns beneath a city called Sereth-Naga.

The presence of a priest caused her to wonder more about the nature of the scene unfurling before her eyes.

"Had some caught in the sea and raised a few more of them here," Sulpinnio exclaimed with the air of a boast. Looking at the forlorn, bound figure, he continued speaking, a cold smile etched on his face, "Brutal things, the Sabatian Eels are ... they latch teeth as sharp as blades into the skin of their prey to draw blood out. Do not take your eyes off. It is a frenzy to behold."

Around Sulpinnio, several of the other guests proclaimed their agreement. The captive looked terrified, and rivulets of urine ran down his legs and dripped from his loincloth. Despite his continued strain, he could not budge the iron grip of the two slaves.

"We will show the fate that awaits a slave who seeks to run away from his master," Sulpinnio stated, the look in his eyes growing crueler by the moment. "We will also make it an offering to the Divinity of the Imperator, with the blessing of one of his sacred priests."

At Sulpinnio's words, the man in the long tunic came forward to stand behind the doomed runaway. After looking toward Sulpinnio, he raised his hands high.

Everyone in attendance fell quiet and any smiles among the guests faded into solemn expressions.

"All is done for the empowerment of the Divine Imperator, the one who provides for those loyal to him," the priest declared in a low-pitched, resonant voice. "Let this offering be dedicated for the glory and power of the Imperator."

Stepping back, the priest lowered his hands and once more clasped them together in front of him.

Sulpinnio then nodded to the men holding the recaptured

slave. "Into the pool with him. He belongs to the Sabatian Eels now. Do not forget to remove his gag. His cries will be exquisite to our ears."

Smiles returned to the faces of many guests and their eyes radiated bright with expectation.

One of the large slaves ripped the gag off, bringing a look of sheer anguish to the condemned man. The muscular pair lifted the man off the ground without delay and flung him out over the water.

Screaming, the man plunged into the surface with a big splash that spattered everyone gathered about the pool.

An instant later, the water churned and frothed violently, turning darker in scant moments. His head breaking the surface, the ill-fated man shrieked in agony and went under again.

The glistening skin of the eels broke the surface in many places, submerging again as the hapless slave thrashed and writhed in throes of torment.

The cheers and laughter of Sulpinnio's guests echoed off the garden walls. Taking in the unabashed glee and elation toward the man's extreme suffering, Rayden promised herself that their kind would be made to answer for the travesty. Somehow, she would see that they experienced the same kind of fear that they drew amusement from.

Ripped apart inside, Rayden could not do anything to stop the horrific display.

Without weapons, she stood almost no chance of overcoming all of Sulpinnio's slaves and guests. Rayden would likely be killed or taken captive in the end, and everything that she had come into the city to achieve would be cast into ruin.

Even if by some miracle she did prevail against a throng loyal to Sulpinnio, Rayden would not be able to stop the eels in their blood-crazed frenzy. It was too late the moment the hapless slave's body fell into the water.

Rayden remained conscious that the lives of Hamilcar, Erethea, Alcedan, Annocrates, and all of the people now approaching the city walls could well come to depend upon the mission that Rayden and her companions had undertaken. Thousands upon thousands of lives teetered on a precarious, brittle edge, and Rayden could not throw herself away in a reckless action that would do nothing to spare the unfortunate slave.

The crimson-hued waters settled, leaving a glistening froth behind, and the dead body of the slave bobbed at the surface. Splashing and coiling about the corpse, the eels continued to gorge themselves.

Apart from a few splashes, the air grew quiet and a lone breeze whistled through the trees.

The woman who had been positioned directly across from Rayden in the dining chamber looked toward Sulpinnio.

Breaking the silence, she asked, "I am sure that is not all, is it, Sulpinnio?"

Exhibiting a merry countenance, Sulpinnio chuckled. "It is apparent that you are a regular attendee of the games, Desrinnia. I must say, they are such a wonder, a demonstration of the empire's power, like no other."

"I do go often, and I agree with you," the woman replied, a grin dancing on her lips. "They show all eyes the strength of the Teveren Empire."

"Then you know that the greatest events at the games are not the ones that take place first," Sulpinnio replied, grinning back at her.

Desrinnia smiled.

Raising his hands, Sulpinnio clapped.

Several more slaves emerged, holding small, single-edged knives that they began handing out to the guests. Not knowing what they were to be used for, Rayden accepted one of the blades.

"Does everyone have a blade?" Sulpinnio asked, looking

around at his guests.

Nods and murmurs of confirmation met his query.

"Then let us proceed to the greater event," Sulpinnio announced, leading his guests away from the pool toward another corner of the garden.

Past some thicker foliage, a young man had been chained tight between two small columns of dark granite. Secured at the wrists and ankles, he could not move his limbs to any significant degree.

Like the other slave, his body exhibited the evidence of extreme whippings, including recently inflicted wounds.

"After the invocation, I invite all of you to participate," Sulpinnio proclaimed. "Nothing shall remain hidden anymore with this wretch who dared to strike me after being caught in the arms of another one of my female slaves ... one that had expressly been forbidden to him. The cur will now pay the price."

The defiant, fiery look swirling in the eyes of the chained man convinced Rayden that he would strike Sulpinnio again, without hesitation, if his hands were free.

A light squeeze on her arm drew her eyes to the left, where Polybius stood. Catching her gaze, he shook his head.

"Hold back, Rayden," he whispered, leaning closer to her ear.

"I know," she replied, knowing that she stood in the face of an impossible situation once more.

The distraught look reflecting within Polybius' eyes gave her more reason to dread what was about to take place. Gazing down at the knife that she had been given and eyeing the finely-honed blade, Rayden understood its malicious purpose.

"Let us give the invocation," Sulpinnio announced. "This too shall be an offering to the divinity of our glorious Imperator."

Once again, the priest stepped forward, raised his hands, and proceeded to claim the chained man as an offering to the divinity of the Imperator. The guests listened in a dutiful hush, resuming their chatter and looks of fervor when the priest had concluded.

"This is too far," Rayden whispered to Polybius, sensing the atrocity about to happen.

"Hold fast, Rayden," Polybius stated.

Looking around at the faces surrounding the chained man, Rayden did her best to commit each of them to memory. She could only hope that her path would bring her to a place where she could mete out true justice and honor the lives of the tortured slaves.

"Come forth now, and strip him to true nakedness," Sulpinnio proclaimed, a smile on his face that held no trace of kindness. "Let nothing be hidden."

Striding forward, Sulpinnio lifted his knife to the shoulder of the chained man. Slow and methodical, he sliced a palm-sized piece of skin off, bringing a pained cry from his immobilized victim.

Holding up the thin shred of skin, Sulpinnio stated, "I have claimed the first fruits. Come, my guests, and join with me in this delight."

Realizing that they were about to flay the man alive, Rayden girded herself for the only action she could take that would not put her companions and the mission that they had undertaken together at risk.

Abhorring the thought of watching the poor young wretch before her being skinned at the hands of sick-hearted individuals deriving pleasure from the abominable act, Rayden took a step forward.

Moving in with the other guests, Rayden angled for the front of the man. Laughter intertwining with another agony-filled scream, a woman shaved off a long strip of the man's forearm. In the wake of the blade's path, blood and exposed muscle gleamed in the firelight.

At first, Rayden made it look like she was intending to take a portion of skin from the man's chest. Pressing closer, she whispered quickly into the man's ears.

"I cannot stop this evil, but I will end it for you," Rayden told the doomed slave.

Trembling in the raw pain wracking his body, his eyes met hers for a moment. A desperate plea brimmed within them.

Rayden understood and knew that her intent embraced his desire.

Grim-faced, Rayden lifted her hand. Cutting into the skin at his neck, she applied more force and drove the blade deeper. Blood spurted out and began streaming down his chest.

"No! No!" a male guest cried out in alarm from where he had been on the verge of cutting a swathe of skin from the slave's right leg.

"Not now, you barbarian fool!" Desrinnia exclaimed from where she had begun to carve into the man's buttocks. "What have you done!"

Gagging, and slumping down, the light of life began ebbing from the man's eyes. Ignoring the outcries of the irritated guests, Rayden kept her eyes locked with those of the man whose throat she had cut.

Extending him a final mercy, Rayden held his gaze until the last spark fled his eyes and he could feel pain no more. A wisp of relief and peace could be seen in the last look that he gave her.

She had set him free.

"What is this?" Sulpinnio cried out, agitation rife within his tone.

"Forgive her ignorance, Sulpinnio, she does not know our customs and ways," Polybius replied, exhibiting a placating demeanor.

Rayden turned her eyes to Sulpinnio. "He committed an

offense with a woman, and you were executing him, yes?"

"He should not have died so swiftly," Sulpinnio replied to her, irritation splayed across his face. "What pleasure is there in a quick execution?"

"He is dead, is he not?" Rayden asked, feigning confusion. "Is that not what you desired?"

"The manner of his death was for our pleasure," Sulpinnio responded, anger clouding his face.

"I do not understand your ways," Rayden replied, her words carrying a deeper level of truth than a man like Sulpinnio could detect.

Sulpinnio glared at Polybius and then turned his heated gaze back to Rayden. "You were given a knife. Not knowing our customs, you could not be expected to understand this. It is nonetheless a great disappointment for all of us."

"You should not let barbarian savages participate in an exercise of justice like this," Desrinnia told Sulpinnio, casting a hateful look toward Rayden.

Several murmurs of assent rose from the other guests. In their eyes and faces, Rayden could see nothing human. All of them seethed at being denied the chance to inflict extreme torture on the young man.

Knowing that she had thwarted their chance to sate cruel hungers, Rayden took a little pleasure at their outrage and frustration.

Her eyes now circles of frigid blue ice, Rayden stared back at Desrinnia. "I promise you that I will not forget what I have learned here."

Missing her true meaning, Sulpinnio replied, "A lesson has been learned. Let us finish with this cur, nonetheless. His life is still an offering to the divinity of the Imperator."

A subdued atmosphere hovered over the macabre scene as the guests resumed the grisly skinning, though now they cut into a corpse instead of a living, suffering body. Many terse glances and muttered curses told Rayden that the guests continued to simmer with resentment toward her.

Unwilling to keep her eyes on their vile handiwork, Rayden pulled away from the group and stood in silence, several paces back. Coming over to her right side, Doros joined Rayden.

Polybius walked up to the other guests and proceeded to make a couple slices on the dead body. Bearing him no ill will and understanding his actions, Rayden knew that the Teveren participated to maintain appearances and deflect further attention toward Rayden.

She had chosen the best path available. Rayden's foreign nature had given her a way to spare the unfortunate slave great suffering without causing a full provocation of Sulpinnio and his guests.

When the guests had finished stripping the skin off the dead slave's body, Sulpinnio called for his servants to enter with cloths and pitchers of water. Collecting the gore-coated knives, the slaves tended to the guests, washing away any traces of blood that had gotten onto them.

Rayden watched the cleaning in a terse silence. In her eyes, none of the guests could begin to wash away the dark stains they undoubtedly had incurred on their spirits.

Sulpinnio walked up to Rayden and Doros before going back inside. The flush of anger had ebbed from his face, but his eyes remained cold.

After staring at Rayden for a moment, he stated, "What is done, is done. You have learned, and the next time you will know what is expected. Do not let it happen ever again, or you will take the place of the slave."

Rayden nodded back to Sulpinnio. Inside her mind, she committed every detail about his face that she could to memory.

Polybius strode over to join them. Looking to Sulpinnio, he

declared, "I shall make up for this with an extra allotment of our finest red, the best in all of Trasterro, as soon as the matter of the barbarian invasion is dealt with. Many amphorae, to be my gift to you in the hopes of continued friendship."

"You are too kind and generous," Sulpinnio replied in a polite air, though the cold gaze in his eyes remained. "All can be forgotten in time, and we must not forget that the Alettani will be helping to rid our lands of these cursed invaders."

"That is quite true," Polybius replied with a smile.

"Let us go back inside," Sulpinnio told him. "I am still well-stocked with delectable wines that need drinking. There are also some supple, warm delights of another kind to be had before this night is through."

Stepping forward, Sulpinnio started back for the dining chamber.

"You are fortunate, Rayden," Polybius remarked to her in a voice barely above a whisper, a look of relief upon his face. "We could all be dead right now."

"I saw the only action I could take to spare the man's agony, and I took it," Rayden replied in a similar volume.

"Sometimes it is a good thing to be deemed a savage barbarian," Doros observed, looking toward Polybius.

"At times it can be," Rayden agreed.

Leaving the gruesome displays of Teveren cruelties behind them, the three turned to go back into the dining chamber. Trailing the others, Rayden focused on calming her mind in the aftermath of the atrocities that she had witnessed.

A few paces from the edge of the garden, a ripple of movement within one of the flower beds on Rayden's left drew her attention.

Out from the mass of flowers skittered an elongated shape covered in dark hair. Turning its tapering snout in Rayden's direction, the creature's black eyes had a glistening sheen in the moonlight.

"I have heard talk that rats are everywhere in the city these days," Polybius told her in a low voice, having come to a stop with Doros at Rayden's halt.

The rat continued to sniff at the air and stare in their direction.

"I am more concerned about the other vermin that walks through this garden," Rayden replied, keeping her eyes on the rat.

"If only I had my bow with me," Doros lamented.

Showing no urgency, the rat continued forward, disappearing within another bed of flowers.

"It seems they are well used to people," Polybius remarked.

"It does seem so," Rayden replied, her gaze lingering on the swishing line of flowers marking the passage of the rodent through them. Looking back to Polybius and Doros, she forced a grin onto her face, "Enough of rats, let us go back inside."

Upon returning to the dining chamber, they found that the guests had spread into other areas of Sulpinnio's home. Another passage running from the back of the chamber led to a private bath and a few small rooms, with most of the latter containing bedding.

Wherever they encountered them, the other guests showed no inclination to interact with Rayden or Doros. A few exchanged some words with Polybius, but it stood clear that the night had been ruined for them when Rayden slit the condemned slave's throat.

After accepting a silver cup filled to the brim with wine from one of the household slaves, Rayden broke away from her companions for a short time. Taking slow steps and sipping the flavorful wine, she strolled along the hallway, desiring to be left to herself.

Niches in the walls held lit oil lamps while alcoves holding statues or busts, the latter resting upon marble-topped stands, accented the sides of the hallway. Their expressions permanent and solemn, the faces of the various carved figures held no trace of welcome or kindness. She found their stern, lifeless countenances fitting in a place that held such little regard for human life.

Rayden did not catch sight of Sulpinnio for the rest of their stay in the wealthy man's home. Overhearing a couple remarks from guests, she learned that he had gone to his private quarters in the company of a pair of young, female slaves. Nobody expected him to reappear anytime soon.

After a little more time had passed, Rayden found the priest that had presided over the ritualistic element of the two executions in the garden wandering through the narrow hall alone. Saying nothing, he glared at Rayden when his eyes fell upon her.

Brushing past her, he quickened his step and headed down the passage.

After draining her cup of wine, Rayden rejoined Polybius and Doros back in the dining chamber.

"We were about to come looking for you," Doros said when Rayden approached them.

"I just needed a few moments to myself, nothing more," Rayden replied.

"I think it has been long enough that we can politely excuse ourselves," Polybius stated, looking between the two women.

"I was hoping that you would say that," Rayden said. "I have no desire to stay here any longer."

"I wanted to leave a long while ago," Doros stated, a dour expression rising on her face.

"Then let us not waste a single moment more," Polybius replied. "I am certain Crassor will not argue with us to remain longer."

The remark and the thought of Crassor's usual irritability brought Rayden a much-needed chuckle, though the lighthearted moment proved far too ephemeral.

Polybius, Doros, and Rayden left the dining chamber. Finding the head slave of Sulpinnio's house, Polybius expressed his gratitude for the invitation and took leave to return home, citing the need for rest before taking on a full day of business.

Expressing his understanding, the slave commanded others to assist with the return of their footwear. He then guided them to the domicile's front entrance.

Hearing the doors to Sulpinnio's home shutting behind her, Rayden had no desire to ever return again, no matter how bountiful the feast had been. The mere thought of setting foot in the wicked man's home elicited revulsion within her.

***

During the entire ride on the litter through the twisting, narrow streets back to their apartments, a cascade of thoughts filtered through Rayden's mind.

The presence of a priest dedicated to the Imperator placed the two slave executions in a ritualistic light. In hindsight, both appeared far more sacrificial in nature than merely the acts of a master carrying out brutal forms of justice upon wayward slaves.

There remained little mistaking that the two instances of blood sacrifice served a much larger, darker purpose.

In light of the night's blood-soaked events, Rayden thought about what Sulpinnio had said about the games being a demonstration of Teveren power.

A part of her suspected something on a much deeper and insidious level surrounding the games than just an open display of imperial power. Blood flowing on a grand scale could channel immense flows of dark energies toward the monstrous things of the abyss.

While knowing the experience would be loathsome, Rayden would have to set her eyes upon the games for herself. Only then could she glean understanding of the deeper level things taking place within the Imperial City.

Rayden also needed to continue her assessment of the walls from inside the city. Knowledge of them would become invaluable when the massive tide from the north arrived at the gates.

Watching the slaves with torches walking ahead of the litters, driving back the shadows pervading the empty streets, Rayden took in a deep breath of the chilly air. After holding it captive in her lungs for an extended moment, she let the air out slowly.

The summons from the sorcerer Dreaghen to return to the lands of the north seemed so distant and long ago. A journey that had begun with just herself and Ammanus, from lands far south of the Mystic Kingdom, now saw her at a point of convergence for vast multitudes of lives.

A decisive conflict loomed nigh that would have severe implications for lands far and wide. A failure to stop the continued rise of the Imperator would unleash dark furies upon the world that few could even hope to contend with.

The great power coalescing around the Imperator had been cultivated at the behest of sorcerers exploring the depths of the abyss' mysteries. Those same sorcerers had already unleashed great abominations into the world, in the forms of the Arguntier.

There was no telling what further horrors born of dark sorcery would be unveiled in the time to come.

Rayden admonished herself, knowing that she could not allow worries of the unknown to consume her mind. Her exploration of the Teveren city needed her utmost focus in the time that she spent behind the walls.

Easing back into the cushions of the litter, Rayden set her eyes on the alleys, streets, and buildings they passed. A few times, she caught the sight of figures lurking within pools of shadow, but if any of them had ill intent they did not dare threaten the large contingent marching through the streets.

Throughout their trip back, the night air carried the clopping of hooves and creaking of wheels, along with the occasional bray, bellow, gruff voice, or cracking of a whip. The bevy of sounds did not come as a surprise to Rayden.

The development reflected the nature of other large cities that Rayden had experienced throughout her widespread travels. For the duration of the night, carts and wagons would be given free rein to travel the streets, while firm restrictions prevented the wheeled objects from adding to the congestion so widespread in the city under the tenure of daylight.

Finally, the litters came to a halt before the building that held their quarters. Showing great care and deference, Sulpinnio's slaves assisted with the disembarkation.

After a few moments Rayden, Crassor, Doros, and Polybius stood together near the building entrance, watching the slaves carrying the empty litters away. After proceeding a short distance, the slaves marched around a bend in the street and disappeared from view.

"Let us go inside," Rayden said to the others. "I have had far enough of the city for this night."

"You will find no argument from us," Polybius replied.

Approaching the primary entryway for the tenement, they encountered a different guard than the one they had met when Polybius rented their quarters. Of middle age, gruff in manner, and still possessed of a strong build, the guard exhibited similar qualities to his daytime comrade.

After Polybius presented a key and identified himself, the guard stood aside and allowed them to proceed into the building. The four climbed the stairs in silence.

The only noises to reach their ears during the climb up were muffled voices coming from within other apartments, including the sounds of a couple in the throes of passion. Rayden expected

Crassor to make a jest or ribald comment about the latter, but even he looked to have had more than his fill of the Imperial City for the time being.

Upon reaching their quarters, Polybius fitted the key in the lock, opened the door, and entered. Without servants inside, no lamps had been lit and the interior remained shrouded in darkness.

Watching him address the matter, Rayden saw that Polybius had thought ahead and placed a lamp close to the entrance. Like a blooming flower, light rose from within the bronze lamp a few moments later, spreading outward and pushing the darkness aside.

"A dull night," Crassor remarked in a disgruntled voice, once they had closed the door behind them.

"You would not have wished to see what we did," Rayden replied to him. "I wish there were a way to remove it from memory."

"It is hard to believe that, with the oafish louts I had to endure the night with," Crassor grumbled, an irritated look on his face. "I wish I had bashed a few of their skulls in. I have seen oxen with more of a wit."

"I am glad you did not do so," Polybius commented.

"I know what is expected," Crassor replied with a resigned air. "I can control myself, Polybius."

"We are all in need of some rest," Rayden told the others. "Tomorrow is a new day."

"What will we do?" Doros asked, looking to Rayden.

"I want to get out and explore the city," Rayden answered. "Have a good look at the walls and gates. I also want to see about the games. I need to get a better sense of them. I have my reasons."

"They are not something that you would find any pleasure in, Rayden," Polybius stated with a somber edge. "The same cruelty you witnessed tonight is present there, only on a much larger scale."

"I know," she responded, looking him in the eyes. "But it is something that I need to see, in light of the things we saw tonight."

"Is it necessary?" Doros asked.

A solemn look on her face, Rayden nodded. "I know what I am looking for. You have to trust me in this."

"You know I trust you, Rayden," Doros replied.

"Then we will see about going to the games in the arena," Polybius declared. "We have means, so it should not be difficult to secure advantageous seats for a good view."

"It would be better than anything I endured tonight," Crassor added.

"Then we are all in agreement," Rayden said. "I will use the morning to explore the city and then we will attend the games."

"Get some rest, then, all of you," Polybius said.

"You will get no dispute from me on that," Doros replied. "I am beyond weary and I have had too much wine and food tonight."

"Three of you might have," Crassor replied to her. "My stomach begs for some food. I am going to get some bread and cheese before I sleep."

"There is plenty left of both," Polybius said to him. "I will also make sure to get more food and drink for here tomorrow."

"After I eat, I will get to my door watch duties," Crassor told the others with a grin, looking over toward the mattress lying on the ground to the right of the front entrance.

While Polybius had taken care of its purchase and arranged for the mattress to be ported to the apartments, Crassor had chosen its location. He had determined the place it had been set down to be as good of a place as any, giving him an advantageous position should anyone try to break in during the night.

"I will see all of you again, soon enough," Rayden told her companions. "Have a good rest. I am going to my bed."

Striding forward, she made her way across the black and white mosaic floor to her room. A chill clung to the air, but not to the degree that she had a need to light a brazier.

Taking her sandals off, Rayden eased onto the mattress. Slipping under the covers, she lay her head down upon the soft, feather-stuffed cushion.

Weary in body, exhausted in mind and spirit, Rayden took little time in drifting into a needed refuge of deep, dreamless sleep.

CHAPTER 3

First light brought with it a sea of mist blanketing the streets and buildings of the massive Teveren city. Rayden peered out her bedroom's small window, gazing at the drifting, dense vapors cloaking the awakening city.

Refreshed in body, Rayden still carried some of the heaviness of heart that she had incurred from the previous night's events at the home of Sulpinnio. She wondered what the coming day would add to that weight, if she made it into the arena and witnessed what took place there.

Knowing what Sulpinnio and his guests had taken great delight in, nothing could be ruled out.

The brightness of a new sun always helped to invigorate her during such times. Turning her face to the right, she closed her eyes and let the golden rays bathe her skin for several moments.

Her mind eased. In a few moments, she reached a solid equilibrium, readying to confront anything she encountered once she stepped outside the apartments and entered the city streets.

Closing the shutters and leaving the window behind, she exited the bedroom.

Making her way to the kitchen, she found Doros sitting at the table, eating some figs and cheese off a small platter lying in front of her. A cup of wine rested to the side of the meager fare.

"Ready to take a look around?" Rayden asked her.

"I am, but have you gotten anything to eat yet?" Doros asked, raising an eyebrow.

Rayden shook her head. "I am eager to begin this day. We will find a tavern a little later, if hunger bothers me enough."

Doros looked past Rayden. "Will Crassor be going with us? Or Polybius?"

Rayden turned her head and set her eyes on the large man slumbering near the door. Again, she shook her head.

"It is best that he stays with Polybius," Rayden said. "It will keep appearances and make certain that our Teveren friend is well-protected."

Doros nodded, finishing the last morsel on her platter and washing it down with the remainder of the wine in her cup.

"Let us begin!" Doros announced in an exuberant manner, setting the cup down and getting to her feet.

Keeping their steps quiet, Rayden and Doros exited and shut the door behind them. At the bottom of the stairs, they edged by a female servant busy emptying the contents of a small vessel into the much larger container occupying the corner.

Wincing at the strong, rancid aroma of urine in the air, Rayden found herself relieved to step onto the street outside. Acknowledging the doorman to the right with a glance and slight nod of her head, she set off with Doros for the morning excursion.

Doros walked along at her right side. From the outset, both of them remained engrossed in observing the elements of the city around them. Exchanging few words, they kept to their intended aims.

Reaching the outer walls of the city, Rayden began her assessment.

Stopping several times along the way to gain an extended look at the various gates, Rayden and Doros followed the course of the walls. A few times, they had to detour around some areas where shadowing the wall would appear too conspicuous to an observer.

The composition of the walls told Rayden that the barrier had been constructed in several phases. Everything from blocks of travertine and tufa to kiln-fired bricks had been made use of in building the walls, with the bricks utilized in what looked to be the most recent fabrications.

Open galleries along the inside of some wall sections showed their multi-level nature, displaying small windows and slits for archers on a level beneath the wall-walk.

Other sections had closed inner facings. Some of them solid in construct, a few had windows looking into the city, indicating some kind of lower passageway running inside the wall.

Looking at the design, Rayden could tell that the Teverens could move their soldiers along the walls without exposing them to arrows, stones, or other missiles from attackers.

The various gates that Rayden observed exhibited a wide range in size.

What looked to be the city's primary gates were aligned with the main roads; the broader, stone-paved thoroughfares running into the city along key directional points. The prominent gateways consisted of wide single arches, or were double-arched in nature, the tile-faced entrances set between large, square towers.

Other gates were aligned with smaller, unpaved roads. These consisted of single-arched gateways flanked by projecting towers.

Another kind of entrance that Rayden observed involved an arched gateway close in size to the second. These were situated at midpoints between intervals of the regular wall towers.

Though she could not see them, Rayden knew that many small postern gates and concealed doors also existed along the walls. No city of such immense size would be without them; to give soldiers and laborers additional points of egress for upkeep, resupplying, or even defensive needs.

The walls themselves had a few salient points where they reached outward to protect a couple of key areas. One extension on the western side of the city warded a hill with many stout, rectangular edifices clustered upon it. Another protected what looked to be a two-level bridge designed with arcades coming into the city from the northwest, though no traffic of any sort moved along its upper surfaces.

After leaving one of the larger gates behind, Rayden and Doros had to get around a walled compound situated close by. The pungent scent of horse manure, neighs, and whinnies identified the place's nature easily enough. Whether the stables inside were used for markets, travelers, or soldiers, Rayden could not tell, but the area stood an obstacle all the same.

Following a route taking them a short distance from the walls and deeper into the city, Rayden and Doros sought to go around the large compound. The higher tenements and greater preponderance of rougher-looking individuals surrounding them told Rayden that they had entered a much poorer section of the city.

Some of the tenements looked to be in a precarious condition, a few with makeshift timber braces set in place to hold up a leaning side.

Stopping and glancing down an alleyway in response to a loud curse coming from within it, Rayden saw a man looking upward. Far above him, a woman leaned out of a window six stories high with an upturned vessel held in her hands. From his ranting, Rayden gathered that the man had come within a wisp of becoming bathed in discarded bodily waste.

Showing no contrition for the near incident, the woman cursed back at the man and disappeared inside the upper level window.

Before starting forward again, Rayden noticed movement

within the shadows, close to the alley's mouth.

A disheveled, dirt-smudged man in a filthy ragged tunic shuffled out of the alley and proceeded into the street. Cradling a large rat in his hands, the man had a crazed grin spread across his weathered face.

Bony and gaunt, the man had a starved appearance. Yet his eyes had an alert, piercing quality, showing no hint of fatigue or weakness born of hunger.

Those nearing him in the street altered their course to avoid contact. Stroking the fur of the rat, he laughed, fixing his gaze upon Rayden.

"Who are you?" he called to her, stepping a little closer. Baring his teeth like a feral dog and exposing a rotted set of teeth, he asked in a scratchy voice, "Why can I not see you? What mystery do you hold?"

"A madman," Doros remarked, standing at Rayden's right shoulder. "He is staring right at you and claims he cannot see you!"

Rayden knew otherwise. Whatever dwelled inside the man had been stymied by Dreaghen's sorcery. It could not determine her nature or identity, and the confusion vexed the malevolent, hidden entity.

The man shuffled a few steps closer. Spittle sprayed from his lips. "What are you? Why are you here? Who are you? What do you want?"

The rapid barrage of questions accompanied an increasingly agitated expression on his face.

"Leave him be, we will continue," Rayden told Doros.

Rayden and Doros strode forward, heading down the street. Turning, the man began to follow them.

"Get out of here! What have we told you?" a large man yelled, his face contorting into an expression of severe irritation.

Rayden looked back just in time to see him reach the man

from the alleyway, a few paces behind them. Shoving the smaller man backwards, the newcomer kept advancing.

A couple of other tough-looking brutes following in the wake of the large man joined in, pushing the rat-carrying scoundrel toward the alleyway.

Eyes wide and looking like something feral, the scrawny dreg hissed, cursed and screeched in anger. But he could do nothing against the trio of burly men herding him back into the alley.

Breaking away from his stout companions, the tall, thick-built man hurried across the street toward Rayden and Doros.

"Do not worry yourselves, we will make sure the scum does not return to this area," the man announced to them.

Farther behind him, Rayden could see his two comrades forcing the crazed man into the maw of the alley and out of sight.

"The Brotherhood of Malpicus keeps this area free of such miscreants," the man announced. "He must have wandered in. I have not seen him before."

Square-jawed, with a large nose that showed evidence of previous breakings, the man had a rugged appearance. The granite look in his eyes told Rayden that he was no stranger to scuffles and altercations.

"Thank you, but we are capable of defending ourselves well enough," Rayden replied in an even tone, glancing down to the sword and axe resting at her waist.

"I am sure that you are," the man replied, a coy look on his face. "I am called Stramma. I used to fight in the arena. I survived and gained freedom. Now I work with my brothers to keep order in this part of the city. Not an easy task, during normal times. Much worse when the city is flooding with many fleeing the barbarian invasion."

Rayden recognized his type. Little more than a criminal that had banded together with others of a like mind, Stramma held a unique position at the crossroads of rumor and reality. Knowing what moved within the shadows and the open daylight on the streets, he would have a strong sense of the city's true heartbeat.

Most importantly, Stramma was the kind of man who would have answers and the kind of perspective that would benefit her mission. Though midday approached, Rayden decided to tarry a little longer.

"We are of the Alettani, a tribe in alliance with your Imperator, and we find many things about this city strange and unfamiliar," Rayden told Stramma. "Would you have a few moments to speak with us? We were just about to search out a little food and drink."

"Come with me, and let us have some good Teveren wine," Stramma replied. "I will make sure you are not given the watered-down swill that is all too common in this area."

"That would be welcome," Rayden replied, nodding to him.

Taking the lead, he started down the street in the direction they had been headed in. Rayden noticed more than one person parting aside to avoid bumping into Stramma.

The anxiety apparent on their faces told Rayden more than enough. The local populace had a significant fear of the man walking a pace ahead of her.

Rayden could not ease her guard and would have to keep wary at all moments.

Stramma guided them into a tavern straddling the intersection of two narrow streets. A number of tables with stools had been set outside the open-faced establishment.

Several men raised cups or called out greetings to Stramma as he entered. He acknowledged a few of them by name, while a host of gazes fell upon Rayden and Doros.

Taking a place at a table in the corner, from where he could see everyone within the tavern, Stramma gestured for Rayden and Doros to sit down. A serving woman with a tumbling mass of black hair approached them a few moments later.

"What will it be today, Stramma?" she asked, a broad smile on her face. Her eyes shifted over to his two female guests. "And for them?"

"The best wine you have, Ledellis," Stramma replied. "For all of us."

She nodded. "Will you two be eating? A bountiful catch of aspius was pulled from the Golden River just this morning. You will not find anyone in the Imperial City who can season aspius like we can."

"Yes, I would like that very much," Rayden answered her.

"As would I," Doros added.

Ledellis nodded to Rayden and Doros and left the table. She headed toward the long marble counter running down one side of the tavern's interior space.

A heavyset woman tended the other side, where the fires of a couple bronze braziers burned. Chains and hooks on the wall held an arsenal of pots, pans, ladles, and other cooking implements.

After speaking with the woman behind the counter, Ledellis returned with a copper pitcher of wine and three earthenware cups. Behind her, the other woman turned and began taking a few items down from the assortment on the wall.

Raising her cup to her lips, Rayden tasted the wine. It had a robust, fruity taste, and it had not been watered down. Looking to Stramma and Ledellis, she smiled.

"It is very good," she told them. "Just what I needed, right now."

"You see, we do not serve water with a few sprinkles of wine like so many others in this city do," Ledellis replied, laughing. "I will be back soon with your food."

Ledellis walked away, returning to the counter. Rayden watched as she got out a mortar and pestle, along with a few jars.

In a few moments, Ledellis began grinding up leaves taken from one of the jars.

Rayden held no doubts that the seasoning of her coming meal would be quite good.

Stramma took an extended draught from his wine cup. Some of the contents trickled from the corners of his lips, running through the stubble on his face and dripping down to land on his tunic.

"Ahhhhh! ... So good!" he exclaimed with a satisfied air. Looking up, an amused expression rose upon his face.

Two men approached the table. A meek-looking, smaller man walked a step ahead of a stocky brute with cold, dark eyes.

The smaller man set a pouch down on the table before Stramma, and the muffled clink of coins sounded from within it.

"Here is everything owed to you," the man stated in a voice that teetered on shaking. Raw fear gleamed in his eyes.

Smiling and looking at ease, Stramma replied, "This pleases me. See, Ferranus? It is not so hard, and your contribution helps us to keep order in our neighborhood. I have guests now, but I will visit your shop soon. Make sure that next time you do not make it more difficult for yourself."

"I will not, Stramma," the man replied, a look of relief coming to his face before shuffling off.

The larger man remained in place. Stramma gazed toward him.

"All looks to be settled, nothing further is needed," Stramma told the man.

Showing no change in expression, the big man nodded and strode off.

Stramma picked up the pouch. Giving it a little toss in the air, he caught it in his palm.

Looking to Rayden and Doros, he stated, "Do not mind all of that. Our business never sleeps. That man has a chair making shop close to here. He does not yet appreciate what we do for everyone."

"I am sure his understanding has improved," Rayden replied, keeping her own distaste about the matter from showing. She imagined it took high extortion to ensure low crime in the area Stramma and his brotherhood controlled.

Stramma laughed and made another short, vertical toss of the pouch. Landing in his palm, the coins jingled

"It has ... yes, it has improved," Stramma said.

"It is good fortune to have met you. You know a lot more about the city than any others I have met since arriving here," Rayden replied, her words intended to nourish the man's ego.

"I do make it my priority to know what is happening in the city where I live," Stramma replied, looking across to her.

"It looks like you have a well-established presence," Doros said.

"It has not been easy," Stramma replied. "Life in a city is no different for a human than a beast in the wild. You have to fight for everything that you get ... and then defend it from being taken."

Nearby, a group of men around a table erupted in cheers at the result of a dice roll. Stramma looked over toward them, watching in silence for a few moments.

"Every day involves a roll of the dice," he continued, his face taking on a serious countenance. "The choices we make. The stands we take."

"Wise words," Rayden told him.

"I am guessing that your choices are often very different in nature than mine," he replied, the hint of a grin on his lips.

"We walk different paths," Rayden told him, working to keep the air between them polite.

"Whatever you think of my path, I am a free man and I have carved out a life here," Stramma stated, his gaze sweeping across the room. "It is a life far better than I thought I would ever have at one time."

"When you were a fighter in the arena, where did you live?" Doros asked him.

"In the household of a man named Erridus, who owned and trained fighters for the arena," Stramma answered. He shook his head after a moment, and a rueful grin spread across his face. "Those days seem so distant now."

"Did you only fight in the arena, or were there other duties?" Rayden asked him.

"Too many other duties," Stramma answered, the grin leaving his face. "We helped round up those involved in sorcery who were not priests of the Imperator, and we often provided guards for those priests, when they went about the city. Their thirst for blood-sacrifice is unquenchable and those they took for their blood rituals ... I cannot speak of it further."

A haunted look crept into the eyes of Stramma. Rayden knew she would have to alter the direction of their discourse.

"But you do not serve them anymore," she stated.

"They can take at will from an area like this," Stramma replied, lifting his eyes to meet Rayden's. "No one of power is going to defend the poorest in this city. I cannot stop them from taking, but I no longer help them."

Rayden could sense the revulsion in Stramma toward the practices of the Imperator's priesthood. It never ceased to amaze her how even criminals often had a kind of moral code, one that included areas of behavior they regarded to be unacceptable.

Ledellis returned and set platters down before Rayden and Doros. Each of the platters displayed an ample portion of fish, along with a small mound of grapes, wheat bread, and olives.

The scintillating aroma emanating from the seasoned fish caused Rayden's mouth to water. Taking up a piece in her hand, she raised the chunk of fish and placed it on her tongue. Chewing slowly, she savored the burst of flavors drawn from the morsel.

"You will not find better aspius anywhere in this city," Ledellis declared, gazing toward Rayden.

"I cannot imagine anyone could best this," Rayden replied, her compliment genuine.

"Anything for you?" Ledellis asked, edging toward Stramma.

"Perhaps," he answered her, chuckling.

Grinning, Stramma gave the woman serving them a firm squeeze on the buttocks. Showing no trace of irritation at his ribald behavior, she smiled back to him.

During the short time that she had been inside the place, Rayden had observed a great level of familiarity between the tavern patrons and those running it. Many bawdy interactions like the one before her hinted at an unfettered atmosphere with few limits.

Even so, Rayden could take no offense at the behavior of those like Stramma. The serving women proved to be just as crass and aggressive as the men were.

Observing them, Rayden could see that the women had their boundaries and enforced them without hesitation.

One man at a table nearby, who behaved no different than Stramma toward one of the serving women, received a stern rebuke and had his hand smacked away. Evidently new to the tavern, he was given a reprieve, but the woman made it abundantly clear that the next infraction would see him thrown out to the street in an unceremonious manner.

Rayden watched another inebriated ruffian get slapped hard across the face, before finding himself tossed out of the establishment at the request of the serving woman involved. It stood apparent in the tavern that the women had firm control over what actions were permitted and who could make them.

Eyeing Rayden, Stramma remarked, "You and your friend look like tough women, but that is nothing new to us here. Our women are not fragile little mice drenched in perfumes like you find in the north of the city. This is a different kind of wilderness, and they have had to fight to survive too."

Overhearing his remarks, one of the serving women wrapped an arm around Stramma from behind. Setting her eyes on Rayden, she pulled him close and probed his ear with her tongue. A salacious spark danced within her expressive brown eyes.

"Here, we just take what we want," she quipped, giving Stramma a soft caress on his right cheek, letting him go, and laughing.

Twisting to his right, Stramma leveled a firm smack on her rear. "Yes ... yes we do."

Looking each other in the eyes, the two of them laughed heartily.

"But I do not think you are too interested in our banter," Stramma said to Rayden and Doros, turning back to face them. "What might you wish to learn about the city?"

"You have things in this city that I have never seen," Rayden commented, welcoming his offer to change the course of the discussion. "Just today, I saw what looked to be a bridge coming into the city, over the walls. Yet I know it was no bridge."

Stramma nodded. "One of the new aqueducts. The Imperator had that one built. A massive task that involved the labor of many thousands. Keeps water plentiful in the city. Along with some tunnels they made that come from the river, it is how we keep the baths and fountains in this city full."

"A bridge that brings water," Rayden responded, thinking upon the idea. "That is an incredible thing."

"Another of the reasons why the Imperator will rule the world one day," Stramma exclaimed in a casual tone.

Rayden decided to press for another answer regarding her morning observations. "What of the hill that the wall changes course to protect? The one over on the western side of the city?"

"What of it? You speak of the mills, I am sure," Stramma responded. "They are gathered in a suitable place for taking in grain from the barges traveling the river."

Rayden nodded. "That is what they are. I was curious."

"There is a lot for you to see in the Imperial City beyond grain barges and aqueducts," Stramma said. Pausing, he looked down at his wine cup and chuckled. "Sometimes, a few things you wish you did not see."

For the slightest instant, Rayden caught a sliver of fear within Stramma's eyes. She wished that she could ask him further about what he had experienced and seen when carrying out his duties around the Imperator's priesthood.

An abrupt shriek from the back of the tavern drew her attention away from Stramma.

"Get out of here, you little greasy bastard!" one of the serving women yelled, hurling an earthenware cup that shattered into a multitude of pieces along the tiled floor.

An elongated dark shape scuttled out of sight, close to where the cup had landed.

"More of those damnable rats," Stramma vented, scowling. "Feels like they are overrunning the city these days."

"Maybe the Imperator should have a large number of cats brought in," Doros said.

"You would need a few legions of cats to deal with the vermin," Stramma remarked in a dour tone. "The rats have grown fast in number over the past year."

Rayden sensed another opportunity for more pointed information.

"It sounds like the Imperator is already bringing in the kinds of legions that he needs at the moment," Rayden commented, taking a sip of wine and fixing her eyes upon Stramma.

Stramma looked at Rayden and smiled. "Yes, he is.

Peronnius has a couple of legions at full strength camped outside the walls. But I suspect they will be allowed in the city soon enough, when the horde from the north arrives here."

"Why are they not allowed in the city now?" Rayden asked, seeking confirmation on what Polybius had spoken of when she had seen the fortress extending from the city walls in the northeastern section.

Stramma replied, "It has long been tradition that our legions remain outside the city walls, except for one. That legion has its own stronghold within the city ... the Imperial Legion. They are quartered here and serve the Imperator, though I am sure they could be placed under Peronnius' command as well."

"Three legions strong, and more are coming with Marus," Rayden said. "Including our Alettani brothers and sisters, and the Sarrimena. Should be more than enough to defeat the invaders."

"They will crush them with ease," Stramma replied, grinning. "But what a nuisance the barbarians are causing for everyone right now. More and more Teverens are fleeing their homes across the countryside. They are pouring into the city to seek the safety of its walls. Gives the Brotherhood a lot more to keep an eye on and worry about."

"I imagine so," Rayden replied, taking another drink of the wine. Looking toward the back of the room, she eyed a man fondling a serving woman as they made their way up a staircase. "But it looks like life is still going on around here."

"Unless the barbarians were to storm through the streets, which will never happen, we will continue to live as we have," Stramma told her. "The barbarians cannot sustain a long siege, so I am not worried."

"What if they could?" Rayden inquired.

"The city would soon grow hungry," Stramma answered her, his expression turning somber. "The common people receive gifts of grain from the Imperator already. If that came to an end, great sections of the city would grow restless fast."

"I imagine that would make things difficult for you and your Brotherhood," Doros stated.

"If it were to happen, then yes it would," he said. Waving his hand in a dismissive fashion, Stramma continued, "But let us not worry ourselves over things that will not happen. There are far better things to put our thoughts to."

At a signal from Stramma, Ledellis came back over with a full pitcher of wine. In moments, all three sitting at the table had refilled cups, with wine perched on the brim of each vessel.

Leaning over and resting her elbows on the table surface, Rayden picked at the remnants of her meal. Popping a grape into her mouth and relishing the burst of sweet flavor that followed, she chose not to press Stramma for any further information. She and Doros needed to be getting back to the tenement soon, to rejoin Polybius and Crassor.

Not long after, Rayden and Doros took their leave of Stramma. Looking reluctant to see them go, he extended both of them an open invitation to join him again in the evening.

Though parting in an amicable manner, Rayden had no affinity for the kinds of endeavors that Stramma and his Brotherhood engaged in. Nevertheless, she could still see many respectable qualities in the man, and she walked away carrying an overall liking for the rough-hewn rogue.

Rejoining the flow of traffic in the streets, Rayden and Doros started back for their quarters.

***

Returning to the apartments shortly after the sun had reached its zenith, Rayden and Doros found their companions waiting for them. Looking relieved at their presence, Polybius and Crassor both had a restless air about them.

"I wondered when the two of you might be getting back

here," Polybius stated.

Smiling wide, Polybius held up four rectangular pieces of bone. Each of the pieces had distinct markings carved into their surfaces.

"No easy task ... but I was able to obtain access to today's games," Polybius announced. "These will provide us with seats in the lower part of the arena, placing among those of higher wealth and status."

"Then let us not waste another moment," Rayden replied, pleased with the news. "We will go and learn what we can."

"What exactly is it that are you looking for?" Crassor asked Rayden.

"I am looking for the things that connect everything together in this city," Rayden said. "Everything that is taking place serves the Imperator's purpose."

"Or venerates him," Crassor remarked. "Polybius and I have seen more than one statue bearing his resemblance."

"Probably a small army of them, if you gathered all the statues made in his likeness together," Doros said.

"I am certain that he receives plenty of veneration at that massive temple near his palace," Polybius added. "I suspect that a giant idol of him is within it."

"Not a place that I have any desire to see," Rayden responded, turning back toward the door. "Now, let us proceed to the arena. It is a long walk, and it is best that we get this done and over with today."

Crassor shrugged. "There are no other demands on our time."

Leaving the apartments, Rayden and the others set out through the winding streets, heading toward the arena.

***

After passing a high-walled compound, from which a multitude of bestial sounds emitted, ranging from roars, to deep grunts, screeches, and bellows, Rayden and her companions found themselves standing before a colossal edifice. Exuding an aura of strength, power, and prestige, the facing of the massive, circular structure rose several levels high, containing two rows of alcoves harboring statues bearing the likenesses of various male and female figures.

Pausing for a moment, Rayden watched the clouds drifting over the incredible construct. Conflicting sensations of dread and astonishment mingled within.

As intricate and beautiful its construction might be to her eyes, it had been created to entertain vast crowds with the mass shedding of blood.

"It is one of the newer wonders of the Teveren Empire ... the Imperator had this built," Polybius remarked, standing at her side.

"This is like no arena I have ever seen," Rayden replied, stunned at the magnitude of the construction.

A great din rose from within the arena, the kind of sound that only thousands upon thousands of voices blended together could create. A spectacle of blood and death beckoned.

"Come, let us go inside," Polybius said to the group, taking a step in the direction of the arena.

Solemn-faced, Rayden nodded and continued forward, heading with her companions toward one of the many portals in view.

Polybius, Rayden, Doros, and Crassor handed their rectangular bone pieces over to the men overseeing the entrances to the arena. After examining the tokens of admittance, the men handed them back and waved the holders through.

Like the crashing of a great wave upon a shore, a loud roar swelled and ebbed from the end of the barrel-vaulted tunnel ahead of her. Staring forward and following Polybius down the tunnel, Rayden had no idea of what to expect when they emerged from the other end.

Shouldering through the congested passage, she ignored the many looks cast her way. Taking a glance back, Rayden saw Doros pressed close to her back, with Crassor glowering just a step behind.

By the time she reached the end of the tunnel, it seemed that it had stretched for a league. Walking out into the sunlight, Rayden found it hard to believe her eyes.

Rows upon rows packed with men and women filled the arena. Thousands upon thousands gathered in attendance, the enormous crowd watched a sprawling melee of beasts and warriors taking place within the huge, sand-covered pit below.

"Our places are close to here, follow me," Polybius told Rayden and the others, leading them down some steps.

After descending a few rows, Polybius turned to the right and edged across to an open section large enough for the four of them to sit comfortably. Rayden endured a few irritated expressions when passing in front of other spectators, blocking their view of the ongoing bloodshed.

Not far from where they were seated, a large group of lions, a throng of hyenas, a trio of massive, horned bulls, and around two dozen armed warriors clashed on the sands. The swirling, chaotic violence covered the entirety of the pit.

After getting situated, Rayden took a deep breath and set her eyes upon the brutal melee. An orgy of violence, the scene drew feverish responses from the spectators.

Hyenas rushed at lions, snapping at their limbs. Men stabbed with sword or spear at the hides of snorting bulls. Lions sprang upon hyenas, men, and bulls alike.

Disorderly and blood-soaked, the frenzied violence raged across the sand. Dead, wounded, and dying creatures scattered everywhere, the casualties from the savage contest mounted fast.

Hooves shattering bone and pulping flesh, a bull trampled a man to death, and then found itself covered in lionesses a few moments later.

A hyena ripped the throat of another man out, only to be impaled through the side by the spear of a remaining fighter.

A male lion with a full-grown mane pounced on a hyena, overpowering the creature in an instant and taking it to the ground. After finishing the creature off with a vicious bite to the neck, the lion whirled to face another that had bitten at one of its rear legs.

The hyena could not scuttle off before being engulfed by the lion. Rising up from the kill, the lion snarled and gazed about, displaying blood streaks along its face resembling a warrior's battle paint.

Springing into motion, the lion then brought down a bull in an extraordinary feat of dexterity and power. Claws dug in and jaws locked tight on the bull's throat, the lion held onto the massive beast until it breathed out its last.

Once more, the lion stood and swept its gaze around, drawing a loud cheer from the crowd. Charging forward, the lion barreled into a cluster of hyenas that had a lioness in mortal danger. Swiping its claws and knocking the smaller creatures away, the lion freed the sorely beset female.

Taking advantage of the lion's distraction, a man scurried in with a sword and delivered a gash to the side of the creature. Roaring in pain and fury, the lion lunged at the man.

Bringing its jaws together, the lion ripped over half the man's face off. Still alive and left with a horrific visage, the man screamed. The lion spread its jaws and lowered its head, bringing an end to the struggle.

Straddling the dead man, the lion lifted its head high. Looking defiant and still unconquered, the creature bared its bloodied fangs while glaring at the masses of onlookers filling the rows to the heights.

For a moment, Rayden feared that the majestic lion was the same as the one that she had freed from the Teveren camp in the north. Seeing an assortment of old scars all over its face and the darker hue of its mane, she came to realize it was not the same creature.

Padding away from the corpse, the lion rallied again to continue its fight. Engaging new attackers, the lion slew two more hyenas and then another of the armed warriors.

Receiving yet more wounds in the intense fighting, the lion showed signs of wearing down at last. Bleeding from a glut of wounds, the lion's slowing movements reflected a beast that was finally nearing the end.

Seeing the creature's desperate fight for survival, it pained Rayden to witness the proud, bestial warrior suffering the withering onslaught of blades and fangs.

Limping, and issuing one final, defiant roar, the lion hurled itself at a trio of approaching warriors; the armed men were the last of the humans still alive in the grisly melee.

Mauling one from chest to gut, the lion exposed its sides to the blades of the other two men. Stabbing and slashing, they delivered the killing blows.

The regal beast collapsed to the ground and lay still at last, bleeding from many wounds into the sands.

The two men that had slain the lion had no time to celebrate their kill.

Charging in fast, three lionesses assailed the pair. Leaping onto the men and bearing them to the ground, the lionesses tore into their bodies with fangs and claws. Both men met a swift, savage death.

With the slaying of the two men, the fighting on the sands came to an end at last. A pensive stillness descended across the carcass-riddled ground.

A throng of soldiers then emerged from one side of the pit. Shouting and banging their weapons upon the facing of their shields, they formed a wall and herded the few surviving lionesses toward the open gateway at the far end.

Having the appearance of a veteran warrior, exhibiting a severely tattered right ear and a visible gash on her side, one of the lionesses turned and bared her fangs in defiance at the soldiers. The line of Teverens kept shouting, jabbing, and pressing forward behind their shields. The lioness roared once more, before exiting the sands of the arena.

Knowing that the lionesses would be brought out until they were slain by other beasts or weapons, Rayden's burdened heart filled with disgust. Loathing the nature of the arena already, Rayden found it difficult to keep her composure.

At her side, Doros remained silent. The lines of tension visible along her jaw line gave ample evidence that she viewed the carnage in the same manner as Rayden.

A small horde of slaves entered after the soldiers had removed the lionesses. Some bearing litters, the slaves worked to clear the pit of the corpses. The bodies of the three massive bulls had to be dragged out by teams of slaves using ropes.

Along with the slaves, a conspicuous pair of robed figures emerged, taking up positions to either side of the tunnel. Raising their arms skyward, they appeared to be praying.

"To the divinity of the Imperator!" a crier proclaimed in a booming voice. "To the glory and power of the Empire, all that takes place upon the sands is offered."

Drawn to the crier's voice, Rayden found him positioned low and to the right, in the center of the arena. He stood within a projecting, extended section that had a partial covering to provide shade and shelter from rain.

Around him, a number of prominent-looking men and women seated in chairs beheld the activity. Laughing and conversing amongst each other, several held cups, and small tables to the sides of their seats held an assortment of food items.

Standing close behind each of the seated figures, many other men and women in much plainer attire displayed somber, attentive looks. Rayden saw one of them using a silver ewer to refill the golden cup of an older man occupying one of the seats.

Several Teveren soldiers in gleaming, polished helms stood guard at both ends of the long section.

Shaven of head and face, and attired in robes, the crier had the look of a priest, as did the two men with arms outstretched in the pit below.

After the crier had finished his address, the pair of robed figures lowered their arms and departed through the tunnel. Behind them, the slaves continued to labor, ridding the pit of the remaining carnage.

Once the slaves had finished with their gruesome task and exited the pit, the gate shut.

Rayden stared at the empty sands, pondering what she had just witnessed. She had no desire to talk with anyone, including her companions.

Around her, the crowd began getting restless, a sense of anticipation surging in the air.

Following a short delay, a bevy of horns sounded.

The crowd erupted, roaring its approval.

The bars of the large, iron gate to the right rose slowly upward. Coming to a halt, the tapering ends of the bars made the tunnel look like a maw lined with jagged teeth.

All eyes turned toward the dark opening.

A few moments later, a man clad in a loincloth, holding nothing more than a short dagger in his right hand, stumbled into view from the shadowy interior. Entering the arena and looking around with the sheen of raw terror filling his eyes, he had none of the balance and poise of even an average warrior.

Seeing the way that he carried his lone weapon, Rayden knew that the man had no proper training. She had no doubts that the Teverens did not intend for him to have a chance of leaving the arena alive.

"Behold, the condemned murderer Magranius!" the crier announced, his voice projecting strong and echoing throughout the arena. "Magranius shall be offered up now for the divinity of the Imperator and the power and glory of the Empire."

A booming chorus of vitriol erupted at the announcement of the man's criminal nature. Their faces becoming masks of hatred, most of the people filling the rows cursed and jeered at the condemned man.

His face brimming with fear and panic, the man continued looking around at the hostile crowd.

At the opposite end of the pit to Rayden's left, the other iron gateway began lifting upward. The noise of the crowd lowered, and all eyes looked toward the open tunnel.

Shambling out from the darkness, a massive form ambled into the arena. A titan among its kind, the brown-furred mountain bear set its gaze upon the man standing in the open ground, across a stretch of sand that would take little time to traverse.

A boisterous uproar from the crowd greeted the mountain bear's entrance. Rayden could sense a ravenous bloodlust rippling through the teeming thousands of onlookers.

Lurching into motion, the bear charged across the sand toward the ill-fated man. Taking off at a run, the man hurried toward the wall behind him and then kept running along the edge of the pit.

Shifting its course and bounding along the wall, the bear pursued its human quarry. The gap between beast and man dwindled fast.

Casting glances over his shoulder, the man screamed, his

distress drawing a deafening cheer from the audience.

Gazing around, Rayden grew sicker inside.

Everywhere that she looked, Rayden could see eager looks of anticipation on the faces of the spectators. They desired to see a fellow human torn apart, and she knew that their craving had nothing to do with the execution of justice.

The man's criminal status merely gave them a rationale for their hysteria. His condemnation excused their bloodlust.

With the bear about to reach him, the terrified man suddenly leaped upward, trying in desperation to grab the top of the pit's wall. Falling short, he tumbled back to the ground.

The bear overtook him a moment later.

Cries of raw terror turned into shrieks of agony as the bear thrashed the man's body. Even after the man had fallen silent in death, the bear continued pulverizing his corpse.

Engulfing the man's head within its jaws, the bear ripped it free of the neck in one powerful wrenching of its jaws. Shaking its head and spraying blood and gore all around, the bear then flung the head to the side.

The morbid display drew a euphoric reaction from the crowd.

If the man had indeed been a murderer, then he deserved death, but what Rayden had just witnessed represented something other than justice. She could never countenance an execution being conducted in a manner intended for the entertainment of a crowd.

Careful and patient, a group of soldiers standing shoulder to shoulder and using long spears cajoled the mountain bear back through the gateway that it had entered from. The moment that the enormous creature padded into the depths of the tunnel, the iron gate lowered back into place behind it.

Exhibiting ritualistic behavior like before, two robed priests entered and stood to the side of the opposite tunnel, while a cluster of slaves gathered up the head and other remains of the slain criminal's body.

Rayden and Doros shared an extended look that made it clear that her companion had not derived any sort of pleasure from the events in the pit. Beyond Doros, Polybius had a somber expression, while Crassor looked sullen and morose.

After a brief wait, the crier announced the next event in the same manner as he had done before, making an offering of the looming bloodshed to the divinity of the Imperator and power and glory of the Empire.

In the next exhibition, a throng of condemned criminals in loincloths, armed with short blades or spears, found themselves pitted against a pair of well-trained warriors. The criminals entered the sands through the gate to the right, while the warriors entered through the left.

Both of the warriors tall and muscular in build, one had a dark skin tone, with the other's being light in hue. Announced as champions of the arena, the two were greeted with thunderous accolades.

The dark-skinned warrior carried an oval-shaped hide shield and a distinctive spear, both of the types used in the lands across the sea and far to the south. Fur-tasseled upper arm and ankle bands decorated his brawny limbs.

In his right hand, the other warrior gripped a wider, inward-curving blade, like those found in places like Thrakkia, one of the stronger kingdoms in the lands of Griaca to the east. A round, bronze-faced shield held in his left hand displayed the image of an eagle upon the polished surface.

The warriors held the favor of the crowd from the outset.

Rayden knew the outcome before the fighting even began. In her eyes, the exhibition was far more a massacre in nature than it was any true clash at arms.

Despite having a significant advantage in numbers, the

criminals stood no chance. Severing heads, ripping guts open, and hewing limbs off, the two warriors meted gruesome ends out to the criminals.

Rayden could see the skillful pair extending the slaughter for the entertainment of the feverish, exhilarated audience. Honed and disciplined, the two fighters avoided broad openings offering easy kill strikes; instead waiting until they could deliver a more spectacular blow to one of their heavily outmatched opponents.

Abandoning the brutal massacre in the grip of sheer terror, the last two criminals still alive had to be chased down before they were finished off.

The spear-bearing warrior mounted the head of his last kill on the blade of his weapon. Thrusting the spear upward and standing tall, he displayed the ghastly trophy to the adulation of the crowd.

After setting his shield and weapon down on the sand, the other warrior lifted the final criminal in his arms. Finishing the exhibition, the warrior dropped down and broke the man's back on his right knee.

The crowd reacted to the dramatic finish with a dizzying ebullience, filling the air with a rabid cacophony coursing with raw bloodlust.

Striding side by side across the blood-spattered sand, the two warriors exited the pit through the tunnel to the left.

Allies at the moment, they could well be facing each other across the same sands on another day. On such a day, only one of the two would leave the sands with breath in their lungs.

Limbs, heads, and mutilated bodies were then collected up and carried from the arena, leaving numerous blood-stained patches on the ground behind. As before, two priests entered and raised their arms skyward.

Everything within Rayden warned of a deeper purpose to the contests taking place before her. Underneath the public veneer, something very important to the Imperator and the sorcerers in league with him transpired.

Once the pit had been cleared and a little time passed, a group of Teveren soldiers marched through the gateway to the right. Leading a large batch of ragged-looking men and women chained together, they headed toward the center of the arena.

A cold wave of apprehension passed through Rayden at the sight. All around her, the crowd began cheering in heightening anticipation.

The men and women being herded forward did not exhibit the harder edge of violent criminals. With several of them clutching onto each other, they looked far out of place on the sands of the pit.

Horns blared and a call for silence followed, settling the exuberant crowd down.

The voice of the crier then rang out to the heights of the arena.

"Fools that refuse and deny the divinity of the Imperator will now be offered up to his divinity. In our next exhibition ... featuring creatures never before seen within the arena ... a greater sacrifice offered to the divinity of the Imperator, for your pleasure!"

A jubilant frenzy met the announcement.

Seeing the cruel, merciless expressions on the faces all around her, Rayden grew even more revolted at the spectacle. A part of her wished to get up and leave the arena right then, but another instinct told her to bear witness, no matter how difficult.

Tears poured down the face of haggard-looking woman of middle years. An older man near to her dripped steadily from a soaked loincloth, having emptied his bladder in the grip of terror. Closing her eyes, a young woman in tattered garments trembled.

Another young woman clutched onto a man of about her age. Hugging each other tight, both of them began to weep.

The sight of their sorrow and fear brought a deep, burning agony into Rayden's heart.

She could do nothing.

Surrounded by a mob of so many thousands, with no weapons, Rayden found herself helpless for the second time in the Imperial City to stop an evil about to take place. Powerless to intervene, she struggled to brace herself, a couple of tears sliding from the corners of her eyes and crawling down her face.

The crystalline tears carried a blend of compassion for the victims and rage toward the Teverens; the wrath encompassing those providing the spectacle and the crowd taking pleasure from it.

Rayden could not understand how any man or woman deemed human could take pleasure in the wretched display. Yet in a crowd of tens of thousands, she, Doros, Polybius, and Crassor were among a tiny handful not cheering.

All that Rayden could do was bear witness and set her mind toward bringing an end to the vile displays through the vanquishing of the Imperator and those serving him.

Two men within the group about to be slaughtered then caught Rayden's eyes. Both had their arms stretched wide and their heads raised toward the sky. In a way, their manner resembled the behavior of priests.

In stark contrast to all the others, the two men had placid expressions, devoid of all fear and anxiety. Looking unruffled in the face of the looming spectacle, they invoked Rayden's memories.

Rayden doubted her eyes for a moment, but the identities of the men manifested and remained unmistakable.

She had last seen the enigmatic pair when walking with Hamilcar along the Boreus Way. The two men had been offering prayers over crucified slaves lining the notorious road for many leagues.

Their presence had driven off the malevolent figure that had been skulking among the decaying bodies and stalking Rayden and Hamilcar. Mocking Rayden, and displaying an unnatural presence within, the possessed figure had shown no fear of her. Yet it had scurried off like a wild beast singed with fire in the face of the two priests.

The other gateway then rattled open. Rayden tensed, and then she turned her head, wondering what kind of horror would emerge from the dark maw to her left.

One after the other, a pack of grotesque creatures trotted out from the tunnel and continued onto the sands. Gasps and exclamations broke out through the crowd.

Looking as if they had loped from the depths of a nightmare, the creatures snarled and growled, eyeing the captive group of humans at the center of the pit.

Rayden leaned forward, staring at the strange beasts. She had never seen anything like them before, in any of the lands that she had traveled.

Fanning out wide when they entered, a couple of the creatures passed close to Rayden, affording her a few moments to scrutinize their unfamiliar forms.

Cadaverous gray in hue, the bizarre creatures had long, lean bodies with narrow limbs. Flatter in profile with upturned snouts, their visages looked akin to those of bats. A pair of large, triangular ears adorned their heads, set above eyes of solid black.

A pronounced set of fangs accented the dense array of spiky teeth filling their broad jaws. A crest of coarse, black bristles ran down from the middle of their heads, continuing along the central ridge of their backs.

At the ends of their forelegs, the beasts had extremities similar to elongated hands, each with six digits, one of them thumb-like.

Their hind legs ended in a similar kind of structure, though larger and even more elongated in form.

Behind the upper segment of their forelegs and the higher portion of their hind legs, the creatures had leathery membranes of skin spanning from limb to body. While not wings capable of flight, the four distinct sections of membrane looked well-suited for gliding.

A few of the creatures in the forefront, nearing the chained humans, demonstrated another formidable trait. All twenty-four of their extremities, both in front and back, harbored retractable claws.

Unsheathing the curving, sharp, prominent weapons, the lead creatures exhibited fearsome natural arsenals.

Displaying great quickness, several of the creatures then bounded around the huddled mass of impending victims, surrounding the unfortunates completely.

Watching the creatures encircling them, many of the men and women screamed and cried out, their pitiful utterances trailing off in the upper rows of an audience ravenous for the spilling of blood.

All the while, the two priests that Rayden had recognized among the victims continued to hold their arms wide and gaze toward the skies above. An oasis of calm in a stark desert of terror, their demeanor in the face of such a horrific fate attested to something that reached far beyond the arena's sands.

Stepping forward, the beasts converged on the trapped, chained humans.

The most fortunate among the hapless victims died swiftly.

Some tried to strike at the beasts, making feeble attempts to fight them off. Drawing laughter and derision from the crowd, their efforts merely enraged the bizarre creatures, bringing savage attacks upon them.

The two apparent priests continued with their quiet supplication after the carnage began, but they were not spared the doom of the others. If anything, the priests' serenity appeared to ignite a fearsome wrath in the creatures assailing them.

Claws grasping and driving deep into flesh, the beasts ripped the two men asunder, limb from limb. To Rayden's eyes, it seemed as if the creatures sought to desecrate the two priests in the extreme, brutal manner of their slaying.

Astonishingly, the two priests did not utter a single cry throughout their evisceration and dismemberment. Life slipped out of their bodies long before the creatures were finished with them, and little that could be recognized of the priests remained in the aftermath.

When all of the humans had been slain, the creatures began to feed.

Rayden could not believe what she was witnessing. The maniacal crowd cheered beasts consuming the flesh of fellow human beings.

A line of soldiers in shining helms, breastplates, and greaves issued through the gate to the right and formed up, shield to shield, with a second line getting into place a few strides behind them. All of the soldiers in both ranks held long spears. After getting into position, the soldiers started marching across the sand, yelling and shouting.

The beasts gorging themselves at the center began moving away from the bodies at the approaching wall of shields and spears. While reluctant to be parted from their feast of flesh, most of the strange beasts funneled into the tunnel exit on the other side of the pit.

Turning and issuing a grating screech, one of the beasts suddenly bounded toward the oncoming soldiers.

Leaping high, the beast glided through the air and cleared the first row of soldiers. A couple of the soldiers in the second row caught the beast on their spears and brought it to the ground. Other soldiers thrust their weapons at the beast, opening up many wounds.

Before it succumbed to the spears lancing into its body, the creature wounded a couple of the soldiers, leaving them bleeding from severe lacerations. The injuries of the soldiers drew more than a few cheers from the crowd.

"I have had far enough of this," Rayden vented, her voice sounding just above a whisper. She had seen all that she could take.

"No more," Doros added in a low voice. "I want to get away from this place."

Polybius leaned over and said to Doros and Rayden in a low voice, "Go, both of you ... I do not wish to stay, but I must remain for appearances, but you can be excused as foreigners."

Tightly clenched jaws and a reddened flush on the glaring face of Crassor spoke loud enough regarding his thoughts of the bloody spectacle.

Rayden and Doros nodded to Polybius, the crowds around them continuing to applaud the events in the pit.

Unable to stomach any more massacres of innocent people, Rayden got to her feet and worked her way down to an aisle leading to a tunnel exit. Doros followed her close behind.

Polybius, with Crassus posing as his slave, remained in place. Rayden knew that Polybius' words had not been patronizing. Both of the men would much rather have departed with her and Doros.

Rayden paid little attention to those around her as she walked through the long tunnel and exited the arena. Coming to a stop a short distance outside the hulking edifice, Rayden took a few deep breaths.

"I can not undo what I have seen, but it shows us what we fight against," Rayden declared. "It gives me further understanding of our enemy's nature. I know one thing with certainty. We must prevail."

"What I saw will haunt many nights, for years to come," Doros replied in a sympathetic air. "To think that people cheer so loud for such cruelty."

"It takes strength to accept scars of memory but know that what we witnessed makes clearer the existence of a deeper, darker purpose to all of this," Rayden replied, returning to the things that she had pondered while in the stands. She recalled the words of the crier, just before the massacre.

'... *a greater sacrifice offered to the divinity of the Imperator...!*'

Rayden did not think that the words '*sacrifice*' and '*offered*' had been idly chosen.

Something venomous and powerful lurked just beneath the words. Laying claim to the wickedness on display to tens of thousands, it fed upon the malignant energies generated.

"A purpose?" Doros asked Rayden, her brow furrowing. "Beyond favor of the people?"

Rayden nodded. "Yes, something more. Much more. This is one vast ritual, just like the man hurled to the eels and the other skinned alive were smaller ones. Everything in this city is connected. It is a city of wicked rituals."

"Empowering the enemy in an unseen way," Doros stated, nodding her head.

"Rituals of power ... hidden in the sight of all," Rayden replied. "This arena ... is nothing more than a giant altar for multitudes of blood sacrifices."

An expression of stunned amazement manifested on Doros' face. She did not speak for several moments.

"Who knows what they prepare in the shadows," Doros replied in a subdued voice, looking daunted at Rayden's assertion.

"The tribes will need more than strength of arms to overcome the Imperator," Rayden declared, staring back toward the arena. "Other kinds of help will be needed. The sorcery that is being worked must be countered."

Another roar from the crowd poured from the massive structure. As if startled from the noise, a couple of large rats scurried across the stones paving the area that Rayden stood upon.

Exhaling once more, Rayden glanced toward Doros. "Let us get away from here and find our way back. I want no more of this ... but a stop along the way to get some drink would be welcome."

"I would find that welcome too," Doros said, nodding, and the two began walking away from the arena and its frenzied occupants.

Striding past a gleaming fountain of white marble, Rayden eyed the arching streams of water coming from an elaborate display of sculpted figures at the center. Cooling the air, the sparkling arcs accented a merry scene of smiling, naked women frolicking in the surf of some unknown ocean. Rayden could almost hear laughter coming from the stone figures.

Rayden eyed a few columns ahead topped with shining bronze statuary. A proud-looking warrior stood vigil with sword and shield in hand. Dressed in loose robes, a regal-looking man had his right arm outstretched with the palm of his left hand pressed to the middle of his chest, as if in the midst of giving an oration. Wearing breastplate and greaves, another majestic figure beyond cast an unblinking gaze northward.

Finding it difficult to match the beautiful, striking displays in the fountain and statues with the wanton bloodlust and cruelty that she had just experienced, Rayden mused about how the Teverens considered her, Doros, and Crassor to be crude barbarians.

Little could be more barbarous than what took place within the Teverens' great arena. All of the elaborate temples, baths, statuary, mosaics, and paintings in the world could not drape the veneer of civility over such loathsome savagery.

Hearing some boisterous laughter and loud banter ahead, Rayden looked in the direction of the voices and saw a tavern on the right side of the street.

"Here is where we stop," she announced.

"I have gained a great thirst myself," Doros replied. "You will find no argument from me."

Rayden waited for a group of slaves bearing a litter to pass before crossing the narrow street.

Once inside, she found an open table with stools along the right side. After she and Doros had taken seats there, a young woman from the tavern attended them.

A little heavyset, the black-haired tavern girl had a pleasant demeanor. Rayden followed her advice regarding a type of wine said to be difficult to get under normal circumstances. The girl lamented that the ongoing war would make it and many other types of wine all but impossible to replace, at least until the fighting had concluded.

Ordering cups for herself and Doros, Rayden watched the serving girl walk off.

Close by, a few men shouted in response to a tumble of the bone dice that they had been gambling with. A groan from one and a raucous cheer from the other proclaimed who had gotten the better of the toss.

An older man sitting alone in a corner stared in silence at the cup before him. Barely moving, the grim look on his sunken face told of a man drowning his sorrows in wine.

At another table, a group of men listened to one of their number telling a story about some exploits of his as a soldier. Boastful in tone, he elicited a lively response from his companions, who all raised their cups high to him.

The tavern had a far different feel than the one overseen by Stramma and his brotherhood. Located close to the arena, its patronage likely had a far greater variance to those anchored within a more residential district of the city.

Outside, the bustling activity of the city continued to stream past the tavern. Rayden could not imagine living among such a swarm of motion, day after day, and year after year.

The serving girl returned and set down two earthenware cups, both filled to the brim with a deep red wine.

Telling the serving girl to wait for a moment, Rayden quaffed her first cup down in one draught, ordering another right after. The girl smiled cheerfully, took the empty cup, and strode away.

A few eyes glanced in the direction of Rayden and Doros, with some of the attention from male patrons more libidinous in nature, but no one chose to bother them.

For their sakes, Rayden was glad that the men stayed to themselves. In the wake of the arena, she knew that her temper would be short when it came to a provocation from Teverens.

Drinking together, as the light of day passed from the late afternoon into the gloaming of dusk, Rayden and Doros spoke together about a number of things. Their conversation ranged from tales of Doros' family to a few of Rayden's more harrowing travels.

A dish of seasoned pork and an assortment of stewed vegetables staved off a few pangs of hunger. Though simple, Rayden found the small meal satisfying.

She could not begrudge the Teverens when it came to food. The more that Rayden partook of Teveren fare, the more she appreciated just how much variety it contained.

Tables emptied and filled back up again, with the old man in the corner the only tavern patron remaining in place besides Doros and Rayden. Other than a short fight breaking out between a pair of inebriated men, nothing eventful occurred, much to Rayden's preference.

Rayden needed the extended respite at that moment.

Nursing cups of wine, Rayden let the toxic gloom infecting

her spirit seep out. There would be time enough to revisit the things she had experienced earlier that day.

Not long after night had fallen, Rayden and Doros got up and left the tavern. Having paced herself well-enough after the first cup of wine, Rayden had not lost hold of her balance or faculties for the way back.

A few roguish-looking individuals peered at them from the shadows of nooks and alleys but did not attempt to waylay them. A pair of foreign women carrying weapons at night proved enough of a deterrent to overcome any temptations they may have harbored.

Wafting from uncountable cook fires and braziers within the lofty tenements, the scent of burning wood accented the evening air. A few wagons and carts trundled along the streets, the first budding signs of the night traffic that would blossom across the city in little time.

When Rayden finally reached their quarters, entered her chamber, and lay down on her mattress, sleep evaded her at first. Alone, thoughts of the day percolated once more, troubling her spirit to its most intimate depths.

Lying in the dark and staring up at the ceiling, Rayden had one small request for any merciful god that would listen.

With all of her heart, she desired the brief refuge of a dreamless night's sleep.

The faces of the two priests and the people chained together with them arose in her thoughts once more. The monstrosities that had slain them pervaded her mind in a cascade of vivid imagery.

Rayden could still hear the crowd baying for the blood of the chained victims.

A few more tears slipped from her eyes, running down the sides of her face to the soft pillow that her head lay upon. Alone in the darkness, she wept for the innocents.

Turning onto her left side a little later, she curled up and focused on her breathing, trying to drive the tormenting memories away. For a long while she did not succeed, but gradually the horrid visions began receding as her weariness mounted.

At long last falling into the depths of sleep, Rayden lost consciousness, her exhaustion finally overcoming her unsettled mind.

Whether an act of mercy or protection involving some unknown deity, or sheer chance, no dreams of blood-soaked arena sands teeming with stark displays of death haunted her that night.

CHAPTER 4

Opening her window shutters, Rayden looked out upon the sea of mist engulfing the Imperial City. A new day had arrived, bringing along with it great potential to learn more about the city and its people.

After tending to bodily needs and breaking her night's fast on some bread, cheese, grapes, and a little wine, Rayden found Polybius in the room to the right of the entrance. Seated in the chair behind the table, he leaned over the surface with an intent expression.

Dipping a quill feather into a little jar, he scribbled upon a sheet of parchment. Looking up and seeing Rayden, Polybius smiled.

"A good new day to you, Rayden," he greeted her, looking to be in a buoyant mood. "I thought I would get some practice in at letters, before the day unfolded."

"What do your words say?" Rayden replied, looking down at the parchment.

"Nothing much," he answered, chuckling. "A few words about the morning sun in an attempt to construct a poem. It will take a little more work."

"A good poem is like a smooth wine for the ears," Rayden replied, smiling at him. "You will have to share it with me when it is finished."

"You will be one of the first," Polybius responded, grinning.

"What does the day hold for us?" Rayden asked, curious about his ideas.

"Something far more enjoyable than what we went through yesterday," Polybius answered. "We cannot have two days in a row of that. Today, we will go to the baths. A proper Teveren goes daily, and I have been remiss in attending. Come with me, it will be a pleasant experience for you. I am sure of it."

"I have scouted the walls and gates," Rayden said. "I would like to study them a little more, but that can wait if you see some importance in these baths."

"I think that a sojourn to the baths today would be good for all of us," Polybius responded, his countenance growing serious. "We had our fill of dark things in our visit to the arena yesterday."

"It is nothing more than an enormous sacrificial altar," Rayden told him, frowning. "A vast temple of blood sacrifice."

"Doros spoke with me about your conclusion," Polybius replied. "If that is true, it is troubling. Even dismaying."

"They have created sources of power for their sorcery, everywhere in this city," Rayden responded. "The tribes bring enough warriors to counter several legions, but what is there to oppose this?"

"I cannot say," Polybius replied in a low voice, looking away from her.

"A way must be found," Rayden declared, her words coursing with determination.

"Then it is even better to go to the baths today," Polybius said, bringing his eyes back to her. "It is a place to clear the mind and think."

"Sounds promising to me, and needed," Rayden told him, thinking of her difficulty gaining sleep the previous evening.

Polybius inserted the quill in the jar and stood up. "Then let all of us go. We will first need to purchase a few clothing items to align with custom."

"A visit to the markets would also be a welcome thing," Rayden replied.

"Then let us not tarry long here," Polybius said, his lips spreading into a smile. "Let the day begin, and may it be one we can find some enjoyment!"

***

The aroma of burning wood thickened the nearer that they drew to an enormous compound of buildings surrounded by an outer wall. A cluster of smoke columns, all of the same size and pattern, reached skyward from farther inside.

"Astounding," Doros commented, staring upward.

"Not something you get to see every day," Rayden replied to her, watching the dense coils of smoke spiraling upward.

"It is another construct of the Imperator's," Polybius remarked. "Nothing to rival it that I have ever heard of."

"I have been to Teveren baths," Crassor stated. "None of them were of this scale. This is something like no other."

"Keep your ears open inside," Polybius said. "This is where the most powerful in the city come every day, and a great amount of business is conducted here. It is a place to enjoy, but there is abundant opportunity. Tidings, rumors, secrets ... a trove abounds for those who listen."

Rayden nodded. "We will follow your lead in here, Polybius, but we must all remain alert and attentive."

Grand arches marked the entryways into the massive bath complex. Some entering and others leaving, large numbers of men and women strolled through the arches.

Those exiting had a relaxed, refreshed air about them. For Rayden, the sight of them boded well for her impending experience.

Polybius paused to give a few coins over to one of several plain-clad attendants standing at the entrance.

Following Polybius, Rayden and the others strode through one of the arches and gained their first sights of what lay beyond the outer walls.

Slowing to a halt, Rayden stared at a gigantic pool of water, filling a greater portion of the vast, open courtyard before her. The sun's rays gleamed brilliantly off the clear water's surface.

Holding a depth of about waist-high to a man of average height, the pool contained a multitude of people. Wading and conversing, with some splashing each other and indulging in playful displays, the men and women in the water looked to be enjoying each other's company within the splendid, irenic environment.

Gazing upon the pool's occupants, Rayden found it hard to believe that they came from the same populace craving the spectacles of violent death in the arena the day before. More than likely, a few of those within her view had been in the stands, screeching for bloodletting.

A portico spanned the left side of the courtyard, with what looked to be half-domed structures in the corners. Several alcoves in the wall were occupied with individuals or small groups, and the faint sounds of a stringed instrument carried through the air from that direction. A group in one alcove broke out into applause as a speaker concluded an oration.

Archways led into a massive edifice looming at the rear of the pool.

Through a colonnade to the right spread a colorful sea of flowers, trees, statuary, and fountains. The bounteous garden beckoned to Rayden with promises of repose and tranquility.

Men and women strolled beneath the boughs of trees abundant with colorful blossoms. Others laughed and talked while sitting upon stone benches and the edges of fountains, the latter's water glittering in the embrace of the sun.

"We will start here," Polybius declared, leading them toward the building at the back of the pool.

Engaging in another exchange involving a slave attendant, Polybius paid for their garments to be looked over. Then, they separated briefly, with Doros and Rayden entering one area to disrobe and change, while Polybius and Crassor entered another.

Rayden and Doros donned narrow stretches of cloth that wrapped about their upper bodies and covered their breasts. Their lower garment consisted of a variant to the loincloth worn by men. The different clothing piqued Rayden's curiosity over what was to come.

Crassor and Polybius wore nothing more than loincloths when they regrouped in the courtyard with the pool.

"I suppose it is now time to experience the baths," Polybius addressed the others with a grin.

"Where do we begin?" Rayden asked, looking around.

"We can get a little exercise first, if you would like," Polybius replied. "Let me show you."

Rayden and the others followed Polybius into an arcaded passage on the side of the building where they had just changed cloths.

Walking along the arcade, they passed several niches where others were occupied in a variety of activities. Slave attendants bearing food and drink navigated about the people in the recessed spaces, offering refreshment.

From fierce debates to performances of music and the giving of speeches, a number of options beckoned to passersby.

"Do not let appearances deceive you in here," Polybius remarked in a lower voice as they walked close together. "This may look like a place for idleness and indulgence, but it is where important matters are conducted and decided upon."

"I can imagine," Rayden replied, taking notice of the number of small groups engaged in intensive conversations. "It looks like a place that makes it easy for one to think and talk."

"Never have I seen the like," Doros added, gazing around with a look of amazement.

"Even the Imperator is known to visit these baths, in person," Polybius added.

Sunlight pouring through the columns beckoned to another large courtyard just ahead. Rayden could hear shouts, grunts, claps, and other sounds of activity coming from it as they neared.

Peering into the open space, Rayden took in the sight of numerous men and a few women engaged in physical exercise and athletic contests of all kinds.

In one area, several men and a woman lifted stone weights. In another, a trio of men played a game involving the hurling of leather-covered balls at each other while standing at equal distances apart. In yet another area, pairs of men competed in wrestling contests, their bodies slick with oil and sweat.

"Here we can get a little exercise before we relax in the waters of the baths," Polybius announced.

Turning to Doros, Rayden grinned. "I think this spot could be enjoyable."

"I agree," Doros replied, looking off into another part of the courtyard. "I would like to explore this place."

"I am wanting to give my muscles a little work, and Crassor will be able to participate too," Polybius said, gazing toward the area with the stone weights.

"I think we will all find something to do here," Crassor stated.

"Then I will find something to get myself into," Rayden told her companions. "Go and choose something to your liking!"

Polybius stretched his arms wide. "I have already made my decision."

"As have I," Crassor responded.

"A few things catch my eye, but I will settle on one soon enough," Doros added, looking around.

Doros, Polybius, and Crassor strode away. Doros approached the part of the courtyard with the larger group games, while Polybius and Crassor walked straight toward the stone weights.

So many options lay before Rayden.

Hearing the thump of fists on a stuffed canvas sack, Rayden observed a young man throwing a barrage of punches for a few moments. Sweat glistened on his arms and shoulders, and it looked like he had been training for awhile.

About to start in his direction, Rayden stopped herself, catching movement at the edge of her peripheral vision.

A tall, broad-shouldered woman approached Rayden.

Her black hair pulled back in a long, thick braid, she had an intense look embedded within her dark brown eyes. Her limbs displayed an excellent muscle tone that heralded the presence of considerable physical strength.

"You are a foreigner ... you look barbarian," the woman said in a mid-toned voice. Nothing more than a declaration, her words carried no traces of insult. "But surely, you are not of the hordes descending upon the city."

Looking her in the eyes, Rayden replied in an even tone. "I am a foreigner and of a tribe to the north, but I am Alettani, allies of the Teveren Empire."

"You have the air of a warrior about you," the woman declared. "Do you fight in war?"

"I do," Rayden stated.

"I am prevented from fighting in the legions, but here there are no such rules," the woman responded. "Would you agree to a match in wrestling? I have few challenges from fellow women, but you look like you would test my ability."

"I would enjoy a chance to measure my own skills," Rayden answered without hesitation. "You look strong."

The woman smiled. "That is good to hear. I regard myself so."

"What are the rules of this match," Rayden asked, unsure of Teveren customs in such a circumstance.

"The match will go until one of us submits," the woman said. "It is a contest of grappling ... no striking."

"I consent to that," Rayden replied, nodding.

The trace of a grin formed on the woman's wide lips. "You are a gift from the gods. I had feared not finding an opponent today."

"I am pleased that I can allay your fears," Rayden replied with a grin.

"Come with me, there is a good space for a match over there," the woman said, gesturing to an open area within the sprawling, sand-covered courtyard.

"What is your name?" the woman asked as they walked toward the space together.

"Rayden."

"I am Ingassa," the woman introduced herself. "I live in the city helping my father, a butcher of swine."

"Labor that requires strength," Rayden observed.

Ingassa nodded. "It is fortunate for him that I grew strong. My two brothers fight in the legions and can not help him."

"It sounds like it is good you are here for him," Rayden said.

"It is, and he has needed me," Ingassa stated, though something about the look in her eyes told Rayden that the woman viewed her position as a familial duty alone. She exhibited no signs of desire for the occupation that her father had pursued.

Nearing the designated space, Ingassa held up a pouch and took a couple of small bronze vials out. She handed one over to Rayden.

"This will add a little more challenge to our match," Ingassa told her. "Nothing more than an oil for the skin."

"You come well prepared to this place," Rayden remarked. "You even have two vessels."

"Both must apply the oil, or it should not be used at all," Ingassa said. "Not all who come here carry it with them, so I bring an additional vessel along with me."

"Your forethought makes possible a purer contest of skill," Rayden replied in an amiable fashion.

"Which is a better way for one's true ability to be measured," Ingassa said.

"Agreed," Rayden responded, impressed with the woman's mindset.

Ingassa then removed her tunic, revealing garb similar to Rayden beneath. Removing the wood stopper from her vial, she poured some of the contents into her left palm and rubbed her hands together.

Rayden did likewise.

Slicking their skin with oils to make gripping flesh more difficult, the two prepared for the bout. A few onlookers began to gather in the vicinity, though they kept a comfortable distance from the contestants.

For her size, Ingassa moved with considerable speed. From the outset, the Teveren woman demonstrated excellent ability.

More than once, Rayden found herself in momentary peril, only to escape the hold and apply one of her own to her skillful opponent.

Initiative and advantage shifted back and forth between them, with concentrated bursts of energy and stretches of prolonged strain. Breathing hard, Ingassa and Rayden exerted themselves using legs and arms to counter and flip each other over. The skin oil made every hold more difficult, their slippery body surfaces proving helpful in evasions time and time again.

Ingassa exhibited a resilient, determined warrior's heart throughout the contest.

At last, Rayden slipped around Ingassa and locked a firm chokehold onto her. Refusing to concede the contest, the tenacious woman continued to struggle, doing all that she could to break the iron hold upon her.

Her movements slowed, bit by bit, but Ingassa did not surrender. At last, Rayden sensed her opponent's body become limp and she relaxed her taut hold at once.

A smattering of cheers broke out from the spectators that had assembled nearby.

Releasing the hold fully, Rayden clutched the woman and prevented her from falling to the ground.

"Wake up, Ingassa!" Rayden exclaimed, smacking her lightly on the face. "Wake up!"

After a few moments of further cajoling, the woman's eyes fluttered open. Taking several breaths, Ingassa said nothing at first.

"I had never been beaten," the woman finally stated in a leaden tone, a melancholy look within her eyes. "That includes some matches that I have had with men."

"You are a warrior, Ingassa," Rayden told her, smiling, sweat dripping from her own body. She helped Ingassa into a sitting position. "It is an honor to have you as an opponent."

"Rayden, you are gracious in victory," the woman said, her breathing now steady and relaxed. "Are all the women where you are from like you?"

Rayden shook her head and grinned. "No, you would fare well in contests like the one we had in the lands that I am from."

"That is good to hear," Ingassa replied, though her eyes still conveyed great dejection with the outcome.

Looking around, Rayden espied Polybius and Crassor among those lifting the stone weights, while Doros had joined in with some women running about with hoops. All three of her companions appeared to be immersed in their pursuits and she had no desire to interrupt them.

"It does not look like my companions are finished yet," Rayden said, turning back toward Ingassa.

"A long time can pass by you in here before you realize it," Ingassa remarked. "Is one of your friends the dark-haired one in the lead of those with the hoops?"

"Yes," Rayden answered. "Her name is Doros."

"I have learned today that the Alettani women have great physical ability," Ingassa commented, continuing to watch Doros. "If the women of the other northern tribes are similar, then we face a far more dangerous adversary than I thought."

Rayden could see the shadow of worry passing across Ingassa's face. She reflected the fear of most people in a time of war.

Ingassa, and most all living inside the walls of the Imperial City, just wanted to go about their days without disruption. They did not share the minds of the wealthy and powerful in seeking new lands to exploit, conquer, and subjugate.

Yet those like Ingassa would pay the most terrible price if the storms of war were set loose in full fury through the streets of the city. The thought filled Rayden's heart with sadness, but the war to overcome the Imperator had to be waged.

To allow the Imperator to continue would be to doom the people of many lands.

"May this conflict pass swiftly and see few come to harm," Rayden told Ingassa.

Ingassa looked into Rayden's eyes. "I do not think that it will be so, but when the moment comes, I will show that I am a warrior."

Rayden nodded and replied in a low voice. "I know that you will."

A smile with a bittersweet edge spread slowly across Ingassa's lips. "I have only met you this day, but I sense a kinship between us. If the gods had chosen differently, we might have been sisters."

Rayden smiled. "I am not one to understand the ways of gods."

"I am not either," Ingassa said. Her voice then lifted, and a spark returned to her eyes. "What do you say to getting cleaned off! We are both well-covered in dust, sand and sweat!"

"It sounds good to me," Rayden replied, standing up. "But guide me, the Alettani do not have any places such as this."

"Then I will help you," Ingassa said, getting up to her feet. "Follow me."

Ingassa led Rayden over to an area of the arcade running along one side of the courtyard, where a number of slaves attended to men and women finished with their physical activity.

Using his hands, a slave rubbed sand on Rayden's skin, spreading it all over her body. Working the gritty handfuls down her arms, legs, back, and torso, the slave created a layer of sand grains clinging to sweat and body oil. Taking out a small implement that had the appearance of a knife, the slave carefully scraped the sand off, taking the sweat and oil along with it.

When the slave had finished with the thorough task, Rayden found herself in a refreshed state with her skin cleansed.

"Feels so good, does it not?" Ingassa asked, when the slave tending to her had completed his work.

"Very good," Rayden answered.

"Now, it is time for the baths," Ingassa said.

"I had better wait for my companions," Rayden told her, looking back to the courtyard.

Ingassa looked a little disappointed at her response. "I have to go inside and see to a bath, as I have to return to my father soon. He will need a little more help before this day is over."

"At the markets?" Rayden asked.

Ingassa nodded. "Only I like dealing with buyers less than

he does. Always arguing to pull another coin or two back from the price."

"I can imagine," Rayden said, having no doubt that haggling became an insulting and irritating experience for many sellers.

"It is an honor to have met you, Rayden," Ingassa stated. "Thank you for the contest, though you bested me. I shall pray to the gods that our paths cross again one day."

"It is my hope that they do, too," Rayden said. She extended her arm out, palm open. "In the manner of many in the north, let us acknowledge each other as warriors before we part."

A little hesitant, Ingassa mimicked Rayden's gesture.

Rayden clasped the woman's forearm, and she returned the grip a moment later.

Elation swelled within Ingassa's eyes when they let go. "Thank you, Rayden."

"You earned it, Ingassa," Rayden said.

The surface of Ingassa's eyes glistened. "May the gods have you in their favor, always."

Turning, Ingassa strode away, a little abrupt in manner. Rayden took no offense at the parting, suspecting that the Teveren woman did not wish for her to see an outburst of raw emotion.

Rayden turned around to watch her companions. She did not have much longer to wait before the others concluded their exercise. At Polybius' lead, they went through the process involving the slaves and sand scraping.

When all of them had finished, they gathered together.

"It is now time for you to experience the baths themselves," Polybius declared.

"So far, all of this has been pleasant," Rayden replied, taking one more look around the open space with its flurry of activity.

Walking together, the four companions left the courtyard behind and continued into the main building.

***

Marble columns of various colors soared upward, supporting cross-vaulted ceilings painted in bright, vivid colors. Large windows set high on the walls allowed the sun's rays to flood into the huge, rectangular chamber.

Small, circular pools, ringed with a couple of steps beneath the surface for immersing and sitting, occupied spaces along the right and left sides of the room.

A light, veiling mist filled the room, and the robust heat permeating the air clung to Rayden from the moment that she stepped into the spacious chamber. After a few moments, sweat beads began forming on her skin.

Most of the pools had a full compliment of occupants. Rayden and her companions had to endure a short delay until a few men climbed out from one of the pools and cleared enough space for all of them to sit together.

The water hot to the touch, Rayden lowered herself into the pool slowly, easing onto one of the ringing steps. Acclimating to the heat, she looked across at a pair of women whose appearances proclaimed their higher status.

Both had colorful facial makeup and ornate hairstyles, the latter displaying ascending layers of curls that rose to a point. The hair of the woman to the left had been dyed crimson, while the hair of the one to the right was a natural, deep black.

Polybius exchanged a few pleasantries with the women as he got situated in place.

"Where are your companions from?" the crimson-haired one asked him in a casual tone, eyeing Doros and Rayden.

"Alettani, allies of the Teveren Empire, from the north," Polybius answered her. "They helped me reach the city when the barbarians swept down from the far north. Kept me safe."

"It is said the barbarians are nearing the city walls," the other woman stated. "Maybe another day or two before they arrive."

"Dire tidings indeed," Polybius replied, sounding concerned.

The crimson-haired woman laughed. "My husband is an officer in the Imperial Legion. There is nothing to fear."

"I would love to hear some good tidings," Polybius replied. "I was forced to flee my home in the north with the barest of warnings."

"Peronnius will pull his legions inside, and when Marus' legions get here, the barbarians will find themselves trapped," the crimson-haired woman replied. "Teveren jaws will grind the mongrels apart."

"Do not forget the Imperial fleets either," the dark-haired woman added. "Word has been sent to recall them. Another force will arrive by sea, soon enough."

Both of the women brimmed with confidence, with no trace of worry in their eyes or voice.

"You are certain of this?" Polybius asked.

The dark-haired woman laughed. "Her husband may be an officer in the Imperial Legion, but mine is on the Imperial Council."

"You will find no envy from me, as long as I get to visit you on your coastal estate when the barbarians are crushed," the crimson-haired woman stated to her friend in a merry tone.

"Perhaps select a few choice male slaves from the captives taken," the dark-haired woman replied, a lascivious gleam flashing in her eyes. "At my expense, of course. We are dear friends, after all."

"That would be so delightful," the other responded with an excited air.

"It will be enough for me just to return home," Polybius remarked.

"You have no idea of what you are missing," the dark-haired woman stated. Both she and her friend chortled.

The two women returned to conversing among themselves.

Her gaze following the green and yellow marble columns upward, Rayden gazed at the cross vaults spanning the ceiling high above. Light streamed through the windows just beneath the colorful, intertwining patterns covering the vaults like a host of vines abundant with blooms.

It did not take long for the sweat beading on the surface of Rayden's forehead to begin trickling down her face and shoulders. While the air remained thicker to the lungs from the heat and vapor pervading the long chamber, the bite of the water ebbed as her body acclimated to its touch.

Not long after, the two women excused themselves and got out of the pool. Slipping their feet into wooden clogs and toweling themselves off, they strolled down the length of the chamber.

Watching them go, Rayden thought about the tidings they had gleaned from the women about Marus, a Teveren fleet, and Peronnius. Polybius had been right. A lot could be learned while in the baths, for those who chose to listen.

A couple of older men took the place vacated by the women.

Looking across, one man's eyes spread wide in response to the sight of Rayden and Doros.

"Barbarians?" he exclaimed, and a glimmer of fear danced within his eyes. "What are barbarians doing here?"

"They are of the Alettani, allies of the Imperator," Polybius explained quickly. "Nothing to worry yourself over."

The man's friend replied. "You will have to forgive his alarm. He barely reached the city. The swarms of vermin from the north were close on his heels."

"It is understandable, I came from the north myself," Polybius replied in a polite manner. "My vineyards are up there, just outside of Trasterro. These two helped me reach the city in safety."

"Dark times have befallen us, but we must put our faith in

the Imperator," the other man declared.

His agitated friend nodded, but said nothing, casting a few anxious glances at Rayden and Doros.

As if taking the older man's discomfort as a cue, Polybius looked to Rayden, Doros, and Crassor. "I think it is time we cooled ourselves off!"

Nodding to the two men, Polybius stood up. Rayden got out of the pool, slipping her feet into wooden clogs and taking up a soft, woolen towel.

Polybius then led them down the chamber, between the pools.

"We have had plenty enough heat … but know that we have not been in the hottest place inside here," Polybius told the others. "Come with me, for a few moments."

He guided them down a narrow passage into a circular room filled with a near-blistering heat. It held no pools, but instead had alcoves arranged around the perimeter with places for sitting. A few people, pouring with sweat, looked up to them from where they sat.

Rayden and the others walked back out. Having no desire to stay in that room, she judged that the heat was so great that her feet would have burned were it not for the wooden clogs.

"Not where I desire to spend time," Polybius quipped when they emerged from the passage to the hot room.

"I can see why," Rayden said.

Polybius guided them down a short hallway into an even more capacious, rectangular chamber, arrayed in a similar fashion to the one they had left behind. Cold air greeted Rayden, enveloping her body and draping its soothing, cool touch all over her skin.

This time, they found an unoccupied pool to sit together in. Rayden eased into the frigid water, soaking in the chill.

Polybius closed his eyes and looked a little ill at first.

"What ails you?" Rayden asked him, becoming concerned fast.

"It happens to many, going from hot to cold," Polybius replied, keeping his eyes shut and breathing deep. "I will be fine. Give me a moment."

Rayden kept an eye on him while they sat together. No others joined them, there being plenty of pools and space for the other visitors to the chamber.

At long last, they climbed out of the icy waters and dried off again.

After leaving the colder pools behind, Polybius took them through another corridor to a large space filled with marble-topped, rectangular tables. All over the area, slaves attended men and woman lying lengthwise upon the surfaces.

"What is this?" Rayden asked him.

"Something you will enjoy," Polybius told her. "Allow them to work upon your body, and you will see. Trust me in this."

Slaves guided Doros, Rayden, and Polybius to open tables. At a gesture from the female slave with her, Rayden disrobed and climbed up onto the table, emulating those near to her.

Lying flat on her belly upon the marble surface, Rayden sighed when the woman attending to her began kneading her taut muscles and applying oils to her skin. The blended oils gave off a pleasant aroma, making each intake of breath something to savor. Closing her eyes, Rayden listened to the light smacking of hands on skin at the other tables.

The strong fingers working on her body hurt a little in some places, but the aftermath left Rayden with supple, loosened muscles and a relaxed, dreamy state. The entire process took some time, and Rayden had to muster additional willpower to get up from the table, when all had been concluded.

One look at Doros, who had been on a table close to Rayden, told her that she had been through a similar experience.

"We will sleep well tonight," Rayden said, walking up to Doros and proceeding out of the area with her.

"I have no doubts," Doros replied, her eyelids drooping. "I am drowsy already."

"Give us a couple cups of wine and we could take to sleep right here," Rayden said, grinning.

Finding a bench on the outskirts of the place with the marble tables, the two women sat down and waited. Continuing in her blissful state, Rayden said nothing to Doros and remained content to watch the people around them.

She eyed the large outer pool in the main courtyard, and a part of her desired to wade in its gleaming, transparent waters. Yet she knew it would not be much longer before Polybius was finished with his body massage.

Tamping down her impulse, Rayden waited.

Polybius emerged from the area with the tables a short while later, a content look upon his face. Only Crassor looked tense.

"If we ever come here again, I am playing another role," Crassor told the others under his breath.

"When we get back to the apartments, I will work the knots out of your muscles," Doros told him. "I have some skill with that, taught to me by my mother."

"I would welcome that," Crassor replied. "It has been unpleasant watching what slaves are denied. Memories are called back to mind."

"Not for much longer, Crassor," Rayden told the tall, muscular man. "We will bring their enslavement of others crashing down around them."

"Yes, we will," he replied, a fiery glint in his eyes.

"It is probably time for us to return now," Polybius said. "We have been here for a long time."

"I am famished now," Crassor said.

"I am too," Polybius said.

"Count me among your number," Doros added.

"Then we will need to seek a tavern or inn, where we can get something to fill our bellies," Rayden said.

"We can purchase a good pot of stew and take it back to our quarters," Polybius said. "I am sure we have all had enough of the crowds."

"Crowds in cities are not something I am used to," Doros commented. "Give me a solid boat on a river or lake."

"Then let us not tarry here any longer," Rayden told the others.

Giving one more look to her companions, Rayden took a stride toward the entrance to the bath complex, and the others started forward along with her. Glancing once more at the pool, she imagined floating atop the glimmering surface without a care in the world.

No day brought a guarantee of survival, but Rayden promised herself that she would return to the pool on a day when the Imperator no longer held authority in the city. For the time being, she would have to give everything that she had within her to see that day realized.

Walking through the arches at the front of the courtyard, she eyed those approaching to enter the compound. A few wealthy and accompanied by slaves, many of modest means, and others poor, all of them came to avail themselves of a true wonder of the city.

Without thinking about it, Rayden shook her head.

"What is it, Rayden?" Doros asked her.

"To think that the same people who built that arena are the same people who built this place," she replied.

"A colossal place of bloodshed and a colossal place of healing, health, and harmony," Doros said. "Both arising by the same hands."

"They do not realize how close they are to creating a place

that brings out the best of our kind," Rayden replied, a rueful undercurrent to her words. "Imagine such ambition, inspired and guided by a different spirit than that behind the Imperator."

"It would be a city of even more wonders, I think," Doros stated.

"The full liberation of every man and woman would bring about an age of wonders," Rayden told her friend. "But being truly free is something that people have to choose in their hearts and then live by. The shackles of bondage come in many forms. It is not just those that are visible to the eye."

"What do you mean?" Doros asked.

"For some it is envy, for others it is greed," Rayden replied. "For some it is drink. For others it is anger. For still others it is indifference. Enslavement of our spirit comes in many unseen forms. The Imperator merely makes use of many masters, seen and unseen, to keep the people in thrall."

"And if the Imperator falls?" Doros asked.

Rayden looked over at Doros with a grim expression. "The people will have an opportunity to choose liberation, in all of its forms. Then, they will have to maintain the discipline to live free. It is no easy thing, but it opens the path for us to reach our highest potential. Only time will show if the people have the courage to truly be free."

Looking ahead, Rayden fell into silence and continued onward.

***

Another night passed and Rayden headed into the city with Doros after the pervasive early morning fog lifted. Having slept well after the previous day's visit to the baths, Rayden intended to cover a lot of distance, seeking to undertake further observation of the city's walls and gates.

Despite the bright sun, smooth blue skies, and drifting

patches of snow-white clouds high above, it seemed like a dark pall had fallen over the streets of the Imperial City.

Faces agitated and fearful permeated the streets, and many appeared to be in a hurry to get to their destination. Tempers flared and many curses were exchanged within the anxious throngs of pedestrians.

From the bits of conversation that she gleaned, Rayden learned the reason for the unease quickly enough.

The tribes from the north had arrived at the walls of the city.

"They are here," Doros commented, walking along at Rayden's right side.

"It is not long before the fighting begins," Rayden said, glancing to her friend.

"No, and it will not be long before the other legions arrive," Doros replied in a somber tone.

"The ones under the command of Marus," Rayden stated, nodding.

"The mood in the city is going to change fast," Doros said, casting her gaze about.

"It already is changing fast," Rayden said, looking around at the passersby.

"I am thinking we will attract even more attention," Doros said.

"It will not be long before many no longer care whether we are seen as allies of the Imperator or not," Rayden replied. "It will be enough that we are from tribes to the north to justify a hostile intent toward us."

"Then we must try to finish our observations, as soon as possible," Doros replied.

"Let us finish with the walls and gates today," Rayden told her.

Rayden and Doros passed through the better part of the morning and continued until mid-afternoon taking more assessments of the gates and walls.

Signs of heightened activity could be seen everywhere they went. More soldiers occupied the wall-walks and towers, and all the gates had been closed to all traffic. No one could enter or leave the city through the usual portals.

A part of Rayden wished that she could get a look from the wall-walk and set her eyes upon the northern host that would now be establishing their camps. Hamilcar, Annocrates, Erethea, Alcedan, and all the others were out there beyond the walls, somewhere within the vast multitude that had finally reached their destination.

The sheer enormity of the northern force resonated within many of the remarks that she heard from the nerve-wracked crowd flowing about them.

"A guard I know told me it is like looking upon a living sea!" exclaimed one older man to another. "Can you imagine that?"

"They say they number more than twenty legions!" a woman proclaimed to a female companion, both of them wide-eyed. "Maybe more!"

"It is said they can surround the entire city if they wish to!" a young man said to a pair of comrades, the three exhibiting looks of disbelief. "That surely is not possible!"

Rayden knew that most of the Teverens would strive to maintain their routines, but the atmosphere had shifted in a significant manner. A much different air would permeate the streets of the Imperial City going forward.

Grain distributed to the poorest districts would become increasingly rationed. Many items purchased on a regular basis in the markets would grow scarce fast, while selling prices rose ever higher. Those holding the advantage of wealth would hoard, and those with little would go without.

The needs of the soldiers would take precedence over almost everything else. Even greater hardship than what so many lived with during times of peace would descend on the greater populace.

Scavenging, theft, violence, and callousness would soar in an increasingly desperate climate, tearing at the fabric of the civil order itself. Rayden had no desire to witness the transformation from civility to ruthlessness that would soon be taking place, but she had seen enough of war and sieges to know what happened throughout a larger populace.

Before calling a halt to their evaluation of the gates and walls, Rayden made her way back to the walled area in the northeast section of the city serving as the garrison site for the Imperial Legion.

A strategic area of the city, the fortress now swarmed with activity. Tasked with protecting the Imperator and reinforcing order in the greater populace, the Imperial Legion would be strained to its limits in the shadows of a massive, besieging force encamped just outside the walls.

For a long while, Rayden observed the movements through the fortress gates accessing the interior of the city. At her side, Doros watched in silence.

Again, and again, disciplined formations of soldiers bearing shields and spears issued from the gates and headed into the city. The gleaming ranks marched in a variety of directions, ranging from western districts to those located more central or south.

The sheer numbers that Rayden observed marching from the fortress gave evidence to a development that she had been expecting. The variances in shield color and the insignias displayed upon their surfaces further confirmed her suspicions.

The formations of marching soldiers derived from more than one legion.

Before the arrival of the northern host, Peronnius had vacated his encampment outside the walls and marched his legions into the city; joining them with the Imperial Legion inside the capacious fortress.

***

Walking inside the front door to their quarters, Rayden turned to the right and stepped into the room with the table and writing implements. Sitting behind the table, Polybius held an inked quill in his right hand, writing upon a sheet of parchment.

"Welcome back, Rayden," he greeted her with an amiable countenance, looking up. "I am certain your day has been far more exciting than mine."

She replied, "I would not call it exciting, but I have many more reasons for concern. I also have a need to quicken our experiences of the city, in a way that could help us."

"What do you mean?" Polybius asked, his brow furrowing. Setting the parchment down, he returned the writing quill back to its slot in a carved, wooden holder. "Did something happen?"

"The tribes have arrived and are now outside the walls," Rayden informed him.

"Is that not welcome news?" he asked her, the puzzled look remaining on his face.

"It is, but it will not be long before anyone that looks like myself, or Doros, will be under constant threat," Rayden told him. "We do not have long before it will be all but impossible for me to walk around in the city like I am able to now."

"That does present a problem," Polybius replied, a frown forming on his face. After an extended pause, he asked her, "What do you need to gain knowledge of the most, now?"

Rayden looked Polybius direct in the eyes. "Get us into another gathering of those with great power and influence in this city. I am sure they will not cease in their luxuries."

"No, they will not," Polybius answered, clasping his hands together and laying them on the table surface. "At least not for a long while. They might even indulge more in the days to come, in order to forget what looms beyond their walls."

"See what can be done," Rayden stated.

"I will secure us an invitation with the right hosts," Polybius assured her, getting up to his feet. "I will leave to get this done at once. Crassor could do with an excursion too."

"Thank you," Rayden replied.

"Do not thank me, Rayden," Polybius said. "We all have our roles to perform, and, with the tribes arriving, time grows very short."

CHAPTER 5

Once more, Rayden took up the guise of an Alettani guest. She accompanied Polybius on an early-evening outing to the home of another wealthy Teveren family.

While relieved to learn that they would not be returning to the house of Sulpinnio Onnidaccus, Rayden harbored little doubt that the new host would be similar in nature. Where the bloody depravities at the end of the feast in Sulpinnio's house had caught her by surprise, Rayden set her mind to face whatever abominations might arise in the night ahead.

Doros and Crassor came along with them, both assuming their previous roles. The other three riding in litters, Crassor once again marched with the slaves alongside the column, displaying a sullen look upon his face.

The ride in the litter took a little longer than the previous one had. The noble's domicile where they were headed was located much closer to the great hill crowned with the Imperator's palace.

Arriving at their destination, Rayden, Doros, and Polybius took a few moments to disembark from the litters. After proceeding through the front entrance of their host's domicile, Rayden found that the layout of the residence proved similar to the other she had visited.

Stopping for a few moments within an atrium to have their

feet washed, they proceeded through a chamber beyond and entered an outdoor area filled with plants, flowers, statues, and an ornate fountain. Welcoming the wave of pleasant scents that engulfed her, Rayden listened to the steady cadence of water arcing from spouts down into the square pool at the fountain's base.

Making their way across the well-ordered garden, they entered a capacious dining chamber opening off from one side. Within, long, low couches had been arranged in the manner Rayden had seen before, with two parallel to each other and another spanning between at one end.

Upon their entrance, a male slave with a deep, sonorous voice announced Polybius, Rayden, and Doros to those reclined on the couches.

As before, Rayden drew a lot of scrutiny from the assembled guests. Some of the looks that she received went far beyond curiosity or cautious apprehension.

When Rayden had taken her place on one of the couches, a woman revealed to be the wife of a prominent magistrate extended her a coy, lingering smile. Meeting Rayden's eyes, the woman's skin flushed to a tone rivaling the carmine hue of her lofty hairstyle.

Taking a look around, Rayden caught desirous looks coming from a few other men and women in attendance. Gauging the prevailing mood in the chamber, Rayden had a strong notion of the direction that the evening would take.

Having no inclination for sharing in the activities that she suspected to be coming later, Rayden knew that she would eat well at the very least. As she had already experienced, the Teverens held feasts that surpassed those held by kings in many lands.

For the time being, Rayden had a wide array of foods to pick at from the low round tables before her, including choice olives, grapes, and cheeses. A slave provided her with a silver cup filled with a flavorful red wine.

Light conversation flowed between the guests. After a little while, a slave with a melodious tone of voice recited a series of verses to the accompaniment of both flute and stringed instruments.

The skillful poet told the story of a pair of lovers who went to great lengths to keep their dalliances hidden from the eyes of their spouses. A little ribald humor and periodic carnal references kept the oration in line with the direction of the night's festivities.

When he had finished, a woman a few places down from Rayden asked aloud, "Why do we tarry so? I am getting quite famished."

Her query seemed like a cue. The older slave overseeing the banquet called for the guests' attention, waiting for them to quiet down before announcing the presence of a new arrival.

A young man with a clean-shaven head and face, dressed in a flowing white tunic that reached down to his sandaled feet, stood at the slave's side. A shiny, silver amulet hung from a leather cord about his neck.

His narrow face, higher cheekbones, and larger nose bestowed him with an eagle-like countenance. Thick eyebrows, dark eyes, and a thinner set of lips lent his resting face a stern mien.

Darsellius, the master of the household and host of the feast, proceeded to introduce his son, Plinnian, a recent initiate into the priesthood devoted to the Imperator. Darsellius' voice rang with pride, conveying the high status and prestige of such a position.

Rayden found the presence of a cleric at a sumptuous banquet with carnal overtones an odd pairing. Nothing ascetic could be found in the ostentatious gathering around her.

Like his father, the young man had a haughty, pompous bearing. Basking in the acclaim from the guests around him,

Plinnian had none of the look of a humble, pious acolyte focused on serving a deity.

Rayden found herself taking a keen interest in the young man, suspecting that he would speak openly of things that others of his priesthood might keep concealed. A lot could be learned from the loose tongue of a boastful individual, and Rayden intended to find a way to speak with him later.

After Plinnian settled in place, the banquet commenced.

The evening's first offering consisted of a massive lobster straddling a prodigious mound of oysters. Darsellius claimed that the impressive specimen had been taken from just off the coast near to the Mystic Kingdom, across the Great Sea to the south and far to the east.

The guests marveled at the cost and origin of the lobster, before reducing the prominent offering to pieces and fragments, many of which they flung onto the mosaic-inlaid floor. Slaves approached and took away the platter, now piled with empty oyster shells.

The next course of the dinner consisted of a roasted, well-fattened goose; the centerpiece presented within a ring of smaller birds that Rayden could not identify until a woman near to her proclaimed them to be parakeets. Tender and spiced, the meat of both goose and parakeets proved delectable.

Another course followed, consisting of a large yellow eel, a creature with formidable-looking jaws that drew a considerable amount of enthusiasm from the guests. A rare delicacy from the ocean waters to the east, the eel had been secured at high expense on the part of Darsellius; a fact that he shared without hesitation or a trace of modesty.

Rayden welcomed the next course featuring sausages made from ground pork and a blend of several herbs and spices. Flavors burst within her mouth upon each luscious bite, and she wished that she could simply indulge in the scrumptious meat, to the exclusion of other offerings.

Toward the end of the extensive meal, a few slaves approached bearing platters exhibiting strange, dark shapes arranged in a circle. The objects were revealed to be upturned camel's feet, much to the delight of most guests. Rayden did not find the unusual cuisine to her liking, but, having eaten much worse while surviving in the wilderness, she tried a few mouthfuls.

From the outset of the banquet, servants bearing silver ewers maintained a constant flow of the red wine to the cups of the guests.

Rayden found the wine in her own silver vessel exquisite. Swirling it in her cup, she savored the robust scent before each sip.

It took a little willpower to keep her pace slower, so that she did not mar her clarity while listening to the discussions of the other guests.

Powerful and prominent in Teveren society, the guests had a lot to offer Rayden and her companions. Their conversations provided her with further information and also confirmed a few other things that she suspected.

Peronnius had pulled his three full legions from their encampment into the city, joining them with the Imperial Legion quartered inside the fortress. Four legions now defended the city from within, in addition to whatever else could be mustered from the populace in support.

Rations of grain to the greater populace had already been cut as a precaution to the specter of a prolonged siege. The northerners had set their encampment, but they had not yet encircled the city. At the moment, some food and other materials continued to arrive through the wharves and quays down at the banks of the Golden River.

Most of the guests believed that the invaders would be

crushed in the jaws of a trap when the legions under Marus arrived. With the additional Alettani and Sarrimena cavalry at his command, Marus could strike fast.

Despite their advantage in sheer numbers, the northern tribes faced a dangerous predicament. They had little to counter the cavalry of the Teverens and their allies. Wagons and carts could be utilized as makeshift camp fortifications, but they would not hold for long as a barrier against well-trained, disciplined Teveren legions.

The forces of Peronnius could not be allowed to unite with those of Marus. Yet if the northern tribes marched to engage Marus, Peronnius' legions could issue from the city gates to attack from behind.

An earthen rampart crowned with stakes surrounding the northern encampment would be a better defense against the enemy cavalry, but it would also allow the besiegers to become the besieged.

Rayden thought about how to counter the enemy's strengths while also preventing them from combining their forces. Doing her best to follow the conversations around her, she found her mind drifting away from her surroundings and focusing on the plight of the northerners.

Following the end of the multi-course feast, the guests continued with their libations. Slaves continued to keep the river of wine flowing.

An atmosphere of gaiety and frivolity swelled within the chamber. An undercurrent of tension took increasing hold; a tension of a more prurient nature.

Before long, the guests began getting up and spreading out from the dining chamber, making their way into the garden, the atrium, and a few other chambers within the large household.

Along with Doros and Polybius, Rayden was among the last to leave the couches in the dining chamber. Having kept an eye on the young priest, Plinnian, she did not get up until he did.

Keeping to a distance, Rayden followed him out into the garden. Accompanying the continuous pattering of water from the multiple spouts of the fountain at the center, the night air whispered through the leaves of the abundant foliage surrounding Rayden.

Placid and tranquil, the atmosphere would not be marred by bloodshed, but Rayden sensed that something else loomed involving power and ritual.

Plinnian made his way across the garden and continued back into the home. Losing sight of the priest, Rayden followed after, and soon found herself back in the atrium where her feet had been washed.

In pairs and trios, a few guests strolled about, their exchanges full of slurred words and tittering laughter. Rayden knew it would not be much longer before the night took a much different course.

A number of slaves, both male and female, appeared soon after. It took little imagination for Rayden to discern their purpose.

Young, attractive, and devoid of any clothing, the slaves fanned out among the guests and began to mingle with them. The scents of fine perfumes emanated from their supple bodies, and their smooth skin glistened with oils, accenting every toned muscle line and contour.

Notes of music from wind and string instruments floated throughout the chambers. Rhythmic and sensual, the music heightened the mesmerizing atmosphere.

Moans and sighs soon began drifting through the air, followed not long after by grunts and shrieks of ecstasy. Rayden did not let her eyes linger upon the undulating bodies that she came across while continuing about the chambers and atrium.

Rebuffing a few advances from both slaves and guests alike,

Rayden kept to herself, having no desire to participate in the wanton displays of lust unfolding around her. One older man that tried to fondle her received a firm grip on his wrist and a sharp warning from her eyes that proved enough to deflect his advances and make him seek pleasure elsewhere.

Rayden found Plinnian at the side of a bed with the legs of a female slave hoisted high, her ankles resting on his shoulders. His naked rear flexed in rapid succession as he pounded into her with vigor, building into a furious crescendo that culminated with his head flung back and an extended, loud groan.

Breathing heavy, he took her legs from his shoulders and let them flop down to the bed. Turning his head and catching sight of Rayden, he smiled at her.

"The height of ecstasy, followed by a touch of death when spent," Plinnian declared to Rayden, dismissing the slave with a brisk wave of his hand.

Taking up his tunic, Plinnian pulled it over his head and straightened it out on his body. While he dressed, the naked girl worked to get off the bed and to her feet.

Noticing a trace of a slur in the priest's words and a flush to his skin, Rayden deemed Plinnian a little intoxicated.

Giving the priest a low, extended bow, the female slave shuffled away and exited the bedchamber, her bare feet slapping against the tiles.

"You are one who enjoys the part of the voyeur, yes?" the priest asked, grinning and showing no sign of offense or discomfort.

"I am a good observer," Rayden answered, feigning an amiable tone.

"I should give you more to observe, but I am a little fatigued at the moment," he responded, wiping sweat from his brow. "Come, let us walk together. I did not get to speak to you at the feast. I have not had an opportunity yet to speak with one of our

Alettani allies."

He led her out of the chamber.

"Do all the priests like you partake in things like this?" Rayden asked him.

"The wise ones do," he stated, laughing.

"Why so, I am curious?" Rayden asked, sensing more than jest in his words.

"The joining contains great power, if you know how to harness it," the priest replied with the hint of a grin. "Life and death course side by side within this act. There is power there. More power than you might realize."

He nodded to the right, indicating an older guest rutting like a beast with a nubile female on her hands and knees nearby.

"No matter the intent, the power to invoke new life is present in the act ... a power to call something out of nothing ... to summon consciousness out of the oblivion of death itself," the priest stated, glancing toward Rayden. "Is that not like a work of sorcery?"

Rayden nodded. "Indeed, it sounds like one."

"To seed life into death," the priest said a moment later. A strange look crawling into Plinnian's eyes, he proceeded. "What one could do with the mastery of such power. The Catacombs themselves could be awakened."

The wistful tone in his voice told Rayden that he no longer was conversing just with her, but rather giving voice to greater desires harbored within. Listening to Plinnian, while knowing what the sorcerers in league with the Imperator had already achieved in the form of abominable things such as the Arguntier, she wondered what further diablerie they might be exploring, or preparing to unleash within the world.

"Is this related to other kinds of sorcery in your eyes?" Rayden asked, probing a little further. She then added, appealing to his arrogance, "The things that you master now, as a priest? I am curious."

Plinnian grinned, and his reply had the air of a proud boast to it. "Blood flowing out with the ebbing of a life upon a sacrificial altar ... the eruption of euphoria at the kill in the arena ... the heights of ecstasy followed by the little taste of death in this act. All of it is centered on power ... and all of it serves our purposes. We channel and gather every last bit of it."

"It is hard to understand," Rayden said, pretending total ignorance. "But you seem to have a hold of it."

"All you need to understand is that your tribe was wise to ally with us," the priest said with a condescending air, laughing. "Those who kneel to the Imperator will gain the world! Those who do not will perish! It is a simple matter!"

Forcing a smile onto her lips, Rayden said nothing in reply.

"I must excuse myself now," Plinnian announced in an abrupt manner, eyeing a cluster of writhing bodies in an alcove set off to one side of the atrium. "It has been good to speak with one of our newest allies."

Absorbing the things that he had said, Rayden watched Plinnian walk away. The enormity of the dark sorcery behind the Imperator staggered her mind.

Everything about the Imperial City fed the power that it wielded.

It had a comprehensive nature, drawing strength from all corners of Teveren society. The blood flowing in the arena and the euphoria of an orgiastic gathering both empowered the same, abyssal sorceries.

Blood sacrifice, whether in the form of a ritual or veiled in a spectacle like the arena, generated tremendous power for dark sorcerers to draw upon. Given the scale of it all, Rayden did not want to think of what the Imperator and his servants prepared within the shadows.

Like a gigantic parasite, they fed upon everything possible.

Worse, such a hunger could never be sated.

Entering the alcove, Plinnian stepped to the side and raised the bottom of his tunic. Kneeling behind a slave woman pleasuring another man, he grabbed onto her hips and set himself in place.

Listening to the ongoing chorus of grunts and moans, Rayden looked away from Plinnian. Walking back through the atrium, she passed the alcove.

The priest had told her enough. She knew what had to be done.

Everything involving the dark sorcery would have to be uprooted, laid bare, and destroyed, or the massive undertaking of the northern tribes in marching south and striking at the heart of the Teveren Empire would be for naught.

***

After the dawn's mists had subsided and unveiled the city that its embrace had shrouded, Rayden headed out from the tenement alone. Needing some time to herself, she tarried just long enough to inform her companions that she would be absent for a little while.

Polybius, Doros, and Crassor all gave her quizzical looks, but none of them sought to impede her, or insist upon their company.

Striding through the Imperial City's streets, Rayden could sense the mounting tension caused from the arrival of the northern tribes outside the walls. Shopkeepers still remained open, but everywhere that Rayden looked she observed a noticeable decline in the usual fervor surrounding the street-encroaching establishments.

The only laughter to be found came from the voices of children running about or playing in small clusters. Even then, the children appeared a little more subdued than before, perhaps sensing the pervasive apprehension clinging to the air.

Tempers flared quickly, and numerous angry exchanges took place within the flow of traffic, but Rayden could see the fear in the eyes of the people shouting curses and invectives at one another. Their displays of ire simply gave an outlet to release their own unease and fright.

Rayden drew many looks and knew that her time in the city would soon have to end. Fewer gazes held curiosity. Far more carried a hostile edge. A couple bordered on aggression.

Rayden wrestled with her own high level of stress, born of her concern for the Gessa and all of the other tribes facing a dangerous, precarious situation.

The previous night's events had left her with an uneasy spirit. The encounter with the priest, Plinnian, had given her more understanding of the sorcery underlying the Imperator's power.

Removed from the bawdy gathering and having the benefit of a night's rest, Rayden could think upon the moment at hand with sharper clarity and detachment.

She had achieved everything that she had hoped for in coming to the Imperial City.

Within the shadows of the Teveren Empire, a horrific darkness had been growing and gathering strength. Its roots spreading and thickening, the rising darkness channeled increasing power to everything branching off from its soaring, broadening trunk.

Though the specific nature of it remained veiled to her eyes and understanding, Rayden could see that everything surrounding the Imperator was coalescing toward something unprecedented in scale and degree. Once manifested in the world, the wicked dominion spawned from the depths of the abyss would be even more difficult to resist, much less overcome.

Rayden could not allow the discomforting thoughts to sap

her resolve.

She had evaluated the Teveren walls from the inside, gaining a much better understanding of the kinds of gates and wall segments in the process.

Even further, she knew the full strength of the Teveren forces, both inside the city and approaching it from without.

All of the information that she had gathered would be valuable to the northern chieftains like Alcedan.

Pungent scents engulfing Rayden, an unpleasant, aromatic blend of dung, opened entrails, blood, animals, and many other elements announced the presence of the city's sprawling livestock market. A labyrinthine mass of corrals, tents, and other structures filled an enormous open space bordered with colonnades.

Rayden wished she had more time, wondering if Ingassa labored somewhere within the vast market area, helping her father.

Quickening her stride, Rayden hastened to bypass the area. The grunts and squeals of pigs, bleats of goats, and noises of many other animals carried across the fetid air.

In a protracted siege, the area would grow increasingly quiet without an influx of animals to fill the vast market. Even the weakest specimens in each sector would command tremendous prices with scarcity taking dominion.

Rayden took notice of three plain-clothed men coming from the direction of the market, all of them holding the legs of several live chickens in each hand. They followed an older man wearing a crimson mantle atop an unsullied tunic.

She did not have to see the group before her eyes to know that the wealthy in the city had begun to hoard. They would still be eating the usual types of meats when the rest of the populace had long since turned to filling their bellies with the rats pervading the city.

Beyond the animal market, Rayden came upon another

kind of market that would also decline in activity during an extended siege.

She did not seek to bypass the area, but rather slowed her pace, setting her eyes on the buyers and sellers gathered around a series of timber platforms arrayed along one end of the space.

On the platforms, wearing little to cover their bodies, stood a number of men and women. Of all skin tones and physical characteristics, their appearances told Rayden that they hailed from lands all over.

A pale-skinned, strong-looking man with long red hair stood next to a thin, dark-haired woman, a beauty with skin of a light brown hue. Both stared downward with dejected, resigned countenances.

Near to them, a lean man with curly locks of black hair and a more olive tone of skin peered across the crowd, though Rayden could tell that he looked at nothing in particular. He stood next to a round-faced, short man with almond-shaped eyes, who had undoubtedly come from lands far, far to the east.

To the right of the far easterner stood a striking-looking, tall, muscular figure. The man had the dark skin of the tribes dwelling in the open grasslands deep in the south of the lands across the sea.

At his side stood a blond-haired woman with a hue of skin matching Rayden's own. Also, like Rayden, she had piercing blue eyes, though no spark of flame could be found anywhere within her despondent gaze.

All of the men and women on the platforms looked subdued and disconsolate. Each wore a small wooden sign about their necks, though Rayden could not read what had been written upon the surfaces.

Men in finer attire moved among them, shouting to the crowd while emphasizing some attribute of a particular individual. Holding up the arm of a well-muscled man or grabbing the rear or breast of an attractive female, the sellers proclaimed the value of their living wares.

"Stronger than a mule and ready for the fields!" cried one of the sellers.

"Sensual and silken skin, she would provide you with a stream of coins in any brothel!" shouted another.

"A smart one, who can write and read, suitable for a household!" called yet another.

Rayden edged through the crowd, drawing closer to the platform with the blond-haired woman.

Thoughts ran through her mind. Gazing upon the woman, she began seeing herself.

A different place of birth and path in life could have seen Rayden standing upon that same wooden platform; a living piece of property to be sold off to the highest bidder.

The siege would bring a slowdown in the transaction of slaves, but if the Teverens prevailed it would resume at its former level. Further, if the Teverens triumphed, they would have an abundance of new slaves at their disposal after taking captives.

Rayden found it difficult to imagine the fear that many of the slaves contended with. None of them knew what kind of fate awaited them.

The cries of the sellers shed light on a few likely fates.

Some of the luckier ones might go into a household and live in relative comfort, but others would be sent to hard labor on large farms, quarries, or mines, until their bodies gave out.

A few of the more beautiful might find themselves condemned to serving in a brothel, forcing violations of their body each and every day until the mercy of time caused their looks to fade.

Without recourse to any protection from laws, the slaves could be killed outright or used for the pleasure of their masters and mistresses. They could only hope to fall into the possession of an owner with a kinder heart or sense of justice.

The pudgy seller on the platform before Rayden grabbed the chin of the blond-haired woman and lifted it in a rough manner. Calling out to the crowd, he started the bidding for her.

The first bid exceeded the few coins that Rayden carried in a pouch at her waist.

While voices rose to proclaim new bids and the seller worked to coax out more from the audience, the gaze of the blond-haired woman drifted across the crowd. She seemed to be staring toward a far horizon, somewhere well beyond the walls of the city, until her eyes met those of Rayden.

Her eyes widened for a moment.

Rayden did not look away. Finding an element of kinship with the woman, she kept her eyes fixed to the other's gaze.

The sheen covering the surface of the woman's eyes conveyed sadness, fear, and resignation. Every part of Rayden wished that she could give her some consolation in the knowledge that a war to overthrow Teveren authority had reached the gates of the city.

At last, the bidding drew to a halt, and a short man near the front was proclaimed the winner.

A burst of loud curses and yells off to the right caused a momentary distraction, as a few within the crowd reacted to a trio of large rats skittering across the ground. Brushing against the legs of several bidders, the rats caused many in the throng to jump or crash into each other, before finding safe refuge beneath one of the platforms.

Following the brief disturbance, the winning buyer handed his payment over to the seller. A tall, young man at his side, presumably another slave, stepped forward and lifted the blond-haired woman down from the platform.

Shaking and looking even more afraid, the woman hesitated for a moment. An instant later, she found herself slung over the shoulder of the impatient slave, who carried her off in the wake of the buyer, already striding away.

Watching the crying woman being taken away like a mere sack of goods, Rayden's anger simmered. The troubling sight struck at the core of the fight against the Teverens and represented the dire cost of failing in the struggle.

The building tempest within Rayden sought liberation through axe and sword. She burned with the desire to cut down seller and buyer alike for the abomination they made possible.

"You are of our tribal allies," a voice interrupted her darkening thoughts. "One of the Alettani, I believe."

Turning her head, Rayden recognized one of the men who had attended the first feast that she had been to in the city, at the home of Sulpinnio Onnidaccus.

His attention and comment drew the focus of many bystanders. Rayden could feel their eyes weighing upon her. She took a breath in and released it, letting her furor recede.

"I am," Rayden replied, keeping her tone even.

"What of Marus, is there any new word?" he asked.

Rayden answered. "I cannot tell you the day, but I have learned that Marus is drawing close with his legions, as well as my tribe and the warriors of the Sarrimena. I would say that he will be here within a few more days."

Relief flooded the face of the man before her and those within range of hearing. A joyful smile then crossed his face.

"Those are welcome tidings, now that the barbarians have reached our gates," he replied. "We have not been able to learn anything since we last met at the house of Sulpinnio Onnidaccus."

Rayden forced a smile onto her face in response, to perform the role that she had to assume.

Inside, she chafed. Her words gave comfort to several men who bought and sold others of their own kind; yet she could do nothing to bring relief to those standing in loincloths and scant attire atop the wooden platforms.

The thought sickened Rayden, but she could not display her true feelings to the man before her.

"I must take leave now," Rayden told him in a polite tone. "I seek to rejoin my people soon."

Her words resounded with truth. She had to return to Alcedan and the other tribal leaders, to relay all that she knew to them.

"Smash the barbarians against the walls of the Imperial City," the man exhorted her, murmurs and nods of assent coming from those listening nearby.

Rayden nodded and then took her leave. With more bids shouted into the air, as another auction got underway, Rayden worked her way through the crowd to the streets.

Everything seemed a blur on her walk back to the tenement. A seed of impatience had sprouted within, giving rise to a fast-growing restlessness.

Rayden had to get out of the city and seek the northern tribes.

CHAPTER 6

Night deepened and the Imperial City fell into a restless slumber. Within the dark tenements, brooding multitudes tossed and turned, wrestling with nightmares of barbarian hordes storming through the streets in an orgy of blood and fire.

On the barren streets outside, a lone figure moved swift and silent through the shadows. Avoiding the few drunkards that she encountered with ease, and evading the robbers and cutthroats prowling the shadows, Rayden made her way toward the walls facing the north.

With all eyes focusing on the encampments of the besiegers, few within the city looked for a single figure to seek escape from inside the walls.

The bellows of oxen and creaking of wheels brought Rayden to a halt for a moment. Recognizing the sounds as coming from a few streets over, she continued onward.

At last she came to the end of the lofty tenements, entering a less congested section of the city that offered her a more open view. Colonnades, statues, and fountains decorated a long stretch of open space beneath the shadows of august temples and grander structures.

Pressing herself against a wide plinth supporting a marble statue of a regal-looking man clad in formal robes, Rayden took notice of a small group of figures heading in her direction. Piquing her interest, the group walked down the street that climbed the great hill adorned with the Imperator's massive palace complex.

All four attired in the long garments typical of priests, one of them bearing a torch, the group did not proceed toward the city when they reached the base of the hill. Rather, they turned right and started for the northern walls; heading in the same direction that Rayden had been going.

Eyeing their garb, she guessed the figures to be priests, or possibly sorcerers. Even if they were not of a higher rank, she found the sight of four priests or sorcerers striding toward the northern walls unusual so late in the night.

Hurrying after them, Rayden kept to the columns and statues along the way, concealing her form with ease.

Heightening her interest even further, the figures ahead then angled toward the portal known as the Hunter's Gate. Rayden and Doros had studied the Hunter's Gate well during their reconnoitering.

A single-arch gateway without flanking towers, the portal stood at the midpoint of a regular section of wall. From all outward signs, the wall itself looked to be solid in construct, without any enclosed passages.

Rayden adjusted her direction, heading for a section of the wall not far from the gate. A staircase running up the interior facing of the wall from the ground to its summit drew her attention. Giving those on the wall-walk closer access to the gate, the stairs offered Rayden a simple means of gaining the top.

While keeping watch on the progress of the robed quartet, Rayden took an assessment of the wall, identifying every guard position along it that she could. Eyeing the regular wall towers within sight, she focused on the one closest to the place where the staircase culminated.

Gauging the distance from the tower to that spot, Rayden

determined that if guards on the tower sighted her atop the wall, it would take several moments for them to reach her.

Their steps purposeful, the torch-bearing group approached the gate. A guard positioned on the wall-walk above the gate called down to the approaching figures.

Rayden could see the attention of other guards on the wall near to the Hunter's Gate shift toward the nearing robed figures. None of them were looking in the direction of the staircase.

A brief exchange ensued between the guards and the priests. Moments later, three of the guards descended from the wall-walk, using a staircase on the other side of the portal. Shortly after, the metallic squeaking of iron hinges and the creaking of wood rose into the night as the Hunter's Gate opened.

Seeing her opportunity, Rayden took a final glance at the wall-walk and sprinted toward the staircase. For a few heartbeats, she bounded across open ground, exposed to the view of any that might happen to look away from the gate area and back toward the city.

No outcry meeting her attempt, Rayden reached the base of the staircase undetected.

With no hesitation, Rayden scampered up the stone steps. Nearing the top, she lowered to a crouch and slowed to a halt. Lifting her eyes just above the wall-walk, she looked around.

The attention of the guards on the wall-walk remained fixed on the robe-attired quartet, who were just now issuing through the gateway. Once through, the gate would shut, and the guards would resume their patrols along the wall.

Rayden then took off the pack carrying the length of hempen rope that she had bought soon after arriving in the Imperial City. Sliding the coiled rope out, she took up one end and formed a loop.

Remaining in a crouched stance, Rayden surmounted the last step, and moved over to the edge of the wall.

Slipping the loop around one of the square merlons warding the wall-walk itself, Rayden tightened the rope in place. Then, she let the rest of the coil's length fall down the other side of the merlon, along the wall's outer facing.

Satisfied that her knot was secure, Rayden took firm hold of the rope. The rough texture of the tight-woven fibers pressed into the skin of her palms and fingers. Mindful to keep her profile low, she climbed over the side of the wall between two merlons and let herself dangle for a moment.

Bracing her feet against the wall and keeping a robust grip on the rope, Rayden walked her way down the wall in a methodical, controlled manner, until she came to the end of the rope.

A short drop remaining to the ground, Rayden let her body extend full-length from the last handhold of rope before letting go. The swift fall took only a moment.

Feet touching the ground, she absorbed the impact, bending her knees and lowering down into a crouch.

Standing upright, Rayden looked up the wall. Guards had begun to stroll along the wall-walk again, but none threatened to see her.

Taking a few deeper breaths, she turned and looked into the night. Farther off, a single torch bobbed, indicating the group that Rayden had been following.

The clerics had proceeded a fair distance beyond the gate, the latter closed shut once more. Marching toward the northeast, they headed straight in the direction of the Catacombs.

Her curiosity kindled into flame, Rayden made the decision to continue following the quartet, rather than making her way to the tribal encampment immediately. Suspecting the Catacombs as their destination, every sense within told her that the priests were engaged in something of importance tied to the underlying darkness pervading the Imperial City.

Loping forward into the shadow-draped expanse of open

ground beyond the walls and fixing her eyes on the torchlight, Rayden pursued the quartet of priests.

A chance for gaining more knowledge of her enemy beckoned, and knowing an enemy brought the greatest chance of defeating that enemy.

***

A single, billowing torchlight her beacon in the night, Rayden followed the dark-robed quartet at a distance. Keeping her footfalls light and nimble, she concealed her pursuit as much as possible.

After a while, the stretch of open ground came to an end. A line of trees silhouetted in the moonlight loomed. The priests took a broad pathway into the midst of the woods.

Staying out of the open, Rayden positioned herself close to the foliage and trees that they walked through; ready to blend into the shadows at the first hint of a pause from those ahead of her.

Keeping to a brisk gait, the robed figures continued onward, showing no signs of suspecting that anyone followed them.

After crossing almost half a league, the ground sloped downward, heading into a wide tunnel entrance. Broad enough for several people to enter side by side, the large portal engulfed the figures after just a few strides.

Striding down the short, rocky slope and entering the Catacombs, Rayden continued after the others. Heading down a long, dark passageway, she espied the torch once more.

Once underground, she took up her weapons. A dank, musty scent pervaded the air, the latter growing colder the farther that she proceeded.

A few higher-pitched, chittering sounds echoed throughout the darkness, signifying that more than corpses dwelled within the passages and chambers of the vast necropolis.

Passing the openings to several other tunnels, leading to other areas within the Catacombs, Rayden kept her blades at the ready.

A place of death attracted the kinds of entities and creatures that inhabited the hellish depictions of a malevolent god's abyssal realm. Things that hungered for the flesh of the living prowled and stalked the cold, lightless passages below the surface.

Shunning the touch of the sun and lying in wait for those daring or foolish enough to brave the nether regions of the world, the diabolic breathed the essence of death.

Coming from the darkness ahead and deep in pitch, a melodious chant reached her ears. The continuous incantation giving her a little more cover for her footsteps on the rough surface of the passageway, Rayden increased her pace. Keeping her eyes locked to the flame carried among the figures ahead of her, she gained some ground.

The torch and its afterglow suddenly disappeared from sight, the robed figures turning aside and heading into another passage to the right. Momentarily enveloped within an impenetrable blackness, Rayden slowed, but still continued forward.

Glancing to the right, she regained sight of the flame once more. Before starting down the side passage, she raked the edge of her axe and sword blades across the hard-packed dirt surface, carving a pair of furrows. She then added two more, creating a total of four distinct, parallel lines in the ground.

Entering the passage, Rayden picked up her pace, the group ahead having regained some distance on her. The sound of the chanting growing louder and a little more pronounced, Rayden knew that the priests' destination lay near.

Slowing her progress once more, the quartet made another turn, this time to the left. When Rayden reached the entrance to the tunnel that they had taken, she saw a new flickering light, coming from farther down.

The chanting now prominent and filling the confines of the passage, Rayden steeled herself for whatever depravity or abomination the light farther ahead would reveal.

As before, Rayden used her blades to cut four parallel furrows into the ground. Then, she resumed her pursuit of the priests.

The robed figures reached the firelight and disappeared from view.

Rayden hurried forward.

Nearing the end of the tunnel, she slowed and edged along the left side. Step by step, she made her way to the end of the tunnel and peered in.

The passage culminated in a large, circular chamber. Shadows billowed along walls teeming with niches. Each of the recessed spaces displayed piled clusters of human skulls, casting lifeless stares above their fixed grins of death.

At the center of the chamber rose a stone table. Standing before the gray, rectangular slab, with their backs to Rayden, two robed men flanked a little girl of no more than eight years of age. The men gripped her arms, holding her firmly in place.

Struggling against their hold, she looked around and Rayden saw her face. Eyes gleaming with raw fright, the little girl had several tears streaking down her cheeks. A length of cloth tied about her mouth kept the girl's crying muffled.

A long tunic of pure white covered her trembling body. The girl's well-combed, dark brown tresses had a luxuriant sheen, showing that she had been carefully prepared for the ceremony now taking place.

On the other side of the stone table, a black-robed figure wearing the broad, horned skull of a bull faced the girl, holding a curving dagger in the right hand.

Around the perimeter of the chamber, in back of the girl and two priests, several other robed figures stood in place. Adding their voices to the building chant, the quartet that Rayden had been following took places among them.

Keeping low and to the shadows, Rayden knew the purpose of the girl and stone table. For a moment, she thought of Hamilcar and the widespread accounts of children being sought by the Teverens.

She did not want to think of how many similar scenes had taken place within the macabre, skull-filled chamber before her.

Arms outstretched, the one wearing the bull skull called out an invocation, speaking in a commanding tone of voice. The two holding onto the girl dragged her forward and lifted her onto the stone table.

Taking up positions at either end of the table, they held her down by the ankles and wrists. Squirming and twisting, the girl strained to break free, but could do nothing to dislodge their steely holds.

Taking a step forward and arms raising higher, the figure wearing the bull skull gazed down upon the girl. A frigid chill seeped into the air, and the chamber appeared to darken before Rayden's eyes.

Sensing the manifestation of something much worse, and far more powerful than the priests, Rayden could wait no longer.

Her left arm reaching back and up, Rayden sent her axe whirring through the air in a tight spin. Crossing the distance fast, the blade drove into the chest of the one wearing the bull skull.

Wavering in place for a moment, the figure dropped the curved dagger and toppled backward.

The chanting ended at once, and many cries of alarm erupted.

Her eyes twin pools of cold, blue ice, Rayden lunged forward, striking at the two still holding the girl in place. Her blades opening their throats and spattering the altar with their blood, both of the priests fell in swift succession.

Turning on the robed men in the chamber, a look of wrath filled her face. The priests hurried to escape, but Rayden cut down three of their number before they could all exit.

Rayden pursued them a short distance down the passage beyond the chamber, bringing down two more of them from behind. The others kept running, showing no inclination to turn and resist despite the darkness that swallowed them.

Standing still for a moment and catching her breath, Rayden listened to their footsteps fading in the distance. She wondered how they would find their way through the Catacombs in the pitch dark.

Returning to the chamber, Rayden went over to the girl, who had gotten off the stone table and backed up to the edge of the room. Standing beneath rows of leering skulls, a look of fear spread on her face, the girl stared at Rayden with wide eyes.

Taking slow steps, Rayden told her in a low, gentle voice, "It is over, you are free. They are not going to hurt you. I have stopped them."

Still looking terrified, the girl trembled and whimpered, but could say nothing with the gag in her mouth. Hands behind her head, she worked frantically at the knot.

"We will leave together, I will get you out of here," Rayden continued, keeping her voice calm. "You are going to live and be free again."

Glancing about, seeking to make certain that the chamber had remained empty, Rayden listened for any sounds of breathing or the scrape of a footstep. It appeared that the priests had indeed fled, though she knew they would return with guards soon enough.

Rayden stepped over to the side of the figure who had been overseeing the ceremony. She crouched down.

Ripping the bull skull off, Rayden exposed the face of an

older man, clean-shaven, with a prominent nose and dense eyebrows.

To her surprise, he still lived.

Wheezing, he did not look to have much life remaining within him.

"What do you think ... you have stopped?" he managed to say, his breaths growing shallower. The ghost of a mocking smile rose on his face for a moment. "Everything is a sacrifice ... foolish woman ... everything."

Following a slow, extended gurgle, his chest went still, and his breathing ceased.

Whether a trick of the ears or something of a nature that she wanted no part of, Rayden believed that she heard a faint wailing. The icy chill in the air ebbed and the room returned to its former ambiance.

Whatever had been manifesting in the presence of the priests had departed.

Staring toward Rayden, the little girl had removed the cloth that had been gagging her. Still wide-eyed, she continued to say nothing.

"Come with me," Rayden said to the girl. "Stay close. This is no place for us."

After wiping her axe blade off on the robes of the one that she suspected to be a high priest, she slid the weapon back into the loop at her belt. Stepping over to the bull-skull headdress that she had taken off him, Rayden raised her right foot and stomped down, shattering the ornate headdress into pieces.

"No children for you, abyss worm ... rot in your darkness," she whispered, hoping that the vile entity that had been just denied a blood sacrifice heard her words in a deafening roar.

Taking up a torch in her left hand, Rayden kept her sword in her right and led the girl from the chamber. Down the passage, coming to an intersection, she illuminated the marks that she had cut into the ground easily enough.

Turning right and proceeding carefully, Rayden paused at the mouths of other tunnels, wary of the possibility of ambush from the men that had fled the chamber. Adding to her caution, the commotion that she had stirred up could have attracted other, more unpleasant things that lurked in the dark passages and chambers of the Catacombs.

Rayden found the second set of marks indicating the location of the main passage that she had taken at the outset. Turning left, she maintained her heightened caution, guiding the girl forward and continuing all the way through, until the Catacombs came to an end at last.

The first touch of fresh, cool night air came as a welcome relief. Glad to leave the sprawling necropolis behind and return to the world of the living, she strode out of the entrance.

Breathing in deep and expunging the last vestiges of the decay-ridden air from her lungs and nose, she looked toward the girl.

"I imagine that it is good to look up and see the stars again," Rayden said to her in a gentle tone.

Her eyes no longer brimming with fear, the girl nodded back.

Refreshed, Rayden started up the incline. The girl followed close behind.

***

To avoid any mistakes of identification on the part of those warding the tribal camp, Rayden decided to forgo approaching them until the next day arrived. Any warriors on watch would be on edge so close to the Teveren city, expecting enemy scouts and probes at any moment.

Until morning's light took dominion across the skies, Rayden holed up with the little girl in the lee of a large rock jutting out from a hillside. Despite the absence of further threats, Rayden slept lightly, poised to react to any disturbance.

Exhausted from the horrific trial that she had endured, the little girl succumbed to her fatigue and fell asleep, but she exhibited a fitful rest. Rayden had little doubt of the cause.

Despite being freed, the little girl's ordeal had not come to an end. The night in the Catacombs would undoubtedly give birth to haunting nightmares for a long time to come.

Rustling the little girl awake in a gentle fashion, when morning's light spread across on the eastern horizon, Rayden set out at dawn.

Coming upon an abundance of wild berries near a stream, Rayden picked many, giving several to the girl while consuming a few handfuls herself. The berries had a bitter, sour edge, but she knew them to be safe. While not enough to assuage her hunger entirely, the berries gave a lift to her energies.

Cupping her hands, Rayden splashed cold stream water on her face before drinking enough to slake the edge of thirst.

The chirping of birds and trilling of insects provided a pleasant accompaniment to the long march through the low, wooded hills. Breezes weaving through the boughs of the trees whispered in the presence of unsullied beams of light descending from above.

Tranquil and reverent, the atmosphere had a timeless quality that soothed Rayden. Delighting in the moment, she put aside her concerns for a little while.

CHAPTER 7

A little after midday, emerging from the hills into an expanse of low grassland, a most welcome sight met Rayden's eyes.

The might of the northern tribes lay before her eyes.

Sprawling masses of wagons and carts occupied the open ground. Thousands upon thousands of people could be seen moving about, and the smoke from countless fires spiraled and wafted up toward the blue skies above.

Rayden looked over to the girl, whose eyes had spread in a look of amazement.

"They have come to break the power of the Imperator," Rayden told her. "They are our friends."

The girl looked up, into Rayden's eyes, and the hint of a smile came to her lips as she nodded. Rayden smiled back to her.

"Come with me," Rayden said. "We will get you some proper food and new friends."

Starting down the slope of the hill, Rayden and the girl headed toward the vast encampment.

***

Before they reached the edge of the encampment, several armed warriors approached. Tall, long-haired, and thick-bearded, wearing belted tunics and woolen cloaks, the warriors hailed Rayden and the girl.

After a brief interaction, Rayden learned that the warriors were of the Pannimbri. Two of the men offered to lead her to where the Gessa had gathered.

Not knowing the locations of the various tribes in the sprawling host, Rayden accepted their offer. Without delay, the Pannimbri warriors guided her into the heart of the vast multitude that had descended from the north.

Rayden passed through a sea of wagons, carts, cookfires, makeshift shelters, animals, and people. An abundance of eyes peered toward her as she passed through the midst of thousands.

More than a few looked to each other and began talking, no doubt having heard of the blond-haired, female tempest from the Gessa who carried axe and sword.

The scents of burning wood, stews cooking in pots, and the musk of animals pervaded the air. The aroma of the stews caused Rayden's mouth to water, but she could not attend to matters of hunger just yet.

Walking among the northern people brought some joy to her heart. After living among Teverens for a while, Rayden found it wonderful to be surrounded by the people of the north once more.

Crossing through a short span of open ground, they paused for an exchange with some armed men warding the camp of the Marren. The warriors let the men of the Pannimbri and the two they accompanied through with no trouble.

Watching the smooth cooperation between the warriors of two tribes, Rayden could see the chance for prevailing in the war against the Teverens. Old enmities and quarrels had been one of her greatest concerns, in addition to the situations where a few tribes had been warring with each other not long ago; such as her own Gessa with the Runi.

To defeat the Teverens, the tribes would have to fight together like never before.

The people of the Marren eyed Rayden in a similar manner to the Pannimbri. A few hailed her from their campfires, and Rayden acknowledged their greeting with a nod and raise of a hand.

Rayden kept an eye on the girl striding close to her side. Looking around at masses of unfamiliar people, as far as the eye could see, the girl undoubtedly wrestled with a host of anxious thoughts and feelings.

Reaching out, Rayden ruffled the girl's hair, smiling when she looked up to her.

Though Rayden could see the discomfort within her dark brown eyes, the girl mustered a slight grin in response.

"You are a brave one," Rayden told her in a low voice. "Remember, you are safe here."

The girl nodded back but made no reply.

Rayden looked ahead and saw the end of the Marren encampment ahead. Passing beyond, and crossing another stretch of open ground, they encountered yet another group of warriors standing watch.

Rayden smiled wide, recognizing a few of the Gessa men. Their faces beamed with gladness in return.

***

Alcedan rose to his feet at the sight of Rayden. A broad smile forming upon his face, the young chieftain of the Gessa stepped forward.

The two warriors grasped each other's forearms in greeting.

"A most welcome sight to see," Alcedan exclaimed, elation showing in his eyes.

"I should be welcoming you," Rayden replied to him, grinning. "Though I am one of the few from the Teveren city that would do so."

Alcedan laughed. "I am sure there are many inside their walls who are not pleased to see us here."

"Wickedness confronted rarely is," Rayden remarked, lingering thoughts of her experience inside the Catacombs prompting the response.

"Who is this with you?" Alcedan asked, taking notice of the young girl standing just behind Rayden.

"One meant for blood sacrifice to their vile gods," Rayden answered him, her face shadowing over with a scowl. "I stopped them, but she needs a home that I cannot give her myself. She is a very brave young girl and has endured a nightmare."

Alcedan nodded his understanding, but his look turned grim. "We will see that she is cared for, though I cannot promise the safety of anyone among us here. The Teverens will surely attack soon, now that we are taking up a position."

"They will, it is inevitable," Rayden responded, in full agreement with the Gessa chieftain. "When do you move to surround the city?"

"It has already begun, this very morning," Alcedan replied. "Several tribes, the Borreni, Cirna, and Lanassa among them, curl around the eastern and western sides of the city, even as we speak. Other groups are ranging into the surrounding area, to gather up whatever can be gained from the lands around the city."

"Many of their wealthiest nobles have land and estates just outside the city," Rayden told him. "There will be much to take and many more former slaves to join your ranks."

"They are a strong and dependable force already," Alcedan said. "I know that you have many friends among their ranks. If you wish to find them, they are camped aside the Tega."

"There are a few I wish to set my eyes upon this day," Rayden replied, thinking of Hamilcar, Annocrates, and several others that she had come to know well when fighting in their uprising. "How are the tribal leaders faring since I departed for the Imperial City?"

"Common purpose has kept harmony," Alcedan said. "We have had no setbacks or quarrels of any substance, which has been good for the morale of all."

"Food must be rationed now that you are outside the city," Rayden cautioned him.

"Much has been gathered, and much was taken along with us, but all leaders agree to be careful," Alcedan said.

"That is good to hear," Rayden said. "Our people are not experienced in the way of sieges. It often becomes a contest of wills."

"How fares your companions? Have you learned much since dwelling within the enemy city?" Alcedan asked.

"I have much to share with you, and the other leaders," Rayden replied, nodding. "Polybius, Crassor, and Doros are safe where they are, inside of the city.

"We must gather the tribal leaders so that I can tell all of you what I have learned, but it must be done soon. I also wish to offer some counsel.

"I cannot stay for long. I must see to a task of great importance to the north of here. I will be returning to the city afterward."

"Will you be able to get back into the city?" Alcedan asked her. "With our warriors encircling them, they will be more watchful than ever on their walls."

"There is always a gap," Rayden told Alcedan, giving him a smirk. "Have some confidence in me. I will find it."

"I speak before I think, sometimes," Alcedan replied with a laugh. "You are not the usual warrior that one encounters in this world."

"My path in this world has been far from the usual one," Rayden lamented.

"It has forged you into something that is a blessing of the gods to all of our people," Alcedan stated.

"Sometimes I think that even a sword likes to rest for a little while within its sheath," Rayden responded.

"May the blade that you speak of find some time to do just that," Alcedan replied with a knowing look in his eyes.

"No blade can seek rest until the Imperator falls," Rayden stated. "Gather the tribal leaders this night, and I will share what I have learned while in the Teveren city. For now, I will go visit with a few that I hold in my heart among this great multitude."

"I will see you this evening," Alcedan replied. Walking over, the tall Gessa chieftain came to stand by the little girl. With a smile, he looked down upon her and said to Rayden. "I give you my promise that she will have a place to call home among us, before the sun sets."

Turning to the girl, Rayden looked her in the eyes. "The days ahead will not be easy, but you will find your way forward. Remember ... small steps in abundance cross great distances. The Gessa gave me a home among them when I was very young ... even younger than you are now ... and I know they will give you one too."

"Thank you ... for saving me," the girl responded, in a voice barely above a whisper.

They were the first words that the girl had spoken to Rayden. The girl's eyes glistened over, a wellspring of emotion reflecting on their surfaces.

"I had no other choice," Rayden said, giving her a warm smile and setting her right hand down on the girl's shoulder. "Your life is worth protecting, to the best of my ability."

Suddenly, the girl lurched forward and embraced Rayden. Wrapping her arms tight about Rayden's waist, she buried her head into her liberator's midsection.

Heaving sobs reverberated against Rayden's stomach

moments later. Relieved to see the little girl giving release to long-restrained emotions, Rayden knew that she had put up a brave face for long enough.

Rayden reached her arms around the girl's shoulders and hugged her close. Waves of powerful memories passing through her, Rayden remembered a time long ago when a little blond-haired girl, in the wake of a heart-wrenching, horrific tragedy, had taken a step forward to embrace the wife of a revered northern chieftain.

Having once received the light of consolation within the darkest depths of despair, Rayden now did the same for another.

∗∗

Rayden spent the better part of the early afternoon visiting with others among the Gessa. After spending a little extra time with Erethea and listening to her give release to a few irritations concerning her husband Jarut, Rayden headed onward to find the encampment of the former slaves.

After passing through the Tega and crossing the mid-point of the open expanse beyond, a number of faces turned in her direction from the outskirts of the next encampment. Zealous shouts rang out through the air, and in scant moments many more individuals began gathering at the edge of the wagons, carts, and shelters ahead.

Running so fast that he stumbled and nearly fell down, Hamilcar raced across the ground toward Rayden.

"Rayden!" he cried out, his face shining with joy.

Catching Hamilcar up and enfolding him within her arms, Rayden hugged the boy tight before setting him back down in the grass. Tousling his dark, curly locks, she smiled and laughed, shedding all concerns for a moment.

"You almost knocked me over!" Rayden exclaimed.

"I have missed you so much, Rayden!" Hamilcar replied, his

face exuding a jubilant fervor.

"And I you," Rayden replied, looking upon him and savoring the moment.

"I did not know when you would be returning to us," he stated, the excitement still rife within his voice. "Nobody knew."

"Not even I knew," Rayden replied, chuckling.

"You are back, though!" Hamilcar stated, sparks of hope dancing in his eyes. "Will you stay with us now?"

"I have only a little time here, but I could not leave without setting my eyes on you," Rayden answered.

"I am glad," Hamilcar replied, though a little disappointment shone within his eyes at the news that she could not stay.

"What have you been doing since I saw you last?" Rayden asked him.

"Wait until you see how I handle a sword now," he declared to Rayden, a flare of pride coursing through his voice. "I have trained a long time every day with Annocrates. I have worked very hard on everything that you taught me."

Rayden patted him on the right shoulder. "I would love to see how far you have come."

"Rayden!" a familiar voice called, prompting her to look up from Hamilcar.

Annocrates trotted across the ground toward her, bringing another smile to her face.

When he reached her, Rayden grasped his forearm in the manner of fellow warriors. "It gladdens my heart to see you again!"

"It has been a long march through lands I did not wish to return to," Annocrates replied, his expression growing a little more serious. "Unpleasant memories stir again and the days seem to go on forever."

"At least you will get a little rest for your legs now," Rayden said. "A siege will ask a different kind of endurance of you ... one that is less physical in nature."

"I hope that we defeat the Teverens soon, so I can get back to building my own home," Annocrates responded. "I have gathered many quality timbers from the trees on my land. I have a field of my own to till as well!"

Hearing the former slave speak about building a home on his own land and growing crops brought Rayden great joy. "I look forward to visiting this new home of yours when it is built."

"I hope that you are the first to stay in it, as an honored guest of mine," Annocrates replied. "You made it possible."

"Many made it possible," Rayden said, thinking of the many that she had fought alongside after choosing to help the slave uprising.

"You were the guiding light to our victory and to the finding of a place to settle," Annocrates said, his timbre turning deferential. "None of us who were freed from bondage and settled in the Tega lands will ever forget that."

Having no words to respond to the enormity of the praise just given to her, Rayden glanced toward Hamilcar. "It seems that you have kept him active, Annocrates. His body shows it."

"The boy never tires," Annocrates replied, chuckling. "I find myself envious at times. He has bountiful endurance."

"One of the most glorious gifts of youth," Rayden observed, laughing. "I wish that I still had that endless fire too."

"How soon do you have to leave?" Hamilar interrupted them, a hint of anxiety showing upon his face.

"I must head to the north tomorrow," Rayden answered him. "I came here to share what I have learned among the Teverens, and then I must go to seek more help for all of us. It is a mission that cannot wait."

"I understand," Hamilcar said after a moment in a lower voice, looking a little downcast.

Rayden ruffled his hair. "Hamilcar, do not be dismayed. I

am here now, and I would love to see how you have improved with the sword."

Hamilcar's look of disappointment fled. Excitement surged within the boy's eyes once again.

"You will be pleased!" he boasted, straightening up. "Come, let me show you!"

"Very well," Rayden answered, laughing, as Hamilcar started back for the encampment.

"The boy works hard to make you proud," Annocrates commented, walking alongside Rayden.

"The skills he is honing will do him well in a world such as this," Rayden replied, sharing a knowing glance with her friend.

An enemy that would not hesitate to cut the boy down loomed nigh.

"Everyone will have to fight soon enough," Annocrates remarked, echoing her sentiments. "Teveren legions will be coming to defend the Imperial City. I am certain of it."

"It is definite that they will be, I have learned of this already ... to add to the legions already quartered inside of it," Rayden stated in a somber voice. "We will have the numbers, and they will have a better armed, more disciplined force. It is best to find a way to get inside that city and keep the siege as short as we can."

"Agreed," Annocrates responded.

Reaching the encampment of the former slaves, Rayden received warm welcomes from numerous men and women that she had come to know and fight alongside, ever since becoming a part of their rebellion.

Hamilcar led them past many campfires and shelters. Taking them to a wagon, he pulled out a couple of crude, wooden swords.

Tossing one to Annocrates, he exclaimed to Rayden, "Tell me what you think!"

The sharp clacking of wood on wood erupted a few

heartbeats later as Hamilcar launched a vigorous attack. Annocrates defended against the slashes and thrusts, but Rayden could see many improvements in the boy's stances, strikes, and overall movement.

The boy had not exaggerated in his claims to Rayden. Only regular drilling and training could have produced such an effect.

When the demonstration came to an end, Rayden walked up to Hamilcar and clutched his left shoulder. Sweat dribbling from his brow and breathing hard, he had a nervous look when he raised his eyes to meet hers.

"Well done, Hamilcar," Rayden commended the boy. "You have taken many steps forward since last we met."

Relief flooded the boy's face at her words, and his eyes lit aflame with exultation. "Really? Do you think so?"

"You know me well enough to know that I do not give unearned praise," Rayden told the boy, raising an eyebrow and growing a little sterner. "To do so would be to invite you toward weakness ... and weakness is a path to peril and death. I invite you to become strong in all things of mind, soul, and body ... and strength in these things is a path to a life free and of true worth."

"I know, and I do not forget the things you have told me," Hamilcar responded to her in a low voice, taking in her light admonishment.

"Then celebrate the harvest of your labor," Rayden encouraged him, smiling broadly once more.

Annocrates put an arm around the boy. "Well done, Hamilcar. I am proud of you as well."

Seeing the fatherly manner of Annocrates, Rayden found comfort and reassurance that she had chosen the boy's guardian well. Hamilcar had been left in the best of hands to receive the right guidance and upbringing.

An honorable man, Annocrates truly cared about the boy. Even more heartening, Rayden could see that Hamilcar looked to

Annocrates as a father figure.

Rayden spent the rest of the day in the camp of the former slaves, until summoned by Alcedan near to dusk. Hamilcar's eyes glistened with the onset of tears when she finally had to leave, making the parting more difficult.

"Your stay was not long enough," Hamilcar muttered, his voice starting to waver.

"Stay strong, you are becoming a warrior," Rayden told him, maintaining a firm tone and expression, despite the fact that she wished in her heart that she had some more time to see him.

"I will do all you ask, Rayden," Hamilcar replied, nodding his head.

Looking into his eyes, Rayden instructed the boy, "Heed Annocrates' will. In all things. It is a dangerous and uncertain time, and he will do his best to see you through the trials to come."

"I promise that I will ... and I will keep training, every day," Hamilcar declared to Rayden, trying to look determined, though a lone tear slipped from the corner of the boy's right eye and trickled down his cheek.

With her right hand, Rayden clutched the back of the boy's head and pressed him against her bosom. Holding him there for a few moments, she gazed down upon the top of his head.

"I am so very proud of you, Hamilcar," Rayden told the boy. "Keep to the path that you are on. Every day take a stride forward. Know that I will return to see you as soon as I am able."

Releasing him, Rayden then took leave of Annocrates and the others, starting back for the Gessa encampment where the chieftain's council would soon be taking place.

***

Being of the Gessa herself, Rayden knew that she did not have the full trust of every face now looking upon her. Stepping forward at Alcedan's invitation, she did have the focused attention of every tribal chieftain.

For her, that was a good enough position to start from.

Save for the chieftains of the Alettani and Sarrimena, all the leaders of the northern tribes surrounded her.

Among those present at the council stood a hulk of a warrior named Makabaras, who had become chieftain of the Runi after the previous one had fallen in battle with the Gessa. It had been Rayden herself who had slain the last Runi chieftain, a reality that Makabaras was certainly conscious of.

The menace of the bestial, sorcery formed Arguntier had driven them into the madness of attacking the Gessa, but Rayden could not imagine the Runi having much affection for those who had sent so many of their best warriors into the cold embrace of the grave.

Furthermore, Rayden stood aware of another stark reality. A gathering like the one now taking place had never transpired before; not even once prior to the tribes coming together to march south and drive toward the heart of the Teveren Empire.

In essence and fact, the entire war campaign represented unprecedented territory for all of the northern tribes.

Warring among each other had always been the usual order of things. Cooperating in a unified, long term mission stood an absolute anomaly, in all of their long histories.

Only Ledakia, who stood for the population of former slaves now living in Tega lands, and Alcedan of the Gessa, could be counted upon to understand the absolute necessity of holding together as one body of people.

Everyone else still stood unproven.

Rayden took a moment to assess the faces around her. Grogner of the Tega looked far less suspicious than he had been when she had first gone before him, to seek permission to settle the mass of former Teveren slaves.

Olten of the Cirna, a rugged, craggy-faced man who looked

like he had been formed out of the mountains where he dwelled, had an unreadable expression. But his eyes carried no hint of irritation or defiance.

Reading one look after another, Rayden could see the same absence of resistance in the others. To her relief, the chieftains appeared to have come to listen with open ears, and they had not carried any major antagonisms to the gathering.

Rayden addressed the chieftains, telling them of everything that she had observed within the Imperial City. She told them of what she had learned about the nature of the Teverens' sorcery, the martial strength at the command of Peronnius and Marus, the nature of the walls and gates; in addition to many more things that she had gleaned about the Teveren world.

The chieftains remained attentive throughout her extensive address. Not one of them interrupted her.

Long before she concluded, Rayden could sense the unease percolating among them. Her account had been received in the manner that she had hoped; the deliverance of a severe warning.

Silence hovered over the throng of northern chieftains when she concluded. Several moments passed before another spoke.

"It will not be easy to choke this city," Serivas, chieftain of the Marren, stated, breaking the stillness. "We have a gap in our encirclement, down by the river. Nothing can be done about it."

"Why is that so?" Alcedan asked Serivas.

"The walls of the city draw close enough to a long stretch of the river where their arrows can reach us," Serivas replied.

"Then they can continue to bring some food and supplies in, using their ships," Kellas of the Pannimbri said. "If we try to contest them, our warriors are vulnerable to their archers on the wall."

"We would lose warriors needlessly, and gain nothing," Serivas said.

Alcedan responded, "Then we challenge the Teverens,

whenever they try to bring relief to the city from the river ... and whatever they seek to bring into it will be reduced to a trickle. The Teverens will not rain arrows upon their own."

"We may be able to reduce what they bring into the city, but what devilry are they mustering?" an older chieftain, Peremdurus of the Borreni, asked of Rayden. "We may be able to sever them from the Catacombs that you speak of, but it sounds like they have turned the city into a giant altar of blood sacrifice. That portends something far beyond the experience of any of us."

"Make no mistake, they are preparing something that none of us has seen or faced," Rayden said. "It is the reason that I must leave when the sun rises, to gain us some aid against whatever they intend to conjure."

Her words brought immediate discomfort to the eyes of most around her. Rayden knew they shared her intense dislike of sorcery and things not of flesh and blood.

The thought of a massive, unprecedented act of sorcery would bring them far more unease and concern than anything involving the Teveren legions. Nevertheless, the northern tribes would have to prepare for all weapons of the enemy.

"What of those you seek help from?" Makabaras asked. "Are you certain they do not use dark sorcery?"

"The ones that I seek out do not," Rayden replied, keeping the nature of the ones that she would be seeking quiet. "They strive against the darkness and have great power. I need only gain their help."

"How can you gain their help in this fight?" Serivas asked.

"I did an act of kindness and mercy for one of their number, a leader of theirs who had been captured and tormented by the Teverens," Rayden said. "I was given something to present to the others if ever I needed help. I trust that they will honor this."

"What group of sorcerers is this?" Peremdurus asked, his deep voice unable to mask an undercurrent of anxiety.

"Ones that dwell in seclusion, to the north, in the depths of the hills," Rayden answered. "They will have much to lose if the Imperator is allowed to continue unchallenged, and I will see to it that they understand the grave threat facing them. Our attack on the Imperial City is their best chance for survival too."

"I may not know of the ones you are seeking, but you have proven yourself more than trustworthy in my eyes," Grogner stated, his words carrying clear and loud to the rest of the chieftains.

"Mine as well," Ledakia added.

"Then it stands that you have a good chance of gaining this aid," Olten said to Rayden.

"I am confident that I do," Rayden replied to him, before looking around at the other chieftains.

Some looked assured, while a little doubt reflected in the faces of others. Yet none of them disputed Rayden or argued against her pending trek to the north.

After a little pause, the discussion continued.

"Aside from Rayden's task in the north, there is still the matter of the legions inside the city ... and those marching here now ... along with those bastard Alettani and Sarrimena," Kellas said, his mention of the two rogue tribes evoking a seething reaction from the others.

"To the abyss with those curs!" Olten rumbled, his eyes flashing with anger.

"The sooner we break their traitorous backs, the better!" Belgra of the Arnan thundered.

"We still have three times their numbers, maybe four!" Celterren of the Lanassa shouted. "Let us crush those that march here, and then we will destroy or starve those in the city!"

"It will not be that easy," Rayden said, keeping her voice even in an attempt to mitigate the spiraling fervor among the chieftains. "They are well-disciplined and will fight as one body.

Our warriors will be seeking to hold ground all around the city. We must be cautious. We face a dangerous enemy."

"They have many gates to send their warriors inside the city through, as Rayden has told us," Grogner said, gazing around at the others. "We do not know where they may emerge!"

"Then all of us must put our minds to finding a way to defend against those within and without," Makabaras said. "It would be better to find a way inside the city, soon."

"When I return from seeking help against the sorcery of the Teverens, I will see that a gate is opened for you," Rayden declared.

Looks of surprise and astonishment sprouted on many faces, including that of Alcedan.

"Rayden, you are a great warrior, but those walls will be under heavy guard now that we are encamped," Alcedan stated.

"Stealth often succeeds where an entire army would fail," Rayden said. "You would break yourselves on their walls before you ever pierced one of their gates. Keep your distance from the walls and allow me to enter the city. I will find a way to see a gate opened for you. Until then, keep that city under the tightest siege that you can."

"That we can do," Kellas responded with an air of confidence.

"When I go north, I will see if I can learn anything of the legions marching toward us," Rayden said. "I know that my path will take me close to them."

"You carry many burdens, Rayden," Belgra said. "Yet I think our fates rest within your hands."

"We would be fools to think otherwise," Peremdurus declared to the group. "We have no answers for their sorcery. What few who lived among us that had understanding of such powerful arts have vanished from our lands."

"You know their disappearances are no coincidence," Olten responded, looking to Peremdurus. "What happened to them is tied to what is occurring in Teveren lands."

"Whatever happened to them, there are none left among us who know anything of the most powerful kinds of sorcery," Peremdurus said. "We only have a few skilled in healing, a few whose gaze can pierce the mists of the past or future, and some others with knowledge of lesser kinds of sorcery. They have nothing of use to confront the sorcerers serving the Imperator."

"Then our fates truly do rest in her hands," Celterren stated.

"We must put our minds to what we can do, pray to the gods, and trust that Rayden will prevail in her mission," Ledakia stated. "There is no other choice we can make."

"Ledakia speaks wisely," Alcedan said. "We know that we cannot go back and leave the Imperator in power, or we will face an even stronger enemy in our own homelands, in a time to come. We must do what we are able to do, and Rayden will seek an answer for our enemy's sorcery."

Though none of them looked entirely at ease, the others nodded and murmured their agreement with Alcedan. With nothing further to discuss and a general consensus reached, Alcedan then called an end to the war council.

The chieftains dispersed and walked back to their respective encampments. Watching them depart, Rayden had no doubt that their thoughts would be occupied late into the evening, absorbing everything that she had related to them.

A shrewd and powerful enemy had to be countered in battle, involving both sorcery and force of arms. Rayden's looming trek to the Mist Vale would have to bear fruit, or a massacre would take place outside the walls of the Imperial City; a massacre that would see the treacherous Alettani and Sarrimena the only tribes left intact in the north.

The mere thought of that sickened Rayden. Taking a deep breath and staring out across a sea of campfires, she cast the slithering doubts from her mind.

Everything that remained in her mind centered on prevailing.

***

"Here, you will not object to this," Erethea said with a smile, handing a wooden cup over to Rayden.

Sitting down cross-legged with a cup of her own in hand, Erethea joined Rayden by the fire blazing within a shallow pit before them.

The scent of mead filling her nostrils, a smile bloomed upon Rayden's face. Raising the cup to her lips, she took a light sip. The sweet taste of honey danced upon her tongue before gliding down her throat.

"A welcome boon," Rayden exclaimed, a wave of calm permeating her mind. "You have my gratitude, as always, Erethea."

"I wish that we were sitting together in the lands of the Gessa, with nothing more to concern ourselves about than what foolishness Jarut might be getting into," Erethea replied, staring into the fire.

"I also wish it were so," Rayden agreed, her smile fading. She took another sip of the mead.

Erethea turned her head to look straight at Rayden. Her expression solemn, she asked, "Do you think we stand a chance of victory? Can we truly prevail over the Teveren Empire?"

"Of course, I do," Rayden responded. "Unless the tribes fall into argument and contention, they represent a great force, one capable of defeating the Teverens."

"That is what I thought," Erethea said, looking reassured. "Many others, too. But now that we have had a look at the walls of this city, hope diminishes in the hearts of many. I have never set my eyes on anything so massive or strong in appearance."

"It is a place like nowhere else I have been," Rayden said. "I wish I could show you what is in there, in a time of peace. But it is full of people not so different than us. There is fear inside those walls too, as they have never had a force like ours encamped outside their walls."

"Is that true? They fear us?" Erethea asked, raising her eyebrows.

"I could see it in nearly every eye, the last time I walked through their streets," Rayden told her friend. "They are people who do not wish for war. Most just wish to raise their children, fill their bellies, find a few moments of joy, and live another day. Only those steeped in power and wealth ... the ones who send others to fight for them ... crave war. As it has always been."

"Your words soothe me a little," Erethea said. "It has been a long, hard march to get here, and we find ourselves before such towering walls of stone."

"A way will be found," Rayden assured her friend. "Or I will die in the effort."

"Do not say such a thing," Erethea replied at once.

"Who can ever say what tomorrow will bring?" Rayden queried. "We have this moment, and nothing more is promised."

"No, nothing is promised," Erethea agreed, staring into the fire again.

Rayden grinned. "I would say there is a very good chance the sun will take to the skies tomorrow ... and an even better chance of Jarut doing something to raise your ire."

Erethea glanced back to Rayden and broke out in laughter. "How I miss you, Rayden. I can always speak of the things weighing upon my spirit and you find the one thing to say to turn it all upside down."

"I would think that I know you a little by now," Rayden said, before taking a longer sip of the mead. Licking her lips, she added, "I know that both of us would not mind filling these cups over and over again, throughout the night."

"The soonest that we can, we will do so," Erethea stated.

"We are agreed," Rayden replied, smiling at her.

"One day I must travel with you, to another land," Erethea said. "I do not wish that the only journey in my life is this one ... a long march under a cloud of war."

"A journey with you to another land in a time of peace would be wonderful," Rayden said with a wistful lilt, staring into the undulating, crackling flames.

"I think I would have to undertake a journey to have your company for a longer time," Erethea said, with a rueful grin. "I know you would not grow roots under you, even in Gessa lands."

Rayden kept staring into the fire, thinking of the deep-seeded restlessness that propelled her across land and sea. Though world-weary at times, she knew that the greater journey would continue even if the northern tribes prevailed and returned to their homelands.

She still did not know the destination of that greater journey, but she did trust that it would lead to a place that she could call home; a home in the truest sense.

The thought bringing a smile to her face, Rayden finished the cup of mead while savoring each moment that transpired in the company of her friend.

CHAPTER 8

The next couple of days passed without incident. Trekking northward, Rayden covered several leagues each day, bypassing many large estates and villages nestled within the sprawling countryside.

With all of the upheaval, Rayden proceeded carefully through the wilderness. Eating light, she made few stops, endeavoring to make the most out of the available daylight.

Mid-morning on the third day, Rayden heard something other than the chirping of birds and trilling of insects. Carrying to her through the trees, distinct voices from a casual conversation indicated the presence of multiple individuals, somewhere just ahead of her.

Using trees and brush for concealment, Rayden made her way toward the voices, while keeping an eye out for any signs of movement around her. Her footfalls almost imperceptible, she crept closer and closer.

Three men came into view. Setting her eyes upon them, their appearances and the weapons they carried proclaimed their nature.

One held a scythe, another an axe of the kind used for splitting logs, and the third grasped the hilt of a long knife. Clad in plain tunics and leather shoes, all three had short-cropped hair and nothing beyond stubble on their faces.

Stepping out from a tree and into the open, Rayden's sudden appearance startled the three, to the degree that the one with the scythe nearly dropped his weapon.

Keeping her hands low, to take up her weapons if necessary, she declared to the men, "I am a friend, and an enemy to the ones who enslaved you."

Fear and puzzlement reflected in their faces.

"You are one of the barbarians!" the man with the scythe said.

"Not the word I use, but I am from the tribes of the north," Rayden replied in a steady, firm tone.

Short and stocky in build, the man with the axe stated, "I heard tales of a Valkyrie with hair of gold and eyes of blue flame, fighting with sword and axe, who led an army of escaped slaves to victory over the Teverens."

"From the uprising?" the man holding the scythe queried, his eyes widening.

"Are you her?" the man with the knife asked, tentatively.

"My name is Rayden, and some have called me Valkyrie," she responded to them. "My hair is not made of gold, and I do not have flames in my eyes, but I did have the honor of fighting alongside many who stood strong to take back their freedom."

"You are most welcome among us!" the man with the scythe declared, his expression softening into a welcoming smile. "Many times, we have celebrated tales of you!"

"Rayden Valkyrie, standing right before my eyes," exclaimed the fellow with the axe, looking awestruck.

"It is just me," Rayden replied, taking in their astonishment. "We are on the same side, I am certain, in the ongoing war."

"Yes ... yes we are!" the scythe-wielding man proclaimed. Emphatic, he shook his weapon above his head. "We fight on the same side as Rayden Valkyrie!"

"Are there more of you?" she asked, remaining calm.

"Yes, a camp of us is near," the knife-bearer stated.

"I would welcome a meal, and some knowledge of the lands around here," Rayden told them. "I am on an important task."

"We can help with both things," the scythe-holder told her, an edge of eagerness to his voice.

"Come with us, we will take you to the camp," the axe-wielder invited.

"Thank you," Rayden said.

The men led her off through the woods, heading northeast. Several times they glanced at her, as if in disbelief toward the witness of their eyes.

Rayden strode along with them, wondering how stories about her became so exaggerated in such a short amount of time.

***

Breaking off a piece of bread and softening it in a clay cup full of highly watered wine, Rayden looked to the round-faced man sitting on the ground near her.

"You say that the Mist Vale is located close to here?" she asked, before putting the bread into her mouth.

Nodding, he replied, "You were not far when you came across our men. It is not more than a half-day's march, straight north of here. You are almost upon the river that flows into it."

"I intended to follow the river straight into the Mist Vale." Softening another piece of bread in the wine, she eyed the man.

"You do not want to travel into there at the edge of night or dawn," the man said, staring back at her with a nervous expression. "The mists return, and it becomes impassable."

"I will camp close and go in after morning's light has cleared the air," Rayden told him.

A look of disbelief on his face, he said to her, "You should continue south with us. We all go to join the northern tribes and the large numbers of former slaves that are now fighting to end such bondage as we have long-suffered."

"I will be returning south to fight alongside all of you, very soon," Rayden replied. "I have business in the Mist Vale that must be attended to first."

"I do not wish to suggest you are not right of mind," the man said, eyeing her with a look of incredulity splayed across his face. "But to say that you have business in the Mist Vale ... that is something I cannot comprehend."

"All of you likely believe I am not right of mind," Rayden said, chuckling and looking about the makeshift encampment of former slaves.

Some with the harder, weathered bodies and more gruff appearances of laborers, and others with the softer, cleaner looks of household staff, the mixture of former slaves proved interesting for Rayden to observe. Deserting their previous stations, they had come together in the woods until the entire band numbered well over a hundred strong.

Knowing of the siege taking place at the Imperial City, the newly liberated men and women had decided on joining the ranks of the invaders. Heading southward through the forested hills, they would reach the tribal multitudes in another couple of days.

Surrounded by men and women bearing the marks of severe lashings and worse, more permanent injuries, Rayden could sense the desire for vengeance burning fiercely within the hearts of the former slaves. Even if untrained, they would fight hard.

"I know of no one else here who would willingly venture into the Mist Vale," the man replied, shaking his head. "It is a place for the fae ... and the fae alone."

"I have had my encounters with the fae before," Rayden replied. After a pause, she added, "If that is what you wish the most to caution me about."

"They cannot be predicted ... not ever ... and the forests there are dangerous enough," the man countered, looking worried. "Many have ventured there, and vanished, with no trace."

"I am well-warned," Rayden responded. "Whatever happens to me is the result of my own choices and the fault of no one else. I accept all responsibility for my actions."

"You are not one easily dissuaded," the man stated, shaking his head.

His words brought a smile to her face. "Not when I have my mind set."

"We do not have much here, but I can spare a little more bread for you to take with you on your journey," the man said. "Some of those who have come here looted their former masters before setting out."

"I thank you," Rayden said, finishing the bread remaining in her hand. She then drank down the rest of the wine in her cup. "You have my gratitude for your generosity."

"You are a great warrior of the northern tribes, the tribes who fight against those who enslaved and oppressed us," the man said, a smile breaking across his face. "Many in this camp have heard of you and the defeat of the Teveren legion that tried blocking a passage to the north. How could I ever refuse you?"

Rayden got to her feet and handed the empty cup back to the man.

"May no harm come to you on your journey to the south," Rayden said, extending her right arm. When he held up his, she grasped his forearm in a warrior's embrace. "I will look toward seeing you again, soon, after I am finished in the Mist Vale."

"We have enough of us here to look out for ourselves," the man replied in a tone of assurance. "I also hope to see you again soon, in the south. Something tells me that you are the kind of warrior who wins wars."

"All wars exact such a heavy price that I sometimes think no one ever truly wins a war," Rayden told him, growing more somber. "Yet some are necessary and cannot be avoided. This fight against the Teverens that we are both a part of is one of those kinds of wars. It must be fought. It must be won. All else is meaningless."

"I can never go back to a life of bondage," the man responded, shaking his head. "Never again. But let me delay you no more. Hold for a moment and let me get you the promised bread."

Rising up, the man left her sitting by herself for a few moments while going to retrieve the bread. Seeing him returning with a round loaf in hand, she stepped forward to meet him.

Handing the bread over to Rayden, he said, "Take this, and may it provide you with sustenance."

Gripping the hard, outer crust, she pushed the loaf into her largest pouch, finding that she had just enough room inside to hold it.

"I have one more question to ask before I leave," Rayden asked him.

"Ask what you will," he replied.

"I must know your name, so that I may ask after you when I return south," Rayden responded.

"I am called Oressius," he said.

Reaching out, she clasped the man's forearm once more. "I thank you again, Oressius. May it happen that we see each other again, soon."

"May the gods watch over you, Rayden Valkyrie," he responded to her, a little of the worry that he had exhibited earlier returning to his eyes.

Rayden gave the man a smile before turning and striding away from the sprawling woodland camp.

Setting off to the north, Rayden soon found herself amid tranquil surroundings. Sunlight filtered through the trees and the songs of birds carried through the air.

Setting her mind to wariness, Rayden did not allow the peaceful environment to lull her into a state of complacency. Predatory beasts and outlaws alike could make the most beautiful and inviting of surroundings dangerous.

While maintaining a solid gait, Rayden did not press herself too hard. She did not want to sap her strength too much before reaching the boundary of the Mist Vale.

After she had traveled about half a league, Rayden came upon the river that Oressius had spoken of. The sparkling, silvery ribbon meandered through the wooded hills, flowing at a slow, steady pace.

Following the course of the river, Rayden made good progress throughout the afternoon. Other than startling a few deer that had been drinking at the water's edge, she had no encounters to break the peaceful atmosphere.

Before the sun began its descent into the western horizon, she arrived at the edge of the Mist Vale. The land opening up on both sides, a lush, forested valley spread before her eyes. High hills ran along its eastern and western sides.

Not wanting to proceed any farther with dusk so close, Rayden spent the last part of the day finding an advantageous spot to pass the night.

Making use of the large trunk of an old, fallen tree and gathering up some brush, she fashioned a well-concealed space padded with soft grass inside.

Not far from the site, Rayden found an abundance of wild berries close to ripening. Though a little sour, they proved delectable after a long day's march.

She also availed herself of a few mushrooms whose non-poisonous nature she was certain of. The discovery of the berries and mushrooms allowed her to spare the bread that she carried for a later time.

A chill seeping into the air, the approach of dusk brought with it the reason for the vale's name. Tendrils of gray mist began wafting through the trees, increasing in number until a thick mist had manifested throughout the forest. The dense vapors shrouded everything, reducing visibility down to where becoming lost would be a likely outcome for any who tried passing through it.

Making herself comfortable within the provisional enclosure that she had crafted, Rayden settled down to pass the night. Her sword laying close at hand and sleeping light, she awoke at the slightest disturbance.

Deeper in the night, the light cracking of twigs and faint scuffling of leaves marked the steps of something moving in the dark close by, but it did not investigate the place where Rayden was hidden. The noises disappeared soon enough, and the night fell into silence once more, but Rayden waited a little time before releasing the grip upon her sword hilt.

Far into the night, the scraping of claws on the bark of the fallen trunk, a little farther down from where Rayden lay, prompted her to grab the hilt of her sword again. The creature sounded larger than the previous one that had disturbed her slumber.

A few husky breaths sounded closer to the enclosure. Keeping her mind still, Rayden raised the sword, ready to thrust the honed iron blade should anything try to burrow into her space.

Knowing that it possessed claws, she could take no chances on the creature outside being a harmless denizen of the forest. A moment's hesitation could mean the difference between inflicting a wound that would drive away a large predator and being attacked, with no area to maneuver in, or route of escape.

The creature in the night roved onward, leaving Rayden in a pool of silence. After listening for an extended period, she lowered the blade and returned to slumber.

Nothing else interrupted her rest for the duration of the night.

∗∗∗

A chilly, damp morning greeted Rayden. Engulfed in light gray mist, she had to delay entering the vale.

A light rainfall began soon after, though to her relief it did not advance into a downpour. Remaining dry in her hideaway, Rayden listened to the patter of raindrops throughout the early part of the morning.

At last the rain ebbed and the mists dissipated, unfurling bright, blue skies overhead, accented with patches of puffy, white clouds.

Returning to the place where she had found the wild berries, Rayden harvested a few more handfuls. Eating some of the berries and saving others in a small pouch, she had a little cheese, and some of the remaining bread softened in water, before heading into the vale.

Rested and with no pangs of hunger in her belly, Rayden had a spring to her step and sharpness of mind.

In the aftermath of the rain, the forest had the glisten of something fresh and pristine. Catching the sunlight, water drops on leaves exhibited a crystalline sparkle.

To Rayden, the vibrant look of the forest seemed fitting for an area known to be inhabited by elusive creatures steeped in magical arts. Under no illusions, she knew that every step she made was being observed within the boundaries of the Mist Vale.

Underfoot, softened from the light rain, the forest floor cushioned her strides. Birds of several kinds serenaded her from the boughs of the trees. Dappling the ground in shadows and pools of light, the interlacing canopy above scattered the showering rays of sunlight.

The raw wilderness had a perfect order to it, a completeness that Rayden could sense every time that she immersed herself within its vibrant midst.

She wished that she harbored the gift that some in the world claimed to possess, of being able to speak with the trees. Many of the centuries-old, majestic sentinels that she came across in forests had a perspective unlike most any living thing from the natural world.

The wisdom that could be gleaned from diligent observers that had witnessed the passing of ages far surpassed any hoard of gold, silver, and jewels.

Many such trees thrived within the Mist Vale. With massive trunks and a multitude of stout branches, the old, moss-draped giants beckoned to Rayden, inviting her to peaceful repose and tranquility beneath their watchful, patient gazes.

No matter what inclinations she harbored, Rayden could not stop or relax her guard. The faeries of the Mist Vale had to be found and entreated.

The promise of a king during his final breaths compelled her forward.

Around the outer edges of her vision, Rayden began to perceive periodic movements. The instances proved fleeting and ephemeral, every time that she shifted her eyes to focus in the direction of the things detected.

Noticing that the forest around her had grown quiet, Rayden slowed her pace. The shift in atmosphere furthered her suspicions that whatever played about the boundaries of her sight was no mere mirage.

Those she sought had drawn close.

Breathing steady, Rayden kept her axe and sword at her waist. She did not want to present a threatening posture, not when she had come seeking the help of reclusive creatures adept at avoiding humans.

A short distance ahead, within a small clearing, a broad

ring of colorful toadstools came into view. The bright red mushrooms had grown thick around the perimeter of the open space, encircling a lush, deep blue shade of grass.

Towering in height, thick of trunk, and regal in nature, the trees bordering the clearing were all ancients of their venerable kind.

Every instinct within Rayden counseled her to display a reverent demeanor as she approached the edge of the distinctive clearing. Ground sacred to the fae lay within the toadstool ring.

Powerful emotions churning within, she thought of the little winged creature sacrificed on the altar, in the temple back in Verranus. A king of his kind, the diminutive being had succumbed to the atrocities committed upon him.

Though thwarting the wicked designs of those who had captured Roggar, the faerie king, Rayden had been unable to save the creature from the embrace of death. Keeping Roggar company during his final moments, she had not allowed the faerie king to die alone.

Thinking of Roggar, Rayden stepped to the edge of the clearing, but she did not enter it, sensing the mushroom ring and blue area that it contained to be forbidden ground. Looking around, she kept her movements slow, taking out a distinctive ring from the small pouch at her waist.

Given to her by Roggar just before his spirit left the world, the ring felt warm to her touch. The faerie king had given it to her for the purpose of seeking help among its kind within the Mist Vale, but she knew nothing more of its use or properties.

Opening her palm, Rayden exposed the ring to the view of any that might be looking upon her.

"I stayed with King Roggar, during his last breaths," Rayden announced in a firm tone. "I found him in a temple, a captive of wicked priests who sought to offer him in sacrifice. I fought against the priests and their creatures, and they failed in their

185

ritual, but I could not save your king.

"Before he died, King Roggar gave this ring to me, and bid me to use it here in the Mist Vale should I ever need the help of the faerie folk.

"I am in great need of that help now, to help overcome those that the killers of Roggar serve. I stand here at your mercy and judgment."

Rayden continued to keep the ring displayed after falling into silence. Not even a breeze stirred the pensive stillness permeating the area. No insect chittered, and no bird sang a single note.

Rayden waited, until at last something stirred within the ring of toadstools.

Blinking, Rayden sought to clear her eyes. The ground within the circle appeared to shimmer and blur, causing her to wonder whether something was happening to her own vision.

At the center of the clearing, a slim fold of golden light expanded and brightened, revealing a winged creature within. Having an appearance aligning it with the kind of fairy that Roggar had been, the faerie displayed feminine attributes in its slender face and body.

"You carry King Roggar's ring," the creature declared, her voice melodious and resonant. "That ring can only be given, and never taken."

Wings beating against the air, the faerie rose into the air and drifted closer to Rayden. Reaching the inner edge of the mushroom ring, the faerie came to a halt, hovering mid-air.

Looking Rayden direct in the eyes, the faerie then continued. "Roggar was taken from us, by those who are slaves to dark powers. I sensed in my heart that he had passed the Veil, but you bring grave tidings to us. We have lost our king ... and I have lost the greater part of myself."

A stinging undercurrent of sorrow flowed through the

fairy's words in a manner that Rayden could sense in a profound way. Unable to respond, she had no words of comfort to offer the little creature.

"If he passed the ring to you, Roggar deemed you worthy of friendship with our kind," the creature continued, drawing closer and keeping her gaze to Rayden's own. After a moment, she asked, "May I have the name that you are called by?"

Staring into the depths of the faerie's mesmerizing, golden eyes, Rayden answered, "I am Rayden."

"I am Roggar's queen, Muirithesos," the faerie replied to her.

Lowering her eyes toward the ground, Rayden extended the small being a respectful bow of her head. "It is an honor to have this audience with you, Queen Muirithesos."

"Dark times bring unlikely friendships into life," Muirithesos replied. "It is the way of things."

Raising her head back up, Rayden looked back into the faerie's eyes. "A genuine friendship is among the greatest of fortunes that one can receive in this world. No matter what path led to it."

"You speak with wisdom," Muirithesos responded.

"I have seen enough in this world to know the folly of those who count their fortunes in land, coins, or jewels," Rayden commented.

"Many such fools bring horrors into this world in their lust for riches," Muirithesos stated with a sharp air of distaste.

"Many Teverens among that number," Rayden said, nodding in agreement.

"Their Imperator is not one of them," Muirithesos replied. "He is of an even more dangerous kind ... he is one who hungers for power, for its own sake."

"Under his authority, uncountable atrocities have been committed," Rayden said. Frowning, she thought of the crucified slaves displayed in grisly fashion for leagues along the Boreus

Way.

"All of these abominations have taken place for a purpose," Muirithesos replied. Wings beating faster, the faerie queen crossed over the mushroom ring and fluttered past Rayden. Glancing back, she added, "Come with me."

Rayden turned as Muirithesos proceeded away from the clearing. She knew enough about the ways of faeries to understand that the queen was demonstrating her trust of Rayden in leaving the sacred, protective ground within the circle of mushrooms.

The faerie continued forward and landed upon the branch of a nearby tree that placed her about eye-level to Rayden. Her wings became still, the two elegant appendages having a gossamer appearance that glimmered in the sunlight's radiant touch.

"The Imperator gathers ever more strength," Queen Muirithesos remarked.

"The Imperator is engaging in blood sacrifice on a massive scale," Rayden declared. "All manner of living beings have had their blood shed on dark altars and within the sands of his arena ... and even in the homes of the powerful beholden to him. All of the dark power created through the spilling of blood flows to his purposes."

"He has gathered the powers of the Abyss like no other human I have gained awareness of," Muirithesos replied in a grim tone. "A sorcerer of great power, who possesses knowledge of rare, dark mysteries guides him. There is only one reason to gather such a tremendous amount of dark energies. The Imperator and those serving him seek to cross the boundaries between worlds."

"They have already done so," Rayden responded. "In the north, they channeled fell spirits into captured beasts, and changed them into nightmares that walked upon two legs. Their new creations would have caused the extinction of entire tribes had we failed to stand together and gain help from the Varganir. It took everything within us to stop them."

"We were told of such monstrosities roving the north," the queen acknowledged. "It is good that they are no more, but the gathering of dark powers continues, unceasing. Something else looms."

"What else are they seeking to bring into this world?" Rayden asked.

"Who can say?" the queen responded. "The only thing that can be known is that it will be an even greater transgression of the natural order of things."

Rayden stared again into the depths of the queen's spellbinding gaze, but she maintained her wits. "This is why I seek the help of the faerie folk. None among the tribes can match the sorcery being wielded from the Imperial City. If the tribes fall, there will be nothing to stop the Imperator's legions from swarming the north.

"In time, they will bring their dark magic to bear upon all things that refuse to bow to Teveren might. The faerie folk of the Mist Vale will fall under their shadow, eventually."

"I cannot argue against that," the queen replied. "But what can my kind do against them? Their sorcerers now wield a staggering level of dark magic. We would be slaughtered in going against their sorcerers openly."

"Bring your full power to bear upon the greatest among our enemy, when they are in a weakened state," Rayden told the queen. "There will come a time when they expend a great amount of power, and they will be vulnerable in the aftermath. Strike in that moment. Do not let them recover. Let us hope that the warriors of the tribes yet stand strong when that happens. Together, there is a greater chance we can break the Teverens' power."

The faerie queen held Rayden's gaze, but said nothing for many long moments. Her unchanging expression gave no hint of her thoughts.

At last, Muirithesos broke the extended silence. "I hold no

illusions. If we do not break the power of the Imperator and his sorcerers, then all of my kind will face the same kind of fate as Roggar."

"If we fail, the tribes of the north will be shattered and enslaved," Rayden said. "We both face the same threat and enemy."

"Even so, you ask much of us," Queen Muirithesos replied, remaining solemn in demeanor. "This is a much larger entreaty than one seeking help for a matter involving just yourself."

"It is," Rayden admitted. "I know that it goes well beyond the promise invoked by the ring given to me."

"Nevertheless, I understand why you have come to us," the queen replied. "The Imperator and his servants have brought great pain and sorrow to both of our kinds, and they are a deadly adversary."

"Their hunger will never be fed," Rayden addressed the queen. "No matter how much they devour, they will remain starved, and ravenous to consume more.

"If the tribes of the north fall to them ... if the Kartajenians are overcome ... if all others are subjugated and placed in bondage ... they will turn their eyes elsewhere, looking for new conquests.

"I know that the magic of the faerie folk has great power, but not even the Mist Vale can remain hidden from their sight forever."

"Again, I cannot argue with what you have said," the queen responded. After becoming quiet for a few moments, she asked, "Where will you go, when you leave the Mist Vale?"

"I must return back to the south, to where the tribes now besiege the Imperator," Rayden answered. "A way into the city must be gained soon, or time will labor against us."

"Before you depart, take a few moments to rest for a little while, and drink of the nectar of faerie-kind," Muirithesos invited. "Let us restore you for the journey back."

"I must leave before the mists rise to engulf the vale and its borders," Rayden replied. "The forest is impassable when the mists take hold."

"Perhaps I can implore you to leave in the morning, after a full night's sleep under our watch?" Muirithesos responded.

The offer tempted Rayden. A chance to be the guest of a faerie queen did not occur often among humankind. She would be also able to allow herself a deep, restorative sleep, without concern for wild beasts or the entities of darkness.

Yet she had made her supplication to the queen and needed to return south. Nothing could be assumed when it came to the Teverens; whether involving their sorcerers, or the legions that she knew would be coming to break the siege.

"I can only spare a little while longer here," Rayden replied after thinking upon the queen's offer. "My place is back with the tribes of the north."

The queen nodded. "Your wish will be respected. If a better time comes in future days, know that you can return here as an honored guest."

"You have my gratitude, and my wish is for that better time to come in future days," Rayden replied.

"You did say that you could spare a little while longer, though," the queen stated.

"I do have some time left," Rayden confirmed. "But I must leave well before the mists come."

Setting her face aglow, the queen smiled, her mood becoming more buoyant. "Then we will make sure that is so. Now, come with me!"

Sunlight casting a luxuriant sheen upon her gossamer wings, the queen started forward, fluttering slow and allowing Rayden to keep pace with her at an easy stride.

All around them and no longer concealed, a wide array of faeries had gathered. Some extremely diminutive, no larger than a fly, and others the size of the queen, the mixed throng moved along with their queen and Rayden.

Looking like a swarm of bright crystals, a batch of the smallest kind passed through a pool of sunlight. Continuing into a stretch of deep shadow, they took on the appearance of little stars manifesting out of the dusk.

Many of the various types in view around Rayden had faces echoing those of humankind, while other kinds had appearances far less human. One palm-sized fairy had a pair of nostril slits above elongated jaws filled with spiky teeth. Another type of similar size had protruding, muzzle-like jaws and upright, triangular ears, giving the faerie a canine appearance. Rayden almost took one kind to be a butterfly, were it not for the creature's delicate-looking arms and legs.

Everywhere that Rayden looked, the glints, sparkles, and glimmers of faeries bestowed a magical ambience to the forest surroundings.

The queen guided Rayden to a large pond of clear water, cradled within a grove of trees. The still surface mirrored the trees and clusters of white clouds drifting across the skies far above.

A mass of faeries converged near the edge, attending to a broad swathe of tall grass. When they dispersed, the faeries left behind a compact, bowl-shaped space, large enough for Rayden to be seated within.

"With the little time that you have left, take some comfort among us," the queen told her, while alighting upon the ground.

Rayden lowered herself down into the space, easing into the soft, cushioning grass.

Moments later, several faeries of the queen's type approached Rayden. Bearing a small clay bowl through the air, the faeries exhibited great care with the contents in the vessel.

Slowing to a stop before Rayden, the faeries hovered in

place.

"Drink of the nectar of faerie-kind," the queen invited her.

Rayden smiled and carefully took the small cup from the faeries. The vessel contained an amber-hued liquid that gave off a distinct floral scent.

"Will this cause me to shed my wits, in the manner of ale or wine?" Rayden asked, looking over to the queen.

"No, but it will bring strength to your limbs and sharpness to your mind," the queen responded. "This drink brings together many gifts of the forest."

Raising the cup to her lips, Rayden took a slow sip. The cool liquid had a mildly sweet taste and slid down her throat in a smooth fashion.

After taking a couple more sips, Rayden began to feel a warm sensation running throughout her body and limbs. Brimming with energy, she had an urge to spring to her feet and bound through the woods.

Everything around her took on a vivid clarity; a sharpness of focus that surpassed that of a full night's rest.

"Astonishing," Rayden exclaimed, gazing at the liquid and then looking back to the queen.

"The nectar of many kinds of leaves and flowers is collected to form Elysian Wings, the drink you now partake of," the queen told her. "We have our own ways in the creation of it, but it is nothing that humankind could not prepare. Remarkable gifts surround you, in abundance, yet most humans fail to accept what is freely offered."

"My kind are often blind to many things," Rayden replied to the queen with a rueful edge. "So many put their hearts toward the things that will destroy them and ignore that which can restore and sustain them."

"That is a path that many of our kind have taken," the queen responded, her expression growing more somber. "The darkness is seductive and often appears in beautiful raiment."

"Leading so many astray," Rayden lamented. "To betray and dishonor themselves ... and finally ... to condemn themselves."

"But not all fall to the lures of the abyss," the queen responded, smiling once more toward Rayden. "Some rise far above the temptations of darkness."

Nodding, Rayden replied, "No, not all fall prey. Some still take the better path, though narrow and more difficult it may be to travel."

"Sometimes, we all need to be reminded of the destination," the queen stated, a different lilt entering her voice. "Those of us bearing the burdens of inner weariness ... and those of us bearing the burdens of sorrow."

Understanding passing between them, Rayden held the eyes of the queen for several moments with her gaze. Nowhere did she perceive the craving for power that she had found in most human rulers.

Rather, the small winged figure standing before Rayden displayed the quiet confidence born of a strong heart guided by compassion and wisdom. In a world fraught with tragedy, peril, and wickedness, such a leader represented a rare and inestimable blessing.

Rayden found herself wondering whether the brief span of human life hindered the emergence of such leaders. A human had only so many years to sate an appetite.

When ambitions could be spread across centuries instead of a few mere decades, perhaps the fires of greed and impetuous desires could be tempered in the hearts of many. Wisdom could then be cultivated and grown.

Yet another part of Rayden reminded her that some of the most wicked and power-hungry entities she had encountered during her far-ranging journeys possessed an immortal nature. Patient and calculating, some of those entities had made great use of the passing of ages to pursue their aims in a meticulous, painstaking fashion.

"The destination is what everything comes to, for faerie-kind and human alike," Rayden observed, lifting her head and staring across the pond. "The question of what all of this is for ... the toil, the sacrifice, and the striving of a lifetime."

"That is a question that none of us on this side of the Veil can answer in full," the queen replied. "But we can gain glimpses, visions, and hints of something much greater ahead, if we calm our minds and spirits."

"Beacons in the darkness," Rayden stated, nodding her understanding. "Such have given me a tether to hold onto during times of great darkness."

A somber expression came over the queen's face. "Even then, we fail at times to perceive rays of light, when all becomes shrouded in the discord of a weary or troubled heart."

"It is then that we have to look deeper inside our own hearts," Rayden said. "There, at the center of everything that we are, is a spark that can never be extinguished so long as we draw breath."

"This is why all of us can be a light for another," the queen responded. Muirithesos looked away from Rayden, and a smile returned to her face. "Now, let us become lights for you."

A group of faeries then arrived, carrying a thin, flat stone that held a pair of cooked fish and a trio of small round cakes. The scent of both caused Rayden's mouth to water.

"Take sustenance, and let your mind and spirit be at peace," the queen told her. "Let your ears and eyes fill with the beauty of life. Be open to glimpses, visions, and hints of another reality."

Light, melodic notes from a pair of stringed instruments glided and danced through the air. Several high-pitched voices joined in, forming enchanting harmonies that flowed around the instrumental progression.

In her heightened state of alertness, Rayden savored the faerie music enveloping her. Each note clear and resonant, the music flowed into her ears in a way that she had never before experienced.

Alone, in smaller groups, and in larger throngs, faeries carried out an enthralling spectacle of acrobatic displays and cohesive movements through the air, out over the pond. The elegant, airborne dancing paired with the music to create an enrapturing atmosphere.

Like starbursts of light, concentrated groups of faeries flared outward against the backdrop of large, sparkling swirls formed by others of their kind. Many formed curling, luminescent streams that caressed the outskirts of the larger formations.

Reflecting the multitudes of faerie lights, the pond surface transformed into a glittering portal of dynamic brilliance. Rayden could imagine the heavens that she had heard of containing such resplendent ponds.

Partaking of the fish and sweet cakes given to her, Rayden delighted in every moment watching the dazzling pageant, a celebration of life and light. A visual ecstasy, the radiant performers appeared to be taking just as much pleasure in the exhibition as she did.

Soaring elation and comforting peace flowed through Rayden. The enchanting music seemed to be reaching deep inside her, all the way to her innermost spirit, bringing restoration and renewal to areas grown heavier with inner weariness.

An encompassing timelessness pervaded the profound experience. In the midst of it all, Rayden could not tell if she had been seated for a few moments or many days.

At long last, the faeries began drifting away from the area over the pond. The music ebbed, with voices trailing off until only the notes of the stringed instruments remained. Those too then fell silent, leaving their final tones ringing out across the glistening, still waters.

Gazing across the pond, Rayden could not speak for several heartbeats.

"It is like I have been allowed to have a taste of the heavens," Rayden finally said, in a low, reverent voice.

"In some ways, maybe you have been," the queen replied. "Glimpses, visions, and hints ... the eternal spirit of life whispers to each of us in a different way."

"This is something that I will never forget," Rayden said, keeping her voice softer and quietly getting up to her feet. Turning, she looked down into the queen's eyes. "Thank you, Queen Muirithesos. This has been an honor and a tremendous gift."

Wings fluttering, Queen Muirithesos lifted into the air, rising up to Rayden's eye level. "You have my undying gratitude for what you did for Roggar in his final moments."

"I only wish that I could have saved him," Rayden replied with a trace of lament.

"You did," the queen said in a firm tone. "You saved him from being used for a wicked purpose. You gave him peace at the end of one journey ... and the beginning of another."

"It was my honor," Rayden said, giving the queen a bow of her head.

Muirithesos drifted forward several paces and rotated back toward Rayden. "Now, let me guide you to the end of the Vale, so that you may begin the journey back and rejoin your people in the south."

Rayden nodded her assent, and the queen resumed moving forward.

Walking along with the queen, Rayden remained silent for a little while. Looking around, she took in as much of the Mist Vale as she possibly could. Even without spectacular displays by throngs of faeries, the vale had an enchanting beauty to it.

The return to the end of the Mist Vale seemed to pass much more swiftly than the walk into it. Not having to proceed in a state of caution and wariness, Rayden had ease of mind in the company of the queen.

The queen slowed and came to a halt close to the end of the vale.

"We have reached our borders," Muirithesos declared, gazing southward.

Rayden girded herself to continue forward, through the wilderness beyond.

Yet one question remained.

"Will you be able to aid us against the Imperator's sorcerers?" Rayden asked the queen.

"I will send messages to other kingdoms of my kind, and a council will be called," Muirithesos answered. "Know that help will be given to you, to honor Roggar's wishes in the placement of his ring in your care, but the extent of it I cannot say at this moment."

"I thank you, Queen Muirithesos," Rayden said, extending the faerie another bow of her head. Straightening back up, she then asked in an amiable tone, "Do you desire to have this ring returned to you? I would freely give it back, should you wish."

Looking upon the faerie in that moment as Roggar's wife and not as a queen, Rayden desired to give Muirithesos a chance to reclaim the ring if it happened to possess an intimate, private meaning to her.

Muirithesos gazed upon the ring and a crystalline sheen formed over her eyes.

"The ring is yours to keep," Muirithesos stated after a few moments had passed, a smile forming on her delicate lips. "It was freely given and will tell other fairy folk ... those who have not turned their hearts to dark magic ... that you are a friend to our kind."

"It is a great honor, one that I will never take lightly," Rayden told the queen. Giving yet another short bow, she returned the ring to the pouch secured at her waist. "I will do all that I can to remain worthy of this friendship."

"That is all that could ever be asked," Muirithesos said. "I can already sense what Roggar saw within you. My life is over three centuries long, as humans measure the days and nights. In that time, I have known of few among humankind that Roggar would even think of bestowing his ring upon."

"I wish that I could have come to know him in another way," Rayden told the queen.

"We have little control over circumstances," the queen replied.

"No, we do not," Rayden agreed. After a pause, she then asked the queen, "How will I be able to speak with you, or those who serve you, after I return south? How will I know when you have arrived?"

"Do not worry yourself, we will find you," Muirithesos told Rayden. "We will do our part to help defeat this abomination that has risen to such power in the world of humans. Those that serve the powers in the Abyss will be made to answer for what was done to Roggar."

"Yes, they will be made to answer in full," Rayden responded with a flare of iron-hard determination in her eyes.

"Before you depart, there is one warning that I must give to you," Muirithesos then said, her expression remaining solemn.

Rayden nodded to the faery queen.

"The minions of the enemy keep watch upon our borders," Muirithesos said. "Dark fae will have great interest in a human leaving from our domain, after passing a great part of the day here."

"An ill-tiding," Rayden said, frowning at the queen's words. "I saw nothing of them when coming into the Mist Vale."

"They were not able to gather numbers to confront you ... or you somehow managed to slip by them," Muirithesos replied. "Their eyes are on the Mist Vale and the approaches to it. It is hard to think that not one saw you."

"Perhaps rare chance can repeat and I can slip by them once more," Rayden said. "If I cannot, then there are other measures. If they are fae, they will not like the taste of iron."

"No, they will not," Muirithesos replied. "But, like our kind, they do have other powers to wield."

"Not all fae are the same," Rayden said. "What is a weakness to one kind is not the same as another. Does this kind have any weakness?"

"The ones we know of skulking about our borders are of a kind that loathes water, and they will not cross over a running channel of it," Muirithesos said. "You can be certain of that. Use streams, creeks, or the river if you must."

"What is their strength?" Rayden asked.

"They do not have the strength to challenge our borders," Muirithesos said. "These are scouts and watchers, but there are enough of them to swarm a single being."

"Then let us hope that I can pass through them without drawing their attention," Rayden said. "Or they will be fed honed iron."

"These accursed dregs deserve no less," Muirithesos replied, an edge of animosity rife within her face and voice. "They have long since turned upon their own kind, and I know that Roggar would not have been taken without their help."

"I thank you for warning me of them," Rayden told the queen.

"I am certain they are in the service of the same enemy that we are pitted against," Muirithesos said. "I see that the war being waged is bringing many together, on both sides."

"It gladdens me that we stand together in this war, on the

same side," Rayden stated.

"It gladdens me as well," Muirithesos replied, a smile coming to her face.

Rayden looked away, peering toward the south. "Now, I must return to the others."

"May you return unscathed, and know that I will be seeing you again, soon enough," Muirithesos stated.

Turning back to Muirithesos, Rayden replied, "Yes, we will see each other again, soon. Farewell, until then."

Rayden gave one final bow of her head to the faery queen and began the journey back, striding across the border of the Mist Vale.

CHAPTER 9

No layers of mist impeding her view, Rayden could see downriver through leagues of forest.

Despite the warnings given to her by Queen Muirithesos, Rayden remained in an uplifted state after leaving the faerie kingdom. Her mind refreshed and body rejuvenated, she had a limber step from the outset.

Traveling along the eastern bank of the river flowing into the Vale, Rayden settled into a swift pace without undue exertion. Behind her, the Mist Vale began to recede into the distance, a stride at a time.

***

Maintaining a rapid stride, Rayden pressed forward throughout the middle part of the afternoon. Keeping to the eastern bank of the river, she intended to follow the course of the broad channel for as long as she could.

The skies remained clear, and she calculated that she would be clear of the area containing the dark fae before twilight fell. If the creatures hated flowing water to the extent that Muirithesos had indicated, Rayden doubted that they would be lingering close to the river.

After venturing for another half of a league, Rayden's increasing hopes of slipping through undetected crumbled when a series of new, distinctive noises arose, from the trees off to her left.

Faint and ephemeral, strange voices began carrying to her ears from the depths of the woods. Whenever she turned her head to the left, looking into the forest, Rayden caught only glimmers and flitting shadows darting about the trees.

Rayden knew at once what the sounds and movements represented. Dark fae were shadowing her from within the trees.

Keeping to her faster pace, Rayden proceeded southward. Every sense told her that the dark fae lurking close intended full pursuit, having selected their quarry.

In an unsettling tone, like claws scratching timber, voices spoke words in a language unknown to Rayden.

Whatever roved the woods and stalked her had the essence of a predator and pack hunter. Wolves would have concerned her far less than the sentient entities that continued to remain shrouded to her eyes.

The number of voices increased over the next half-league and she espied more frequent movements within the woods. Rayden could only conclude that the dark fae's numbers were swelling.

Before long, Rayden knew that she was in great peril from the entities that Muirithesos had warned her about. She began thinking about the action that she could take.

Pondering her situation, Rayden marched onward.

Rayden could not chance the currents of a river, especially one flowing at a robust pace like the one to her right. Even the best of swimmers stood no match against the overwhelming strength of a powerful undertow.

The things lurking in the woods had her trapped against the shore, unless she departed from her path and entered their domain.

More voices filling the air, the forest grew increasingly alive with movement. Soon, she would have no options available to her.

Left with no other viable choice, Rayden turned and charged away from the riverbank, heading straight into the woods. Taking up her sword and axe, she found herself among the trees after only a few bounding strides.

Slowing down, Rayden allowed her eyes to adjust to the dimmer ambience beneath the tree canopy.

No longer disguising their presence, the entities that had been tracking Rayden began emerging into open view. Though not large in size, each one about knee-high to her if standing upon the ground, the creatures had gruesome appearances.

Bony and spindly of body, the creatures had leathery, dark gray skin riddled with bumps of a violet hue. Elongated faces held small mouths bristling with jagged teeth.

Large, deep-set eye sockets contained pools of solid black, the hue like a manifestation of the abyss itself.

Creatures given to wickedness and cruelty, the dark fae gathering before Rayden's eyes had little resemblance to the kind that she had encountered within the Mist Vale.

The creatures still maintaining some distance from her, Rayden kept moving forward. The vocalizations of the dark fae continued, with some speaking the unknown tongue in whispers that sounded more like hisses, and others of their number emitting bestial growls and snarls.

The hackles on her neck standing up, Rayden sensed the spiraling tension all around her. She knew that the creatures would not keep back for long.

Massing in number, the dark fae were poised to attack at any moment.

A broad, shallow stream then came into view, crossing her

path a short distance ahead. Before reaching its edge, Rayden slowed down, recalling the words given to her by Muirithesos.

'The ones we know of skulking about our borders are of a kind that loathes water, and they will not cross over it.'

Quickening her stride, Rayden covered the rest of the distance remaining to the water and stopped at its edge. Behind her, a throng of dark fae had gathered. The air filled with their eerie whispers and guttural sounds.

On the other side of the stream, another group of dark fae emerged from the shadows, brush, and trees. Some on the ground and a few flying, they approached the water.

Facing a situation that she could not fight her way out of alone, Rayden had to trust in Muirithesos' guidance. Her mind remained calm and focused.

Knowing an attack imminent, Rayden stepped out into the flowing water. Her feet sinking a little into the mud of the stream's bed, the soft, cool touch of the water enveloped her skin from the shins down.

Walking with the current, the latter slow and presenting no threat to her balance, Rayden turned headed down the middle of the stream. Weapons at the ready, she eyed the creatures encroaching upon both sides.

Though baring their teeth and growling, the dark fae made no move to violate the edges of the banks. Hovering close, the fell creatures drifted along and shadowed Rayden on both sides.

"Come a little closer, if you dare," Rayden challenged one that looked to be on the verge of testing the boundary between land and water.

Gnashing its teeth at Rayden, the creature drew a little closer and then recoiled, as if stung. A torrent of words poured from its little mouth in the unknown tongue, drawing responses from a few of the others.

A little farther down, alarm spiked within Rayden as her feet nearly slipped out from beneath her. Having stepped upon a slab of moss-covered rock, Rayden found herself on the equivalent of a solid sheet of ice.

The slick layer of moss spanned the stream, leaving her with no option but to continue onward. Slow and methodical, shortening her stride, Rayden made her way across the treacherous surface.

The throng of dark fae continued to menace Rayden and shadow her, but she paid them little heed. A major slip and fall could well see her sliding over to the edge of one side or the other, bringing her within range of their claws.

Keeping her breath steady, Rayden kept moving in a slow, controlled manner. The moss-covered stretch of rock came to an end, and her sandals pressed into a cool layer of mud once more.

Continuing down the center of the stream, Rayden gave some thought to the barriers protecting her from being swarmed. Large groups of dark fae sought to beset her from both sides, but the water's edge to her left and right stymied them.

Thoughts of Marus, Peronnius, and the plight of the northern tribes crossed through her mind. With their numbers extended around most of the city, the tribes stood vulnerable to a concentrated attack at any one point.

Water could not shun the Teveren forces on two sides like the dark fae, but a pair of earthen ramparts could block them. A massive undertaking would be required to build them, but the tribes could shift their encampment into the space running between two ramparts encircling the city.

Such a construct would hinder enemy cavalry and ward against being overwhelmed through a concentration of force on a single area of the encirclement.

The idea intrigued Rayden. With time precious, she wished that she were back among the tribes outside the Imperial City's walls, so that she could present her thoughts to the chieftains.

Minding her steps, Rayden followed the course of the stream for a little while longer without incident. Finally, the end of the channel drew into sight; the culmination presenting her with an advantage.

The stream emptied into a larger creek coming in from a little father east. The confluence of the two channels of water blocked the group of dark fae stalking her on the left, putting barriers on both sides of them and sealing off their forward path, where the waters merged.

A few moments later, the dark fae on the left realized their approaching predicament. Many shrieked and screeched, their ear-piercing cries filling the air.

Reaching the juncture where the creek and stream merged, Rayden took a few steps forward, putting a little distance behind her. The water deepened, reaching up to her mid-thigh.

Shifting toward the left bank of the creek, Rayden worked her way out of the water. Voicing their rancor, the dark fae that had been to her left continued venting their rage behind her.

The ones following on her right had no new obstacles. The creatures could continue along the opposite bank, but they could not pursue after Rayden left the channel of water behind.

Heading south and east, with her legs freed of the drag of water, Rayden took up a brisk gait. The shrill cries of the dark fae reached her ears for a little while longer, but even those faded into silence as the afternoon marched onward.

The chirping of birds returned to the air along with the trilling of insects, joining with the whisperings of the wind through the trees.

Rayden welcomed the natural sounds. In a way, they heralded that she had passed through the territory inhabited by the dark fae. Other dangers roved the wilderness, but she had slipped the grasp of the creatures menacing the border area of the Mist Vale.

Adjusting her path due south, Rayden still endeavored to put as much distance as she could between herself and the Mist Vale before dusk.

The shadows lengthened, and the descending sun cast its rays through every opening in the tree canopy that it could find. The scattered beams of light throughout the shadowy environs made for some beautiful displays in the waning afternoon.

Rayden pressed onward as long as she could before coming to a halt, giving herself just enough time to create a small enclosure to pass the night within.

Moonlight filtered through the trees when she finally allowed herself to partake of some bread and cheese. The food had such a bland taste in contrast with her last meal as a guest of Muirithesos.

Though famished after the exertion of the day, she restrained herself from consuming it all, making certain that she had some food saved for the next day.

Curling up in the brush-covered enclosure, Rayden slumbered without any major disturbances throughout the night.

***

Awakening near dawn, Rayden undertook a little scavenging in the immediate area and found some edible roots and mushrooms. After breaking her night's fast, she headed south, stopping only to avail herself of a little water to drink and splash on her face, the water taken from a narrow stream that she came across.

Even though no threats of dark fae loomed, Rayden took up a rapid pace, desiring to get back to the northern tribes as soon as possible.

A late-morning sprinkling of rain preceded the emergence of a bright, clear day. Rayden made great progress southward through some low, wooded hills, until a stark, daunting sight brought her to an immediate halt, just after midday.

Ascending the slope of a nearby hill, Rayden diverted from her path to gain a higher vantage from which to take in the massive scene.

***

Riddled with thin columns of smoke rising from cooking fires, a sea of tents arrayed in precise rows filled the low ground. A ditch and rampart arranged in a vast square with four entrance points, the latter set at the midpoint of each side, marked the encampment as Teveren in nature.

It took little time for Rayden to identify the presence of others quartered within the encampment. Most of the interior reflected the rigid, meticulous order of the Teverens, but two particular areas held wagons and carts arrayed in a manner that Rayden could recognized well-enough.

Great clusters of horses could be seen in more than one location within the earthen ramparts. Rayden identified three distinct groupings, two of which had markedly different appearances than the other. The third, undoubtedly Teveren, reflected the pristine order comprising most of the encampment.

The enormous size of the encampment left little doubt in Rayden's mind that she was gazing upon Marus' veteran legions.

Without question, the encampment before Rayden's eyes also quartered a large contingent of cavalry, one that was Teveren, Alettani, and Sarrimena in nature.

Rayden concluded that at least three Teveren legions of full strength were quartered within the ramparts, in addition to several thousand Alettani and Sarrimena warriors.

Moving southward, the feared Teveren commander approached the besieging tribes from behind, while Peronnius remained poised behind the walls of the Imperial City to strike at any opportunity. The jaws of a deadly adversary being set in place, the northern tribes would soon find themselves hard-pressed, if not trapped.

She found it intriguing that the Teverens, Alettani, and Sarrimena had all encamped within the ramparts. The inclusion of the two allied tribes within the main encampment told Rayden how vital the Teverens regarded the horses, and how much of a threat the other northern tribes stood in their eyes.

No hints of recklessness or overconfidence could be seen. Rather, a disciplined, focused enemy reflected from every aspect of the encampment.

Rayden would have to get word of everything that she observed back to the tribal encampments, before Marus could reach them.

She still had a little time. Marus had drawn close, but Rayden knew that he would break camp one more time and establish another, closer to the Imperial City, before engaging the northern tribes in open battle.

Staring down at the encampment, Rayden wondered how many other legions existed in the various regions of the Teveren Empire, and how far they had to journey to reach the Imperial City. Marus and Peronnius stood dangerous enough, but if others could return in time to join them, the chances for the northern tribes to prevail would deteriorate quickly.

The city would have to be taken as soon as possible.

Time favored the Teverens.

Rayden would have to get inside the city and open a gate without delay, after her return.

***

Hearing a faint swish of grass behind her, Rayden kept still. A moment later, a little closer, the lightest rustle of dry grass underfoot reached her ears.

Rayden waited.

Hearing another step and the trace of an intake of breath,

she held her place. She did not have to turn her head to know the threat closing in behind her.

Another faint step sounded while Rayden maintained the ruse that she was still focused on watching the encampment. A light step and the barest sound of a breath drawn told her that her adversary had poised for a strike.

Twisting and rolling to her left, Rayden vacated the spot where a spear lanced into the ground. Getting to her feet swiftly, Rayden took up her sword and axe.

Cursing, the attacker yanked the spear free and shifted his stance to face Rayden. A little farther beyond him, a second warrior stood, holding a long sword.

Clad in woolen tunics and trousers, bearded, and wearing their hair long, her adversaries were not Teveren.

"Alettani? Or Sarrimena?" Rayden questioned the pair, her eyes becoming two pools of blue fire. Surging in anger, she continued, "Only two of the northern tribes grovel and lick the boots of Teveren masters. Traitorous wretches."

The warrior that had failed in his strike at her laughed. "Who is the fool? You are with that rabble about to be crushed on the walls of the Imperial City."

"I am with those who shall live longer than you, a true craven fool!" Rayden countered, sneering at the brazen warrior.

Yelling out and wild-eyed, the warrior rushed at her, his companion following close behind. Gnashing his teeth, he thrust his spear toward Rayden.

Sweeping his weapon aside using her axe, Rayden slashed her sword blade down on the side of his neck. The warrior crumpled to the ground.

Rayden stepped forward to meet the attack of the second warrior. Blocking his sword with her own, she brought him down with a vicious chop of her axe to his exposed right side. Tearing her weapon free, Rayden broadened the gaping wound, blood gushing in the wake.

Gasping, her remaining attacker slumped to his knees, where another slash of her sword finished him off.

Undertaking a brief search of their bodies, Rayden found a couple of pouches with coins and a pair of rectangular wooden pieces inscribed with Teveren letters. Rayden suspected that the latter objects, suspended from leather cords about their necks, served as some kind of allegiance marker. Combining the coins and markers into one pouch, she tied it to the belt at her waist.

In the trees, not far from where Rayden had been observing the Teveren camp, she found the horses that had belonged to the scouts. Both had been tethered.

Though a part of her wished to ride one of the steeds fast through the night, Rayden could not risk any sounds that might alert guards and scouts from the Teveren camp to her presence. An errant neigh or snort, or mere hoofbeats, could betray her presence at any moment along a still, silent road. Her discretion swayed her to take the path of stealth and caution, even if it meant slower travel.

Speaking in a low voice, she approached the horses. Both exhibited a little agitation at the presence of someone unfamiliar to them, but she ignored their whinnies and snorts, while continuing to address them in a gentle tone.

After turning the animals loose, Rayden chose to resume her southward trek. Nothing more could be gained from observing the Teveren encampment; and Marus would have his legions marching south soon enough.

Rayden had to reach the tribes ahead of him.

***

Rayden traveled west for a little while before turning south, desiring to give the Teveren encampment a wide enough berth to reduce the chances of being sighted, or encountering further scouts. Skirting thousands of enemy warriors, Rayden maintained a swift pace, desiring to be far south of the Teverens when night arrived.

Throughout the rest of the afternoon, the sun continued its steady march across the skies. Rayden took a brief respite at a creek to slake her thirst and eat most of the remaining food that she carried.

If clear skies persisted, Rayden determined to journey through the night. Having been made to deviate from the course that she had taken to the Mist Vale, Rayden sought to mitigate the longer route of return.

Slowing her pace down a little, Rayden watched the shadows lengthen, spread, and deepen as the sun descended in the west. Twilight passed, violet hues giving way to darkness as night fell across the land.

A bright, waxing moon rose above the trees, ascending into skies brimming with stars. Unobstructed beyond a few wisps of clouds that drifted across its face from time to time, the silvery orb would reach a full state in a matter of days.

Coming across a broad dirt road carved with furrows from the passage of wheeled carts and wagons, Rayden followed its course. Heading southward, the path was all but certain to lead to the Imperial City.

Rayden would have to keep wary for the occasional brigand, but she doubted the road had much night traffic with the siege of the Imperial City underway. Taking advantage of a direct route, she knew that she could gain some ground that night.

Seeing the buildings of an estate crowning a hill in the distance, far to her left, Rayden wondered who would take possession of such places should the northern tribes prevail in taking the city. The fall of the Imperator would leave some chaos in the aftermath, a precarious time that would have to be addressed with care, or the seeds of another threat to the northern lands could be sown.

Rayden pushed the troubling thoughts aside. All of her mind had to remain on the battles to come.

The city would have to be taken, or all would be for naught.

Filling her lungs with the night air and breathing out, she strode onward.

***

Cresting a low rise, Rayden saw a flurry of movement and came to a halt.

Several dark forms could be seen within the rolling terrain ahead of her. From their elongated forms, the extended shape of their snouts, and their four-legged nature, she knew them to be marsekkels.

Pack scavengers and opportunistic hunters, marsekkels avoided people under most circumstances, but the prospect of one human alone at night could prove tempting to the creatures.

Rayden suspected a place of burial or recent carrion to be near, though no scent of the latter carried to her along the chilly night breezes. Often seen slinking about graves and battlefields, marsekkels had a close association with death.

Starting forward, Rayden gripped both of her weapons. The road continued downward, and before long she lost sight of the creatures.

Rayden could hear their grating screeches from time to time, echoing through the low hills. Keeping at the ready should they attempt to assail her, Rayden stayed to the road.

Reaching lower ground, the road leveled out, passing through some rises.

Off to her left, in the side of a hill, Rayden espied the gaping entrance to some manner of graves or catacombs. An iron grate blocked the portal.

A pair of old, weathered statues flanked the entrance.

Sightless eyes gazing toward her, the stone figures maintained their unceasing vigil.

A flicker of movement to the right of the catacomb entrance sped the blood within Rayden's veins. A gust of cold wind tossed her hair about, but the rest of her remained as still as the stone of the ancient sculptures.

Crouched behind the broken statue of what once had been the image of a prominent man, a thin, cadaverous figure sneered at Rayden.

On first glance, the figure appeared to be a man, wearing filthy, tattered vestiges of clothing. Head bare, save for a few wispy, scattered remnants of hair, the figure's emaciated, diseased look reminded her at once of the being that she had encountered with Hamilcar along the Boreus Way.

Skulking about the rotting bodies of the slaves crucified at the hands of the Teverens, the other being's gaze had carried the same miasma of madness, rage, hunger, and keen alertness that the eyes of the figure before her reflected.

Further, the look reflected that of the being that she had encountered in the northern woods, while seeking the aid of the Varganir. Rayden had barely escaped a grisly fate that night, bringing the entity down among a ravenous pack of wild boars that it had summoned to tear her to pieces.

Rayden knew that she faced something inhuman, intelligent, and powerful.

Stepping out from behind the statue, the figure glared at Rayden while baring his broken, blood-stained teeth at her.

Opening his thin, cracked lips, the figure's voice sounded like a fusion between a snarl and hiss. "Did you think you could hide from us forever? Leave us in the belly of boars? Wait for saviors to run us off?"

Strands of hair billowing in the wind, the figure took a step forward, gazing upon Rayden like a hunter about to corner its prey.

"You watched those saviors ripped to shreds ... in the arena of sacrifice to our Master!" the figure shouted, its timbre akin to a grating screech.

A look of triumph blazed within its crazed, glittering eyes.

"Rayden ... we know you," the thing declared. "You are no longer hidden to us."

The statement sent a cold thrill through her. Something far beyond her ken and dangerous lurked beneath the slithering words.

"The weak magic could not hide you forever ... it veiled you for a time, but we see you," the figure stated with a mocking edge, its countenance taking on a look of pure malice. "You cannot evade us. Dominion is ours."

"You have no dominion over me," Rayden replied in an icy, low voice.

Her words appeared to agitate the figure.

It shrieked, "We are many! We will bear you to the realms of death!"

"Try if you wish," Rayden responded, her left foot sliding back into a fighting stance.

The creature's next words came forth like a rattling hiss. "Wherever will we go? We can not drift and wander the world and its wastelands. Is there a place for us to go? Yes, there are places! Many, many places."

Staring at Rayden, it cackled with a gleeful delight. She sensed that the figure anticipated something imminent.

Holding her position, Rayden glanced about, but saw nothing to justify the figure's crazed merriment.

"When shadows fall under our dominion, death rises!" the figure proclaimed.

Slumping down, its expression frozen into a mockery of a smile, the figure became silent and still.

Rising from his corpse like tendrils of black mist, several vaporous forms emerged and took to the air. A horrid stench filling the area, the temperature around Rayden plunged to a freezing cold. Her ensuing breaths emerged in ghostly, grey wisps.

The dark, spectral phantoms began circling around Rayden and the dead body. Hissing in the manner of serpents, the apparitions rose higher into the air.

Distorted, skeletal visages formed where heads would have been. Leering at Rayden, the phantasmal entities continued to circle, lifting even higher.

Hearing movements in the brush and an outbreak of heavy, panting breaths, Rayden looked beyond the wraiths to see a number of marsekkels striding into the open ground, emerging from the trees at the edge of the cemetery. She had no doubts that the creatures were the same ones that she had espied from the hilltop.

With rat-like visages and long, low bodies covered in black, coarse fur, marsekkels had shorter legs ending in broad claws; effective for digging into hard ground or ripping into flesh.

Tongues lolling and sides heaving, the beasts had run hard over a long distance. Rayden knew with little doubt that the marsekkels had been summoned; and had been hastening toward the cemetery while the depraved figure spoke to her.

Sounding like a multitude of voices, otherworldly howls and cries erupted from the apparitions drifting about in the air. Darting toward the marsekkels, the wraiths were upon them before the animals could begin to flee.

One per marsekkel, the wraiths seeped into the bodies of the animals. At first, the creatures stumbled and fell onto their sides.

Kicking their legs, snarling, and frothing along their jaws, the beasts looked to be enveloped in throes of great pain, at first, but after a few moments all of the marsekkels became calm.

Breathing steady, the animals got back up and turned to face Rayden. A strange glint, not born of any reflection of light, shone from within their eyes.

Rumbling louder, a chorus of growls erupted. Baring their teeth, saliva dripping from their jaws, the creatures padded forward, heading straight toward Rayden.

Casting the approaching beasts a burning glare, Rayden let her mind settle into the warrior's calm, the state of mind that appeared to slow the quality of time itself. Her grip tightened on her weapons, and she readied for the first of the beasts to charge her.

In some far recess of her mind, she knew that the creatures would swarm her, in overwhelming numbers, but the thoughts remained far from her mind's focus.

A loud roar shaking the night, a mass of muscle and claw hurtled into view, slamming into the marsekkels and scattering the beasts apart in an instant.

Rayden looked on in amazement, watching the maned lion bearing down on a marsekkel before pinning it to the ground. Raging, the lion tore into the hapless creature, shredding it apart in moments.

Spinning about, the lion swiped at another marsekkel and mauled its side. Enduring the bites of others at legs and sides, the lion became a tempest of savage fury.

No longer facing overwhelming numbers, Rayden moved in, hacking and slashing, her blades quenching their thirst for the marsekkels' blood.

Any other pack of marsekkels would have run off, but the creatures no longer had command of themselves. A murderous sentience that cared nothing for the animals pressed the attack.

Marsekkels hurled themselves against the lion and Rayden, drawing blood more than once, but one after another fell under the martial storm of the rampaging pair.

Rayden drove her sword deep into the open mouth of one marsekkel at about the same instant that the lion leaped upon another, clamping his powerful jaws onto the back of the creature's neck. A moment later, life fled the bodies of the last two marsekkels from the large pack that the wraiths had taken control of.

Bleeding from a few places on her arms and legs, and breathing heavy, Rayden straightened up. The freezing bite within the air dissipated.

A few strides away, the lion faced her; the same creature that had intervened before on her behalf.

Sides heaving, the great beast exhibited several light wounds.

"We survived," Rayden said to the lion in a low, gentle voice. She gave a bow of her head to the creature. "You have been my guardian in the wilderness, more than once."

The last time that the two of them had been close, Rayden had remained in place and let the lion approach her. This time, she stepped toward the beast.

His eyes reflecting moonlight, the regal creature did not move, allowing her to walk right up to him. The lion brushed his great mane against Rayden and made the distinctive chuffing sound that she took to be an expression of affection, of a kind recognizing bonds of friendship, or possibly even family.

Rayden leaned forward and pressed her forehead between the lion's eyes, running her hands deep through his mane on both sides of his head. Pulling her head back a little, while continuing to stroke his mane, she looked into the creature's golden eyes.

"I wish I could guide you to a kingdom of your own, one with many lionesses," Rayden told the brawny creature, whose gaze remained fixed upon her own. "Know that the world is your own, nonetheless, to roam as you please."

After caressing the lion's mane a few more moments,

she pulled her hands away. The lion nuzzled her one more time, turned, and then padded away, entering the brush and disappearing into the night.

Rayden stood in the quiet aftermath, paying no heed to the marsekkel bodies strewn all about the ground. She did not understand how the lion had become a guardian for her, but she carried gratitude in her heart.

More than once the beast had manifested to balance a fight against otherworldly adversaries. She could not help but think that a deity of some kind had taken an interest in protecting her.

"Whoever you may be, I thank you," Rayden whispered into the night.

After taking a little time to clean off her blades, using unbloodied fur on the bodies of a few marsekkels, Rayden set out once more toward the south and left the carnage behind.

CHAPTER 10

Keeping to the road, Rayden continued through the night, covering a great distance before daybreak arrived. Graced with a beautiful, resplendent sunrise, she gave no thought to stopping for rest.

Though she passed a few more estates and farms, Rayden did not encounter any other people throughout the morning. After the dark fae, Teveren encampment, and the pack of marsekkels, she preferred a solitary path for the rest of her journey.

A little after midday, Rayden finally saw tendrils of smoke rising in the distance ahead. Quickening her pace, she blocked the mounting fatigue from her mind.

An opportunity for rest would come soon enough.

Late in the afternoon, Rayden set her eyes on the vast, sprawling encampments of the northern tribes. The sight brought a smile to her face.

Though exhausted, she had found her way back.

***

With the night clear and harboring no threats of rain, Rayden chose to sleep under the open sky.

The low murmur of conversations around campfires nearby

prevented the kind of silence that she would have preferred, but Rayden knew that she could be at ease for the first time in many days.

Her return to the tribal camps had sparked a swelling tide of excitement. Word had spread fast, and it had not taken long for many to seek her out.

Hamilcar had been overjoyed to see her, along with Annocrates and several other warriors from the force of former slaves.

Jarut and many of the Gessa visited for a short time with Rayden. Even Alcedan had come at once to see her.

No longer on the open road or in the wilderness, Rayden did nothing to resist the weariness pervading her. Eating some roast pork and drinking some ale while talking with those who came to see her, she had filled her belly, but her need for rest would not be dissuaded.

A gathering of chieftains would be convened in the morning, but Alcedan saw to it that Rayden had no obligations for the duration of the night. When she had found a suitable place to lay down, her eyelids fluttered under a great heaviness.

Gazing into the starry depths far above, Rayden started to fade from the waking world and began the crossing into other realms of consciousness.

***

Sight returning to her eyes, Rayden found herself standing on the summit of a great hill overlooking the Imperial City.

Fires outside the walls marked the positions of the northern tribes encircling the heart of the Teveren Empire.

A solitary figure strode up to Rayden and came to stand at her right side. Turning her head, Rayden beheld a half-translucent, ghostly specter with a familiar visage.

Within the dream, Dreaghen's presence did not startle

Rayden in the slightest. Neither did the form that he had taken.

"You come to me looking like a ghost," Rayden declared, lucid and conscious of the dream-state that she stood within. "I hope that does not have greater meaning."

"It does not, though I am not far from that state of being," Dreaghen replied to her.

"This does not seem like a dream," Rayden commented, looking out toward the city.

"You may be asleep and awake at the same moment," Dreaghen replied with a shrug and the trace of a grin. "Laying in one place … and standing in another. Who can say?"

"Asleep or awake, I am too weary for your riddles," Rayden responded, a slight frown showing on her face.

"My essence wanes and the veil thins," Dreaghen replied, his face growing somber. "Do not allow the wicked to hold the city for much longer."

"I would overthrow them this very night if I knew a means of doing so," Rayden countered, glaring at the apparition.

"I cannot keep my eyes upon you from the heights," Dreaghen stated. "Nor can I whisper of dangers to maned guardians. I have expended my last shred of strength."

Rayden's brow furrowed. "The lion?"

"Bears great affection toward you, and the creature knows you are the one who gave him freedom," Dreaghen answered. "I could only warn him of dangers in your path. I did not control him. He came to you of his own accord in the night."

"You warned him in just enough time, lest I fall to the minions of the filth underlying that city's power," Rayden said.

Dreaghen looked at her with a grim expression. "I cannot say whether I will remain for much longer in this world or not. It is not for me to decide."

"It is not for any of us to decide, we only have the present moment," Rayden responded.

The sorcerer nodded. "Open a gate soon. I know not what, but the enemy musters tremendous power for some unknown devilry. I cannot discern their intent."

"The fae of the Mist Vale will aid us," Rayden told him.

"I do not know if that will be enough," Dreaghen replied.

"We will fight them, no matter what," Rayden said.

"Do not wait long to enter the city," Dreaghen stated, his voice growing weaker. "Time grows very short."

Like mist taken up in a gust of wind, Dreaghen's form dissipated, vanishing from sight.

Rayden awoke with a start. Despite the penetrating chill of the late-night air, sweat glistened along her brow and trickled down the sides of her face.

The conversations around her had long since fallen silent, and blazing campfires had been reduced to little more than piles of glowing embers.

Somewhere in the dark, Dreaghen still drew breath, but his warning unsettled her. The enigmatic sorcerer had called to her from across sea, mountain, desert, and plain, and Rayden had crossed them all in the journey that led to the walls of the Imperial City.

The enemy continued to gather power for the unfurling of some kind of unprecedented, diabolical sorcery. Rayden had no idea of the form that it would take, but she knew that it would be fearsome in nature; and at a level to threaten all of the besieging tribes.

Settling down once more, Rayden cleared her mind again. Morning had not yet arrived, and she intended to get as much rest as possible.

Shutting her eyes and slowing her breathing, she eased back into a relaxed state. Before long, Rayden took to sleep once more.

This time, no dreams disturbed her rest.

When Shadows Fall

***

Sunlight gleamed from the loose strands of Rayden's hair buoyed within a passing breeze. Her piercing blue gaze took in the faces of the tribal leaders gathered about her.

"The Teverens heading this way have great numbers of horse-mounted fighters," Rayden stated. "Some are of their own, and many are those of the Alettani and Sarrimena."

"We can use our wagons and carts to defend against those on horse," Alcedan replied, sounding unconcerned at her assessment of the enemy cavalry.

"This is a large, disciplined force, but do not forget that another waits for the right moment to strike, from within the city walls," Rayden replied, thinking of Peronnius' legions.

"A stout rampart will give pause to those on foot and horse alike," Ledakia stated. "One could be built fast, with the thousands and thousands of us who are here."

"Which side of the rampart should we stand behind?" Alcedan asked him. "A force can fall upon us from either side."

"Why not have ramparts facing both of the enemy's main forces?" Rayden then asked in a loud, resonant tone, for all to hear, giving voice to the notion that had been building inside of her mind, ever since her precarious encounter with the dark fae. "Build two great ramparts, with a broad space in between. Within them, encamp all of the tribes. You will be fortified on both sides."

A hush fell over the tribal leaders. Alcedan and the others looked to Rayden. Confusion filled their faces at first, but gradually the puzzled expressions began receding, as they thought further upon her words.

"Two ramparts," Alcedan stated, beginning to nod. "We could hold the siege of the city in place, even if we are under siege from outside."

"You will have to be careful about foodstuffs and drink,"

Rayden replied. "You will be unable to forage and hunt. The city will have to be taken before too long. But, for a short time, two ramparts will prevent them from ensnaring you between iron jaws."

"Do we have enough time to raise these ramparts?" Belgra of the Arnan asked in a raised voice.

"All can labor in the digging," Peremdurus of the Borreni responded. "Use every wagon and cart. Every warrior and member of a tribe can give their labor."

"At a pressed march, Marus' legions could arrive here in a couple of days," Rayden said. "He would be a fool to attack at once. Marus will first set camp before striking at us. That will allow us a little more time."

"There is still the matter of the gap down near the river," Celterren of the Lanassa said. "We will still be unable to close it off."

"It would remain open, but we can do what we can to choke off any attempts of our enemy to bring food and supplies into the city," Olten of the Cirna declared.

"Then we close off the ends of the walls and make passages through them, should we have need to attack anything trying to pass between," Grogner of the Tega remarked.

"It is all we can do," Rayden stated. "Once we have a barrier in place against Marus' legions behind us, we can look to enter the city."

"Wise counsel," Alcedan stated. After a pause, he asked, "Do you still intend to go back into the city?"

"I will see that a gate is opened to you," Rayden told him, before sweeping her gaze across all of the chieftains' faces. "Then, you will be able to enter the city unhindered."

"We must not delay in our defenses," Alcedan declared. "Let us raise ramparts on both sides of the line that we have put in place, surrounding the city."

Statements of assent and acclamation met Alcedan's words, bringing Rayden a great sense of relief. The northern tribes could not afford to make the wrong choice, and the cohesion that she saw before her had to hold for them to stand a chance against the Teverens.

Without any precedence in their histories, the northern tribes continued to tread upon unfamiliar ground, but so far, they had demonstrated wisdom.

Looking around at the chieftains, at the conclusion of the morning war council, Rayden had increasing confidence that the tribes would continue to do so.

Rayden watched the chieftains disperse, knowing that the coming day would be filled with physical labor.

***

Before the sun reached its zenith in the midday skies, every able-bodied man, woman, and child from the encamped northern tribes had joined in the massive effort ringing the Teveren city. Every possible implement that could be used for digging had been put to the task of breaking up ground and shoveling soil.

The course of the double-rampart followed the path of the encirclement already set in place, connecting the various tribal encampments together in a grand continuum.

With the dedicated labor of thousands upon thousands, it did not take long for a broad channel to take form, bordered on each side by the beginnings of earthen ramparts. Trenches lining the outer facings of the nascent ramparts deepened, the excavated soil being used to build the walls higher and higher.

Running all around the north, east, south, and much of the western side of the Imperial City, the ramparts continued rising on both sides of the channel. Only the gap along the eastern bank of the Golden River remained open.

Using ox-drawn carts and wagons, sacks, and buckets to

move loose soil, the people labored with an urgency that begged little rest or sustenance while daylight held dominion. All knew that the shadow of the enemy drew nearer, with every waking moment.

The ramparts represented a chance at survival, keeping the hope of victory alive within the hearts of all working to build them.

A multitude labored in a concentrated effort to dig the wide trench running along the outer bases of the two walls. Unless attackers could span the trench by some means, they would have to go down into it, before trying to surmount the other side and ascend the steep slope of the ramparts.

The incessant thwacks of axes on wood sounded throughout the rising walls. Harvesting trees from the forested areas close by, large numbers of tribal people fashioned sharp-pointed stakes to crown the top of each rampart.

Narrow passages through the walls, blocked with removable timber barriers, were formed at strategic points all along the ramparts. Faced with a layer of wicker covered in mud, the barriers for the access points were difficult to see from the outside.

Walkways made of rough-hewn planks were fashioned and stored inside the ramparts near each of the passages, to be used for crossing the outer trench. Shorter wooden platforms were also crafted, for spanning the top of an opened passage.

All the while, thick, hard-packed earthen walls continued to grow taller.

***

The tribes continued to labor under firelight, stars, and moon, raising the two extensive walls without the work ever coming to a complete stop. Groups began forming and organizing rotations, so that the people could gain a little rest from time to time.

The walls grew higher throughout the next day and night.

Warriors kept their weapons close at hand should the Teverens within the city attempt an assault, but the enemy appeared content to remain behind their own walls.

Rayden built up a great sweat laboring alongside the Gessa. During the short, periodic respites, she devoured the apportioned meat, bread, and cheese given to her, taking no more than any of the others involved in the arduous endeavor.

Her presence among the Gessa lifted the morale of those around her. Children sought to impress Rayden with the amount of work that they could do, and other warriors jested with her in good humor. Many contests took place in filling wagons and carts with dirt.

More than one of the Gessa approached and thanked her for working alongside them.

"Do not thank me any more than I thank you," Rayden told those individuals. "We must all work together in this great task and in the fight to come."

Her responses bolstered the efforts of those around her even further, and the walls continued to grow.

***

Standing atop a finished section of level, hard-packed dirt serving as a wall-walk, Rayden saw the pair of scouts running towards the ramparts, long before they reached the new fortifications.

Rayden did not have to hear their words to know the cause for the urgency reflected in their faces and movements. Their cries carried to her, nonetheless, bringing the tidings that she had been expecting.

"The enemy legions have come! They are setting camp! Less than a day's march from here!"

With the announcement, Rayden knew that a battle loomed. The walls would face a severe test from the outset, as the Teverens would assail them from both sides.

Descending a short flight of wood-covered steps to the ground, Rayden called out, "Get all stakes available in place along the top!"

Responding to her directive, many hastened to the many stacks of finished wooden stakes located close by.

Rayden walked down the channel between the ramparts, gazing upon the new constructs. While not completely finished, the walls were now in a state where they could fulfill their intended purpose.

Wide and almost three times the height of Rayden herself, the walls would be a formidable obstacle to the enemy legions.

Looking farther ahead, she espied Alcedan heading in her direction. Quickening her pace, Rayden shortened the distance between them.

"They have come!" Alcedan called out when had drawn closer to each other.

"Battle will be upon us soon, but not today," Rayden told him, slowing down to a halt. "The labor on the wall must continue, but the warriors must also gain rest tonight. Do not waver in keeping an eye on the Imperial City. Peronnius is always a threat."

"We have a close watch on the city, on all of their gates," Alcedan stated. "Horns will sound if anything is seen that may hint of an attack."

"That is good to hear," Rayden stated. "I have little doubt that the legions of Peronnius will strike tomorrow, at the same time Marus assails these ramparts."

"We must be ready for them," Alcedan replied. "It is just a matter of where along these ramparts they will strike."

"I expect them to attack here," Rayden said. "Marus will not risk a force slipping between his legions and their camp. But Peronnius, I can not say."

"Horns will alert us, and the chieftains can shift their warriors to wherever the battle may erupt," Alcedan said.

"Another strength of this double wall ... they will be able to move under protection," Rayden observed.

"What do you advise of rations?" Alcedan asked.

"A little extra for the warriors," Rayden said. "They will need to recover all the strength that they can for tomorrow."

***

Armor gleamed bright in the morning sun beneath the tasseled, square standards held throughout the orderly rectangular and square formations arraying to the north of the ramparts.

Standing atop the outer rampart, facing the north, Rayden squinted, taking account of the marshalling enemy force. Marus had deployed his full strength, conveying an intention to bring the siege of the Imperial City to a swift end.

Rank after rank of infantry in square formations displayed lines of rectangular shields emblazoned with the images of eagles, crescent moons, or serpents. Positioned along a broad front, the soldiers stood with spears in hand, awaiting the signal to advance.

At the left end of the square formations, set toward the rear, two formations of Teveren cavalry rested upon their mounts. Before them, a small cluster of riders surrounded a man wearing a breastplate and helm of what appeared to be gold. Those in back of the prominent figure held long, narrow horns at the ready.

Above them all could be seen a conspicuous standard, bearing a crimson square inscribed with golden writing. Its wings outstretched and jaws open in mid-roar, the gold-cast figure of a dragon held dominion above the square.

Rayden's gaze lingered upon the small group of riders for a few moments. The unique standard represented a tremendous prize, and the man in the golden breastplate and helm could be none other than Marus himself.

Standing to the left and right of the infantry squares were pairs of broad rectangular formations. Each several ranks deep, they were arranged with one formation set at the forefront and the other behind. Filled with archers, slingers, and javelin throwers, the outer formations did not exhibit the larger shields and heavier armor of the infantry formations between them.

Looser throngs of horsemen had gathered to the outskirts of the rectangular formations, forming the flanks of the full battle array. From their attire, longer hair, and beards, Rayden knew the masses of riders to be the Alettani and Sarrimena contingents allied with the Teverens.

Marus had arrived at last, and he had wasted little time in deploying for battle. Only a day before, tribal scouts had returned with the word that Marus' legions had stopped about half a league from the city and were establishing their camp.

Yet to attack so soon told Rayden that the enemy commander was likely overconfident, viewing the northerners as an undisciplined rabble of barbarian tribes lacking the cohesion to match Teveren discipline.

Every detail that the scouts had reported later on the previous day concerning Marus' forces matched up with Rayden's own assessment. The absence of unpleasant surprises in the reports encouraged many of the tribal leaders who, Rayden could see, had feared additional enemy contingents beyond the ones that she had observed.

"His strength is as I saw, and as the scouts reported," Rayden said to Alcedan, who stood to her right, staring outward.

Expressing his need of Rayden's knowledge and keen sense of the Teverens, Alcedan had positioned himself close to her. Down behind him, standing on the low ground of the channel between the ramparts, several men with signaling horns waited.

Rayden had helped a slave uprising defeat a strong Teveren force before. Now, she intended to help Alcedan and the northern tribes prevail over another.

"They will seek to coordinate their attack with those in the city," Rayden continued, glancing toward Alcedan.

His eyes having a steely glint, Alcedan's face brimmed with determination and a righteous anger. The sight of the Teverens had not evoked even the slightest hint of distress in him. Rayden could see the young warrior becoming a leader like Eigon more every day.

As Rayden had been expecting, a wave of horns blared from Marus' ranks, filling the air. A second wave answered, sounding from the direction of the Imperial City.

"Peronnius will strike at the other rampart, as I thought," Rayden told Alcedan while turning around.

Looking back toward the south, Rayden watched as one of the most prominent gates in the wall, one of those protected with flanking towers and aligned with a stone-paved road, opened wide.

Issuing forth, Peronnius' legions marched through the wide portal and continued into the open ground, maintaining tight, disciplined ranks. Spreading outward, to either side of the gate, the forces emitting from the city began deploying into battle formation.

Peronnius' forces arranged themselves in a similar form to those under Marus', with the exception of having no significant cavalry formations among them. Well-armored infantry in square formations lined up with a broad, rectangular formation of lighter-equipped missile troops to either side.

Peronnius himself was mounted, his shining golden helm and breastplate identifying him among a small group of riders. Another prominent standard bearing a dragon figure of gold could be seen in their midst, and several of the riders behind Peronnius had the same long, narrow horns as those behind Marus.

Veteran legions now stood poised for battle upon both sides of the ramparts. The concentration of Teveren forces outnumbered the tribal warriors by a wide margin along the area shielding the northern section of the siege.

Having to keep their encirclement of the Imperial City in place, the tribal defenders could not bring their ultimate advantage in numbers to bear upon the looming clash. Within the ramparts, the tribes were spread thin, and those defending the northern section against the legions of Peronnius and Marus would have to hold.

The hosts of mounted warriors at the flanks of Marus' formations remained back for the moment, and a ponderous silence fell across the entire expanse.

Rayden took a slow, calming breath, keeping her eyes fixed on Marus' formations.

"The storm is about to break," Rayden told Alcedan.

"Then let the rain come, we cannot stop it from falling," Alcedan replied in a steady voice.

A few moments later, a chorus of horns broke out among Marus' ranks. Just afterward, a similar eruption took place within Peronnius' formations.

Like an intake of breath, a moment of silence transpired across the entirety of both ramparts and the ground outside of them.

Then, a deep rumble coursed through the air and ground. Their steps falling solid and rhythmic wherever they tread, thousands of Teveren soldiers advanced.

Holding tight order, the legions closed in on both sides of the ramparts.

Northern warriors packed the wall-walks along both ramparts, readying a host of javelins and arrows to greet the oncoming Teverens.

More horns brayed from within the Teveren ranks.

A sound like rolling thunder rippled through the air as the two masses of allied cavalry surged into motion from Marus' flanks. Fanning outward, the Alettani and Sarrimena riders charged toward the ramparts.

On the side under Marus' command, the long rectangular formations slowed, and then another wave of horn blasts brought them to a full halt. A flurry of movement took place as archers moved to the forefront, notching arrows and drawing bowstrings back.

Between the ranks of archers and other missile troops, the square infantry formations continued tromping forward.

Several short horn blasts released the holds of the archers.

Arcing through the air, a lethal hail of arrows passed over the rampart and rained down into the area behind. Those warriors with shields held them over their heads, and those without pressed themselves tight against the rampart's inner facing or the stakes running along the wall-walk.

The thuds of arrows striking the ground, thwacks of iron burrowing into wood, and cries from pierced flesh combined to form a hellish dissonance. Keeping low, Rayden listened to the hisses and thumps of incoming arrows burying themselves in the wooden stakes shielding her.

On the side under Peronnius, the rectangular formations neared the place where they would be within arrow range of the ramparts.

Deep horn blasts, different in tone from those of the Teverens, erupted from within the ramparts.

The defenders answered the Teverens' storm of arrows with a tempest of their own. Loosed from both wall-walks, masses of arrows soared through the air.

Commands shouted throughout the Teveren infantry formations brought shields up at haste. In moments, the concerted response formed a stout barrier both in front and above the marching ranks.

A hail of missiles riddled the two approaching Teveren

multitudes. Despite the disciplined overlapping of the shields among the infantry, several of the arrows found living targets.

Horns blared and the Teverens resumed their full advance, involving all of the formations across the entire front. Archers continued to send arrows toward the warriors along the ramparts, moving forward between each release of bowstrings.

Shortly after, the slingers and javelin throwers among the archers came within range of the ramparts. Without delay, they added their own missiles to the growing aerial onslaught, now being answered with javelins hurled down from the wall-walks.

During the furious exchange, Rayden risked a few glances above the palisade to keep apprised of the enemy positions.

In many places throughout their formations, Teveren infantry carried planks to span the trenches and high ladders to aid in climbing the ramparts.

Calling for archers and javelin throwers, Rayden shouted instructions to those around her. Other leaders among the tribal warriors took up her directive and helped carry her message down the lines to each side.

Missiles had to be concentrated toward those carrying ladders and platforms.

Keeping her head beneath the pointed stakes, Rayden looked over to Alcedan, who crouched low a few places down from her.

"Do we set the attack loose now?" he asked, catching her eyes.

Rayden shook her head and shouted back to him, "Wait until they are tangled along the top of the ramparts! Then we will strike!"

Looking back to her with an unwavering, hard glint in his eyes, Alcedan nodded.

Though many Teverens fell to javelin or arrow, planks were set across the outer trench in many places. After setting ladders in place, soldiers began climbing the outer facing toward the wall-walks.

Behind them, Teveren archers did what they could to disrupt attempts to dislodge the ladders. Yet in several instances, ascending Teverens screamed as tribal warriors shoved the ladders that they held onto backward, sending many soldiers falling a long way down to the bottom of the trench.

Teveren soldiers reached the top of the ramparts in many places. The sharp clang of blades clashing rang out along the wall-walk amid a new torrent of cries and screams.

Arrows, javelins, and stones continued to fall upon the defenders, the lethal rain now reduced to a much lighter degree with the Teveren soldiers engaged in close combat with the tribal warriors.

Rayden worked her way over to where a Teveren soldier had just reached the top of a ladder, bringing his helm into view. Seeing her approaching, the soldier thrust his medium-length blade at her. Sweeping his weapon to the outside with her sword, she thrust the top of her axe into the midst of his face, the impact knocking him back and sending him plunging down into the trench.

Another warrior near to Rayden leaned over, grabbed the ends of the ladder, and flung it outward with a great heave, much to the chagrin of the three Teverens still climbing it.

Peering to both sides along the rampart, Rayden could see the enemy gaining the wall-walk in many places. Below, the infantry had massed at the trench's edge, with more planks being set and ladders carried across.

Rayden looked back to Alcedan, who had risen to engage another Teveren reaching the top. She waited as he struck the enemy soldier with a vicious downward slash of his sword. The heavy blow took the man's right arm at the elbow and the long blade cleaved deep into his upper leg.

Alcedan ripped his blade free of the soldier, spattering blood about. Screaming and bleeding, the Teveren fell from the ladder.

"Alcedan! Release the attack!" Rayden called to him. "Now is the time!"

Glancing back with a quick nod, Alcedan shouted down to the men with the horns below him.

A long, low-pitched, resonant signal carried from between the ramparts, the distinctive call setting new forces into motion.

While the Gessa and Cirna battled furiously against the Teverens on both sides, from atop the walls, barriers were removed to clear passages in the ramparts.

Warriors of the Tega and Borreni sallied forth from the inside rampart, rushing to engage the legions of Peronnius on their flanks.

At the same time, warriors from the contingent of former Teveren slaves and warriors the Arnan tribe exited the outer ramparts. Rayden watched their attack unfold.

Crossing their own portable platforms across the trench at several points beyond the ends of the Teveren formations, the former slaves and Arnan warriors curled around to assail Marus' legions.

The air filling with guttural war cries, the warriors fell upon the exposed enemy flanks, consisting of the more vulnerable, lighter-armed missile troops. Hacking and slashing, the charging warriors began cutting through the enemy ranks. Teveren morale started to crumble as fear rippled through the outer formations.

Short, frantic-sounding horn signals blasted. The signals caused many of the deeper, square formations of infantry to shift outward, positioning themselves toward the flanks to counter the new and unexpected threat.

A large number of skilled javelin throwers and archers exited the outer ramparts within the outflow of warriors. All of them focused on harrying the Alettani and Sarrimena cavalry now trying to slow the unexpected assault on Marus' flanks.

Wheeling their mounts about and galloping off amid a barrage of javelins and arrows that claimed many of their lives, the Teverens' tribal allies could do little to stymie the ongoing attack.

Taking a look to the other side, Rayden could see that Peronnius had made the same shift as Marus within his ranks, moving fast to protect his missile troops using the deeper formations of infantry.

The pressure on the ramparts decreased swiftly in the aftermath of the pincer-attacks. It did not take long for the defenders to regain full control of the wall-walk. Shoving the remaining ladders back, tribal warriors jeered and cursed the Teveren soldiers.

Extended horn signals then carried through the air, coming from the Teveren ranks on both sides. At once, the enemy forces began receding from the earthen walls.

Cheers erupted throughout the ramparts and ground just outside of them.

"We bloodied those bastards good!" Alcedan exclaimed, watching the Teverens pulling back in good order.

The tribal warriors that had issued forth from the outer rampart did not pursue the Teverens, lest they find themselves vulnerable to the still-numerous cavalry of the enemy.

The bottom of the trench and ground close to it held a multitude of dead Teverens. Warriors from Ledakia's force roved through the bodies on the ground, finishing off those few still clinging to life.

Rayden took a look around, assessing the carnage.

"We have wounded them," she declared. "But they will return."

"They will need some time to lick their wounds," Alcedan replied.

"Do not expect them to take long," Rayden told him.

Turning about, she watched the soldiers of Peronnius passing through the large gate, heading back into the Imperial City.

"We have lost many warriors too," Rayden commented, a somber look upon her face. A few moments later, she added, in a lower, melancholic tone of voice, "Tonight, many pyres will burn."

"Yet our warriors know we can fight them, and we can defeat them ... much has been gained on this day," Alcedan replied, glancing over to her. "I have learned much."

"Every day offers lessons, some bittersweet," Rayden responded.

"What is your counsel now?" Alcedan asked her.

"We must begin at once to prepare for tomorrow," Rayden advised him.

In her mind, Rayden wondered what form the next strike would take. Even more worrisome, the enemy sorcerers could unveil whatever they had been preparing in the shadows at any time.

No sign of Queen Muirithesos had manifested yet. The northern tribes remained vulnerable to the enemy's great advantage in sorcery.

Rayden could only hope that the Imperator's sorcerers held back for the moment.

Reminding herself that she could do nothing about the things beyond her control, Rayden battened the troubling concerns down.

"Many burdens weigh upon your mind," Alcedan said, a slight frown on his face. "I can see it in your face."

Rayden nodded. "I can not deny that. But I cannot allow my focus to waver."

"Not an easy task, as I have found since becoming chieftain

of the Gessa," Alcedan replied in a tone laden with hints of his own inner burdens.

"I know that you understand," Rayden said. Looking into his eyes, she stated, "You grow each and every day. You are becoming everything I foresaw in you."

Alcedan smiled, and an echo of the younger boy who had beamed at praise from Rayden in earlier times shone within his face.

"I have no choice," Alcedan replied, his momentary smile replaced with a rueful grin. "Do I?"

"None of us truly do," Rayden admitted. "To become stagnate is to slowly erode and weaken. The things of the dark never rest."

"No, they do not," Alcedan replied, the trace of a frown forming again. He looked around and took a deep breath. "Yet we need to rest, at times."

"Tonight is one of those times," Rayden said. "We cannot celebrate today in ale or song, but a little more in rations for those who fought would help."

"No one will begrudge that," Alcedan said.

"I do not think so either," Rayden said. "It is incredible to watch what is taking place. The northern tribes have put petty things aside and see each other for the brothers and sisters that they are. If they continue in this way, we can defeat the Teverens."

"We must not become divided, or distracted," Alcedan replied. "Standing shoulder to shoulder, we can overcome them, as you have said."

Reaching out, Rayden gave Alcedan a firm pat on the back with her right hand.

"We can," she assured him. "Now, let us make certain that those who fought today get some rest and extra food. Then, you and I can do the same. To be a leader of others often means you will be the last in line."

Together, they walked down the channel between the ramparts. Overhead, the sun beamed down through clear, blue skies.

***

The following day passed without incident, though the warriors of the northern tribes remained alert for any sign of attack by the Teverens.

No sign of the fae from the Mist Vale surfaced either.

Rayden chose to hold back from going into the city and opening a gate, judging that it would be ideal to do so when she knew that Queen Muirithesos was in the vicinity. A part of her warned that it would do no good to enter the city, only to have the Imperator's sorcerers spring a massive attack using their dark arts in an unknown, unprecedented manner.

Rayden had seen what they were capable of in the form of the bestial Arguntier. She could not afford to underestimate what they could bring to bear upon the tribes.

She passed the uneventful day in a state of restlessness and found it difficult to get much sleep that night.

When Rayden awoke for the following day, she had only a little time to herself before word arrived that the enemy was forming up for battle.

The tidings jolted her into a state of full alertness. After a quick visit to a latrine pit, Rayden hurried to where the enemy was reported to be mustering.

***

Forming up once more in the morning sun, the forces of Marus and Peronnius arrayed for battle. Gleaming formations faced the ramparts on both sides, the fabric of their standards rippling in the breezes.

Shortly afterward, the forces of the two commanders launched a coordinated assault on the double ramparts along the northern side.

At first, Rayden wondered why the two veteran commanders would repeat an attack that had failed to breach the ramparts. Then, another purpose for the broad attack on the northern side became clear, bringing to light an intent that did not seek to overcome the ramparts.

With the Teverens' full-scale attack tying down a large portion of the tribal warriors, to prevent their ramparts from being stormed, fewer defenders could be diverted to confront the emergence of new threats.

An unwelcome, sudden development took place later that morning, down by the river.

Urgent horn signals from the Rugara, encamped close to one end of the western ramparts, abounded with alarm.

Knowing that the northern wall could be held against the Teverens, Rayden hurried down from the wall-walk and broke into a sprint. Many warriors eyed her as she raced through their midst, keeping her legs churning fast.

Having no idea of what kind of scene awaited her at the end of her run, Rayden wondered if the Teveren sorcerers had finally unveiled what they had been preparing for so long in the murk of secrets, shadows, and dark ambitions.

Coming to a halt at the end of the ramparts, where the vulnerable gap in the siege lines began, Rayden peered toward the river.

The sight that met her eyes gave cause for apprehension.

Large eyes painted just above the waterline bestowed the approaching vessels with the appearances of sea monsters surging in for the kill. Sails furled upon the galleys, banks of oars pulled in rhythmic unison at the cadence of thundering drums propelled the warships.

A raised bulwark along the sides of each vessel protected the soldiers massed on the main part of the deck. High platforms at bow and stern teemed with even more soldiers, in addition to stone-throwing devices.

An entire Teveren war fleet filled waters of the Golden River, presenting a new, grave danger to the tribes of the north.

The waterborne horde advanced closer and closer to the shoreline, commencing an attack before they reached the river's edge.

Catapults on the raised platforms of the Teveren war galleys launched a hail of large stones. Hurling through the air and arcing downward, the heavy projectiles pounded into the ramparts and space between them.

Rayden tensed at the reverberation from one stone slamming into the facing of the rampart a few strides from where she gazed upon the river.

Behind her, a few screams cut the air as another stone tore through a cluster of Rugara warriors, taking several lives in a gruesome fashion.

Cries of agony persisted where the stone had ripped through the warriors. Rayden glanced back, and her eyes widened.

Bleeding profusely and disfigured, two warriors had been maimed horrifically in the strike and still lived. Both would have been far better off dead.

Begging for liberation from a torturous, slow death, the mortally wounded men received it quickly from nearby comrades.

Booming drums maintaining a steady rhythm, the beats sent oars dipping into the water to pull the war vessels forward. The forefront of the great fleet homed in on the riverbank where the gap in the ramparts lay.

At close range to the shore area, archers gathered at the bow of the galleys showered the end sections of the northerners' double ramparts.

Rayden had to crouch and press tight against the stakes crowning the wall-walk to avoid being riddled with the missiles. Arrows hissed through the air all around her, burrowing into wood and hard-packed dirt alike.

The inner rampart and ground area between emptied fast. Warriors scattered about, some flattening themselves against the outer rampart and others racing farther up the channel to get free of the arrows' reach.

Rayden cursed her predicament. Pinned down under the shower of arrows, she could do little other than watch the enemy's advance.

She could not deny having some admiration for the Teveren fleet. It operated with the same kind of cohesion and discipline that its counterparts on land did.

One after another, forming a broad row along the shore, the war galleys lodged themselves onto the beach. In moments, planks were set in place running from the decks to the ground.

Wasting little time, Teveren soldiers began disembarking and rushing up the beach. Without delay, they began organizing into square formations, with officers barking orders among them.

The formations at the front began advancing up the beach, heading toward the city.

Rayden observed a large group of tribal warriors sallying forth from a narrow gateway set in the other end of the ramparts. Her heart sinking at the sight, she knew their folly before the warriors clashed with a single Teveren.

In swift fashion, the warriors found themselves overwhelmed and driven back. A loose rabble, the warriors could do nothing to break the tight cohesion of their advancing enemy.

A wall of overlapping shields faced the charging warriors, and a bristling host of blades greeted them. After many of the tribal warriors had been cut down, the rest pulled back and sought refuge inside the ramparts.

More and more Teverens pouring from the ships created additional formations and joined their comrades farther up the beach. Thickening their ranks, the Teverens pressed closer and closer to the city walls.

On both sides of the formations, clusters of Teveren archers shadowed the flanks. They maintained a constant harassment on the two ends of the rampart while the swelling ranks advanced farther.

Then, after a bevy of succinct horn blasts, large numbers of soldiers from the formations at the front broke away and began repositioning along each side of the path they had just taken. Shields facing outward and standing shoulder to shoulder, the Teverens formed a living wall.

The forefront of the Teveren advance then reached the double-arch gateway facing the riverfront: the well-fortified River Gate. Warded on both sides by towers, the tall, iron-banded gates opened.

Before much longer, a broad, clear corridor, running all the way from the gate down to the ships, had been established. Still held down by the continuing barrage of arrows, Rayden did not like the look of the new development at all.

Wasting no time, rowers from the ships began lugging sacks, amphorae, chests, and many other containers and vessels to the city. With the River Gate open, the inhabitants of the Imperial City soon contributed many more porters to the intensive effort.

With a strong force in place on each flank, enough to deter counterattacks, there remained nothing to inhibit the offloading of the beached galleys. A few carts pulled by mules or horses were brought out of the city to help with heavier loads.

A constant stream built up, moving back and forth from the beach. Prodigious amounts of food, wine, and other supplies were hauled and carried into the city.

Chafing with fury and helpless to do anything about it,

Rayden watched the traffic flowing into the city.

The attack along the northern ramparts had taken away all spare warriors. Those now huddled behind the ramparts around her did not have the numbers to challenge the large Teveren force from the sea.

An outright attack could cause some disruption to the offloading of supplies, but it would become a bloodbath for the tribal warriors. The tribes had been caught unprepared to counter the scale of the ship-borne maneuver being executed by the enemy.

Rayden knew what would come. Having demonstrated a robust means of resupplying the city, the Teveren fleet would be pulling back from the shore and heading downriver before long, unscathed and able to return again.

Most everything carried into the city would be utilized to bolster the legions and those of great power and wealth. It stood to reason that very little would find its way to the multitudes of poor dwelling in the towering, overcrowded tenements that Rayden had seen while in the city.

The ability of the Teverens to establish corridors from river to gate had other implications. The enemy could also provide a solid means of escape for the powerful in the city, even the Imperator himself.

Rayden doubted the Teverens would even consider such a thing at the moment.

Behind their high walls, with an effective means of gaining more food and supplies, the Teverens faced an opponent trapped inside ramparts with finite quantities of food and drink diminishing further every day.

***

Slumping down, Rayden rested on the ground with her back leaning against the outermost rampart from the city. All around her, exhausted warriors sat, lay, or trudged onward.

A fire pit not far from Rayden provided a little light, a boon now that night had fallen across the city, ramparts, and lands beyond.

Carts trundling through the channel brought the meager rations of bread and cheese, along with a small portion of ale. Blood-spattered, sweaty, and grimy, Rayden gave no thought to her condition, devouring her allotment of food swiftly.

"May I sit with you?" a familiar voice asked her.

Raising her eyes, Rayden peered at Annocrates. Like her, he bore all the signs of a day-long battle. He had even suffered a gash, high on his left arm.

"I would like that," she answered him.

Settling down next to her, Annocrates said nothing for several moments.

"A battle neither won, nor lost," he muttered, staring ahead into empty space.

"It is that way in war, at times," Rayden replied, looking downward. She then turned her head toward him and gazed upon his grimy, blood-smeared face. "But we survived this day, and that is a victory in itself."

"It is hard to think of victory when the enemy can bring everything they need into the city, and we are trapped here," Annocrates commented.

Rayden could not argue with him. After watching the Teverens establish their corridor from beach to gate, she had returned to the northern ramparts and rejoined the ongoing struggle there.

Before the fighting had ended, her blades had quenched their thirst for Teveren blood. Like the first assault, Marus and Peronnius had been forced to pull back, unable to gain purchase on the walls and leaving many dead behind.

"Marus returned to his camp today with even fewer soldiers,

and so did Peronnius," Rayden said. "We bloodied them again, and they failed again."

Annocrates nodded slowly and looked back to her. "But so many of ours fell. Pyres burn in the camps of all tribes tonight."

"Not even the fall of night brings peace," Rayden stated, staring toward the flames of the nearby fire.

Carrying the stench of burning flesh from the makeshift pyres, the cold night winds reminded all within the ramparts of the highest cost of war. Moans and cries drifted through the air, coming from those suffering a merciless, relentless agony.

Many of them would join the number of the slain that night, after succumbing to the grievous wounds that they had suffered in battle. For some, death would spare them from the doom of a drawn-out decline, filled with pain and advancing sickness. A few would look to trusted friends or even family to end their extreme suffering.

"The Teveren bastards hold the beach," Annocrates lamented.

Rayden nodded. "That is not the worst of it."

"I know, they seek to put their own ramparts in place," Annocrates commented, glancing toward Rayden. "Many spoke of it when evening fell."

"It is more than seeking to," Rayden countered, looking grim. "By morning they will have a rampart up that is worthy of a field encampment."

While the Teverens held the broad gap between the two ends of the ramparts, another unwelcome development had taken place, not long after midday. When most of the supplies from the ships had been taken into the city, large numbers of Teverens had set about digging the trenches for a new, narrow encampment; one that stretched from the walls to the beach.

"Will we attack them tomorrow?" Annocrates asked Rayden.

"It is likely, unless Peronnius and Marus choose to concentrate another attack, somewhere along the ramparts," Rayden nodded. "But I think the Teveren ships will pull away for a time. They will do our enemy little good lodged on the shoreline."

"The ships can return, and bring more food and supplies to the city," Annocrates replied in a dour tone. After a moment, he added, "And more soldiers."

"Something will have to be done about this gap and the matter of ships, or the city will be able to endure the siege without any trouble," Rayden told him.

"Which would see all of us destroyed," Annocrates remarked.

"Yes, it would," Rayden agreed in a dour tone. "We would become the besieged, and we are not prepared to sustain such a condition for long."

"The stretch of land by the riverfront was just too narrow for us to extend the ramparts," Annocrates stated, shaking his head with a deepening look of frustration. "What could we have done?"

"The Teverens would never have allowed that gap to be closed," Rayden said. "Those walls and the towers warding the gate would have been filled with archers, during every moment of the day. Catapults and ballistas would have been positioned. Beneath that storm of arrow, bolt, and rock, Peronnius could send his forces out again and again. No, we could not have closed that gap without incurring the kinds of losses that would threaten the entire war."

Annocrates shook his head. "But we will have to attack the gap immediately and try to reach those ships. At the least, if we destroy their ships, they cannot bring supplies and reinforcements."

In a slow, methodical fashion, Rayden got to her feet. Aches and pains rippled through her, with stiffened muscles staunchly protesting the notion of being made to labor any more that night.

"I must go find Alcedan," Rayden said, grimacing while she stretched her limbs out a little. "A war council must be convened."

Wincing, Annocrates stood up and looked to her. "I will go with you. I can look in on Hamilcar too."

"That boy better be staying put within the Gessa camp, or he is going to get the flat of my blade on his backside," Rayden declared, looking into Annocrates eyes. "Be unwavering in your discipline of him. Never forget, your discipline gives him a chance to survive all of this."

"The flat of both our blades, you meant," Annocrates replied with no trace of jest. "Trust in me, Rayden. There is no slack in my discipline of the boy. I know what recklessness leads to."

"The whims of war are nothing to tempt in a reckless manner," Rayden stated. Taking a step forward, she added, "And I do trust in you. Now, let us see about mustering a force to take the shore back when morning arrives."

"Count me in the number that assails the Teverens when dawn breaks," Annocrates replied.

Heading in the direction of the Gessa camp, the two warriors strode down the midst of the ground between the ramparts.

Left to her own thoughts, Rayden tried to ignore the inner voice reminding her that no hint of Queen Muirithesos or the fae had manifested that day.

She hoped that it would not be much longer until the little creatures made their presence known. The city had to be taken as soon as possible.

The daunting situation facing the tribes had just grown even more dire.

Rayden did not want to enter the city under any circumstances without something to counter the Imperator's sorcery, but the Teverens would have no need of dark magic when they could win a war of attrition.

Holding her concerns at bay, Rayden kept striding forward. The scent of burning flesh remaining thick in the air, a multitude of groans and cries continued rising into the night.

CHAPTER 11

Morning's light reflected off the spear blades, swords, and axes of a large force of tribal warriors. Gathered near the end of the ramparts, where the two earthen walls had been connected, they waited with iron-hard expressions.

A similar force stood poised at the other end of the ramparts, positioned on the other side of the new camp fortifications set in place overnight by the Teverens.

Rayden stood alongside Annocrates and Alcedan, awaiting the horn blasts that would send them streaming through the narrow portals in the ramparts to begin the assault.

A terrible price in blood loomed, but the enemy could not be allowed to become more fortified or entrenched.

***

Horns blared and a tremendous commotion broke out from the direction of the riverbank.

The distinctive tone of the braying horns told Rayden at once that they were Teveren in nature.

Springing into motion, Rayden rushed over to the outer rampart facing the river. Scampering up the steps dug into the hard-packed dirt and covered with rough timber planks, she halted atop the wall-walk.

Gazing in the direction of the Golden River, Rayden looked to see what had caused the sudden uproar.

Approaching from farther down the river, a large fleet of galleys sliced through the water. Their decks bristling with warriors, the vessels displayed dark square sails.

Fashioned in shining bronze, the heads of bulls, dragons, lions, and other powerful creatures crowned the prows of the approaching galleys.

"Kartajenian! They are Kartajenian!" Rayden shouted, recognizing the nature of the incoming war galleys.

Elated and astonished, she found it difficult to believe her own eyes. With so much pressing against the tribal forces, something in their favor had manifested out of nowhere, in a most unexpected fashion.

From both the ships beached on the shore and their encampment, Teveren horns continued to blare.

Teverens within the encampment rushed down the beach toward their own galleys. Planks were lowered on the sides of the vessels to allow the hustling soldiers and rowers to scramble board.

Soldiers and rowers alike ran up and down the decks of the Teveren ships, hurrying to take their places and respond to the looming Kartajenian threat.

With the Teverens focused on their vessels, an opportunity emerged for the northern tribes. Rayden could see it clearly.

Rayden looked down to where Alcedan stood.

"Attack them, now!" Rayden yelled. "Give the signal! Now is the time! Take the Teveren camp!"

Alcedan looked back to her and nodded. Turning aside, he addressed a few men standing near with horns in hand.

The call to attack filled the air a few moments later. A second round of tribal horn blasts sounded just after, rising from the other side of the Teveren camp.

Having already removed the barriers to a pair of exit passages at the end of the ramparts, warriors began issuing through. Laying down stout planks spanning the ditch beyond, forming makeshift bridges, the tribal warriors began pouring into the open ground on both sides of the Teveren encampment.

After taking a little time to mass in number and bring forward many ladders and planks, the warriors charged headlong at the enemy ramparts.

Before descending from the wall-walk to join in the attack, Rayden looked once more out to the river.

The Kartajenian vessels had drawn close enough that archers gathered at their prows had begun exchanging volleys of missiles with the Teverens on the still-beached ships.

Rayden noticed that many of the Kartajenian arrows had been set to flame.

The Teverens aboard the ships quickly found themselves engaged in extinguishing the roots of fires, all over the wooden vessels.

Split between defending the ships and repulsing the sudden assault on both sides of their camp, the Teverens were spreading thin fast.

Descending from the wall-walk, Rayden joined with the other warriors funneling through the narrow portals.

A tremendous fervor gripped the air. Given the chance to go on the offensive at last, the tribal warriors surged forward in a volcanic fury.

Screaming her own war cry, Rayden sprinted across the open ground toward the enemy camp.

Tribal warriors ahead were already climbing ladders and surmounting the Teverens' smaller earthen wall in many places. Enemy horns sounded in a flurry, the rapid, short blasts conveying alarm and urgency.

Finding a ladder still contested at the top, Rayden ran to its base. Keeping her weapons in hand, she ascended the rungs.

A falling warrior almost knocked Rayden free of the ladder, but she hugged it close, and the body grazed her back and continued downward.

Striving to gain the top, the warrior above her hacked wildly at Teverens defending the rampart. An enemy soldier thrust his blade deep into the side of the warrior, who took another broad swing at the Teveren before collapsing forward.

Recognizing the brief gap that the dying warrior's fall had opened, Rayden hurried up the last few rungs.

Reaching the top, she reared up fast. Her cry rending the air and eyes aflame with a honed intensity, Rayden swept her weapons outward with great force.

Catching one Teveren in the side of the neck with her axe, Rayden cut deep into the arm of another with her sword. Blood gushing from the axe wound and head half-severed, the first soldier toppled backward from the rampart. The soldier with the maimed arm dropped his medium-length blade and shrieked in pain.

Setting foot atop the enemy rampart, Rayden bared her teeth at the man like a savage wolf. Cutting him down with a vicious swing of her axe, her blow opened his neck wide, sending a spray of blood through the air.

A tall, brawny tribal warrior armed with a sword reached the top just behind Rayden. Slashing and bellowing guttural cries, the warrior drove the Teverens behind Rayden farther back, creating even more room for the other warriors climbing the ladder.

Another warrior scrambled up to stand on the wall-walk, followed by another, with more ascending behind them.

"Take the camp and gain the shore!" Rayden exhorted the others, blocking a Teveren's sword thrust and felling the man with a counterstrike from her axe.

As the man fell to the side, Rayden thrust her sword into the exposed throat of the next soldier before he could even set his eyes on her. He staggered back, gurgling and choking.

A tribal warrior reached the top of another ladder, right where the man had shuffled back. Shoving him off the rampart and stepping onto the wall, the warrior cast a quick glance at Rayden before squaring to his right and raising his long-hafted axe.

Afforded a moment to look around, Rayden took an assessment.

More and more tribal warriors surmounting the Teveren ramparts unimpeded, many had already reached the ground below. Charging deeper into the enemy camp, the zealous warriors pressed the attack.

Unable to assemble into tight ranks, the Teverens were forced into a sprawling melee that gave swift advantage to the emboldened attackers. The air swirled with shouts, cries, clashes of metal, and other sounds of battle.

Reaching a ladder on the inside of the enemy rampart, one that the Teverens had placed to access the top of the wall, Rayden climbed downward. Eyeing the wall above, she could see that the Teverens were losing control of the ramparts fast.

Rayden then turned her attention to the other rampart, the one facing the second force of northern warriors. She watched a large, thick-limbed warrior lift up a Teveren soldier and hurl him down from the wall-walk.

Like the rampart behind her, the warriors attacking from the other side were sweeping the top clear of Teveren soldiers.

It would not be long before the northerners had complete control of both ramparts.

Rayden then looked toward the shoreline.

A few Teveren ships had managed to launch from the beach,

but most remained woefully undermanned and had not yet dislodged. Those vessels soon found themselves caught between the northerners storming the beach and the Kartajenian force coming in from the river.

The Teveren galleys that left the shore were far too few in number to threaten the Kartajenian fleet. Furthermore, the Kartajenian war galleys demonstrated greater speed and maneuverability than the larger Teveren vessels, sealing off any possibilities of escape. '

Rammed and boarded one by one, none of the Teveren galleys out in the water escaped the trap closing in upon them.

Warriors continued flooding into the Teveren camp on both sides. Spirited war cries intermingled with the screams of the mangled and dying, the latter a hellish chorus that Rayden was all too familiar with.

Rayden then pivoted about to look in the direction of the city walls.

A small cluster of Teverens able to fight their way through the camp made a dash for the River Gate. Archers on the flanking towers and wall above the gate covered their retreat into the city.

The archers then began releasing arrows in the direction of the shoreline, bringing down tribal warriors and even a few of their fellow Teverens in the swirling melee.

The archers did not possess the clearest lines of sight. Many northerners had been savvy enough during their rampage to start fires all throughout the Teveren camp.

Burning wagons, tents, barrels, and other flammable items sent plumes of smoke upward, creating a sprawling array of obstructions for the eyes of the enemy archers.

Rayden loped toward the beach, where the last of the fighting was taking place.

With the camp awash in northern warriors, the Teverens aboard the remaining beached galleys had become trapped.

Kartajenian galleys drawing close from the river began showering them in fire arrows.

Before long, a forest of dark smoke columns began snaking toward the skies, issuing from more and more burning Teveren vessels.

The blazing ships forced the remnants still aboard them to take to the beach. Rowers and soldiers alike leaped down from the sides of the flaming galleys and rushed away from them; bringing the desperate Teverens running headlong into a mass of waiting northern warriors.

The fleeing Teverens were cut down in swift fashion.

Rayden and the other leaders among the masses of northern warriors then gave the command to pull back to their own ramparts.

With the rout of the Teverens throughout the camp and along the beach, the arrows coming from the city walls increased in volume. Within the stretch of ground spanning between the ends of the northerner's ramparts, there was nowhere safe from the lethal rain.

A few precarious moments passed as Rayden had to wait where the masses of tribal warriors funneled through the few narrow portals accessing their own ramparts. Pressing against each other, warriors shoved and jostled each other in their haste to get inside the protective walls, adding even more burdens to the ordeal.

Teveren arrows claimed the lives of several more warriors, including one standing just a few places behind Rayden, by the time that she finally passed through one of the narrow openings.

Among the last of the warriors to enter, Rayden stood in place for a moment, watching the warriors setting the timber barriers back in place to block the openings. The feverish pace of battle masking fatigue, the first moments of calm unveiled the sapped nature of her body and limbs.

Covered in sweat and the blood of her enemies, Rayden looked around at the other warriors. Though weary from the extended fighting, they had a burning ferocity within their gazes.

They had gained confidence and denied the Teverens their encampment. The time for Rayden to enter the city and open a gate loomed, whether or not the fae under Queen Muirithesos had come.

Wiping off her blades, using a patch of her tunic that remained unsullied, Rayden returned the weapons to their places of rest at her waist.

Her next thoughts focused on the imminent landing of Kartajenian vessels.

***

Watching the Teveren vessels burning along the shore and out in the water, Rayden and Alcedan stood together atop their own ramparts. Knowing it would not be long before the Kartajenian forces moved to come ashore, she intended to be among the first of the tribal warriors to greet them.

After allowing the fires to consume the Teveren galleys for awhile, the vessels from the Kartajen Empire began heading to shore. One after another, they pulled onto the beach, claiming the area so recently occupied by their hated enemies.

Several tribal leaders, Rayden among them, hurried to the edge of the water, the boundary where the arrows of the enemy could not reach. Facing the growing line of galleys, she waited to greet the northern tribes' unexpected allies.

Farther behind Rayden and the other warriors, smoke continued to billow from the overrun Teveren camp. Many more fires had been set to aid in the obstruction of the enemy's view of the shore area.

Under the watch of the northerners, the captains of the Kartajenian galleys began to disembark. Unchallenged by enemies, the galley commanders and attending warriors descended walking planks in an orderly manner, gathering into a larger group on the shoreline.

After assembling, the Kartajenians marched toward the awaiting cluster of northern leaders. Moving along the water's edge, they kept well out of the reach of Teveren arrows.

A proud-looking figure walked at their lead. A gleaming cuirass of bronze scales protected his upper body. Fitted with cheek pieces, the conical helm atop his head rose up to where thick tresses of horsehair sprouted from a narrow finial to fall down his back.

A magnificent cloak of red flowed behind him. Images in the surface depicted a variety of star shapes and crescent moons. An ornate, curving dragon's head marked the handle of the sword resting in the scabbard at his left side.

His long beard and hair had been styled into an array of ringlets. Taking slow strides, the warrior's dark eyes looked over the tribal leaders a short distance ahead of him.

Other prominent-looking figures followed, though none carried the air of the man at their lead. One had a leopard-skin headdress and cloak. A couple of others wore cuirasses of stiffened cloth, around the skirt of which scales of leather had been affixed.

"We welcome the ships of the Kartajen Empire, though we did not expect you this day," Alcedan greeted the man at the front. "I am Alcedan, chieftain of the Gessa tribe. With me are many chieftains of the northern tribes who have joined together to fight the Teverens."

"I am Xanthiros," the Kartajenian leader replied. "I am the commander of the fleet you see before you. Those with me are captains of war galleys, and a few of their guards."

"We share the same enemy, so it follows that we are fighting on the same side in this war," Alcedan responded to Xanthiros.

"What brings you to the shores of the Imperial City this day?"

"The Teverens presented us with an opportunity that we could not overlook," Xanthiros stated. "They ceased their attack on our province of Algenesia and returned to their own territory in Sicillus; a great island south of here that was once ours, abundant in farmland.

"Our spies in Sicillus told us that the Teverens were gathering up everything they could in food, wine and other supplies. Word then came to us of your siege, and we knew at once where the Teverens would be going.

"After gathering up every galley that we could muster, we set forth from Kartajen. We sheltered within some small islands to the west of Sicillus and waited.

"When their fleet left the shores of Sicillus, we set out and followed at a distance. It was a risk with their fleet being larger in numbers than ours, but I knew we stood more than a fair chance of catching them in the manner that we did today.

"Very few of their ships made it off the shore," Alcedan stated.

"You made it easier for us by attacking their camp," the Kartajenian commander replied. "Who knows how many galleys they would have put to water if they had not been hindered by the assault on their camp? We are grateful for your attack. Their entire fleet is now in ruins."

"What are your plans from here?" Alcedan asked.

Rayden watched Xanthiros face and eyes with great scrutiny.

"We will keep to our galleys tonight and depart in the morning," Xanthiros announced. "We are not prepared to join in your siege, but that fleet will no longer be of benefit to them. They have suffered a great blow, and we can return to strengthen Algenesia against the Teverens' next attack."

Rayden did not trust the Kartajenian fleet commander. Xanthiros had not come for the benefit of the northern tribes.

His interests lay with the will of the Kartajen Empire and the council that ruled over it. Rayden had no doubt that he was calculating the situation regarding the heart of their mortal enemies, the Imperial City.

The next time that they appeared, Xanthiros could well have a Kartajenian army with him to take the city itself.

After suffering so many losses to the Teverens, in blood and land, the Kartajenians undoubtedly hungered for a reversal of fortunes. Rayden could see a glint of that craving within the commander's gaze.

Alcedan looked to be taking the commander's announcement in stride, replying, "You are welcome to join with us, but I thank you for what you have done. May a friendship grow between the people of our tribes and your Empire."

Xanthiros gave Alcedan a pleasant smile. "May it be so, and may the future see the destruction of our mutual enemy. The Teverens have shown themselves to be a blight upon the world."

"You will find no argument among us about that," Alcedan replied.

"May your fight against them prevail, Alcedan of the Gessa," Xanthiros stated. "We shall return to our vessels, where we will rest and pass the night before departing these shores in the morning."

Alcedan acknowledged Xanthiros' words with a slight bow of his head.

Followed by the throng of captains and guards, Xanthiros turned and started back toward the Kartajenian galleys. Rayden could not deny finding the vessels lined up along the shore a wonderful sight in comparison to the Teveren display that had been there that very morning.

"You do not like him, do you Rayden?" Alcedan's voice interrupted her thoughts.

Rayden turned her head toward the Gessa chieftain.

"It is good we have no intentions of trying to hold the city, once the Imperator is overthrown," Rayden replied in an even tone.

"He wants the city for their people," Alcedan responded, nodding. "I could see it in his eyes too. He sees taking the Imperial City as a big stride in taking back the lands they have lost."

Pleased at his response, Rayden smiled. "Your eyes are seeing clearly."

Alcedan grinned, though the look carried a rueful element. "Every day that I have walked as the leader of my people has taught me lessons. As you said, some have been bittersweet in nature."

Rayden nodded. "The intentions of people are often veiled beneath the surface. Some very well hidden."

"It will take time for him to gather an army and prepare supplies," Alcedan remarked, gazing out toward the host of Kartajenian galleys.

"By then, our fight here will be resolved, one way or another," Rayden responded.

Alcedan held her gaze for a moment. "May it be that we are marching north to return to our homelands when the Kartajenians return."

"May it be so," Rayden said in a lower voice, laden with weariness.

She looked toward the extensive wreckage and multitude of bodies floating on the water. The currents were already carrying the debris and carnage downstream, but what remained testified to a great loss of life that day.

Most of those who had died were mere fodder for the power-hungry Imperator and those of high status in the Teveren Empire. Wanting nothing more than to return to loved ones, so many would never make their way home.

No burial or blazing pyre would take place. Their bodies would now fill the bellies of the creatures dwelling within the river.

The thought left Rayden in a melancholy state as she turned back toward the tribal ramparts. Water lapped over her feet, bringing its chill touch to her ankles.

Keeping to the water's edge, she strode along the river. The air remained thick with the scent of burning wood.

Rayden could only hope that the war would soon come to an end and that those given to grave evils be held to account for the abominations they had committed.

For her part, she would fight with every last bit of strength left within her to see that happen.

***

Later in the day, with dusk drawing near, the skies blackened over the Imperial City. The massive front spread fast, stretching as far as the eye could see.

Rumbles of thunder, sounding like the throaty growls of a colossal beast, rolled across the skies. A deep, biting cold fell across the tribal positions.

Howling like wolves on the hunt, the winds began picking up. Frigid gusts whisked through the various contingents encamped between the two high ramparts.

Looking upon the forming maelstrom, Rayden frowned, a keen sense of unease settling over her. Nothing about the storm looked natural.

Despite the winds, the forefront of the billowing, dark vapors appeared to be hovering over the Imperial City, when normal cloud masses would have swept westward.

Making her way to the top of the ramparts, Rayden gripped the rough, wooden stakes lining the earthen wall. Spectacular flashes of lightning began lighting up the skies, and the winds continued to surge in strength, whipping through her long golden tresses.

With the coming of twilight, it did not take long before the city, ramparts, and river were plunged into a deep darkness. No rain fell yet, but the usual multitude of campfires failed to appear as the people of the tribes huddled and braced for the torrents they expected to come at any moment.

Rayden stayed in place, enduring the lashes of the wind and watching the anomalous storm continue to unfold. The massive waves of lightning illuminated the city, riverside, and ramparts, as far as her vision could reach.

Thunder boomed overhead. Rivulets of lightning then shot down from the black cloud masses, the host of effulgent white streaks lancing the area around the river.

Soon afterward, the telltale glow of fires began emerging out of the darkness.

The storm intensified further. The fires ignited from the lightning grew, shedding enough light for Rayden to see a dismaying spectacle; the forms of burning galleys being smashed into each other in the grips of rising waves.

Rain never fell, but the lightning and thunder continued in their ferocity, deep into the night. The frequency of the flashes and rivulets then began decreasing, until at long last the lightning came to an end.

The winds abated and the thunder settled into low rumbles. Rayden's eyes remained fixed toward the river, watching the host of fires blazing in the night where the Kartajenian fleet had been located.

A part of her dreaded the sight that dawn would unveil.

***

Wreckage littered the surface of the river near to the shore, where the current had not yet carried off the remains of Kartajenian vessels thrashed in the bizarre storm of the previous night.

The scent of burning wood clinging thick to the air, smoke continued to rise from the husks of destroyed war galleys.

Rayden and a large party of warriors probed through the wreckage, looking for any survivors that they could find. The faintest cry or other sound drew them in a hurry.

Here and there, they pulled survivors from the waters. Several times, they could do nothing but watch helpless as other survivors, some clinging to large pieces of wood, drifted off in the river's robust currents.

Dispirited, Rayden accompanied the others when the search drew to an end. Trudging along the shore, they began making their way back to the ramparts.

Entering the high earthen fortifications through one of the narrow passages, Rayden set her eyes upon a dense throng of Kartajenian rowers, soldiers, and others from the galley crews.

Listless and milling about, most had forlorn expressions on their faces, though a few spirited outbursts met the recognition of survivors that had returned in the company of the search party.

Rayden worked her way through the crowd. Making a quick evaluation, she estimated that perhaps a thousand Kartajenian had survived the night; out of the many thousands that had operated the large war fleet.

She caught sight of Xanthiros, gathered in conversation with some other Kartajenians. Though looking disheveled and no longer clad in a cuirass, mantle, or helm, the man still conveyed the air of a leader. Rayden could see the others listening to his every word.

The survivors would need him desperately in the days to come. Without any means of leaving the shores of the river, and with their hated enemy in command of the ground outside the tribal ramparts, their fate would now depend on the tribal forces prevailing.

Rayden continued forward, shouldering through the multitude of downcast Kartajenians.

"I bet you did not think I would catch back up with you," a familiar voice called to Rayden in a tone of levity that stood in stark contrast to the brooding atmosphere.

Eyes widening, Rayden turned around. The grin already spreading on her face bloomed into a luminous smile when she set her eyes upon Ammanus.

Battered-looking and a little gaunt, Ammanus had a buoyant smile on his own face. His short, light-brown tunic had a rough, well-soiled appearance, ripped and gouged in several places.

Spreading his arms out wide, he stated, "The least you can do is give me a big embrace, after leaving me stranded on the streets of Kartajen."

"You mean when I escaped an entire city pursuing me, to recapture a child they wanted to throw into fire to appease a vile god," Rayden replied, smirking, and not giving a care whether any of Kartajenians near heard her disparaging their bull god.

Striding forward, Rayden embraced her friend tight, lifting the smaller man off his feet for a moment.

"Are you going to carry me off and whisper sweet things in my ear, while we drink wine and pursue wonderful pleasures?" Ammanus quipped, chuckling.

"I am going to give you a solid, proper wallop if you continue to suggest such things," Rayden told Ammanus, laughing and releasing him. "Believe me, you are long overdue for one."

"You know that you missed me," he replied, giving her a wink.

"Even if I was one of the foolish girls that you seduce with your silken tongue and trickery, I would demand you to bathe and get some new clothes," Rayden commented. "You look rougher than when I last set eyes on you. What happened? By all the gods that are worshipped in this world, how is it that you are standing here now?"

"After you left, I had some wonderful times with a few of those foolish girls you speak of," Ammanus said, a mischievous gleam in his eyes. "I heard of the escape of the brazen, blond-haired northerner who stole away a boy intended for sacrifice. I had no doubts of who that northerner was, when you did not turn up anywhere else."

"I have many tales to tell you of what happened after that," Rayden told him, thinking back for a moment on the harrowing sequence of events following the escape from Kartajen.

"Let us get ahold of a good quantity of ale and I will listen to all of them gladly," Ammanus replied. His face took on a serious mien. "I know that you had to escape, and could not seek me out, but I am glad that our paths have brought us together once more. I have often wondered how you were faring."

"How did you find your way here?" Rayden asked.

"Word spread that a Teveren fleet was making haste to gather up whatever food, supplies, wine, and weapons that it could from a large island, taken not long ago from the Kartajen Empire," he answered. "It was said they were going to make haste to return to the Imperial City, because of some invasion from the north. Talk of tribes coming together and besieging the Imperial City reached Kartajen lands."

Ammanus paused, chuckled, and shook his head.

"I should have guessed that you had something to do with the invasion from the north," he remarked. "Only you would dare to strike at the heart of the Teveren Empire."

"I am not the only one who dared to do so," Rayden replied. "There is an army of determined warriors here with me."

"I am grateful for that," Ammanus stated. "Those I came with are pretty stranded now."

"You still have not told me how you came to be here," Rayden said.

"The rulers of Kartajen thought it would be a good opportunity to strike back at the Teverens," Ammanus continued. "So, they rounded up a lot of able-bodied men to help with oars. For some reason, they lumped me into the group that they scraped up on the streets of Kartajen, and I ended up on one of their war galleys. My protest about the matter fell on deaf ears and earned me a few bruises.

"The food was not good at all ... what little there was given to us each day. I was surrounded by foul-smelling men, without a nubile young woman to be found anywhere ... and they worked me to exhaustion without pay."

"Sounds like life as a rower on a war galley," Rayden responded. "But you proved you could handle it, or you would not be standing here."

"Not for much longer," Ammanus told her. "It was awful. They pressed us hard and showed no mercy to those who could not keep rowing. More than a few bodies were pitched into the sea along the way. But seeing you again helps soothe my horrible memories of the nightmare."

"Will I have to fight them to let you come back with me now?" Rayden asked.

"They probably still lay claim to me, but I have had far enough of it," Ammanus said. "Besides, what vessel is there to row out there?"

Rayden thought of the shattered remains of the Kartajen fleet that she had just searched through. The destruction would definitely have a major impact on whatever intentions Xanthiros had previously harbored. No vessel remained in any kind of condition to be put out into the river.

"I am sure they have enough rowers on hand to man what remains to them," Rayden told him with a smirk.

"They say they are going to make an encampment here, while they decide what to do," Ammanus said. "They have been given refuge by the leaders of your tribes."

"Then you can encamp with us, while they figure things out," Rayden said. "If you wish to return to them, you can. If not, you can stay with us. Does that sound good?"

"That does sound very good," Ammanus responded, grinning. "I like to have options, though I already know my choice."

"Come on, and follow me," Rayden told her friend, smiling and starting forward. "We will find you some food and a change of clothing."

Ammanus walked along at her side. Though drawing some curious glances from some of the surviving Kartajenians, none made any move to stop him from accompanying Rayden.

"Getting the weird looks again, walking along with you, Rayden ... just like old times," Ammanus jested, laughing.

***

A grim look on his face, Alcedan looked around at the faces of the tribal chieftains gathered for the night's war council. "We have almost a thousand more warriors with us in the ramparts, but little to nothing of their stores of food were salvaged."

"We cannot spare any food," Belgra of the Arna declared, to murmurs of assent all around him. "We do not know how long we will need to stay here, within these walls."

"Now is the time to strike at the city," Grogner said, shifting his gaze toward Rayden. "If you can open a gate, the moment has come."

"It would be better to have a thousand Kartajenians fighting at our side than turning on us," Celterren of the Lanassa stated.

Rayden looked around at their faces and saw the heightened anxiety in their gazes. The arrival of the Kartajenian fleet had helped to rid them all of one threat, but the storm had created another.

Nodding to them, Rayden replied, "Tomorrow night I will enter the city."

"What do you counsel, once a gate is opened?" Kellas of the Pannimbri asked.

"Before the gate is opened, draw the Teverens to the south of the city, and then enter through their Eagle Gate on the north," Rayden answered him. "We must pull as many as we can away from the fortress they have inside the city. Entering through the north, we will be an immediate threat to the homes of the powerful, and even the Imperator's palace."

"How are you certain we will enter through this Eagle Gate?" Belgra asked, a mocking grin on his face. "Are the Teverens going to help you open it and welcome us into the city?"

"I will see that it is opened," Rayden told Belgra in an unwavering, determined voice. Her piercing gaze drove the arrogant smirk from his face. "After the sun descends tomorrow, I will enter the city once more. When the fog lifts from the city in the morning, let them think they will face an attack on the south ... and prepare to enter from the north."

Her gaze sweeping across the visages of the chieftains, Rayden continued, "Gain a better position using the fog to your advantage. It will conceal the force on the northern side and let you assemble closer to the Eagle Gate."

Many of the chieftains nodded in agreement with her counsel.

Rayden then told them, "Give the Kartajenians some rations. They are our allies and will be fighting with us. They can be helpful to ward against Marus' legions."

"A wise course of action," Serivas of the Marren commented. "The battle will be decided when we move on the city, one way or another."

"What if she is unable to open the gate?" Kellas asked.

"Underestimate Rayden at your own folly," Makabaras of

the Runi replied to the Pannimbri chieftain.

"Just be sure to draw as many Teverens south as you can and have a large force ready in the north to enter," Rayden told him.

Alcedan then spoke up. "We will be ready, Rayden. We have gotten this far together, and together the tribes of the north will storm the Imperial City."

Alcedan's declaration met with strong acclaim from the chieftains, and Rayden knew they would continue the solid cooperation they had demonstrated so far.

The rest of the war council proceeded in a smooth fashion, addressing smaller matters, until Alcedan declared the evening's discussions concluded. The chieftains then dispersed to rejoin their respective tribes.

***

Walking away from the site of the war council, Rayden made her way back to the camp of the Gessa.

One critical matter remained unresolved.

Climbing to the top of the outer rampart, Rayden stared across the rolling, forested landscape. Reaching down to a pouch at her belt, she unfastened the ties and took out the ring within it.

Clutching the ring in her right palm, Rayden whispered into the night, "Where are you, Muirithesos?"

A gust of wind passed over her, flaring Rayden's locks out behind her. For a moment, she forgot about the thousands upon thousands of warriors encamped within the ramparts just behind her and the massive city beyond that those high earthen walls encircled.

A quiet, unruffled landscape spread before her eyes, beneath skies filled with bright stars.

Squeezing the ring in her palm a little tighter, she whispered, "I just want to know you are there, before I go into the city."

Nothing stirred within the moonlight. Rayden's gaze roved

from left to right, desiring to see a flicker of light or something to indicate that her allies from the Mist Vale had come.

After a little more time had passed without any hint of response, Rayden climbed down into the channel between the ramparts and sought a place to sleep for the night.

It took a little time for Rayden to fall asleep with the array of things weighing upon her mind and heart. The tribes still had no counter for the enemy's powerful sorcery, but they could not sustain a war of attrition. The addition of over a thousand Kartajenian survivors hastened the erosion of the tribes' remaining stores of food.

The enemy also had more than one fleet and remained capable of reestablishing another line of supply at any time.

With the Kartajenians fighting alongside them, the tribes stood their strongest at the present moment.

Despite the absence of Queen Muirithesos, Rayden's choice had been made.

When the next night arrived, Rayden would enter the Imperial City, regardless of whether the fae had arrived or not.

CHAPTER 12

*U*nder the light of the rising moon on the following evening, Rayden descended the outer facing of the rampart. In the distance, the walls of the Imperial City beckoned to her.

Etched in the moonlight, the solid, imposing line of walls and towers dared any attacker to assail them.

Rayden did not plan to climb the walls or enter through a main gate. This time, she had her mind on the smallest kind of gate, one of the many postern doorways placed along the walls.

Carefully masked, they were far too small to allow an army to enter. But they were useful for convenient egress in accessing the ground outside the walls and the passage of those with clandestine purposes.

Once more, Rayden would assume a role to perform.

Keeping a lower profile, Rayden crept toward the walls. In the glow of firelight on both the walls and towers, she could see the outline of soldiers keeping watch.

Using the Eagle Gate as her guide, she counted four regular wall towers to the left. Fixing her eyes on the fourth tower, she adjusted her course to head straight toward it.

With the moon shrouded behind a fortuitous layer of clouds, Rayden knew that she would be well-concealed on the last part of her approach.

Patient and methodical, she reached the base of the tower. It did not take her long to find the outline of the postern gate, an entrance little more than a large doorway. The small portal had been set in the right side of the tower, where it opened parallel to the walls.

Scouts for the northern tribes had witnessed the Teverens using that postern gate on a nightly basis. The scouts had observed robed figures entering and leaving, and had also identified the entrance to a small, disguised tunnel, located a little farther away from the walls.

Rayden had little doubt that the tunnel went to somewhere within the vast Catacombs outside the city, where the priests of the Imperator conducted their horrid rituals. She had no time to investigate to confirm her suspicion, but the observed use of the postern gate gave her confidence in her looming ruse.

Weapons in hand and positioned with her back to the wall, close to the door, Rayden waited.

A little deeper into the night, the scrape of a door being pulled open rose into the air, accompanied with the metallic creaking of hinges.

The iron-banded postern, made of thick, timber planks, swung inward, opening wide. A couple of robed priests stepped forward from the dark portal. Neither took notice of Rayden, pressed flat against the wall to their left in the shadows.

"We will return before morning's light," one of the priests said to someone out of Rayden's sight, standing within the portal.

"You risk much," the one in the portal said, with the gruff tone of a soldier. "Marus' camp is not over the Catacombs."

"The barbarians would never find us in the vast labyrinth and our work must continue," the priest replied in a boastful voice.

"I would not want to tread there," the guard replied in a curt manner. "I will be here to see you in before morning's light."

The two priests nodded to the guard and started forward, striding away from the walls. A part of Rayden desired to cut them down, but she could not risk a cry going up that would alert the guards on the walls and towers.

Rayden waited until the priests had disappeared from sight before putting up her weapons and walking up to the door. Rapping her knuckles hard on the rough wooden planks, she listened for a response.

"Who knocks?" the voice of the guard came from the other side, after a few heartbeats had passed.

"An Alettani scout, I used the Catacomb tunnel to get here," Rayden called back. "I have word from Marus' camp that needs to be conveyed at once."

"Do you have a mark?" the guard asked.

"Yes," Rayden answered.

Out of a pouch at her waist, Rayden took up one of the inscribed wooden pieces that she had found on the bodies of the enemy warriors that had attacked her when she had been observing Marus' encampment. Recognizing what the wooden pieces signified, she had kept them safe, conserving them for a moment like the one at hand.

The door opened and a Teveren soldier in helm and cuirass stepped out. Another stood in the doorway. Both eyed her with great wariness.

Rayden extended her hand with the wooden mark resting in her palm.

The soldier standing in front of Rayden took the mark and eyed it close.

Nodding, he said to her, "This is authentic. We did not expect any scouts tonight. Follow us."

He turned to enter the postern.

Rayden slipped out her sword, out of the eyesight of the

second guard in the doorway.

Skirting her sword around the neck of the guard who had his back to her, fast and precise, Rayden ripped the freshly honed blade back, cutting his throat wide open.

In a continuum of movement, Rayden stepped past the dying guard and brought the bloodied sword blade rushing upward, catching the second soldier by surprise and driving the sharp end through the soft skin beneath his chin.

Eyes wide, he flailed for a moment, gurgling on the honed iron skewering him. Yanking downward, Rayden tore the weapon free before the Teveren slumped to the ground. A final, rattling gasp escaped the soldier's mouth before he became still.

Rayden cleaned her blade off on the dead man's tunic and returned the weapon to its sheath. She then pulled the body of the first soldier through the doorway, dragging the corpse alongside the other before letting go.

Turning back, she closed the postern and set a bar in place to keep it shut.

In the darkness, Rayden found the base of a flight of steps heading upward. Keeping her footfalls soft, she ascended them, listening carefully for any hint of other soldiers.

Reaching the top without incident, Rayden found herself in a small chamber, dimly lit from a copper oil lamp set in one corner. Some bone dice lay on a cloak where they displayed the result of their last roll.

Walking over to a door to the outside, Rayden listened for a moment and heard nothing to indicate the presence of anyone close. Maintaining caution, she opened the door partway and peered outward.

A short stretch of open ground separated her from an elongated building, likely a storehouse belonging to one of the wealthy merchants desiring closer proximity to the Eagle Gate.

Higher above, a couple of guards strolled along the wall-walk, close to the tower. They would be the most likely to see her, so Rayden delayed until they had their backs to her before she departed the chamber and headed across the open ground.

Though keeping her stride long, Rayden did not sprint. A fast, sudden burst of motion more likely to attract unwanted attention, she walked as if she belonged within the city.

No outcry erupted from behind her. Reaching the building, Rayden lost herself within the shadows and began making her way to the tenement where she expected Polybius, Doros, and Crassor to be staying.

The city slumbered under a deeper hush than usual. Rayden noticed far fewer signs of the nocturnal wagon and cart traffic that normally took place in the streets at night. A couple of large rats scuttled across her path, just ahead of her.

The lack of activity cast an eerie edge to the prevailing atmosphere.

When she reached the tenement, the doorman on guard recognized her.

"I have not seen you in some time," he remarked when she walked up.

"I have kept to our apartments at night, for the most part," she replied, keeping her tone amiable.

He nodded, looking grim. "Life will not be the same until the barbarians are driven off. They are even reducing the number of contests at the games."

"A siege affects us all," Rayden responded.

"Aye, it does, and may it soon be over," the man agreed, an edge of weariness to his voice while stepping aside to allow her entrance.

Walking past him, Rayden made her way up to the apartments that Polybius had secured. Balling her fist up, she delivered a few thudding knocks to the front door.

"Who comes this late at night?" Polybius' voice called from

the other side.

"A friend who has returned," Rayden answered.

The door flung wide open a moment later.

"Rayden!" Polybius exclaimed.

Behind him, holding weapons in their hands, stood Crassor and Doros. Both relaxed at the sight of her and lowered their arms.

"You do not need to greet me with those," Rayden jested, glancing at the others' blades.

"We have missed you," Doros stated, a beaming smile on her face.

"It has been far from exciting without you around," Crassor said, grinning.

Rayden entered the apartment and Polybius closed the door behind her. Heart gladdened at the sight of her friends, she proceeded to give each of them tight, extended embraces.

"I am guessing this is not a casual visit," Polybius remarked, after she had finished hugging him.

"The time has come for us to take the city," Rayden announced to the others, growing serious.

"I am guessing that you have much to tell us," Doros replied with a solemn mien.

Rayden nodded.

"Then let us sit at table and have some wine," Polybius said.

The group proceeded into the room to the left of the entrance. Polybius set about getting cups and filling them with wine as the others took places on the stools by the table.

Rayden drained about half of her cup on the first drink, savoring the robust, fruity taste. Polybius finished up and took a seat to her right.

The other three gave Rayden their full, undivided attention as she related all of the things that had happened since they had parted.

Rayden described her journey to the Mist Vale, including her experience within the Catacombs prior to going there. She told them of the harrowing walk down the middle of the stream, pursued on both sides by malevolent fae, and how that led to the idea of raising double walls to protect the northern tribes besieging the Imperial City.

Talking at length of the fighting outside the city walls, she spoke of the arrival of the Teveren fleet and the Kartajenian one that had appeared later to assail the enemy vessels. All three of her companions widened their eyes as she described the mysterious, anomalous storm that had manifested and shattered the Kartajenian fleet.

Rayden then explained her plan for the morning, to open the Eagle Gate and let the warriors of the northern tribes into the Imperial City.

***

With dawn about to break across the eastern horizon, the time had come to head forth and open the city.

A frigid bite clinging to the air, the streets and hills outside lay shrouded in dense fog. Scattered hints of the urban colossus cloaked beneath, the tops of statues and buildings poked through the surface of the drifting, vaporous mass.

Eyes gleaming in the firelight from a small charcoal brazier, Rayden stared into the eyes of Doros and Crassor. Not a single word passed between them, but a question had to be answered.

What she saw reflected within their gazes left her with no doubts of their resolve to carry through the bold strike that they had decided upon.

"This siege ends today," Rayden told them.

"So does the rule of that scum they call the Imperator," Crassor replied, his face darkened in anger. "I swear by all the gods that when nightfall comes my blade will be soaked in

Teveren blood."

"The city must be taken first, and the tribes must not visit the evils of the rulers upon the people," Rayden said. "That includes you, Crassor."

"When you unleash a fire, how will you seek to control it?" Crassor asked her, glowering.

"The thousands upon thousands crammed into those filthy tenements do not own slaves, and never have," Rayden countered him. "They labor for enough bread to last from one day to the next. Their children are sent to bleed and die for those whose granaries and coin pouches are full.

"Many within your own ranks came from those slums and sold themselves into slavery. Do not visit even more suffering upon them than they will face with the collapse of the city."

Crassor stared at her for a moment but said nothing. An uncertain look crept into his eyes, and Rayden knew that her words had resonated with him.

"The fire within you comes from a righteous anger," Rayden continued, her tone softening. "Keep that fire channeled and use it to hold the wicked to account. In doing so, your blade will yet slake its thirst."

"It is so quiet out there ... so peaceful," Doros observed, standing a couple paces away and gazing across the city. "It is difficult to think that great bloodshed will take place here, in these streets, this very day."

"It is the last light of the open sky, before a great storm rolls in," Rayden stated.

For far too many on both sides, that approaching storm would spell the end of their lives.

Thinking on that harsh truth, Rayden could not allow her heart to grow heavy; at least not until the day at hand had concluded. There would be time enough for contending with the sorrows and horrors of war later.

For now, the Imperator had to be overthrown, or a malignant darkness would be allowed to grow, spread, and inflict untold suffering upon the people of many lands.

Rayden stepped over to Doros' side and joined her in looking out toward the north.

Somewhere beyond the wall, concealed within the vast sea of fog, thousands upon thousands of others were waking up from slumber and readying to confront the fears and hopes contending within them.

Alcedan and all of the Gessa, Annocrates and Hamilcar, Erethea, Ammanus, and so many more that Rayden cared about were preparing themselves out there, between the lengthy earthen ramparts. All of them depended on her to tip the balance in the fighting that day and help bring the long, blood-soaked struggle to an end.

She could only hope that the tribal chieftains had deployed a force large enough to be a viable threat outside the southern walls of the city. With no way of knowing whether the force was in place, or if the Teverens had shifted significant numbers of soldiers to the southern walls to confront it, Rayden could not worry herself with what she could not control.

Nevertheless, she knew that if large numbers of Teverens were not drawn away to the south of the city, everything that she did could be for naught.

Even then, other concerns beyond her control nagged at her mind. Not even a hint of the fae from the Mist Vale had manifested, and Rayden knew that the Imperator's sorcerers lay in wait, having prepared something fearsome and unprecedented to release upon the tribal people.

"It is time to go," Rayden declared in a low voice, forcing the lingering worries aside.

Turning away from the window, she set her eyes on Polybius, who stood quietly watching the others.

Walking up to him, Rayden clasped Polybius about the forearm. She held the grip in place for several moments and looked him direct in the eyes.

"Keep this door shut and stay here," Rayden instructed him. "Lay low. Do not go out until we send someone for you. None can predict the passions burning in the hearts of those wronged and set loose within the domain of the wrongdoers."

"I am willing to fight," Polybius replied with an edge of protest.

"You are willing to die for us ... you have already shown that," Rayden told him, giving the words an intonation of praise.

"I am, Rayden," Polybius responded, a sheen of emotion reflecting within his eyes.

"You have shown courage matching that of the greatest of warriors," Rayden told him. "You have done everything asked of you, and we could not have achieved all that we have without you. None of us will forget that."

Polybius asked her, "Then why must I stay huddled down here, in this place of wealth and comfort, while you and the others risk yourselves and fight to free everyone from the monstrosities that we have all witnessed?"

"In this war, we all have our places," Rayden replied. "We go this morning to attempt a task that will demand everything we have in our skill at arms and physical abilities. You know that Crassor, Doros, and I have had to hold back several times and let your wit and skills in interacting with people take the forefront. Now it is time for our skills to take the forefront and for you to hold back. Do you understand this?"

Polybius nodded, but frustration and sadness remained thick within his eyes and expression. "I wish that I had the skills to go with you this morning and stand at your side. It has been an honor to be a part of this journey with you."

Rayden smiled. "It has been an honor to stand at your side,

Polybius. Our journey has seen you weighed and measured ... and you can rest knowing you are among the best of men."

"You have my heartfelt gratitude, Rayden," he replied, looking awestruck at her words.

"It is no gift," Rayden replied, grinning. "Your actions have spoken of the man that you are."

Reaching out, she patted him on the left shoulder in the manner of a comrade. "So, lay low, keep safe, and may we both endure the day to come and see each other once more when all is done. Then, we shall drink more wine together than we can handle."

"That sounds wonderful, Rayden," Polybius replied, a smile coming to his face.

After giving him one last embrace, Rayden parted from Polybius and returned her attention to the others. She could only hope that her words would sooth the hurt and frustration that she sensed in the one person of their number who would remain behind.

Rayden looked to Doros and Crassor one more time, and stated, "Let us go forth and see that gate opened!"

Determined expressions etched upon their faces, the other two nodded back. Rayden led them out the front door of the apartments.

***

Stepping out of the tenement and into the street, Rayden led her companions to the north, heading toward the Eagle Gate. Visibility reduced to little more than a few steps ahead by the mists still clinging to air around them, she had to make certain that they followed a stone-paved course.

Weapons in hand, the trio shed all pretenses of the roles they had assumed when first entering the city. No longer did Rayden and Doros stand in the guise of Alettani warriors, and nor did Crassor assume his former slave status.

All three stood as implacable enemies of the Imperator and the malignant empire that he had built.

Due to the siege and early stage of the morning, they encountered very few people on the streets. Only a couple of individuals heading about their business paid them any heed, and neither looked to have any interest beyond mere curiosity.

Then, a most welcome array of sounds came from ahead. Metallic clinks and the thudding of a great multitude of footsteps filled the air.

Rayden recognized the noises at once.

"To the side!" Rayden told the others in a low voice, hurrying back to the mouth of an alley that they had just passed, on the right side of the street.

Crassor having the most Teveren appearance, Rayden put him in the front as the trio pressed against the walls of the narrow alley.

Shortly afterward, their standards held high at the forefront, Teveren soldiers in a cohesive formation marched past the alley.

Rank after rank in gleaming helms and cuirasses stepped in rhythm. Bearing rectangular shields and carrying their distinctive style of spear, the Teveren soldiers had their medium-length blades sheathed in scabbards at their waists.

Rayden did her best to estimate the size of the Teveren force marching past them. She knew that well over five thousand soldiers had tromped past the alleyway when the end of the dense ranks finally crossed through her view.

The sight of the force told her one thing; the tribes given the task of mustering outside the southern walls had succeeded.

At least five thousand fewer soldiers would be able to respond to a sudden influx of northern warriors through the Eagle Gate.

Clasping Doros and Crassor on the shoulder, Rayden could

see the same realization on their faces.

They remained in place until the low rumble of the marching soldiers faded down the street. Then, the three warriors stepped out from the alley and continued on their way.

The lingering mist afforded them cover the rest of the way to the Eagle Gate, but Rayden quickened their pace, knowing they did not have much time remaining before the fog lifted.

When they neared the Eagle Gate, Rayden angled for the tower to the right of the double-arch gateway. A lioness encroaching on her prey, she slowed and kept every step silent, focused and ready to spring forward in an instant.

The door at the base of the tower drew close.

Glancing back to Doros and Crassor, she whispered, "Kill fast."

Rayden pushed the door open.

Death fell upon the quartet of soldiers inside before they could raise an outcry.

Eyes wide with shock had only an instant to register the sight of the three lethal figures wielding blades in savage fury. Throats and bellies slashed wide open, copious amounts of blood gushed out of the stricken men crumpling to the floor.

Rayden made her way up the staircase at the back of the ground-level chamber, followed by Crassor and Doros. Behind them, blood spread outward from the bodies strewn about the floor.

Entering another open chamber, Rayden looked around and came to a stop. She motioned for Doros and Crassor to stay in place, to ward the doors set on either side of the tower leading onto the wall-walk.

Rayden then continued up to the highest point, finding a short flight of steps leading to the top of the tower. A wooden trap door lay open and the low voices of two men could be heard just beyond it.

Making no sound, Rayden surmounted the steps and came up from behind the pair of guards staring outward. Neither had an inkling of her presence, until her blades tore their necks open, cutting off any calls of alarm.

Rayden eyed the wall-walk spanning the towers flanking the gate, in addition to the other tower. Two guards could be seen on the wall-walk, with another two directly across from her.

Keeping a low profile, she proceeded back down through the trap door.

"It is clear above us," she whispered to her companions, who stood near the door to the section of wall-walk between the towers. "Two guards on the wall, and two more atop the next tower. Give me a moment."

Rayden crossed through the chamber and slid a bolt into place on the other door, opening to the wall-walk running away from the gate area.

Returning, Rayden took her place at the forefront of the three warriors.

Pausing a moment to let Crassor and Doros to situate themselves, Rayden prepared to open the door leading onto the wall-walk.

Opening the door and raising her weapons, Rayden darted forward.

Moments later, two dead Teverens lay on the wall-walk.

Entering the other tower without delay, Rayden headed up to the top. Using stealth once more, she took the two guards there by surprise, bringing them down in rapid succession.

Again, neither of the Teverens got off a single cry.

Looking around, Rayden could see farther down the walls and deeper into the ground beyond. With the fog lifting, she had little time remaining to finish her task.

Rayden then hurried down into the chamber with the doors accessing the wall-walk. She took a few moments to lock the one that could have allowed Teveren soldiers coming from other areas of the wall to enter the second tower.

Then, she descended with Crassor and Doros through the rest of the tower, continuing down to the chamber on the ground level. Four guards engaged in some early morning banter found themselves taken unaware and cut down swiftly.

Catching her breath and standing in the middle of the chamber, dead Teverens lying at her feet, Rayden looked to her companions. "The gate is no longer guarded. Now is the time to open it!"

"And take this city!" Crassor added, his eyes churning with rage.

Rayden nodded to Crassor. "It is time to take this city!"

Leading the other two outside the tower, Rayden strode around to the gate.

***

After removing the interior bars from their brackets, with no one around to contest the effort, Rayden, Doros, and Crassor pulled one of the heavy, iron-banded, timber gates open.

Then, they opened the other.

The entrance to the Imperial City stood wide open, undefended.

Walking a few strides out from the pair of gates, Rayden took up a horn from a pouch at her side. Filling her lungs to capacity with the fresh morning air, Rayden sounded a long, deep blast through it.

Outside the walls, the dissipating fog had been unveiling a sight that elated Rayden. The same vision prompted horns of alarm to erupt from numerous points along the walls.

A vast multitude of tribal warriors, many brandishing their weapons, pounding on shields, and shouting war cries, stood not far from the walls.

At Rayden's horn blast, a swelling roar erupted from the northern tribes. A host of war horns sounded in response.

In a vast wave, the warriors of the north surged toward the Teveren walls and began funneling toward the Eagle Gate.

***

A smattering of Teveren soldiers responding to the horns on the walls beheld a torrent of tribal warriors pouring into the city through the undefended Eagle Gate. Those on the walls ran away from the massive influx, the Teveren soldiers making use of both wall-walks and interior channels to escape the vicinity.

Rayden, Crassor, and Doros joined the advance into the city. In a great flood, thousands of tribal warriors swarmed the streets and alleyways of the Imperial City.

A ravenous beast set free of its cage, the northern host fell upon the wealthier sector of the city with great ferocity.

The contingent of warriors who had once been Teveren slaves rushed forward at the spearhead of the invading masses. Little time passed before the northerners began breaking down the doors to larger domiciles.

Screams of terror and wailing from those who had been haughty, ruthless masters and mistresses only a day before began rising into the air. Those who staunchly refused mercy to others now pleaded for it.

In many of the dwellings, those who had lived and suffered in bondage rose up against their owners, shedding the scourge of enslavement in their first moments of rebellion.

Rayden bounded down the streets with Crassor and Doros not far behind her. She knew that she had to reach a certain tenement before the oncoming horde stormed through the area.

The tenements, shops, shrines, and other structures that she passed stood still and silent. She knew that behind the closed doors and shuttered windows men, women, and children huddled together, hoping and praying for the martial tempest to pass over them.

At last, Rayden reached the tenement that had served as her quarters within the city. The door into it had been closed and locked.

Rayden backed up and ran at the door, leaping into the air and delivering a heavy kick that broke it partway off its hinges. Before she could make another attempt, Crassor charged up from behind and sent another kick barreling into the door, breaking it loose from its remaining hinges.

Rayden and Crassor shoved the broken door aside and entered. Taking the lead, Rayden sprinted up the stairs and ran to the doorway that she had come to know well over many days.

Pounding a specific cadence on the wood, using her fist, she waited.

After a short, pensive delay, the door opened. Polybius stood on the other side with a dagger gripped in his right hand.

Relief flooded his face, and not a little disbelief flickered within his eyes.

"I thought I was to lay low," he said.

"I decided it would be best if I came to get you myself," Rayden replied, giving him a brief smile. "We are not far ahead of the others."

Already, the cacophony that had been following Rayden drew nearer, signaling the arrival of the brushfire that had been set loose inside the imperiled city.

"Stay close," Rayden told Polybius.

The look on his face told her that he would need no reminding.

Rayden at their lead, the quartet headed down to the street.

With no Teveren soldiers defending the immediate area, the homes of the wealthy Teverens became sites of pillaging and looting.

Moving down the street, Rayden eyed more than one scene of revenge.

To one side, several young women held an older woman down, tearing her garments off until she lay naked. From the younger women's anger and curses, Rayden did not doubt the older women to be a harsh former mistress.

On the right, several men caught up to a heavy-set man trying to run from them. He shrieked as they pulled him down and began raining blows on him.

Large throngs of tribal warriors hurried past, shouting war cries and heading deeper into the city.

***

Standing atop the large Wolf Gate on the city's eastern side, Rayden eyed another mass of tribal warriors flooding into the city. To her right, Alcedan observed the warriors with a look of great concentration.

It had not been easy to find him within the swirling maelstrom, but the presence of large numbers of Gessa warriors had helped to guide her. Crassor and Doros stood a few paces away, eyeing the thousands more that were now entering the fray.

Inside the walls, everywhere that Rayden looked, smoke columns of all sizes spiraled into the air. A widespread din created from a multitude of cries, shouts, curses, screams, and other vocal elements accompanied the growing multitude of fires.

"A large force of Teverens has taken up positions near the southern part of the wall," Alcedan stated, a few moments later. "All others that could get away from us have fled into their fortress, in the northeastern part of the city. A strong force yet remains there."

"What of the gates on the city's western side?" Rayden asked.

"The River Gate is open," Alcedan said. "Only those who mustered outside the southern walls now await entrance into the city."

"Their presence has helped keep the enemy in place there," Rayden said. "We will need to regroup the warriors within the city before they run into the Teverens there, or they will be cut down fast."

"Grogner and Belgra have begun massing close to them," Alcedan replied, glancing over to her.

"Any sign of Marus yet?" Rayden asked.

Alcedan shook his head. "The last word brought to me indicated that he still holds back. He has been heavily bloodied, and it is likely he knows of the Kartajenians on our ramparts."

"He does not wish to get showered with their arrows and ours, most likely," Rayden commented. "Marus will know that the Kartajenians are survivors from their fleet, and the soldiers who fight upon their vessels are well-known to be deadly with a bow."

"That is what I think," Alcedan replied, nodding.

Rayden looked away, watching the sprawling forest of smoke columns winding their way upward. She thought of Ingassa, the woman who had proved to be a strong wrestling opponent on the day Rayden had visited the baths.

Ingassa and vast multitudes stood at great risk now. The incoming tribal warriors expected loot after all the hardship and blood that had been spilled in gaining the city.

All efforts would be made to direct the brunt of the pillaging toward the wealthier area of the city. But no tribal leader could entirely restrain the emotions and tempers of warriors who had gone hungry, lost comrades, and risked their lives many times during the long, arduous campaign.

Turning away from Alcedan and the others, Rayden whispered a prayer to any god that would listen to protect Ingassa and those like her. She asked that the conquering wave would pass over the heavily populated tenements that held so little in the way of material value.

"What would you counsel now?" Alcedan asked her.

Looking back to the Gessa chieftain, Rayden said, "Let us go finish off the Teverens gathered to the south. Then, our main quarry will be cornered."

***

Coiling around the Teverens, throngs of tribal warriors filled the wall-walk along the southern wall of the city. The large Dragon Gate remained closed, but a smaller one farther down the wall toward the eastern side had been opened.

The tribal contingents massed outside since the break of day had entered, adding their number to the swelling multitude that now had the Teverens effectively trapped.

Rayden stood alongside the warriors of the Gessa when the attack commenced.

Volleys of javelins and arrows rained down on the Teverens from all sides. A living fortress under overlapping shields, the Teveren soldiers weathered most of the missile storm.

Following the barrage, warriors rushed at the Teverens from three sides, their charge ending in a thunderous clash. Weapons clanged and thudded into shields, and blood began to flow from both the northerners and the Teverens.

Well-suited to fighting in close confines using their medium-length blades, the Teverens held their ground. Though buckling in a few places, they kept their formations intact.

Rayden used the bottom of her axe to hook over the top of a Teveren shield and yanked downward. Thrusting her sword into the opening, she caught the soldier in the mouth and drove the blade through the back of his neck.

Ripping the blade free, she sent her axe down low to the side, chopping into the ankle of the Teveren to the left of the one she had just felled.

Howling in agony, the soldier collapsed to the ground, unable to support his weight on his left leg.

The opening that Rayden created widened in moments, as other tribal warriors exploited the fissure and carved their way farther inward.

Horn signals within the Teveren ranks prompted a coordinated movement. The taut ranks began tromping forward, heading north and filling more than one of the narrow streets ahead of them.

Fighting her way free of the pocket about to envelop her, Rayden joined with the other warriors in harrying the enemy soldiers.

Warriors racing farther ahead of the Teverens made their way to the rooftops of tenements and other buildings. Hurling down whatever they could lay their hands on, and throwing javelins, they menaced the Teverens from above.

With the Teverens filling streets from side to side, the tribal warriors had to strike from ahead, behind, the mouths of alleys, and intersections.

Suffering casualties along the way, the Teverens maintained discipline and kept pushing north.

Running down a street to get ahead of the enemy's forefront once more, Rayden broke into an open space covered in grass, trees, and fountains.

A surge of light from a fountain to her right distracted Rayden, bringing her to a halt. Whirling about, she raised her weapons and took up a fighting stance.

Perched atop a sculpture of an elegant horse, sleek with flowing lines of muscle, a bright, winged form faced in her direction.

Rayden's eyes widened.

"What is it?" a tribal warrior called out to Rayden as he ran past, before slowing down and looking back to her.

"Go on, I will rejoin all of you!" Rayden shouted back to the warrior and a few others that had slowed.

The warriors nodded to her and loped ahead, taking no notice of the figure that had grabbed Rayden's attention.

Rayden strode toward the light-radiating form. Details taking shape, the features of Muirithesos emerged as the radiance ebbed.

"We are here," Muirithesos declared in her melodious voice.

"I have looked for you in the dark, each night," Rayden told the faery, a little frustration coursing through her words. "The battle rages, but their sorcerers have not yet brought forth whatever they have prepared."

"It is close, and I fear that we cannot stop it," Muirithesos replied, her face grim. "We have found their power unassailable, until they have expended it. Many of our kind have fallen already."

The queen's words troubled Rayden. Looking away from the queen, Rayden gazed toward the sounds of fighting in the streets.

"Then we can only brace for the storm to come and strive to weather its might," Rayden replied in a low voice, resisting the despair seeking to work its tendrils into her.

"It is all that we can do," the queen said. "After they have used their power, they will be weakened, and we will have a chance to strike them."

Casting her gaze far beyond the sounds of battle, Rayden asked, "Will it be too late then?"

"I do not know," the queen answered.

Fighting back an onslaught of dismay at the queen's uncertainty, Rayden looked back to her. "The battle yet rages. I must rejoin the others."

Setting her mind firm and turning away, Rayden did not wait for a response. Sprinting across the grass, she raced towards the din of cries, screams, and clashing of weapons.

***

Using the streets to their advantage, the Teverens that had mustered in the south fought their way back to the fortress in the northeastern part of the city. Well over half of the force that had marched early that morning to the southern walls returned intact enough to continue fighting.

The concentration of Teveren soldiers at the fortress and slopes of the hill where the Imperial palace loomed prevented the masses of tribal warriors from advancing. Flurries of arrows kept the northerners at bay, and orderly ranks higher on the slope of the hill presented a living bulwark that would be difficult to overwhelm.

The northern warriors soon began gathering near the fortress and base of the hill.

Rayden eyed the lavish buildings on the hill's summit, wondering what the Imperator intended to do. A strange, unsettling calm settled over the area with the respite in the fighting.

Collecting her thoughts, Rayden strode away from the impasse. Stopping to wipe her blades clean on the tunic of a dead Teveren soldier, she returned the weapons to her waist.

Finding a tavern at the head of a street lined with tenements, she came upon a number of warriors helping themselves to the food and drink remaining in the establishment.

Taking up a cup of wine and a ragged chunk of bread off one of the tables, Rayden softened the latter with the former. Sitting quietly on a stool, she chewed and sipped, waiting, though she did not know for what.

She only knew that the Imperator would not take well to being trapped for long.

Rayden welcomed the bread and wine, along with some olives scrounged up from behind the long counter at the front.

Giving her body a little rest, she let the sustenance replenish her depleted energies.

When finished, Rayden walked back into the street. A sense of unease growing within her, she began making her way back toward the warriors massing near the Teverens' stronghold and the great hill with the Imperial palace.

Crossing through a stone-surfaced expanse filled with statues on columns, fountains, and lined on two sides by continuous arcades, Rayden drew to a halt as anxious cries started to break out all around her.

"A dark sun!" a man shouted, pointing upward. "Look!"

Rayden raised her head toward the skies and set her eyes upon an extraordinary sight, one that filled her heart with dread.

***

The midday sun reaching its zenith, an astounding phenomenon unfolded before all eyes within the Imperial City. Rising in the west, a large, pitch-black orb ascended into the heavens.

Rivaling the size of the sun from the ground's perspective, the dark orb's presence accompanied a bizarre development. As if the sphere cast rays to contend with those of the sun, a gray pall fell across the city, like that from an overcast sky.

Hackles raising all along on her neck, Rayden watched the developing phenomenon in an uneasy silence. Though she could not yet fathom the nature of the dark sphere, she had no doubt of it being a harbinger to something horrific.

Another storm of the type that had thrashed the Kartajen fleet then manifested in the wake of the dark sun's rise, blackening the skies once more. Rayden moved over to one of the columns supporting the arcade, gaining some shelter beneath while she continued to observe the transforming skies.

Thunder snarled within the dark masses of vapors spreading to all horizons. Lightning flashed across the underbelly of the growing cloud mass, illuminating the anxious faces of warriors looking upon the sensational developments in states of astonishment and fear.

Powerful winds began ripping through the area, prompting Rayden to reach out and brace herself against the marble column.

Then, to Rayden's amazement, the ferocity of the winds, thunder, and lightning ebbed. Further, the black skies reseeded in their intensity, dissipating into a drab, featureless gray.

Yet no cloud masses caused the dimmer, gray ambiance.

Where the sun had been, the dark orb now reigned supreme, casting forth its mockery of light. In a manner of speaking, the orb radiated darkness.

Rayden did not know what to make of the incredible spectacle. Something of tremendous power had just been unleashed, but it would take a different form than the furious tempest that had reduced the Kartajenian fleet to shards and splinters.

A freezing cold permeated the air. Rayden shivered as an icy gust passed over her body.

Alarmed cries rose in every direction, heralding yet another surreal development, one that took place on the ground instead of the skies.

Rayden shifted to the left to avoid a throng of large rats scuttling across the stone by her. Hundreds upon hundreds of the rodents scampered through the stone-paved area, paying no heed to the humans hastening to avoid contact with them.

Looking around, Rayden saw more of the creatures coming from all around, heading toward the streets that she had just come from.

Deciding to follow her intuition and the path of the rats, Rayden trotted out from the arcade and shadowed the flow of the creatures. Entering the streets passing through the tenements and shops of merchants and artisans, Rayden took up her axe, but none of the creatures paid her the slightest attention.

All moved with a singular purpose.

It appeared that the vermin were emerging from every building, nook, and crevice. More astonishing, they all looked to be swarming in the same direction, following some call or summons that Rayden could not hear.

Curiosity growing fast, Rayden continued along in the direction that the masses of rats flowed in. Their numbers continued swelling as more and more joined the thickening channel.

Thousands and thousands of rats scurrying forward in her view, Rayden found the River Gate looming just ahead of her. All over, tribal warriors kept a wide berth, looking upon the vast, skittering horde with wide eyes and distressed expressions.

Staying to the side of the rats, Rayden jogged along, fearing nothing from the creatures. She could see they had a dedicated aim, though what it might be yet eluded her.

The vanguard of the rodent horde reached the shoreline, farther ahead of Rayden. Giving no pause, the rats charged into the water, followed by those coming up from behind.

Rayden slowed a short distance past the River Gate and watched the bizarre development. The creatures showed no hesitation in plunging into the waters of the Golden River.

Even stranger, they made no effort to remain at the surface and swim, an ability that Rayden had observed numerous times in their tenacious kind.

Rather, the creatures disappeared beneath the surface.

Unable to make any sense of the rats' peculiar behavior, Rayden could only watch from a distance.

A few black amorphous shapes began rising from the surface of the river in the area where the dense waves of rats had drowned themselves. Others dark forms followed, the numbers escalating until multitudes of the ethereal entities were climbing skyward like so many wisps of black smoke.

Once the dark forms had attained a great height, the wraiths began drifting toward the Imperial City.

The sight reminded Rayden of her encounter with the crazed figure and the marsekkels on her return from the Mist Vale, in addition to the vivid dreams that she had experienced during her journey.

Ignoring the rats that continued running out from the city towards the river, Rayden passed back through the River Gate. Making her way north, she now followed the course of the wraiths above.

Striding fast, Rayden soon found herself in the open ground beyond the Eagle Gate, where her day had begun.

On the horizon, the wraiths began converging above an area farther to the northeast.

A cold sensation filled Rayden.

She knew what lay beneath the dark, swirling forms.

The wraiths were gathering over the entrances to the Catacombs.

Like a surreal, black rain, the condensed mass of wraiths, thousands upon thousands in number, began descending toward the ground.

***

"Rayden!" the voice of Crassor called from behind her.

Turning, Rayden saw Crassor and Doros striding toward her.

Doros shouted, "We saw you heading to the Eagle Gate! What is happening?"

"To the top of the walls!" Rayden called back to them. "We must gain a higher vantage!"

Springing into motion, Rayden raced back toward the Eagle Gate. Once she passed through, she turned to the right, ignoring the calls from Doros and Crassor behind her.

The guards they had slain still lay where they had fallen that morning. Feet pounding against the steps, she hurried up the tower.

Reaching the chamber with the doors to the wall-walk, she saw that they had been opened. Rayden hurried left, passing through the door ahead onto the section of wall running between the towers flanking the Eagle Gate.

The cold winds blowing through her hair, Rayden peered outward, casting her gaze in the direction of the Catacombs.

So many wraiths now streamed toward the ground that it looked like a dark mist was falling from the skies.

"What ... in the name ... of the gods ... is going on?" Crassor asked her, gulping in breaths of air as he emerged from the tower doorway onto the wall-walk.

Chest heaving, Doros walked through the doorway after him. She came over to stand on the other side of Rayden and looked to the northeast.

"This is not over," Rayden stated, glancing to her companions. "Far from it."

"We have beaten them," Crassor responded, a scowl forming on his face. "The last of the Teverens are cornered, and we are about to finish them off."

"Not yet," Rayden replied, watching the last of the hordes of wraiths descending out of view.

"Their storm failed!" Crassor exclaimed. "We all saw it form, and then it stopped. They used their power on the Kartajenian vessels. They had no more to wield."

"Those little black vapors are just the remnants of their attempt," Doros said.

"No, this is something much different ... and far more powerful than the storm that wrecked the Kartajenian ships," Rayden told the other two. "This is what they have been gathering such great amounts of dark power for."

A look of great unease grew upon both of their faces.

A moment later, Rayden and the others found themselves jostled as the ground shook and rumbled.

Keeping her footing, Rayden swayed with the powerful tremors.

"An earthquake!" Doros exclaimed. "It could bring the walls down!"

The violent tremors then ebbed and ceased.

"An ill omen," Rayden stated, her expression becoming grave.

"Was that the intent of their sorcery?" Doros asked. "An earthquake?"

"Then it failed, the walls yet stand," Crassor stated, glowering.

A grim expression on her face, Rayden shook her head. "It was not intended to bring the walls down. It was a signal ... of something that is about to be unveiled."

"Something that does not bode well for any of us, I am guessing," Doros responded, frowning.

"Something of the depths of the abyss is coming," Rayden replied, trying to think of what hellish action the Imperator and his servants could be about.

The Catacombs were the place where the servants of the abyssal powers performed their dark rituals, so it stood to reason that it would be the place where the vast host of wraiths would concentrate.

A place teeming with death, the Catacombs presented an ideal site for the kind of diablerie that the Imperator's sorcerers would be engaged in. But it remained to be seen what form their wickedness would take.

All that Rayden did know in her heart was that it would be massive in nature; powerful enough to be a threat to all who had dared to fight and take a stand against the Imperator that day.

***

After some time had passed, a distant, deep-pitched moaning took hold at the farthest edge of Rayden's hearing. Concentrating on the new sound, she listened carefully.

Before much longer, she could tell that the strange noise was increasing in volume.

At last, the others began taking notice of the unsettling manifestation.

"What is that damnable sound?" Crassor asked, staring toward the northeast.

Unease filling her gut, Rayden gazed outward, listening to the incessant groaning carried along the frigid winds.

"I have never heard the like," Doros remarked, a look of dread forming across her face.

In the distance, far beyond the ramparts of the northern tribes, a shadowy line drew into view, creeping slowly forward.

Once more, Rayden thought of the night that she had encountered the crazed man and the marsekkels. She then thought of the Catacombs and what they contained.

Everything came to her at once.

"All of those left within the ramparts have to come into the city!" Rayden shouted, springing into motion. "Follow me! Every moment counts!"

Hurrying down the tower from the wall-walk, she ran outside and continued through the Eagle Gate. Once beyond the entryway, Rayden bounded across the ground toward the earthen ramparts.

Cold gusts lashed at her body and layers of gray clouds above drifted faster. Oriented in her direction, a few heads came into view along the top of the wall-walk.

The moaning in the distance grew a little louder, increasing the sense of urgency churning within Rayden.

Nearing the outer ditch, Rayden slowed and looked toward the spear-bearing warriors that had gathered to watch her approach.

"Get everyone out of the ramparts and take them into the city!" Rayden called out to the warriors. "Signal the others. Do not delay, or it will mean your deaths!"

"Is the fighting done?" one of the men shouted back, a confused look on his face.

Rayden shook her head. "No, but you are about to be overrun. Leave everything and come into the city! There is no time!"

"She speaks the truth!" Crassor yelled, having run up from behind her. "Get everyone out of there."

Rayden shouted, "A sea of the dead advances upon you now! From the north!"

The deep, resonant din swelled a bit louder.

The men along the wall-walk looked to each other with uneasy countenances. A few of them cast their gazes in the direction of the eerie sound.

Rayden charged across a wood-plank spanning the trench and continued through an opening in the rampart. Making her way across to the opposite rampart, she found a short flight of steps up to the wall-walk.

Once Rayden had reached the wall-walk, she looked toward the northeast.

Her words to the men on the wall-walk described the scene that met her eyes well enough.

It looked as if a dark sea was approaching the double ramparts, the forefront of the incoming tide drawing closer to the outer ditch, farther down to the right. Warriors gathered along the wall-walk there had begun to flee, shouting to all around them.

Along with the horrid groaning sound, the winds carried

the distinctive, pungent scent of death and decay.

Eyeing the shambling, shuffling multitudes, Rayden knew that no ditch would stop them from swarming the ramparts and falling upon the most vulnerable from all the tribes.

Horns broke out from behind Rayden, the signals soon joined by several other horn blasts spreading throughout the ramparts.

The horns continued to blast, contending with the rising cacophony emitting from the approaching horde. Voices cried out everywhere, urging everyone to make haste.

Rayden watched the front edge of the undead ranks drawing nearer and nearer. The ponderous approach gave the people within the ramparts their only chance to escape a hideous fate.

Looking back over her shoulder, Rayden could see the first of the men, women, and children that had stayed within the ramparts beginning to cross the open ground, heading toward the Imperial City's gates.

The sight of them gave Rayden a little relief.

Looking back down to the right, she watched the front of the vast, revenant host pouring into the outer ditch. Others coming from behind continued forward.

In little time the ditch filled with their bodies and the host continued unimpeded, walking across their comrades and clutching onto the rampart's facing.

Along a broad front, the undead climbed upward. Many fell or slid down, but others continued their ascent.

Slow and relentless, numerous revenants began surmounting the palisade crowning the top.

The rampart had been breached.

Crassor gagged next to Rayden and exclaimed, "This stench!"

The noxious odor had worsened, and the macabre cacophony continued to grow louder.

Casting another glance back, Rayden observed a thick column of tribal people streaming toward the city gates. A few carts had been put into use; to carry those who had suffered severe wounds in battle, along with the most infirm and feeble, and the newborn and youngest.

Rayden turned back to Crassor. "I do not want to get a close look at those things right now. I think it is about time for us to go back into the city."

"You will get no argument from me," Crassor replied, gagging once more.

"Nor I," Doros added, her eyes watering.

Abandoning the outer rampart, Rayden made her way down from the wall and back across to an opening within the other wall. Passing through it, she strode across a plank over the trench beyond and headed fast toward the column.

About mid-way between the ramparts and the column, she came to a halt and turned about, eyeing the barrier behind them. Doros and Crassor came to a stop at her sides.

Rayden told Crassor, "Keep them moving ... as fast as they can. It will not be long before those things breach the second rampart."

Crassor nodded to her and then began shouting at the people to hurry along.

"Stay with me," Rayden said to Doros. "We must ward the end of the line."

Rayden and Doros began to gather a few warriors around them, including many Kartajenians. With people still coming from the ramparts, a rearguard had to be formed.

It stood inevitable that the oncoming horde would work its way through the ramparts. Looking often toward the earthen walls while gathering more warriors to her, Rayden expected to see the first signs of the undead host at any moment.

***

"We need to get the gates shut behind us, and the walls defended ... fast!" Rayden shouted to the warriors around her, while watching the first wave of the oncoming horde of resurrected corpses beginning to climb over or pass through the second rampart.

The first drops became a trickle, the trickle became a stream, the stream became a river, and the river became a flood. All along the rampart, the dead poured over the top, skidding and tumbling down the slope into the ditch. Others trundled out through the handful of narrow gaps that had been unblocked for the people to flee.

The writhing mass filling the trench did not take long to sort itself out, one way or another. Whether crawling out or advancing across the bodies of the others in the trench, the dead reached the open ground and took their first steps toward the city walls.

The uproar from the dead sent a panic racing through the extended line of tribal people hurrying from the ramparts. Many screams and cries erupted from terrified people setting their eyes on the vast wave of dead, now beginning to flow across the open ground.

Loping over toward the fleeing people, Rayden exhorted them to hurry, while keeping her eyes on the advance of the dead.

The contingent of warriors stayed close with her, ready to defend the end of the line if necessary.

No one lagged. Those healthy and hale aided those who struggled to go faster.

Rayden, Crassor, Doros, and the warriors gathered with them were among the last to race through the Eagle Gate; the latter barriers shut fast behind them, moments after they had crossed through.

***

Once through the gates, Rayden stopped and rested for a moment. The air now sullied with the stench of rot and carrying the otherworldly clamor of the undead, the warriors of the northern tribes needed no reminder of the new threat facing them.

Atop the city's walls, warriors called down that the undead were at the gates. Rayden could hear the things pounding against the outside of the iron-banded barriers but knew they could not break through. Nor could they climb the walls.

For the time being, all within the city would be safe from the revenant host.

***

A short time later, an unwelcome tiding arrived, one that threatened to change the course of the entire battle.

"The dead are entering the city near the Imperator's palace!" a warrior cried out, running toward Rayden. "The Teverens are letting them through a gate they yet hold along the walls!"

Though many around her reacted in great alarm to the dreadful news, Rayden took the words of the messenger in stride. It did not surprise her that the Imperator would sacrifice the entire populace in order to crush the tribes of the north.

Death or victory the only outcomes, the final stage of the battle beckoned, and Rayden stood ready to meet it.

After bringing together a large force of warriors, Rayden led them forward, heading in the direction of the city's greatest hill. Others fell in with them along the way, and more horns sounded.

Her legs propelling her fast across the ground, Rayden listened to the swelling cacophony coming from ahead. The stench of decay increased as the great hill drew closer.

Emerging into open ground, giving her a broad view,

Rayden slowed down and took in a dismaying sight.

The warrior had spoken true. Great masses of undead were now mustering at the base of the hill.

An unbroken flow of the grotesque entities could be seen coming in from the left, curling around the contours of the hill. Having spread across the bottom of the slope, the ranks of the undead thickened by the moment.

The macabre horde ranged from those in long-decomposed states, many at the cusp of skeletal, to others with bodies still looking much like they did when alive. An animating force controlled each of the morbid figures, one that could see for those without eyes and move the limbs of the ones far decayed.

Eerie moans, wails, groans, guttural cries, and other unsettling vocalizations began rising from the masses facing Rayden and the tribal warriors. A chorus of death itself, the sepulchral, otherworldly rancor chilled the blood inside her veins.

The masses of warriors that had been gathering to fight the remaining Teveren soldiers had pulled back in the wake of the influx of dead. Seeing the arrival of Rayden's force, they came forward once more.

In a short time, two huge forces faced each other, one comprised of living beings and the other comprised of resurrected corpses.

Trudging, hobbling, stepping, or shambling forward, the host of revenants began advancing toward the living.

Thrusting her axe high into the air, Rayden cried out, "Strike them down!"

Charging forward to meet the oncoming wave, Rayden led a massive surge of northern warriors.

Enduring the odious stench permeating the air, Rayden struck hard with her axe and sword. Chunks of bone, decaying flesh, limbs, and other parts of the animated corpses were cast about from her heavy blows.

Sending their war cries toward the heavens, the warriors around Rayden unleashed a storm of fury.

Beheaded corpses fell to the ground and became still, as did those receiving massive head wounds. Otherwise, the revenants fought onward, even when reduced to nothing more than an upper torso.

A putrid reek arose from the more recent corpses opened by the strikes of tribal warriors, the rancid scents of decaying innards intertwining with the other foul odors filling the air. Nauseating many warriors, more than one of the attackers vomited.

Continuing their zealous assault, Rayden and the other warriors hacked and slashed, felling more of the animated corpses.

Savage and relentless, the undead grabbed, clawed, and bit, some pulling the unfortunates caught in their grasp back into their seemingly endless ranks. Their flesh torn into and bodies ripped apart, ill-fated warriors loosed bone-chilling screams, rife with agony.

Footing beneath soon became hazardous with the bodies of fallen warriors and undead mounting upon the blood and gore-coated ground. The danger of slipping or tripping rose with every moment.

It soon became apparent that the enemy numbers were far too great for the warriors to overcome.

Lopping the head off a mostly skeletal figure with her axe, Rayden cast her gaze about. She could see that the warriors had gained no ground. The unbroken channel of revenants coming around the base of the hill continued to add to the enemy ranks.

The tribes could not sustain the pace of the fighting. Limbs would tire, mistakes would be made, and more of the warriors would fall to the undead.

"Fall back!" Rayden cried out, extricating herself from the

fighting after landing a skull-shattering strike of her sword upon a desiccated-looking corpse. Taking a deep breath, she called out again, "Fall back, now!"

Backing up, sparing a few glances for the path behind her so that she did not trip over an obstacle, Rayden exhorted the others to pull back.

To her left and right, warriors broke away from the fighting and retreated back into the city. Catching sight of Doros and Crassor a little farther down to her right, Rayden's assailed spirit gained some needed uplift.

Ears filled with the din and enveloped by the horrid stench, Rayden eyed the revenants. Resuming their massing around the base of the great hill, they did not pursue the retreating warriors.

After putting some distance between her and the undead, Rayden looked skyward. Scattered throughout the heights, more wraith-like forms drifted in the direction of the Catacombs.

A few descended much nearer.

Watching in revulsion, Rayden beheld the dark specters alighting upon the bodies of fallen tribal warriors. A few moments after the wraiths absorbed into them, the fresh corpses spasmed and jerked about, before laboring to get upright.

The hideous development did not come as a surprise to Rayden, but it did concern her. She knew it would shake the hearts of the northern warriors to strike at the resurrected corpses of those who had been comrades and fellow tribal warriors only moments before.

The thought of fighting the corpse of Crassor, Doros, or Annocrates sickened Rayden, and she did not want to even think about Hamilcar.

Summoning the power of her will, Rayden shoved the distressing thoughts aside. She had to keep her mind clear and void of distractions.

Taking one step and then another, Rayden put more distance

between herself and the masses of undead.

***

Continuing their pullback from the frenzied combat, Rayden and the other warriors retreated along a broader, stoned-paved street, until they came to the top of a rise. From the higher position, they could maintain a clear watch of the massed undead.

Rayden and other leaders among them called for the warriors to halt.

"If they begin to move in this direction, raise the alarm at once!" Rayden called to the others.

Breathing hard, she wiped the sweat from her eyes with the back of her left hand, still holding onto her gore-coated axe.

Looking at the dark ranks of the enemy, she wondered why the undead did not pursue them.

To her dismay, Rayden observed more and more of the creatures making their way around the base of the hill to join the swelling host. There appeared to be no end to their numbers.

Rayden turned to a couple of warriors. "Go and see if you can find out what is happening beyond the walls. Let me know what you are able to learn, without delay!"

Somber expressions on their faces, both of the younger men nodded to her. Turning, they hurried off, to carry out her order.

Working their way through the throngs of warriors, Crassor and Doros approached Rayden. Both covered in grime and blood, neither had suffered noticeable wounds in the fighting.

"Rayden," Doros addressed her in a low voice. "You saw what we saw."

"Our slain rise to join them," Crassor added.

Rayden nodded. "They inhabit and control bodies, in the tomb or just fallen."

"How can it be stopped?" Doros asked, an undercurrent of despair beneath her words.

"We can only trust in the fae, who can do what we cannot against the Imperator's sorcerers," Rayden answered her.

"But we face an enemy that needs no food and rest, and stands in far greater numbers than us," Crassor responded. "An enemy that adds to its ranks whenever one of ours fall."

"That is what we face," Rayden told him, the cold truth of the situation irrefutable.

Recalling the multitudes of rats, Rayden could see everything much more clearly. The enemy had invoked fell spirits from the depths of the abyss, to possess the bodies of simple beasts in great numbers, right under the eyes of the populace.

The wicked spirits had destroyed the bodies of their hosts in the river and gone to take a new body from the vast multitudes interred within the Catacombs. Under the rays of the dark sun, the spirits had not been pulled back into the abyss when rendered incorporeal upon the drowning of their rat hosts.

The Imperator's sorcerers had bridged the natural order, empowering the fell spirits to make use of a dead corpse in the same manner as possessing a living body.

Rayden knew that every sorcerer harboring the vile knowledge and ability to do what had been done had to be stopped, whether captured or slain.

Thinking upon the sheer numbers of rats that she had witnessed, each one representing a wicked spirit, Rayden shook her head in frustration. Flinging her head back, she looked skyward, wishing she could cry out to some god or goddess to intervene, but knowing of none in particular that she trusted would do so.

Her eyes settled upon the dark sun reigning in the skies. Looking upon the dark orb, she caught sight of a few more wraiths.

These were coming from the direction of the dark sun.

It took everything within Rayden to hold back an avalanche

of distress as the enormity of what she witnessed struck her in full force.

A portal into the abyss, the dark sun could provide an endless stream of wicked spirits to take up bodies. Even more foreboding, if lesser spirits could cross into the world, then the threat of things much greater and far more powerful loomed.

Rayden could only hope that the nascent dark orb remained limited for the time being. Bringing her eyes back down, she glanced toward Crassor and Doros and kept her thoughts to herself.

They had weathered far enough without the added burden of the new revelation that Rayden had just gained.

***

Streaming with sweat and sorely winded, the two men that Rayden had dispatched returned. When the pair stood before her, she could see a pronounced anxiety on both of their faces.

"We came back ... as fast as we could," one stated, gulping in breaths of air.

"What tidings do you have?" Rayden pressed.

"We are surrounded," the second warrior told her, a look of fear gleaming in his wide eyes. "The dead ring the entire city!"

"Is there any sign of Marus' legions?" Rayden asked.

The second warrior shook his head.

Rayden absorbed the dire news in silence.

The Imperator's ghastly new army had the tribes caught in a trap. Surrounding them on the outside, the undead had blocked all routes of escape.

The great host gathering at the base of the great hill stood in position to begin a sweep through the city. Rayden knew in her heart that no one would be spared.

The masses of poor Teverens packed within their tenements and the tribes of the north would both be slaughtered; providing thousands and thousands more bodies for the fell spirits of the Abyss to inhabit.

Rayden called for warriors close by to gather around her. Once she had assembled a large group, she tasked them with getting word to all of the tribal chieftains about the enemy's intent.

The fighting would resume soon.

CHAPTER 13

Voices rose in alarm all around, causing Rayden to pivot fast and take up her weapons.

Tribal warriors backed away fast, giving wider berth to the small, radiant, winged figure approaching through the air at about waist-height.

"Hold! Do not attack!" Rayden commanded the agitated warriors.

Looking into Queen Muirithesos' luminous eyes, a look of relief passed across Rayden's face, her calm reaction drawing surprised looks from the bystanders.

"Welcome, Queen Muirithesos," Rayden greeted the diminutive figure. "You are a most needed sight at this time."

A solemn look on her face, Muirithesos replied, "I wish I had more time to speak, but we have gathered, and the moment of our strike nears. You must come with me at once."

Rayden nodded, as the faerie queen turned and started up the street, taking her away from the other warriors.

"We are in position and must strike hard before the sorcerers serving the Imperator regenerate and replenish their strength," the queen stated as they proceeded forward together. "Conjuring the dark sun has left them weakened for a short time."

"What is that dark sun?" Rayden asked. "I think that I

understand its nature, but you know the things of sorcery far better than I."

The queen's face took on a grim expression.

"An abomination," she replied. "A breach of the natural order, of the like we have never seen before."

"What power does it give the Imperator?" Rayden queried, raising her eyes to look at the black orb far above.

"You are looking into the abyss," Muirithesos told her. "Fell spirits enter this world, like a gateway, and descend to resurrect corpses under their dominion."

"It is as I thought, then," Rayden replied. "I suspect it will allow much worse to cross in time."

"It will," Muirithesos said. "For now, it allows a trickle of fell spirits. In time, gods of the abyss will be able to cross at will."

"This threatens all the world," Rayden said.

"We move to close it, if we can," the faerie queen responded. "But if they can create such a thing, what other kinds of gateways can these sorcerers conjure?"

"Not something I wish to think about," Rayden stated. She looked over at Muirithesos. "Where are we going?"

"After we strike, to free some who have been held captive a long time," the queen replied. "We only need one with us to represent the tribes, and there is no better for this than you."

"What am I to do?" Rayden asked.

"You will understand soon," Muirithesos answered. "First, you will be a witness."

Muirithesos said nothing more, guiding Rayden along the streets heading toward the eastern side of the city. A few faces gawked from tenement windows at the sight of the faery queen and the northern warrior.

At last, they entered one of the city's lavish parks, filled with flowers, trees, statuary, and fountains. A tremendous brilliance permeated the area, coming from a great multitude of faerie-kind.

"So many," Rayden observed in a low voice, astonished at the numbers assembled before her.

"The fae of three kingdoms are gathered here," Queen Muirithesos stated. With a nod of her head, she indicated two prominent-looking faeries. One male and the other female, they were of the same kind as Muirithesos. "Kin to me, they understand the threat to us all."

Rayden looked to each of the regal figures, rendering them bows of respect. Both returned the gesture, to her surprise.

"They know of what you have done, not just for the Mist Vale, but for all of your kind," Muirithesos stated.

"What is going to happen now?" Rayden asked her.

"We must strike at the dark sun, and then we must free captives of great value to the enemy's sorcerers," Muirithesos stated. "We know where they are being held."

Rayden nodded to the queen. Though she wished to know the identity of the captives, she did not press the queen for answers.

"I shall return to you," Muirithesos declared with an air of resolution.

Muirithesos turned and rejoined the other monarchs. Rayden quietly stepped aside, taking a place beneath the boughs of a tree.

Wings beating fast, the three faery monarchs lifted off the ground and began to ascend. All around Rayden, the light-emitting multitudes took to the air, following the three eminent beings skyward.

Her surroundings darkening with the departure of the fae host, Rayden stood alone, gazing toward the breath-taking display rising into the air. Under any other circumstance, the sight filling Rayden's eyes would have been one to savor and behold.

Against the backdrop of the darker skies, a sprawling host

of lights streamed upward. Converging once they had attained a great height, the multitude of lights began coalescing around the outer boundary of the black orb.

In a unanimous surge of motion, the lights darted inward, swooping in and covering the surface of the black orb. For a moment, the orb looked to be sparkling, with pulses of light flashing all over its surface.

Then, as if the orb was the top of an erupting volcano, the area within it began belching forth a tremendous volume of ash-gray vapor.

Spreading outward from the orb, the roiling mass advanced across the skies, forming a dense layer that hid the clouds.

Having the appearance of a spectacular frenzy of lightning flashes, white, blue, yellow, and green pulses reverberated throughout the dark orb.

An ear-splitting crack then shook the heavens. For a moment, Rayden's vision blurred, and a wave of dizziness passed through her.

Regaining her clarity and equilibrium once more, Rayden looked up again. To her eyes, it appeared that the dark orb was collapsing inward, pulling in upon itself.

Streaking outward from the diminishing sphere, the fae retreated to positions much farther away, forming several large pockets of light.

In a few heartbeats, nothing more could be seen of the dark sphere.

The gray layer spewed from the abyssal portal still covered the sky above, but the outline of the natural world's sun could be seen once more within the thick haze.

A calming sense of relief came over Rayden at the sight. The fae had prevailed.

The host of diminutive lights began descending, heading back in the direction of the city. Most looked to be flying toward an area closer to the Imperator's palace, but others angled straight toward the area where Rayden stood.

A part of Rayden did not settle until she recognized the form of Muirithesos among the small contingent alighting on the ground before her.

Despite the victory, Muirithesos had a somber expression and Rayden needed no explanation. Many of the fae had fallen in the assault on the portal.

"The way into this world has been closed to the fell spirits," Muirithesos announced, walking toward Rayden. "What already crossed still remains, but no more of the dead will rise under their power."

Rayden welcomed the pronouncement of the queen. No longer would they be fighting an enemy that would inhabit and resurrect their own dead.

"Yet it is far from over," Rayden said, thinking of the vast revenant host encircling the Imperial City, in addition to a strong force under Peronnius still defending the Imperator.

"Many of my kind go to draw out their sorcerers," Muirithesos said to Rayden. "I think more than a few of them will be provoked with the loss of their dark sun."

"They will be enraged," Rayden replied, casting a glance toward the reemerging sun above.

"We will go to give them more reasons to be enraged," Muirithesos stated in a grim tone. "Follow me."

Surrounded by a contingent of fae, Rayden followed the queen through the garden. They exited on the north side, proceeding toward the immense, stone-surfaced area where the prominent edifices for the judging of disputes could be found, among a host of other buildings, temples, wide open spaces, grand statuary, and fountains.

Without crowds of Teverens milling about the open spaces, the place had a desolate feeling about it. Crossing through one such area, Muirithesos guided Rayden in the direction of one of the temples dedicated to the divinity of the Imperator.

Rayden climbed the short flight of wide steps while the fae used their wings to drift through the air. The group continued through the large entrance and headed inside.

An altar stood before a towering, golden statue bearing the likeness of the Teveren Empire's ruler.

Scattered about the high columns, a large number of faeries, of several types, turned at the entrance of Rayden, Muirithesos and the others with them. At the sight of their queen, the little creatures gave an immediate bow of their heads.

One of the creatures approached from the other end of the temple. A faerie so diminutive that it could have fit within the palm of Rayden's hand, the little entity's stern gaze belied its delicate appearance.

"Only a few remain below, trapped with the captives," the creature stated in a higher-pitched voice. "We lost many in taking this place. But it is certain they did not expect an attack here."

"They did not think that we knew of this place," Muirithesos responded, an undercurrent of anger rippling through her voice.

The other faerie nodded. "There were still many of their sorcerers and soldiers guarding the captives. The soldiers we overcame swiftly, but it gave warning to the sorcerers."

"Their power has been shattered, fall upon them!" Muirithesos commanded the faerie in a loud voice, her voice carrying throughout the capacious temple.

Without delay and joined by the ones that had come with Muirithesos and Rayden, the faeries spread all about the temple interior sped through the air toward the altar. Passing it and converging, they disappeared into an open door to the right, in the back wall behind the towering statue.

Shouts and cries followed. The doorway lit up with severe flashes of light, and then all became silent.

A few moments later, one of the faeries that had gone below emerged from the doorway.

"The fighting is finished," the little creature declared.

***

Caged behind iron bars in dust and grime-filled cells, a number of bedraggled, haunted-looking figures had been bound in iron shackles on both ankles and wrists. Gagged and with their eyes covered in tight wraps of dark cloth, the prisoners could not see or speak.

Heads raised up, all of the captives were aware that something of great significance had taken place.

Walking through the chamber and stepping around the bodies of dead sorcerers and a few faeries, Rayden looked at the figures held behind the iron bars of three cells.

Rayden's eyes settled upon one captive in particular.

Recognition striking her, Rayden's breath stilled within her lungs, and then she exhaled slowly.

For a moment, all that she could do was stare in astonishment.

Filthy and ragged in appearance, Dreaghen sat on the ground before her eyes.

All of the times that Rayden had seen him in apparitions and dreams contrasted starkly with the image now before her. Dreaghen had been reduced to a pitiful state, an echo of the vision that she had long carried within her mind.

Many times, she had imagined admonishing the sorcerer for all of the times that he had come unbidden to her, whether she had been in a state of wakefulness or slumber. As she looked upon the haggard figure, Rayden could only think of getting him out of the terrible confinement he had been suffering.

"Dreaghen, I am here," she said to him in a low, gentle voice. "Let me get you out of here."

Turning his head and tilting it up toward her, Dreaghen

spread his arms as much as he could and reached out for her. Beginning to tremble, Dreaghen could barely keep the chains connected to his wrist-shackles aloft.

"Do not distress yourself," she told him, keeping her tone gentle. "Give me a moment."

Turning from the cell, she stepped over to the dead sorcerers, looking down at them. Around her, several faeries watched in silence.

Rummaging through the sorcerers' robes, Rayden finally heard the jingle of a larger key ring. Taking possession of it, she started back toward Dreaghen's cell and then hesitated.

The recognition of Dreaghen had consumed her initial thoughts and attention, but she could not overlook the other captives, who had all suffered in a like manner. Rayden turned back to the faeries watching her.

"I will see to it that all are freed," she declared to them. "Please guide the rest upward and take them to a safer place. They have endured far too much at the hands of the wicked."

The small creatures nodded their understanding to her.

Turning back toward Dreaghen's cell, Rayden tried various keys in the lock until she found one that fit. Turning the key and listening to the telltale metallic clicks as the lock released, she pulled on the iron bar door. Hinges creaking, Rayden opened the cell and stepped inside.

Ignoring the pungent scents of excrement, urine, and body odor surrounding the pitiable captive, Rayden unlocked the shackles binding Dreaghen's limbs, letting the ones on his wrists fall to clang against the stone flooring.

Carefully, she unbound the cloth gagging his mouth and then removed the band covering his eyes. With her right hand, she pulled back the scraggly, matted strands of hair falling into his gaunt face.

"You have gray eyes," Rayden stated, keeping her voice low

and giving him a kind smile. "I have often wondered."

"I knew ... you would find me," the sorcerer replied in a weak, scratchy voice.

"You could run to the far side of the world and I would find you, after what I have been through," Rayden replied, a broader grin crossing her face.

"I imagine ... so," Dreaghen replied, the hint of a grin on his own parched lips.

"I am going to have to ask you to wait a few moments longer," Rayden told him. "I must free the others who have been kept prisoner down here with you."

Dreaghen nodded. "Of course, ... but ... help me to my feet ... first. I ... have sat ... in darkness ... far too long."

Doing what she could to avoid causing Dreaghen too much discomfort, Rayden helped the sorcerer get up to his feet. Swaying in place for a moment, the unsteady man wobbled on his first couple of shuffling steps, but in slow fashion he made his way out of the cell.

Keeping a hand on Dreaghen's right arm to help with his balance, Rayden kept close to his side.

Dreaghen looked around at the faerie folk spread about the chamber outside the cells. The hint of a smile returned to his lips.

"You have come ... a far way too," he addressed them. "I ... thank you ... fae who carry ... the light ... of life"

A couple of the larger faeries approached him. Both took up small vials from little hide pouches at their waists. Lifting into the air and nearing the level of Dreaghen's head, they drew up before him.

Carefully, they poured the contents of the vials into his mouth, sending the liquid past his dry, cracked lips.

Seeing him cooperate, Rayden knew that he trusted the creatures.

"Let them tend to you, I must set the others held down here

free," Rayden told him.

"Yes ... of course," Dreaghen replied, before taking in more liquid from one of the fae attending to him.

Rayden then set about liberating the others that had been confined, counting five men and three women in addition to Dreaghen. Speaking to them in soft tones, Rayden could see the gratitude in their exhausted gazes when she freed them to see and speak once again.

She did not have to ask to know that they were also sorcerers of great skill. Though she had no idea of the powers they held or mysteries they had explored, Rayden knew that the men and women had been deemed adversaries by their counterparts, those serving the abyssal powers.

To her, that was enough reassurance that they were not steeped in wicked practices.

One at a time, they shuffled out from their cells. One of the men stumbled and began to fall, but Rayden caught the emaciated figure before he hit the ground.

The faeries tended to each of the freed prisoners, using the contents in the small vials that several of them carried.

The liquid did not restore the bedraggled men and women to full vitality. A state of weariness still clung to them, but the contents within the vials did bolster their focus and strength enough that they could walk on their own accord.

"Are you familiar with the others?" Rayden asked Dreaghen, as they prepared to leave the chamber.

He shook his head. "I am not ... but they ... are like me. I am certain. None ... serves the abyss."

"The ones that had you captive drew upon your power, in some manner," Rayden stated, guessing at one of the reasons that the enemy had kept Dreaghen and the others alive and in confinement.

Dreaghen nodded. "Part of ... their sorcery."

"All this time, even when I was across the sea, crossing deserts and plains, you were bound here," Rayden said, giving voice to the revelation dawning inside her.

"They could not ... subdue all ... my abilities," he replied, the trace of a knowing grin coming again to his lips. "I ... could still ... fly from within."

Seeing the last of the faeries leaving the chamber in the company of the other freed prisoners, Rayden told Dreaghen, "It is time for us to go above."

"The fight is ... not over," Dreaghen said. "Is it?"

"No," Rayden said. "The outcome is still not certain."

"Then ... I will ... do what ... I can," he replied.

A stern look on his face, Dreaghen started across the chamber, heading toward the doorway leading to the flight of steps heading upward. Rayden followed close behind, but she did not have to give Dreaghen any aid.

Though climbing the steps in a slow, methodical fashion, he reached the top without stumbling and proceeded into the temple.

Entering the temple interior after him, Rayden set her eyes on Muirithesos, who stood near the altar. A smile rested on the queen's face.

"I do not think you expected to see him," the faerie queen said, looking from Dreaghen to Rayden.

"Thank you for bringing me here," Rayden replied, understanding more of the queen's purpose.

"Dreaghen conveyed enough to me from afar that I desired to guide you to him in person," Muirithesos said.

"I am glad that you did," Rayden said, giving the queen a smile. She looked over to Dreaghen. "We must go now, though. The battle is far from won ... and could yet be lost."

"A bitter truth," the queen stated.

Rayden and Dreaghen walked together down the center of

the cavernous chamber and exited through the front entrance of the temple. Down the steps before them, the small cluster of freed sorcerers continued forward in the company of several faeries.

"I would not like to think that I am separating you from them, if you wish to be with the others who endured the trial with you," Rayden said to Dreaghen.

"I will ... seek them out ... later," Dreaghen replied. "It is a boon ... to stand ... with you. At last."

"Then let me take you to a place where you can try to get a little rest," Rayden said.

Looking off to the northeast, where the resurrected corpses had massed in position to sweep across the city. Rayden could not promise Dreaghen anything.

***

Upon her return to the tribal ranks, many warriors looked at Rayden with curious or quizzical expressions. Having just witnessed her in the company of many faeries and a handful of ragged-looking men and women, more than a few carried looks that told Rayden they were expecting some kind of explanation.

Doros, standing among the tribal warriors, raised an eyebrow when her eyes met Rayden's.

"The faerie folk have helped us," Rayden stated in a voice loud enough to be understood by the warriors nearby. "You witnessed what happened in the skies. The dark sun is no more. The dead will no longer rise, and we have freed some prisoners valuable to our enemies."

"Those are welcome tidings," Doros said, shifting her gaze to Dreaghen. "Who is your friend?"

"This is Dreaghen, who has been a prisoner of the Imperator all this time," Rayden said.

"The sorcerer of all your visions?" Doros asked, her eyes widening. "The one who has been appearing to you?"

"The same," Rayden answered. "He has been through far enough. Let us get him some food and drink, away from all the fighting."

"I do not wish to be away ... from all the fighting," Dreaghen interjected, looking to Doros and Rayden. His voice emerged clearer and steadier than before. "Perhaps a short respite is needed ... but I must do what I can ... until this fight is over."

"I do not think we could stop you," Rayden told her longtime benefactor, a slight grin on her face. "Come with us now and get some wine and a little food."

"After what we have subsisted on in the darkness, that will come as a welcome feast," Dreaghen replied.

Standing on his right, with Doros on his left, Rayden guided Dreaghen away from the crowded area. She would return to the battlefront soon, but not until she had found the sorcerer a place to drink and fill his belly.

**

Against Rayden's counsel, the tribal chieftains decided to take the fight once more to the enemy, rather than wait for them to sweep through the city. Though against the idea, Rayden took a place at the forefront when the attack commenced.

Within several streets, masses of tribal warriors assailed the undead hordes blocking the way to the Imperator's palace and the fortress holding the remnants of the legions under Peronnius' command.

The resonant din from the groans, wails, and moans of the undead encompassing her, Rayden hacked and slashed in a tempest of battle fervor.

Shattering skulls and severing necks, Rayden sent one undead figure after another to the ground, never to rise again. All around her, the warriors of the northern tribes fought with an inflamed fury, bringing sword, axe, and spear to bear upon the corpse horde.

Many warriors fell during the intensive clash.

Some found themselves pulled into the undead ranks, to be clawed, bitten, and torn limb from limb. Others suffered mortal wounds from the weapons carried by a fair number of the corpse-beings, including many that had watched the sun rise that morning as Teveren soldiers.

This time, no wraiths descended from above to enter and resurrect the bodies of slain northerners.

Though great numbers of the undead were brought down, there still seemed to be an endless number of them. Among the tribal warriors, limbs began to tire, and casualties started to mount.

The streets became hazardous to maneuver in with all of the bodies littering the ground. A warrior losing their footing or balance became easy prey for the dense masses of tireless undead.

Blood-curdling shrieks of warriors having their innards clawed out or suffering a limb being ripped from their body threatened to shake the resolve of many northerners.

Rayden fought on undeterred, wary not to trip over the increasing clutter of bodies on the ground.

Wherever she could, Rayden came to the aid of other warriors, saving quite a few from grisly demises.

In one moment fighting a skeletal figure, and in another facing a fully intact body from a recently slain Teveren soldier, Rayden found herself pitted against many faces of death.

She had to make constant adjustments between the more ponderous, long-decayed attackers and the faster-moving ones still possessed of robust forms.

Reminding her that she contended with adversaries not of flesh and blood, all of the undead entities had bright, spectral glints cradled deep within their eyes. A seething, malicious sentience looked back to Rayden from every set of undead eyes that she gazed into.

The entities that Rayden and the tribal warriors fought were not dull, shambling creatures. A keen intelligence awash in diabolical madness governed each of the bodies fighting the tribal ranks.

After a while, Rayden began to sense the toll on her own body from the extended fighting. Her limbs had begun to tire significantly, and her breathing grew heavier.

Those who had been fighting alongside Rayden all throughout the bloody tempest exhibited advancing signs of weariness. More tribal warriors started falling to the weapons, teeth, and claw-like hands of the undead.

A repeat of the last broad assault was transpiring, just as Rayden had feared when she counseled a more defensive posture to the chieftains.

"We must pull back!" Crassor shouted while beheading a morbid-looking, half-decayed adversary.

Rayden could not dispute him. There seemed to be an endless number of undead and the northerners were tiring fast. Before long, they would collapse and be overrun.

Wrenching her axe free of a skull that she had just buried it into, Rayden cried out, "Sound the horns, pull back! Pull back!"

Moments later, a horn sounded from near to her, the sonorous blast followed in swift succession by many others along the extensive battlefront.

Disengaging from the fighting, Rayden and the other warriors backed up. Once more, to her surprise, the undead did not press their advantage.

To her eyes, they appeared increasingly content in blocking the way to the imperial palace.

Continuing away from the enemy, Rayden and the other warriors made their way back to where they had mustered before starting the assault on the undead horde.

***

"There are too many of the damnable corpses between here and the Imperator," Crassor raged, glaring toward the lavish, hill-top palace that represented the end of the fighting. "We cannot hurl ourselves against them again and again like this."

Sweat poured down his face. Blood trickled from a few scrapes he had suffered at the hands of the undead.

"No, we are not going to get through that ... not even you, Rayden," Ammanus added, eyeing the massive throngs of undead.

No trace of jest marking his face, Ammanus cast her a somber look. The blade in his hands coated in gore, he had fought in the front ranks and not given up a step until the call for retreat had been sounded.

Rayden could not dispute Ammanus. No matter how determined she was, her arms would grow exhausted striking against the undead long before she could get halfway through the teeming horde blocking their way.

The chieftains could not dispute what had taken place.

Under a late afternoon sun, the northerners had taken the fight to the undead again, before the entities pushed through the city. The warriors of the tribes had again failed to break through the enemy ranks.

Having fought hard since the morning with a few short periods of rest, the warriors could not be expected to recover their depleted energies before night descended. Rayden and the other leaders could call upon them perhaps one more time, but then they would need more rest.

All the while, they faced an enemy that would never tire.

A couple of runners stood nearby, having brought the unpleasant news that the thick outer ring of undead surrounding the city yet remained in place.

All gates under the control of the tribes had been closed,

but everyone within the city remained trapped.

Rayden knew that the enemy would not allow the northern warriors time to recover. The battle had to end that day, or the night would bring the destruction of the tribes.

***

While the northerners rested in the aftermath of the failed attack, Rayden, with Ammanus, Crassor, and Doros keeping her company, sought out Muirithesos. The queen of the Mist Vale had taken the freed sorcerers into one of the many public gardens found within the Teveren capital city.

Dreaghen among them, the human sorcerers had gathered together at the edges of a large fountain. All looked up to Rayden as she approached them across the grass.

"We are surrounded," Rayden declared, passing her gaze across their faces. "Their numbers are vast, and they have gathered an enormous horde near the palace of the Imperator. We cannot break through them."

"They will make their move to end the battle soon," one of the sorcerers, a long-bearded, elderly man, stated. "No quarter will be given."

"Can anything be done?" Rayden asked, looking from the humans to the faerie queen standing on the ground to her right. "I do not know your arts, or those of Muirithesos' kind."

"We broke their dark sun, and closed their portal to the abyss with it," Muirithesos said. "But our energies are drained to a point of dangerous weakness. We can do nothing more this day."

"Even if we were hale and rested, what is needed would be far beyond all of our powers," a silver-haired woman with a narrow face stated.

"Surely there is an answer," Rayden replied, doing her best to hold a wave of consternation back from showing on her face.

The others remained silent, but the dour faces on faerie and human alike gave her their answers.

Rayden looked toward the gray skies. She had to think of something fast, but with the fae exhausting their powers and the warriors so fatigued, any scenario involving them would be severely hindered.

The forces opposed to the Imperator needed something unexpected to intervene, like the lion that had rushed out of the night to assail a dark, malevolent enemy that had Rayden in mortal danger.

Rayden thought back to that harrowing experience within a Teveren hilltop camp that she had gone to investigate at night. The recollection brought a rueful smile to her lips.

Even if a lion charged in out of nowhere, it would only be one creature against a sea of enemies.

A thought struck her like a thunderbolt.

There did not have to be just one lion. Nor were lions the only formidable creatures to be found within the kingdom of beasts.

"What of beasts?" Rayden asked abruptly, turning back toward Dreaghen.

The sorcerer looked up to her from where he sat upon the fountain's edge. "Beasts? What of them?"

"You gain their help through your arts," Rayden told him. "You understand them, and they, you. Can you reach out to animals now?"

"I could ... but you are not going to find enough nearby to make any difference," Dreaghen replied in a morose tone. "Even if there were animals close by, they would not be the kind that could tear through the undead. You are in need of savage creatures of the wilderness, not the tame ones kept in Teveren homes."

"Do not be so certain," Rayden replied, the notion

germinating within her sprouting into something more promising by the moment. "It would be a matter of getting the animals to go against their natures and not to turn upon each other. Can that be done?"

Dreaghen stared at Rayden for a moment, and then answered, "It can, though it may leave me on the brink of death."

"Can you work to keep Dreaghen restored in his vitality?" Rayden asked, turning to look at Queen Muirithesos.

"That is something we can do," the faerie queen answered, giving Rayden a curious look. Then, she asked, "What are you thinking of?"

"The Teverens' arena," Rayden stated, looking around to the others. "It is not far behind us. Underneath, it has catacombs of its own, and there are high-walled places located close to it. I am certain that we will find cages and enclosures filled with beasts intended for the grand displays of violence they hold in that accursed sand pit."

"There will be a great number kept in those places near to the arena," Ammanus interjected, nodding. "The Teverens sustained daily fights and executions in the arena, using all manner of creatures. Who knows what we would find down there?"

"Certain kinds of creatures could be worth a hundred skilled warriors," Dreaghen stated, looking deep in thought.

"Then let us see what we can find, and then, if you can, set them all upon the undead," Rayden told the sorcerer.

"Help me to them," Dreaghen implored Rayden and the others. "My condition is too weakened to reach them on my own."

Crassor and Ammanus stepped forward to aid Dreaghen, holding him up on each side.

The other human sorcerers remained behind, while Muirithesos took to the air. Escorted by a large throng of her kind, she followed as Rayden led the group out of the public garden and marched in the direction of the arena.

"Looks like we would have had to move anyway," Ammanus remarked, gesturing back in the direction of the palace.

Off in the distance, movement could be seen along the forefront of the undead ranks filling the streets. The undead shambled, shuffled, and strode forward, heading in the direction of Rayden and the others.

The enemy had begun the anticipated sweep of the city, and Rayden knew that their intent was total extermination.

***

With Rayden at the lead and maintaining a swift gait, Ammanus and Crassor strode close behind, bearing up Dreaghen. Queen Muirithesos, the contingent of faeries with her, and a few tribal warriors followed after them.

Behind them, the surreal, groaning cacophony from the undead masses had grown louder. The frontal wave of the malevolent entities brought with it an ocean behind to flood the streets.

Horns soon began blaring all over, as the northern tribes began to recede from the enemy's advance. In time they would run out of ground to retreat, but the enemy ranks would become a little more divided than they were in the northeast of the city.

Reaching the arena and the buildings adjacent to it, Rayden and the others wasted no time.

From the compounds outside the arena to the labyrinth of passages and cages beneath it, Dreaghen used his arts upon everything that they found.

Individually or in groups, lions, elephants, leopards, rhinos, hyenas, wolves, bulls, and all manner of creatures, including several rare beasts, were freed and let loose into the city.

Muirithesos and the faeries with her attended close to Dreaghen, using their arts to keep his strength up throughout the ordeal.

Rayden could only marvel at the spectacle of beasts leaving their pens, enclosures, and cages, before gathering in a swelling multitude within the open areas near the arena.

Dispatching several warriors, Rayden implored them to carry messages to the retreating forces, some of which had now drawn close, to clear the streets.

The designated warriors bounded off, taking several different streets.

Then, Rayden had other warriors sound urgent retreat signals upon their horns. Everything had to be done to clear the way for what was about to take place.

***

Standing just to the side of the bestial host, Dreaghen said nothing aloud. Eyes closed, the sorcerer faced the animals with a look of deep concentration on his face.

Rayden eyed the nearby streets. Only the undead could be seen to the north with the tribes having pulled back farther, past the area of the arena. Keeping their distance, many warriors looked upon the bizarre assemblage of animals with fearful expressions as they passed through.

Moments earlier, Rayden had called for warriors to run along the eastern walls and continue down the northern walls until they reached the Eagle Gate. Once there, they were instructed to open it wide, and then wait in the flanking towers or on the wall-walk.

When Rayden judged that all stood clear, she called out, "Begin the attack!"

Dreaghen winced and then opened his eyes. Roaring, bellowing, grunting, and snorting, the mass of animals set into motion, building up speed and heading straight toward the oncoming undead ranks.

Amazed, Rayden watched the attack unfold, with throngs of wild beasts charging at full force into the undead hosts.

A huge rhino barreled right through the undead, tossing aside the ghastly entities and creating a broad wedge that predatory creatures racing behind poured into. Fangs and claws ripped into the undead with a savage, primal ferocity.

Flinging undead bodies high into the air with its lengthy tusks, a massive elephant gored another multitude of revenants filling a street. Rampaging through the dense mass, the elephant trampled and pulped many of the entities underfoot.

Hyenas, leopards, and other beasts following in the wake of the elephant finished off any stragglers. Among the creatures that Rayden caught sight of included a white tiger that stood large enough for a human to ride. She also espied a brawny, saber-toothed cat, like those stalking the grassy plains far to the south, in the lands across the Great Sea.

The attacks reflected a wider pattern. The larger animals like rhinos, elephants, and bulls broke apart the ranks of the undead, while the other predators entered the fray in their wake, tearing into the enemy with a relentless ferocity.

"Now, we must attack!" Rayden shouted at those around her. "Signal on the horns! The chieftains will understand!"

"What about the wild beasts?" Crassor asked. "Will they not attack us as well?"

"They are fighting their way through the enemy to the outside of the city," Rayden replied. "The beasts are breaking apart the undead ranks, but they seek freedom themselves. It is what Dreaghen has called to them to fight for. They seek their own liberation. If we follow behind and keep them in front of us, we will not come to harm."

Crassor raised his sword and grinned. "Then let us chop more of these corpse things apart!"

Battle horns sounded once more, spreading the call in a

rapid manner to renew the assault on the undead. All over the city in the shadows of the late afternoon, the northern tribes launched a massive attack up all the streets leading toward the northeastern section of the city.

Cleaving their way through the undead, the polyglot, bestial multitude left a tremendous amount of carnage behind them. Bodies torn to shreds lay everywhere.

Large numbers of the undead had also been passed by in the rapid attack. But what remained was not the unbreakable mass that the northern warriors had faced when pressing their own attacks.

Reinvigorated from the impact of the beasts, the warriors hacked and slashed with great ardor. The tribes suffered some more losses to the undead, but the casualties were on a far lighter scale than before.

Disrupted and shattered apart, the undead host no longer held cohesion or the advantage. Whittled down with every passing moment, the enemy ranks could not overcome, or even stem, the surge of the northerners.

At the back of the undead host, beasts of all kinds broke through and hastened toward the open Eagle Gate.

Rayden caught a glance of three female lions bounding out together, a few strides behind the huge white tiger. One of the lionesses had a tattered right ear.

Fighting forward with the other northerners, Rayden could not stop to wonder about the fate of the creatures. A ring of undead still remained in place outside the city, but she had confidence that most of the animals could fight their way through the encirclement.

Hewing the head off a bony, slow-moving entity in tattered rags, Rayden could see that the end of the long struggle now appeared within grasp. Crying out at the top of her lungs, she exhorted the other warriors to fight forward with everything that they had left within them.

When the northern warriors reached the end of the undead horde, they moved quickly to shut the Eagle Gate and those around the base of the great hill crowned with the Imperator's palace.

The tribes did not delay in attacking the walled-off area serving as the quarters and garrison site for the imperial legion. Javelins and arrows harried the wall-walks, while others labored to break down the small gates accessing the fortress.

Having taken extensive losses, the Teveren defenders could not deter the breaking down of the gates. It did not take long for the attackers to break through.

Pouring into the fortress compound, northern warriors spread through the elongated barracks, stables, storage buildings, and other structures, falling upon Teveren soldiers wherever they could be found.

Meanwhile, swarms of warriors hastened up the slopes of the great hill toward the Imperial palace. Seeing the warriors coming up all sides of the hill, the Teveren soldiers in formation higher up on the southern slope retreated back into the palace complex.

The tribal warriors roared their fury. Nothing stood in their way.

Knowing the end to all the fighting lay somewhere within the palace area, Rayden ran up the hill alongside the others.

Reaching the top, Rayden paused to catch her breath for a few moments, looking around at the massive complex of exquisite quality marble and stone. Ahead of her, warriors flooded into the buildings.

The sounds of intensive fighting erupted from deeper within the complex.

Hurrying forward, Rayden passed beneath the portico fronting a grand, two-story edifice. Inside, she came upon splendid atriums open to the skies, baths and glittering pools, chambers painted with magnificent frescoes, and other trappings of great wealth and power.

Alcoves in chambers and great halls alike held full statues and pedestals that supported busts, the latter depicting the torsos and heads of various men and women. Sculpted with great detail, the statues and busts appeared lifelike at a glance.

All of it had been abandoned. The only noises to be heard in the vicinity came from the jubilant shouts of warriors spreading throughout the depths of the massive palace building.

Striding through a huge dining chamber and making her way into a lavish garden, abundant with colorful flowers, Rayden had her mind set on finding the Imperator, or even Peronnius. She knew that Peronnius would not stray far from the Imperator with the city falling to the northern hordes.

On the far side of the garden, past elaborate fountains and a pool containing an assortment of golden-scaled fish, Rayden entered the palace again. Heading up a flight of steps, she worked her way through bedchambers provided with balconies affording the occupant expansive, breathtaking views of the city.

A tension took root and began growing within her as the empty chambers, halls, and other spaces began to mount. She could find no hint of the Imperator's whereabouts.

After making her way down to the first level, Rayden came to a halt as a familiar voice called out to her.

"Rayden, we found something that I know you would want to see!"

Turning around, Rayden saw Ammanus hurrying toward her, along with Doros.

"What is it?" Rayden asked.

"I cannot make sense of it," Ammanus replied.

"Nor can I," Doros added.

"Is it far from here?" Rayden asked them, impatient to

continue her search for the Imperator.

"It is in another building, very close to here, in a small room," Ammanus replied. "Believe me, you will want to see it for yourself."

"What is in the room?" Rayden queried, chafing to resume her hunt of the Imperator.

"Babies," Doros answered. "A room full of them."

Her brow furrowing and caught by surprise at the answer, Rayden nodded. "Take me there at once."

***

The ground-level room contained a dozen infants. Several of them crying, a cacophony filled the air.

Rayden walked over to the side of one of the small cradles and gazed down.

"Do what you can to find those who nursed them, for the time being," Rayden told Ammanus, Doros, and a few warriors standing nearby. "I do not think they have escaped. They are hiding somewhere on the palace grounds."

Outside, the distant sounds of fighting coming from deeper within the complex of palace buildings had dissipated, signaling the defeat of the last remnants of the Teveren legions.

Reaching into the cradle, Rayden picked up the baby laying within, taking great care to be as gentle as possible.

"There ... there now," Rayden said to the infant in a soft voice, holding the baby close. Lightly rocking the child against her bosom, she smiled and added, "You are safe now, little one."

Looking into Rayden's eyes, the baby ceased its crying and settled within her arms. It did not take long for the baby's eyelids to close, as the little one drifted off into sleep.

Placing the baby back into the cradle, Rayden gazed around the room. The discovery of it demanded a pause in her search for the Imperator.

A look at each of the vulnerable innocents told Rayden that they had been born of mothers from a variety of lands. An undercurrent of dread rising within, she knew that the infants had been kept there for a wicked purpose.

***

After a little time had passed, Doros appeared at the doorway and looked across the room toward Rayden. Ammanus stood just behind her.

Both had grim expressions.

"One of the warriors found a Teveren with a large ring of keys," Doros announced. "We also found another level to this building."

"You are going to want to see this too, Rayden," Ammanus stated in a solemn voice.

Moving in a slow and controlled manner, Rayden laid another sleeping baby that she had calmed back down into the crib by her side. She pulled part of a soft linen cloth within over the infant's body.

Rayden let her gaze linger on the baby's face for a couple of moments. Serene and at ease, the little one slumbered with steady breaths.

Looking up to her companions, she nodded. "Take me there."

Just down the hallway from the chamber with the infants, Ammanus and Doros guided Rayden to a door opening onto a flight of stone steps leading downward. Behind her strode the warrior of the Tega who had discovered the ring of keys.

Doros looked back to Rayden. "It is down here."

"Lead the way," Rayden indicated.

Doros started down the stairs, followed by Rayden and Ammanus.

***

Rayden found it difficult to retain her composure. Little hands gripped iron bars and young faces pressed against the gaps between them, staring at her with haunted, fearful expressions.

Some no more than seven or eight years of age, the children wore ragged, soiled clothes. Their hair stringy and matted, they looked as if they had not bathed in quite some time.

"Get them out of there, at once!" Rayden commanded, finding herself on the verge of shaking in anger.

The Tega warrior holding the keys set at once to unlocking each of the cells. Many of the children were hesitant at first to leave the small, dingy compartments, but several began to come forth at gentle coaxing from Rayden and her companions.

"You are free, little ones," Rayden told them in a low voice, gesturing for the children to come out. "The Teverens have been defeated. You are free."

Casting nervous glances at the Tega warrior, Ammanus, and Doros, the children gathered close around Rayden.

"Who are you?" a young dark-haired girl of about ten asked. By her face and skin hue, she looked to be Kartajenian, and could well have been a sister to Hamilcar. "You have pretty hair. It is like the sun in color."

Rayden gave the young girl a smile. "Thank you. My name is Rayden. I have come from the north with many tribes of warriors to stop the Imperator."

"Thank you, Rayden," said a boy of about twelve, standing next to the girl. A mass of curly black hair atop his head and with a larger nose, he looked to be Teveren. "Thank you for saving us. They came and took some of us from the cages here. But those they took never came back here."

The young girl stepped forward and threw her arms around Rayden, hugging her tight. One by one, other children did the same, until she found herself embraced all around.

Rayden could not prevent a few tears from slipping free of her eyes. Smiling at the children, she gazed upon them with glistening blue eyes.

"Why are you sad?" another little girl asked, a perplexed look on her face.

"I am happy, and sad," Rayden answered her. "Happy because you are free, and sad that you have had to go through all of this."

"But we are free now," another boy of eleven or twelve said. "We can go home now, because of you, and your friends."

His words provoked a couple more tears, both of a sorrowful nature. Rayden knew that few of the throng around her could return to any semblance of a home.

Looking to Doros and Ammanus, Rayden said in the timbre of a firm promise. "We will make certain all are cared for."

"How could they do this?" Doros asked, her own eyes gleaming with sadness.

Rayden turned back to Doros. "The wicked thrive on the defilement and destruction of innocence. I know the purpose of the infants above, and the children here. It is one of their number that I spared out in the Catacombs, before I headed to the Mist Vale."

"The sacrifice of innocence gives evil its greatest power," Ammanus said in a low voice, frowning.

"Not these children, and not the infants above," Rayden replied with the edge of a growl. "Now let us get these children out of this vile place."

"No reason for them to stay a moment longer," Ammanus responded, nodding to her.

"All of you, follow me!" Rayden announced to the children in a raised voice. Sweeping her gaze through them, she met each pair of youthful eyes. "Look out for each other. Hold to each other and stay together. Do you understand me?"

The children all nodded.

Turning and heading back up the stairs, Rayden led the children away from the place of their imprisonment. Reaching the top of the staircase, she proceeded down the hallway.

Warriors stepped aside to clear the way for Rayden. Striding past the room with the infants, she continued out beneath a portico into a garden beyond, filled with green grass, flowering shrubs and trees.

At the center lay a fountain depicting a group of young women frolicking together within an ocean's surf. Spouts had been worked into the ornate sculpture on every side. Arcs of glittering water poured down into a square pool at the base.

Turning around, Rayden looked at the wide-eyed gazes on the cluster of disheveled youth.

"Stay in this garden, but you can explore it as much as you want, and play," Rayden declared. "You are all free now, and we will protect you."

At her invitation, cries of joy and laughter erupted from the children. Rayden wondered how long it had been since the poor children had felt the touch of the sun on their faces. Kept below in filth, shadows, and fear, they had been absent hope.

A few of the children jumped into the fountain and began splashing water on each other. Their shrieks of glee rose high into the air.

The sound and sight of the children enjoying themselves brought a little lightness into Rayden's burdened heart.

Doros and Ammanus stood silent to either side of Rayden, watching the children play and run about.

"Doros and Ammanus, see that these children are kept safe, I am entrusting all of them to you," Rayden said at last, keeping her eyes on the children. "I must go. A hunt still remains."

"Should I not go with you?" Doros asked.

"And I?" Ammanus queried.

"I must know in my heart that these children are under the eyes of those who I trust in my heart," Rayden told her loyal companions.

Doros stared at Rayden for a moment, and then nodded, looking resigned. "I will see that they are not harmed. You have my promise."

"You need only ask of me," Ammanus said, giving her a slight bow of the head.

Reaching out, Rayden set her hands down on the shoulders of her companions. "Thank you both. When you see me again, all of this will be over."

"May all the gods of light, Elysium, and the heavens be with you," Doros said.

"Come back to us, Rayden," Ammanus said. "I desire to go on more journeys with my dear friend."

A resolute look on her face, Rayden nodded to them, and turned away.

Leaving all of the children in the care of Doros and Ammanus, Rayden strode across the garden.

A singular thought occupied her mind.

She had to find Dreaghen.

With a ring of undead yet outside the city, urgency pressed upon her.

CHAPTER 14

"We bring all of this to an end ... now!" Rayden exclaimed, pacing back and forth within a resplendent chamber used for hosting feasts. Turning, she fixed her eyes upon Dreaghen. "I will hunt them down, wherever they may have slipped off to. They can not have gotten far."

"I do not believe they have gotten beyond the walls yet," Dreaghen replied, from where he reclined upon a well-cushioned dining couch.

Her eyes ablaze, Rayden stepped toward Dreaghen. "Then where can the ones responsible for these abominations be found? They must not be allowed to escape to work this kind of vile sorcery... and spread this kind of terror and suffering ... ever again!"

Her voice echoed loud through the large, high-ceilinged chamber.

After a moment, Dreaghen replied, "The greatest among them does not stray far from the Imperator. But if they are separated, there is likely a route of escape through the temple on this very hill. There is much more beneath the temple, hidden from most eyes. I have been dragged through much of it. I committed everything that I could to memory."

"Then we go there at once," Rayden declared. Looking over

to a number of warriors standing around them, she declared, "Come with me, and help Dreaghen. I will need him!"

A pair of warriors strode forward and helped Dreaghen up to his feet. With his arms about their shoulders, they held him upright.

When the warriors stood ready to follow, Rayden led them out of the chamber. A brisk march through the grounds of the palace took her past colonnades of purple and yellow marble, where other warriors milling about watched her pass by.

Keeping her eyes forward, Rayden did not spare a glance for the upper galleries set into the palace buildings. A throng of warriors enjoying the view from them gazed down on the small contingent marching beneath them with an air of purpose.

Once beyond the complex of buildings, Rayden crossed a span of open ground leading toward their destination; a majestic temple larger than any other that she had seen within the city.

Reaching the base of the broad steps leading to its entrance, Rayden did not pause for a moment to admire the soaring white columns supporting the portico. Springing up the stairs, she headed straight through the wide entrance.

***

A towering, golden statue, fashioned in the likeness of the Imperator, dominated a lofty alcove set at the far end of the temple's interior.

Nothing stirred within the shadowy atmosphere pervading the temple. Walking through the middle of the floor toward the colossal statue, Rayden found the stillness within the place a little jarring after being in the midst of all the chaos and fighting outside.

The warriors with Rayden followed a few steps behind, including the pair assisting Dreaghen. Leading them farther in and passing several huge columns, Rayden wondered how any rational beings could deify a man of flesh and blood.

She found the notion preposterous. The Imperator had done nothing to justify his claim. All of his actions had been those of a power-hungry mortal.

When she reached the altar, Rayden slowed down. The other warriors gathered around her.

"I am guessing that there is a concealed door," she said, looking to Dreaghen.

The sorcerer was staring past her, toward the wall at the back. He said to the men hoisting him up, "I can walk from here."

The warriors let him go, and Dreaghen stepped forward. Though taking slow steps, he maintained his balance well.

Rayden followed the sorcerer over to the back of the temple. Coming to a stop a couple paces from the wall, he looked downward.

"I need your keen eyes, Rayden," he stated, gesturing for her to stand next to him. "Do you see any sign of recent passage?"

Looking at the floor, Rayden could see a fine layer of dust, undisturbed. Using her foot, she brushed through it, making easily visible marks.

"Nothing too recent," she told him.

"Good, then we are here in time," Dreaghen stated.

"For what?" Rayden asked, a little perplexed.

"For now, we wait," he replied. "But soon you will catch your prey. They will come to you."

***

Low, muffled voices and the sounds of many shuffling footsteps brought Rayden's head up from where she had been sitting with her back resting for a while against a column near the altar. In a moment, Rayden was on her feet and alert with weapons in hand.

"Spread out, conceal yourselves, and watch for my lead," Rayden told the others in a hushed voice.

The warriors fanned out among the columns, taking up hiding places. Rayden stepped behind one, right as a group of men entered the main temple sanctuary, issuing through a side doorway positioned closer to the entrance area.

A sense of urgency flowing through their movements, a group of robed men strode down the length of the temple. Heading toward the altar at the far end, they surrounded a bald, bearded man of medium height.

Setting her eyes upon the sorcerer, stark recognition gripped Rayden.

A coiled serpent amulet rested beneath the lengthy, dark beard that covered much of his narrow face. His deep-set eyes brimmed with a look of intense fury.

Another harrowing journey in times past had brought the two of them together once before, within a vast subterranean chamber at the heart of a remote city far to the east called Sereth-Naga.

A servant of the cruel, rapacious beings called the Sharir-Mord, the sorcerer had been commanded to head west during a dark ceremony that Rayden had witnessed.

Rayden had seen to the ruin of the Sharir-Mord and the breaking of their stronghold in Sereth-Naga. She now had to bring an end to their malignant influence in the form of the sorcerer drawing near to her.

Taking a couple of steps out from the column, Rayden came to a stop and pivoted, setting herself directly in the path of the approaching group. Seeing her, the robed men drew to an abrupt halt.

Behind them, the other warriors who had come with Rayden emerged from the shadows, blocking the way out of the temple. All of them held their weapons out, in a way that none of the robed men could fail to miss.

"A reckoning is upon you," Rayden announced, glaring

at the long-bearded man standing in the midst of the priests; a sorcerer named Cerranus who had invoked immense evil into the world. "Those you served in Sereth-Naga were uprooted, hunted down, and destroyed, and now the doom that claimed them reaches you here."

A bestial look swarmed the sorcerer's face and eyes, giving him a countenance feral and savage.

"Attack her! All of you!" he cried out in a frenzied voice. "Kill her! Kill her now!"

The robed men around the sorcerer did not hesitate. Pulling daggers from the folds of their robes, the priests shouted and charged at Rayden, ignoring the presence of the other warriors behind them.

Leaping forward to meet them, Rayden cried out and began swinging her deadly blades. Engaged by several opponents at once, she could not stop the sorcerer when he broke into a run.

The priests were not trained warriors and Rayden cut them down fast. Their screams and cries echoed throughout the cavernous temple.

Slashing open guts and necks, splitting skulls, and piercing lungs and hearts, Rayden evaded their clumsy efforts to stab at her.

When the last of the six men fell to the ground, Rayden looked around for the sorcerer. Reaching the back wall and standing at the spot where she had examined the floor earlier, the sorcerer activated some kind of mechanism that opened a concealed doorway. Once the passage beyond stood clear, he hurried through.

Hastening toward Rayden at the outbreak of the fighting, the other warriors reached her as the last of the priests emitted a rattling gurgle and fell silent.

Springing forward and bounding toward the open doorway in the back wall, Rayden gave chase to the sorcerer.

While running, she shouted at the top of her lungs, "Wait in here! Do not follow me! Prevent any from escaping through this door!"

She reached the doorway a few moments later. Exiting the temple sanctuary and starting down a narrow stairwell, Rayden remained wary for the possibility of an ambush.

Farther down in the darkness, she could hear the scuffling on stone from the descending steps of the sorcerer.

Unable to see her own steps, Rayden continued downward. Gauging each stride carefully, Rayden kept her balance back until her lead foot touched upon flat stone.

Closing the distance fast, Rayden reached the bottom just as the sorcerer Cerranus started to run through a doorway a few strides ahead. Her visibility improved through the increased ambience coming from beyond the doorway, Rayden leaped forward and resumed the pursuit.

Racing across a stone surface, Rayden caught up to the sorcerer swiftly. Tripping Cerranus up, using her left foot, Rayden sent the man sprawling hard onto the ground.

Fear coursing through his voice, the sorcerer lifted his head and cried out several words in a language that Rayden did not understand.

Slamming her right foot down into the middle of his back, drawing an agonized gasp from the sorcerer, Rayden pinned Cerranus in place and silenced his words. Only then did she chance a look around at the chamber that they had entered.

A huge pit lay open within the center of a cavernous space. The rough-hewn rock at the sides of the cavity slanted down to a flatter, circular basin.

Rayden espied a large hole in the basin near its outer edge, opposite of the place where she stood keeping the sorcerer in place.

Hearing footsteps approaching from behind, Rayden

glanced back to see Dreaghen limping through the entrance to the stairwell.

"I followed as fast as I could," Dreaghen told her, a pained expression on his face.

"I got him," Rayden replied, keeping her foot pressed hard on her quarry's back, drawing an extended groan from the trapped man. "I was about to finish off this worm and saw all of this."

"Watch the pit!" Dreaghen warned. "When I descended the last steps, I heard him crying out a summons!"

A deep, breathy hiss rose up from the pit, coming from the hole.

"What is that?" Rayden asked, looking back toward the pit.

"A monstrosity comes!" Dreaghen declared, fixing his eyes to the pit. "One that they sacrificed many lives to, casting each victim into the pit while still alive."

Beneath her, the sorcerer began to struggle with an air of desperation, calling out again in the strange voice. Raising her foot, Rayden stamped down hard upon his back once more, knocking the air from his lungs.

Slithering out of the hole, a dark, serpentine creature entered the basin. Like a small crown, a number of sharp tines rose from the top of its broad head.

Large of girth, the creature exhibited numerous marks all along its extensive length, including larger scuffs and an assortment of extended, narrow streaks.

The creature's head oriented toward Rayden. Eyes of solid, rheumy white looked in her direction, the eyes of a creature that could thrive within the deepest darkness.

Thinking fast, a plan formed in Rayden's mind that would solve more than one dilemma, if she could carry it out.

Rayden took her foot off the sorcerer and leaned over him. Grabbing the battered man about the shoulders, she lifted him up to his feet.

"You called upon this thing, you wretch!" Rayden thundered at the dazed sorcerer. "Go then and know the fate of those you offered in this pit! Meet your vile god!"

With a prodigious heave, she flung Cerranus down into the pit. Shrieking in terror, he hurtled toward the serpentine monster.

For all of its bulk, the creature exhibited a fearsome level of speed. Head darting forward, the creature plunged its fangs into the sorcerer and coiled tight around him in scant moments.

Rayden stood in silence, watching. The creature below paid her no heed, focusing upon the fresh meal that she had given to it.

A look of raw horror on his face, the sorcerer gasped, and the coils tightened further. It did not take long for the creature to suffocate the man in its clutches.

Jaws expanding, the creature engulfed the sorcerer's head and began swallowing his torso.

"Let us go," Dreaghen said. "You have cast him to ruin. The creature will descend into the depths once more, and there are others still left to hunt."

"Wait," Rayden told him, continuing to watch the creature consume its prey.

Dreaghen stared at Rayden but did not reply.

The bulge marking the sorcerer's body grew as the creature took in the midsection and legs of the corpse. When the last bit of the sorcerer started down its expanded maw, Rayden took a step toward the edge of the pit.

Keeping her eyes on the creature, she announced to Dreaghen, "Now that this nightmare is gorged and burdened, I shall make certain that it never feeds upon an innocent ... or receives veneration in this world again."

Dreaghen could not get a single word out before Rayden

leaped forward.

With an extended section just beyond its head bulging from the body of the sorcerer that it had just consumed, the creature could not move nearly as quick as before, but it mattered little.

Her sword blade oriented downward, its hilt gripped firm with both of her hands, Rayden used the momentum of her fall and the strength of her body to drive the honed iron deep; burying it into the center of the creature's head.

Skewering its head, Rayden landed hard atop the monstrosity, barely missing the sharp tines. Speared through, the creature shook and thrashed its tail for a moment before slumping down, becoming limp throughout its extensive body.

Taking no chances in assuming a killing blow, Rayden left her sword buried in place and slid off the creature. Using her axe, she proceeded to chop her way through the creature at the base of its head.

Chunks of its flesh and blood scattering in the wake of each blow, she hacked away, finishing the grisly process after several hard strikes. Bracing her foot on the severed head, she then pulled her sword free.

Kicking the head across the basin surface, she turned to look up at Dreaghen. "It will not be feeding on anyone else. The sorcerer was its final meal. A fitting one, in my eyes."

"Very fitting, in all respects," Dreaghen replied, a slight grin appearing on his face. "For a moment I thought you had lost your mind."

"Maybe I did," Rayden replied, smirking at Dreaghen.

Rayden wiped her blades off as best as she could on the hide of the creature's body, before returning them to the sheath and loop on the belt at her waist. Then, she climbed out of the pit, hoisting herself up at the edge near Dreaghen.

"This is an evil, wicked place," Rayden remarked after catching her breath. Standing up, she walked closer to Dreaghen.

"The very air is stained with its cruelty. I wish I could tear it down with my hands."

"It is a place of dark power, given the abundance of atrocities committed here," he replied, nodding. "Once all is done, this pit must be filled, and that hole blocked up. At the least."

"You will find no argument from me on that," Rayden replied in a solemn tone.

Rayden stared for a moment at the hole where the ancient creature had come up from the depths of the world. She wondered what kind of realms lurked farther below, where such monstrosities existed, and even flourished.

"We are not finished yet," Rayden stated, taking her eyes from the pit and beginning to examine the rest of the broad chamber.

Raising her voice, she called to the warriors up in the temple sanctuary, commanding them to come down.

Shortly after, the other warriors entered the chamber. All of them stared at the beheaded corpse of the thing down in the pit, with looks of astonishment and awe forming upon their faces.

"It is time to hunt greater quarry," Rayden announced to the warriors, when they had gathered before her.

***

After a brief search of the cavern, Rayden and the other warriors located a couple of narrow tunnel entrances, located on opposite sides of the pit from each other.

After gauging her position in relation to the temple and palace above her, Rayden determined that one of the tunnels headed straight in the direction of the main palace complex.

"It is time to resume the hunt once more," Rayden said to Dreaghen. "But this will be a matter of iron, not magic."

"Their magic is spent, iron will suffice," Dreaghen replied.

"You need not risk yourself here," Rayden told him. She

looked over to the warriors. "I need just a couple of you to come with me. The rest of you take Dreaghen above and keep him safe from harm. He has done more than enough for all of us."

The warriors looked to each other for a few moments, but after a brief impasse two stood forth; the tallest and strongest looking among them.

"We will go with you, Rayden," one of the stalwart pair proclaimed.

She nodded to the warrior but made no reply.

"I will see you soon enough," Dreaghen told Rayden. "Finish all of this."

"May it be so, on both counts," Rayden countered.

"The victory is yours to take," Dreaghen told her, an intense look in his eyes.

Rayden held the sorcerer's gaze for a moment. Her eyes blazed with a fierce determination.

"All of this ends this day!" Rayden declared.

Dreaghen nodded, turned, and walked toward the stairwell. Taking cautious, balanced steps, he walked without assistance.

The other warriors, save for the two that would continue onward with Rayden, gave bows of their heads to her before following the sorcerer.

***

Rayden looked to the two warriors remaining in the chamber with her. A heavy, ponderous silence surrounded them.

"Follow my lead, at all times," Rayden addressed the warriors. "We will be stalking a dangerous quarry."

Grim-faced, the warriors nodded to her.

She led them over to the mouth of the tunnel that she believed to run back to the palace buildings.

Rayden entered the dark passage, wide enough for her to walk at ease with a little room left to either side. She could only imagine how many times the tunnel had been used by Cerranus and the other sorcerers, moving back and forth beneath the palace to conduct their loathsome ceremonies and rituals.

Excavated out of rock, the tunnel had no adornment or trappings of any kind, a stark contrast to the lavish palace buildings that it connected to. Damp and musty, rough-hewn on both sides and an uneven surface beneath, the tunnel served its purpose; a secluded conduit between the palace and temple.

Rayden proceeded with slow steps through the darkness, until a faint, reddish light in an oval shape pierced the gloom. Picking up her pace a little, she remained careful to keep her footfalls soft.

Behind her, the warriors did likewise, making nary a sound.

The small oval of light farther ahead grew with each step. Able to see her way better, Rayden strode faster.

Nearing the opening, Rayden could see the columns and floor of a well-lit chamber or hall.

Turning her head, she whispered to the warriors at her back. "We will wait in here, for now."

Slowing down, she took up a position at the opening to the chamber. Listening and watching, she waited.

Every instinct told her that her quarry would come.

***

After some time had passed, Rayden snapped to full alertness, hearing footsteps quick and purposeful approaching. They headed toward the one tunnel that could serve as an escape route for a surrounded enemy.

Taking a deep breath, Rayden cleared her thoughts and stepped out from the tunnel entrance. Striding into the open space on an elaborate mosaic surface, she took out her sword and axe.

The two warriors that had accompanied her emerged from

the tunnel and took up positions to either side of Rayden.

In addition to the mosaic flooring, the hallway had two colonnades of marble running the length of each side. The light from several oil lamps set in wall niches at even intervals illuminated the ornate hall.

At a rapid gait, two figures strode around the corner at the far end and started down the center of the long hallway. Seeing Rayden and the two warriors standing at the other end, blocking the tunnel entrance, they drew to an immediate halt.

Rayden's attention fixed upon the second of the figures at once.

She had seen the man's image numerous times in the past. Rendered upon coins, replicated in statues of carved marble and cast bronze, the appearance of the Imperator would be difficult to mistake.

Seeing him living and breathing before her eyes gave Rayden pause for a moment. No longer a towering figure of gleaming bronze within a grand temple, he now stood a creature of mere flesh and blood; a being no different than herself.

A vulnerable air encompassed him. Absent legions to protect him, he had only the sword in his right hand to defend himself.

The Imperator, the highest authority in the Teveren Empire, exhibited an unmistakable look of dismay on his face at the sight of Rayden and the warriors.

Scowling, a tall figure in gleaming armor and a crested helm stepped around the Imperator. Proud of bearing, the Teveren warrior's gaze brimmed with ferocity and steely discipline.

Holding swords in his left and right hands, the warrior took a couple of slow, deliberate steps down the hall, striding toward Rayden and the two warriors.

"Barbarian dogs, come, meet your end here, but know that we will yet crush your rabble!" the warrior declared in a strong, authoritative tone, his voice echoing throughout the hallway.

"Peronnius," Rayden replied in an even tone, her eyes becoming pools of blue flame. "You face your ruin this day."

Square of jaw, Peronnius had a thick neck and broad set of shoulders. Greaves protected his legs up to the knee and a cuirass of horizontal segments guarded his robust chest. Cheek guards attached to his helm shielded the sides of his face.

A mocking smile imbued with frigid cruelty formed upon his face at her declaration. His next words slithered out in a lower tone.

"Barbarian dogs, know that your whelps shall bleed on our altars and be cast into fires to honor our gods."

"This scum must die!" the large warrior to her right erupted, his eyes blazing with fury.

"No!" Rayden shouted at him. "Leave this wretched cur to me!"

Ignoring Rayden and bellowing a war cry that filled the hall, the warrior raised his sword and charged toward Peronnius. A step behind him rushed the second warrior that had marched through the tunnel with Rayden.

Blades flashing and wielded with smooth precision, Peronnius blocked a heavy slash from the first warrior and cut his throat wide open. Dropping his sword, the warrior clutched at his neck in a desperate, futile effort to stem the blood spewing out before toppling to the floor.

Pivoting fast and ducking, Peronnius thrust his blade deep into the gut of the second warrior, whose own slash cut harmlessly through the air above the Teveren. With a violent, twisting yank meant to tear innards to shreds, Peronnius ripped his blade free.

Wide-eyed and gasping, the warrior slumped to his knees, trying to cover the gaping wound before collapsing face-first to the floor.

Peronnius did not have a moment to savor his victories.

Rayden had raced forward in their wake.

Sharp clangs of metal ringing through the hall, Rayden assailed the renowned Teveren general. Axe and sword flashing through the air, she had him on the defensive at the outset.

Peronnius demonstrated great skill weathering the initial storm of Rayden's onslaught, executing a counter of his own after intercepting several strikes. Sliding his right sword off a block of her axe and stepping in, Peronnius landed a hard blow from the pommel flush on the side of Rayden's head.

Pain exploded from the point of impact, but Rayden did not waver in her guard. Deflecting a thrust rushing in from the Teveren's left sword, she sprang back to give herself a little more space.

Head throbbing from the blow, she bared her teeth at the Teveren. Locking eyes with him, Rayden needed no words to convey her rage and hunger to slay him.

For his part, the Teveren's gaze teemed with a murderous fury.

All boasts and insults had been cast aside. Only the voices of blades would speak in the moments to follow.

Peronnius launched an attack, his swords hissing through the air and seeking to bite deep into Rayden. The hall filled once more with the metallic clashes of blades.

Toward the end of the exchange, Rayden swept her sword outward, deflecting a slash of her opponent's left sword. Bringing her axe down, she caught the Teveren's right blade lancing toward her side.

Hooking the bottom of her axe blade about the Teveren's weapon and jerking backward, she disarmed his right hand. Echoing throughout the hall, the sword clattered to the mosaic floor.

An opening beckoned.

Everything that followed afterward transpired fast.

Without a moment to spare, Rayden lifted her axe to strike Peronnius.

Hand lashing forward at the last instant, Peronnius caught the middle of her arm before she could bring the axe down.

The Teveren's left blade flashed, racing downward. Rayden's quick reflexes brought her sword rushing up to block the hard downstroke, the force of the impact reverberating through her body.

Shifting her feet, Rayden pressed in closer to the Teveren, keeping her sword locked tight to his. The heat from his heaving breaths touched the skin of her face.

Her fist, clutching the haft of the axe toward the base, lay tantalizingly close to his face. Yet she could not readily strike at him with her arm caught in his grasp.

The lines of his forearm muscles like iron cords, Peronnius clenched his teeth. Keeping his grip locked on her arm and using his greater physical strength, he had her at a standstill, unless she took a risk.

Loosening her grip, Rayden let the haft slide down through the palm of her left hand until she tightened her hold once more, with her grip set firm against the fitting of the blade. Using the bottom of the axe blade like a short, curving knife, she executed a short, hard turn of her wrist, slicing the blade straight to the left.

Raking the bottom portion of the blade hard across the eyes of the Teveren, she opened gashes across both eyes and blinded him at once.

Screaming and bleeding from both eyes, such that he looked to be crying tears of blood, Peronnius shoved her off of him.

"You dog!" he cried out, slashing wildly with his remaining blade at the air in front of him.

This time, an undercurrent of fear ran through his voice.

Out of the corner of her eyes, Rayden saw the Imperator lunging toward her from the side. A Teveren blade gripped in his right hand, he had the weapon leveled for a thrust.

Slashing downward, Rayden batted his attack aside with ease.

The distraction gave Peronnius enough time to muster his own attack. Advancing toward Rayden, he swung his blade in a broad, horizontal arc.

Bringing her sword up fast, she blocked his assault and countered with her axe. Unable to see it rushing in, he could do nothing to stop the weapon.

The blade lodging deep in the right side of his neck, Peronnius' eyes widened as he cried out in pain. A stream of blood running down the segments of his cuirass, the Teveren general stood in place.

Moving to the left and yanking her axe free, Rayden distanced herself from the Imperator so that she could finish Peronnius off. Another hard chop of her axe to the neck sent the Teveren general to the ground, his half-severed head displaying a lifeless, dull stare when it landed with a thump upon the mosaic floor.

Hearing the sound of pounding footsteps, Rayden broke into a run. Catching up with the Imperator before he could flee the hall, she hobbled him with a deep sword cut across the back of his right leg.

Crying out from the pain of the blow, the Imperator stumbled and almost fell to the ground. Yet somehow, he kept upright.

Unable to bear any weight upon his wounded leg, the Imperator stood in place. Rayden circled around and came to stand in front of him.

A look of sheer malice filled the Imperator's face. Something far from human gazed back at Rayden.

Even then, with his forces shattered and greatest acts of sorcery broken, Rayden sensed grave danger.

Unwilling to give him any time to execute some magical art or call upon another power, Rayden stepped forward and brought her sword racing through the air at the level of his neck. Her blade cleaved through flesh, muscle, and bone, lopping the Imperator's head off in one blow.

Thudding onto the floor, the Imperator's head rolled to a stop a few paces away, the right side of his face oriented down. Walking up to the head, Rayden lifted her right foot and stomped down at full force with her heel, crushing the skull.

"It is over!" Rayden shouted, staring down at the mashed remains of the figure that had willingly served the powers of the abyss, concentrating tremendous powers and wielding them against humanity itself.

A thin, misty vapor began wafting up from the man's crushed head. Forming into a vague human shape, it hovered in the air, facing Rayden.

The air surrounding her grew frigid, to the point that her breaths emitted in ghostly puffs.

Shivering in the extreme cold, Rayden glared at the apparition.

In a commanding voice, she told it, "Your wickedness is in ruin. Go where you belong! To the unending darkness!"

A multi-layered scream brimming with rage and pain burst from the shadowy apparition. Everything shimmered and blurred before Rayden's eyes.

Some unseen force began drawing the apparition backward, distorting its form and funneling it down into a smaller and smaller size until it finally vanished from her sight. The echoes of a faint undulating wail carried down the long hallway.

In the aftermath, the freezing cold ebbed and the air returned back to the state that it had been in before. Her vision regained full clarity.

Walking over to the Imperator's body, Rayden cleaned her

blades off on his luxuriant silken garb and placed the weapons back to rest at her waist. She then walked back over to where the Imperator's head had rolled.

Leaning over and grabbing onto a fistful of the Imperator's dark, curling locks of hair, Rayden lifted the head up from the ground. Making her way to the other end of the hallway, she exited through the tunnel entrance and continued back through to the underground cavern.

Carrying the head of one of the most powerful rulers she had ever encountered, a wide array of thoughts raced through her mind.

A sorcerer's summons had called her across land and sea and pitted her against the might of a powerful empire. Sparking a brushfire of resistance, her indomitable will had seen all of it come to ruin.

The shackles of bondage had been lifted from thousands upon thousands, but thousands upon thousands of others now faced great uncertainty.

Rayden knew that she could not relent in the aftermath of the Teveren ruler's overthrow. Chaos could not be allowed to flood into the void left by the fall of the Imperator.

Taking a deep breath, she reached the end of the tunnel and entered the chamber with the pit. Making her way back up the stairs to the temple above, she saw Dreaghen standing with the warriors that she had assigned to aid and watch over him.

All of their gazes riveted to the grisly object held in her right hand.

"To think that he thought himself a god," Rayden commented aloud, looking back to eye the huge golden statue that bore the same likeness as the head she clutched in her right hand.

"A fool in the end, brought to utter ruin," Dreaghen stated in response, somber in tone. "But only because some chose to confront his wickedness, such as you and all who took the fight to their evil."

"It had to be done," Rayden said. "All men and women must reign over their own lives ... and never become slaves to others."

"I fear that struggle will be much longer than we have years to live," Dreaghen lamented.

"Maybe so," Rayden replied. "But it does not mean we fail to act and do what we can in the time we have."

"You certainly did not fail, Rayden," Dreaghen praised her, a smile coming to his face.

"Come, you bedraggled rogue," she replied, returning the smile. "We will leave this foul place behind and let the others know that what we set out to do is now completed."

"Time for some food, drink, and rest," he said.

"Long overdue for you, my friend," Rayden said. "I may indulge again in the great baths of this city."

"I would like that as well," Dreaghen said in a wistful manner. "But tonight is for celebrating. There will be time enough for bathing and the reckoning of other things."

Rayden, Dreaghen, and the other warriors walked through the temple sanctuary.

Clear skies and the grandeur of a setting sun greeted them outside. Astonished, Rayden could not see a wisp of the thick, gray masses that had blanketed the heavens when she had entered the temple.

"The last remnants of the dark sun's dawn have dissipated," Dreaghen remarked, squinting in the sunset's golden light. He glanced down at the disfigured head in Rayden's hand. "Likely after you slew that wretch."

Rayden basked for a moment in the rays caressing her face. The undead throngs outside the city remained to be dealt with, but she knew in her heart that the ultimate victory had been won.

Descending the steps of the temple, Rayden did not cast so much as a single glance back in its direction.

CHAPTER 15

Rayden knew where to find them.

With the first violet hues of dusk settling across the city, Rayden's footsteps sank into the soft grass, the lush green blades brushing against her ankles. No other humans trod within the secluded expanse and a welcome quiet held dominion.

Continuing forward, Rayden took slow steps, soaking in the tranquil atmosphere, an oasis within a sea of tension and uncertainty. All around the cultivated, well-tended garden, a restive populace wondered about the intentions of the foreign horde holding possession of their city.

Deep within the extensive private garden of the Imperator, in the midst of marble statues, exquisite fountains, clear pools, and bountiful floral displays, Rayden eyed the darting lights with a smile.

Glad that the little creatures had not yet departed, Rayden walked toward the faeries. The diminutive beings flitted about her, exhibiting a playful, carefree manner.

"Celebrating life and a triumph over the things of darkness." Muirithesos' voice came from the midst of a sea of flowers, a living mosaic vivid and rich in hues.

With twilight beginning to take hold, little time remained to appreciate the abundant colors so meticulously arranged.

"It is astonishing how such depraved wickedness could maintain such a place of beauty," Muirithesos continued, stepping out of the flowers.

"Many great evils in the world maintain an appearance pleasing to the eye," Rayden replied. "Sometimes even taking the guise of a creature of light."

"That is true," Muirithesos acknowledged, drawing to a halt just a step to the front of Rayden.

"I had hoped to find you here," Rayden said. "There were no other places in the city that I would think suitable. The public places are full of my kind, and tonight there will be revelry and lots of drinking, among other things."

"This is the only place we could go, inside the walls," the faerie queen stated. "I did not wish to leave until I was certain that we are no longer needed. I watched the skies clear and knew what had happened, but I needed to hear from you that it is over."

"I do not think there are any more unwelcome surprises that the Imperator set in place," Rayden told her. "Our warriors have been all over the city and nothing has erupted among the Teveren people."

"We have sensed nothing to be concerned of," Muirithesos stated. "I have dispersed many of my own across the city, but they have found nothing troublesome, at least of a magical nature."

"Then you need not delay your return to the Mist Vale any longer," Rayden told the queen with a smile. "I am certain you do not wish to remain any longer than necessary in this city."

A bright smile lit the face of the queen.

"No, I wish to return as soon as we can," Muirithesos told Rayden. "Though we may scour the woods around the Mist Vale, to rid it of our adversaries."

Rayden thought of the malevolent creatures that had stalked her along the river.

"I would think their presence so close to be unwelcome

too," Rayden replied.

"It is long past the time we swept them from the lands on our borders," the queen said. Her grin broadened. "I think a human warrior that I count as a friend has had an influence upon me."

Rayden did not know what to say at first in response to the declaration. With their clandestine nature, the fae rarely established any kind of regular contact with a human, much less claimed one to be a friend.

"I am honored, deeply so," Rayden responded at last, giving the queen a low bow of her head.

"Your actions speak clearer than any words," Muirithesos said. "We know you helped to spare the people of this city a bloodbath. The eyes of my kind have been observing everywhere within the walls. The restraint of your people has been astonishing."

The queen then extended Rayden a bow.

"I am just a woman," Rayden said, uncomfortable at the gesture.

"I must give you a little mild admonishment ... as a friend should," the queen replied, her face taking on a solemn countenance. "You are not ... just ... a woman. You are a woman who embodies the potential of humans, both women and men, at a level rarely seen. This entire world would change for the better if more of your kind acted with such harmony of mind, heart, and soul."

"You honor me with such words, but I merely seek to live in accord with the voice that speaks from within," Rayden replied, humbled at the high praise from the faerie queen. "The path I take is one that any can travel, if they listen to the voice that speaks from inside all living beings."

"You have chosen your path, again and again, through acts of will," Muirithesos stated. "It is more than a matter of listening.

A choice must also be made. Every man and woman could choose the same path as you, if they so desired, but so few do."

"We each choose our path, every day that we breathe," Rayden responded.

"Yes, we do," the queen replied, a thoughtful expression manifesting upon her face. "Both faerie kind and human."

"Maybe one day we can all live in the open together, in peace," Rayden said, her gaze taking in the lights darting and gliding through the foliage around them.

"It is wonderful dream that I wish with my heart will come to pass one day," the queen replied after a moment.

"Let us both carry that dream forward with us," Rayden stated.

"Know that you will be welcome always in the Mist Vale," Muirithesos declared. "Know also that I will do what I can to aid you, should you ever have need of it."

"You have my deepest gratitude, Queen Muirithesos," Rayden said to the queen in a lower voice, filled with reverence and respect. "If I can ever be of help to you, or your kind, do not hesitate to send for me."

Wings beating fast, Muirithesos lifted from the ground, rising to eye level with Rayden.

"I will," the faerie queen said. She extended her arm in the manner of a warrior's embrace and a smile broadened on her face. "I wish to bid you well, in the manner of human warriors who are friends.

Though Rayden's hand engulfed the faerie queen's narrow arm, and Muirithesos' own hand could only clutch a small patch of skin on Rayden's forearm, the two executed a warrior's forearm clasp.

"Until we meet again," Rayden stated when they had released their grasps.

"Yes, until we meet again," Muirithesos replied, smiling

again.

Rayden gave the queen one more bow of her head before turning to depart. With her heart uplifted, she started back the way that she had come.

All around, many other faeries flitted about her, shadowing her path. Continuing through the garden, Rayden welcomed their company and knew that few humans ever witnessed such close displays.

Several drew near enough that Rayden could discern the different types among them. From those like Muirithesos to others no larger and no less delicate than a butterfly in appearance, the faeries delighted Rayden.

Approaching the edge of the gardens, Rayden could not see any more lights in the air around her. She knew what the absence of the lights meant.

Coming to a stop, Rayden turned around and waited, looking to the air above the gardens.

A violet hue permeating the lush expanse, a faint light clung to the skies, the last sigh of day before the coming of night.

In a vast, swirling flock of bright lights, the faeries rose high into the air and then sped off toward the north. Rayden watched until the mass of lights reduced into twinkling little specks and then vanished from sight.

Muirithesos and her kind were headed home.

With only the light of stars and the moon to see by, Rayden strode across the soft grass, making her way out of the gardens.

***

Not all acts of violence could be prevented when the warriors of the north had poured into the Imperial City, but no great massacre took place. Most within the city's poorer sections remained unharmed.

The tribes secured all the walls and gates of the city for

the time being, keeping them closed. Outside the walls, thick columns of smoke coiled toward the skies.

Thousands of corpses in massive heaps fueled the fires burning all around the city, out in the open ground beyond the walls.

Prior to the clearing of the skies when dusk approached, the undead surrounding the city had simply dropped in place. Many eyewitnesses had reported multitudes of dark shapes rising from the collapsed undead and heading skyward, before fading from sight.

Rayden determined that the phenomenon had taken place somewhere around the time that she had beheaded the Imperator. Dreaghen had reinforced her thoughts on the matter, surmising that the lesser fell spirits were tied to a much greater one inhabiting the body of the Imperator.

The absence of Marus' forces following the rising of the corpses had also been explained.

A grisly discovery had been made when the corpses had been piled together for burning, the morning after the fall of the city. A large number of Teveren soldiers and many from the Alettani and Sarrimena were found among the bodies ringing the city on the outside.

Teveren stragglers brought with them horrific tales of an undead horde rolling across the camp of Marus. Most of the Teverens within had been slain, in addition to many of their tribal allies. A remnant of the Alettani and Sarrimena contingents had escaped the slaughter on horseback and fled north.

The corpses of the slain had then been resurrected through the power of the dark sorcery, before leaving the camp to join the revenant host encircling the Imperial City.

The macabre stories illustrated the overwhelming threat presented by the dark sun that the Imperator's sorcerers had conjured. The dead would have continued to increase in number and the living would have been overrun.

After an extended tribal council, the warriors of the tribes largely pulled back to the northern area of the city. Only the walls and gates of the other areas remained manned, with movement between them easy enough along the top walkways and interior passages of the city walls.

Hesitant and fearful, the people dwelling in most sectors of the city began emerging after the morning fog had lifted. Though few resumed their full daily routines, perhaps unsure of the intent of the northern hordes, a kind of order began to form among them.

Many who had spoken for the poorer sections prior to the city's fall presented themselves to the tribal chieftains. It did not take long for them to begin acting as emissaries between the Teverens and the city's conquerors.

Satiating the hunger for loot and reward after the hard struggle and arduous journey, the tribal chieftains let all of the warriors know that the property of the Imperator and most of the wealthy nobles stood forfeit; to be gathered up and divided among all the tribes.

A few fires went up after the warriors descended on the Imperial palace and the wealthier section of the city. Given three days to indulge themselves, the warriors pillaged more coins, jewels, and other valuables than they could carry back to their homelands.

Numerous men and women of high rank found hiding were dragged into the sunlight and taken into confinement, many of them in the holding cells below the arena that only recently contained those condemned to violent deaths.

***

In the aftermath of the tremendous victory, Rayden's first thoughts turned to her dearest friends and companions.

After some extended searching, she found Hamilcar in the care of Annocrates. Both had managed to get through the harrowing cascade of events mostly unscathed, save for some minor cuts and bruises.

Seeing the two unharmed brought Rayden great joy along with some needed peace of mind.

Many of the Gessa had fallen during the fighting, but Alcedan, Erethea, and many others that Rayden knew well had survived. Yet for every reunion that she could celebrate, she discovered a loss that she would mourn in the days to come.

Bringing a broad smile to her face, Rayden found Ammanus in the company of Crassor, Doros, and Polybius. She could see the closer bond among the latter three that had been forged during their journey to the Imperial City and the time spent within its walls.

Knowing that Ammanus was in good, trusted company, she had little to worry over beyond the possibility of his wayward mouth garnering him a few lumps and bruises.

Having no desire to partake in the looting and pillaging taking place in the wealthier sectors of the city, Rayden spent most of the following days making certain that the children and infants found on the Imperial palace grounds were safe and cared for. Several of the children took a great liking to Rayden, and she took a keen interest in making certain that they would be left in a stable, protective situation when the time came for her to depart the city.

At last, desiring some time to herself, Rayden took leave to revisit the massive complex of baths and pools that Polybius had first taken her through.

This time, no smoke columns rose into the sky above the largest buildings. Nor were there any servants taking up coins at the entrance.

Men, women, and even a few children moved freely in and

out of the complex. Walking toward the buildings holding the various kinds of baths, Rayden watched many people wading in the large pool beyond the main entrance.

A few men, by the looks of them warriors from the northern tribes, hailed Rayden as she passed. Acknowledging them in kind, she did not slow her gait.

Inside the main building complex, she made her way past the sprawling courtyard where she had wrestled the Teveren woman Ingassa. Rayden wondered how Ingassa had fared following the takeover of the city. The lack of an answer brought a bittersweet, melancholic mood over Rayden.

Continuing onward, she entered the main baths. Without anyone tending them, all of the baths proved tepid.

Rayden opted to go into the chamber where she remembered the water being heated enough to require some time for acclimation.

Easing down into one of the small circular pools ringed with steps, Rayden took a seat and relished the light, relaxing embrace of the water. Though a veil of mist no longer filled the long, capacious chamber with its stout columns, the sunlight flooding through the windows high above gave the space its own mystique.

The banter of others echoed throughout the chamber, but Rayden remained content to have one of the pools to herself. After resting for a while, she got out of the water and made her way outside.

Having not gotten a chance to try the outer pool during the first time that she had visited, Rayden entered the waist-high water and made her way to a vacant area of the expansive space.

Unlike the Teverens she had witnessed, Rayden took to swimming about the clear waters. Taking an easy pace, she went under the surface often, reveling in the encompassing waters.

Then, she floated on her back, gazing toward the bright

blue skies and the white clouds drifting through them. With her ears under the waterline, what little sound reached her became muffled.

After a few moments, it seemed that the only things existing in the entire world were the skies and Rayden. She could have been there for a few heartbeats or several days, for such was the timeless sensation that overcame her.

The weightless feeling in the water took away a sense of space, until at last Rayden perceived that only her consciousness remained, beholding the sunlit heavens.

Rayden believed that she could ascend into the skies in that moment. Everything filling her vision appeared to be a part of her, and she a part of it.

A distant part of her mind told her that she had drawn close to a profound revelation. All fears and concerns fled, and she imagined them being whisked off in the presence of some unseen benefactor that confided with her spirit.

Then, she doubted whether the notion came from her imagination.

In that state, Rayden communed with something that transcended the entire world and the rules governing it. Seeing nothing other than the skies and hearing not a single spoken word, she had the sensation of being healed in the most vulnerable, essential part of her spirit.

At long last, her intimate communion came to an end and she roused herself enough to walk out of the pool. Letting the water drip from her body and allowing the sun to dry the rest, she donned her tunic and high-laced sandals before leaving the bath complex.

A dream-like state still lingered in her mind when she passed through the entryway to the baths. A renewed spirit dwelling within, Rayden entered the streets once more.

**

Strolling through the city later that afternoon, Rayden came upon the tavern where Stramma and his comrades had conducted their nefarious activities. Their criminal mischief seemed so petty in light of the horrors befalling the city in recent days.

Operating once more, most of the tables in the establishment had been filled with patrons. The scent of roasted meat wafted through the air, a succulent aroma that tempted Rayden at once.

Looking up to see Rayden entering, Stramma's eyes widened. Striding up to his table, she took the one chair that remained unoccupied.

At a glance from Stramma, the others who had been sitting with him got up and left.

"You are back," Stramma stated. "So much has happened since I last saw you."

"The Imperator has fallen, but the city need not descend into chaos," Rayden replied.

"No, some order must remain," Stramma responded, before looking up as one of the women serving the patrons approached.

"What will you have tonight?" she asked. "Some things are a little scarcer. It will take time to replenish, even if order holds."

"Just some wine," Rayden replied.

"Thankfully, we still have some, though I hope we can get more soon," she remarked, heading away to get Rayden a cup.

After the brief interruption, Stramma resumed, "The word that I hear is that some who the Imperial Council deemed rabble rousers, because they spoke in the interests of those with little means, have come forth to return us to the days when no Imperator was recognized. The days when this was called the Eternal City. The past is the present again. Maybe there is something eternal about that."

"A promising tiding," Rayden said. "But until then, those such as you can keep this city from crumbling."

"We are doing that," Stramma told her. "We know our

neighbors and now is not the time to think of business concerns."

"There may indeed be something honorable in you," Rayden exclaimed, grinning.

"Seeing this city under attack ... and then realizing that the attack liberated us from a tyrant ... a lot passes through your mind," Stramma stated, exhibiting a serious look within his eyes.

"As it should," Rayden said. "All of you dwelled in the shadow of a great evil."

"One that raised corpses from the tombs," Stramma said, a glint of fear passing through his eyes at the mention.

"Then you know what is at stake, and why this is a fragile time ... if there is to be something different ahead," Rayden told him.

"I do," he replied. "And I might try to step forward and take a more formal position, now that the previous order has fallen."

"There will be plenty of new opportunities," Rayden said. "But I beseech you to help keep order, and do not allow rogues to prey upon the people while this chaos is being wrangled."

"I never thought I would see the day when I was approached to help keep order," Stramma replied to her, chuckling and shaking his head.

The serving woman returned with wine for Rayden, setting an earthenware cup down before her. Raising the cup to her lips, Rayden found the wine to be much thinner in nature, heavily watered down from what she had imbibed there before.

"We have to make what we have last until trade is flowing once more," Stramma said. "Then we can boast of what we serve, once more."

"Which is where you, and others like you, can make sure trade has a faster chance to return to what you knew before," Rayden replied, before taking a draught from her cup.

Stramma looked her in the eyes and said nothing for several moments.

"You are not Alettani, are you," Stramma stated.

Rayden grinned and shook her head. "I once called the lands of the Gessa my home."

"You are one of our conquerors, then," Stramma replied.

"You could say that," Rayden said, the grin remaining.

Taking another drink, she eyed a man pulling a woman up the staircase at the back. Both laughing, their intent stood clear.

"We endured less than I thought we would, when the barbarians took the city," Stramma said. Eyeing Rayden, he then added, in the way of a correction, "Those of the north ... I mean."

"We did what we could to avoid unnecessary bloodshed," Rayden said. "The northern part of the city held plenty of reward for our warriors. Otherwise it would have been much worse."

"I wish I could have taken part in the pillaging of some of those homes," Stramma replied, laughing. "Those bastards amassed tremendous wealth."

"There were more than enough spoils to go around," Rayden said.

"What of those on the Imperial Council and others of the highest levels?" Stramma asked.

"Those found have been rounded up and are held in cages that once held the beasts, prisoners, and fighters intended for the arena," she answered.

"Such irony," Stramma commented, smiling.

"Often it is that way," Rayden said, emptying her cup. Raising it, she signaled to the serving woman for some more.

After the serving woman had poured her vessel full to the brim, Rayden watched the man and woman who had gone upstairs return back to the main tavern room. Looking a little disheveled and sleepy, they both had relaxed grins on their faces.

Rayden turned her eyes back to Stramma. The last time she had visited, she never would have entertained the notion now taking hold in her mind.

This time, she saw a different man sitting before her, a man changing for the better after enduring the harrowing events of the past days. Stramma now had her respect, which made him acceptable for the need at hand.

Standing, Rayden walked over to Stramma and gazed down at him. Another kind of hunger beckoned from within her, impatient and fervent.

"Is there more than one room above us?" she asked him in a low voice.

After a moment's hesitation, he replied, with a hint of confusion on his face, "Yes, a couple."

Though slight, the look in his eyes carried an unmistakable trace of nervousness. She could tell Stramma was not used to being approached so assertively.

"You are fortunate you proved yourself to have some honor, in having an intent to help keep order," Rayden said. "I can already see it reflected around this place and in the street outside."

"Why is that?" Stramma asked.

"Because, otherwise, I would have left after drinking my wine," Rayden said, a grin dancing about her lips. "I do not spend more time than I must with those who have no honor. As it is, I have a need for some release and intend on one more conquest of a Teveren."

Before Stramma could say a word, Rayden seized him by the wrist and hauled him up to his feet. Turning, she tugged him toward the back wall where the staircase led upward.

Voices lowered throughout the tavern as patrons watched Stramma being pulled upstairs by the tall, blond-haired barbarian woman. She all but dragged him up the final two steps.

Once atop the staircase, Rayden proceeded through an open door into a small room, keeping her hold firm upon Stramma. A straw-stuffed mattress lay upon the ground.

Letting go of Stramma, she pulled a curtain over the

entrance, closing off the room.

"What ... is this?" Stramma asked, sounding confused.

"No more talking," Rayden told him, a different kind of fire kindling within. "Are you willing to be my spoils of war?"

"Yes, I am," he replied, a husky, eager undercurrent to his voice.

Turning, Rayden lifted his tunic off. Undoing his loincloth, she left him standing naked before her.

Grinning, she shoved him back onto the mattress and leaned over, taking off her sandals. Shedding her own cloths and setting them to the side, Rayden climbed up on Stramma and straddled him.

Looking down, Rayden declared, "It has been a long journey, and I have almost been killed many times. But I am yet alive ... and now is a moment to live."

Lowering, Rayden covered his mouth with hers. Their tongues intertwined, hers driving deeper and probing with a great hunger. Stramma's arousal pressing against her, she guided him in before starting to ride the man in an escalating rhythm.

Giving herself free rein, Rayden built up a furious pace, abandoning all worries and cares. Waves of heat rippled through her body. More than once she reached a crescendo, crying out in sheer ecstasy.

Beneath her, Stramma groaned and gasped. A couple of times he attempted to change their position, but Rayden grabbed his wrists and pinned him in place both times.

Succumbing to her desires, he remained in place on his back.

After a long while, satiated and galvanized, Rayden changed her rhythm. Her faster pace enabled Stramma to draw closer to his finish, though she reached down and made certain that he concluded himself outside of her body.

Sagging back on the mattress, the sweat coated Teveren

looked thoroughly spent.

Only then did Rayden climb off from Stramma. Donning her footwear and cloths, she smiled down at him. His eyelids looked heavier by the moment, and she knew that he would not stay awake for long.

"After everything that I have gone through, I needed that," Rayden declared aloud, watching the exhausted man's eyes flutter shut.

After smiling at the slumbering man once more, she left the room.

Descending the stairs, Rayden strode through the midst of the tavern. Grinning at the expressions on the faces of many patrons looking toward her, she proceeded outside and started back for the northern sector of the city.

A content feeling encompassed her, one that did not just come from her long-overdue physical release.

In her heart, Rayden had full confidence that Stramma would do his part to hold order in the streets.

***

Casting a shadow over the relaxation and rest that Rayden had begun to allow herself in the aftermath of the city's taking, word arrived that even more cells holding children had been discovered in the bowels of the palace complex.

Haggard and starved, the children were given food at once. Then, they were taken away to be cleaned.

The discovery demonstrated the magnitude of the evil that had been occurring within the shadows under the Imperator's reign. Beneath the veneer of wealth and luxurious opulence, great wickedness had thrived.

The masses in the city had no true idea of what had been taking place, or they would have risen up in fury. The powerful had kept their abominations hidden, reduced to dark murmurs and shadowy rumors passing along the fringes.

Exposed to the light, the vile crimes that the most powerful had been a part of demanded justice. No longer would affluence and status shield the transgressors of humanity itself.

After seeing to the children, Rayden gathered up a number of warriors and sought out Alcedan and the other chieftains.

***

Thoughts of the multitude of children freed from the depths of the palace invoked a simmering rage inside Rayden. Despite the terror that they had suffered, those children had been the fortunate ones.

Whether having their blood spilled upon dark altars, flesh given over to the voracious fires of ritual ceremonies, or bodies still drawing breath thrown to beasts, so many others had been sacrificed to increase the power of the Imperator and the Teveren Empire.

Rayden recalled the sheer opulence and wanton indulgence that she had witnessed during the evenings that she had spent among the high-born Teverens.

Gorging themselves, the influential men and women had induced vomiting just so they could consume more of the exotic fares served to them.

Taking hold of slaves, the wealthy Teverens had satisfied their lusts, holding the power of life and death over the subservient men and women. All of the slaves knew that torture or death loomed if they did not acquiesce to the debauchery and raw violations of their bodies.

Many of them murderers who would never be thrown into the arena, the wealthiest among the Teverens lived through their days far above the reach of justice. Delighting in the most depraved cruelties, they had exercised power for its own sake.

Memories of eels coiling about a hapless victim and another

man being flayed alive for sheer entertainment could never be expelled from Rayden's mind.

Now, soiled, tattered, and bruised, many of those who once held great power, influence, and wealth had been dragged before Rayden and the other leaders of high rank among the tribal masses.

No longer adorned with jewels, fine clothing, facial makeup, or elaborate, lofty hairstyles, the high-born women no longer carried the haughty arrogance that Rayden had witnessed numerous times in the city.

The men no longer presented a prideful bearing. Downcast and haunted in expression, most could not even meet the eyes of their captors.

After extended deliberations, involving witness from many who had just been liberated from the shackles of bondage, a large number of them were released into the streets.

Without a single coin in their pocket, and all of their property seized, each would be made to endure the life of the beggars that they had once mocked and derided.

Like sheep cast among ravenous wolves, most would not last long on their own, receiving a fair recompense for the sorrow, misery, and death they had brought to so many others.

Only a scant few among the high-born were spared the trial of the streets.

With former slaves willing to step forth and testify to their fairness and kindness, the handful were set free to return to their property, after making significant restitution to their previous servants. All were made to give a solemn oath to their gods that they would never again accept someone in bondage to serve them.

A final group remained.

The most cruel, sadistic, and depraved among the Teveren nobles were set aside to receive the justice that their wickedness demanded.

Among their number were Sulpinnio Onnidaccus, Desrinnia, and many others from the first feast that Rayden had attended.

A few sobbed and started to beg for mercy, but Rayden knew that they only sought to save themselves. Others glared with defiance, the looks in their eyes showing that they stood entirely capable of the same atrocities that now doomed them.

More than one tribal warrior lamented that all the beasts had been set free during the fighting against the Imperator's undead multitudes. Rayden could not blame them for wanting to hurl the miscreants to lions, bears, hyenas, and other ferocious predators, but she took great joy from the knowledge that the animals had been set free.

No longer did they have to endure an internment that could only end through their violent death on the sands before blood lusting onlookers.

Warriors and newly freed slaves alike herded the condemned throng into the arena. Shoved, prodded, and at times kicked or punched, the former masters and mistresses now experienced a powerless, defenseless state of being.

Rayden walked along with the multitude, harboring no pity for those who had engaged in acts of extreme brutality and depravity upon fellow humans kept in bondage. Some of the former nobles continued to rage and curse, but most begged and pleaded, putting on facades of sorrow and contrition.

Their cries falling upon the ears of those that they had violated and victimized repeatedly, many for years on end, the once-arrogant patricians received spit in the face and hard blows in return. Rayden did not stop the assaults, allowing the transgressors to reap the bitter harvest that they had sown.

One young woman from the group of former slaves had to be pulled back after raking her fingernails deep across the face of an older man among the condemned. Leaving the left side of his face shredded and bleeding profusely, she would have clawed him to death right there, had she not been restrained.

Rayden could only imagine the kind of horrors that the young woman had been subjected to at the older man's hands to invoke such a virulent response.

The most wicked and cruel of the Teveren high-born were in a bloodied, battered state when they finally reached the sands of the arena.

Rayden eyed the prominent, demarcated areas of seating low in the arena, where those of greatest stature, wealth, and influence within Teveren society had been seated during arena events. She knew that every one of the individuals now standing upon the sands had taken great pleasure from that area at the grand spectacles of death carried out on the arena sands.

Looking at them, Rayden wondered about the kinds of thoughts now running through their minds. For the first time in their lives, they experienced the perspective of those who had been condemned to die upon the sands.

Rayden could only imagine how many times the men and women before her had relished, cheered, savored, and taken joy from the horrific suffering incurred by so many. A large number of those unfortunates had simply been disobedient slaves, or followers of another deity who had refused to venerate the Imperator's claimed divinity.

She thought of the two priests who had maintained a calm demeanor all throughout their ordeal in the arena, in contrast to the blubbering, shrieking cluster now gathered in the middle of the sands.

The priests, like those brought into the arena with them, had been innocent of any true crimes.

The high-born on the sands merited every last speck of what now loomed before them.

The former slaves were held back by the tribal warriors. The young woman who had clawed the older man's face kept crying out, asking why the warriors blocked her from the man who had tormented her for years.

She would have only a few moments to wait.

Alcedan stepped forward and raised his voice.

"I call forth a Teveren, so there is no mistake about the judgment taking place," Alcedan proclaimed, his words echoing throughout the empty rows of seats all around. "Eddarinias, step forward."

At the invitation, a Teveren man of about middle age stepped forward from the crowd behind the line of tribal warriors. A somber look on his face, Eddarinias nodded to Alcedan and came to a stop facing the condemned patricians.

Many men and women among the former nobles began cursing the Teveren. Several accused him of being a traitor.

During those moments, the masks of sorrow fell from their faces and the monsters beneath showed their true countenances to all.

"You who stand in the midst of the arena," the Teveren proclaimed, ignoring their outbursts. "Where are your gold and jewels now? Where is your authority now? You, who took regular pleasure in cruelty and gave no mercy when your victims pleaded ... where is your power now?

"You do not deserve to be deemed human any longer. You are less than beasts. You are things of malice and the abyss is your true home. Receive your recompense at the hands of those you willingly harmed."

At his final words, a number of warriors walked up to him, each carrying many weapons. Daggers, Teveren swords and spears, cudgels, and short-hafted axes were placed down on the sands around Eddarinias.

The warriors stepped away as the line of warriors blocking

the former slaves parted and moved to the sides.

"Carry out the justice that each of these monsters deserves!" the Teveren cried out to the former slaves. "Vengeance is yours!"

Many of the men and women in the throng exhibited some hesitancy at first, but full realization came to them after a few moments. Those who had been subjected to torture and grave violations at the hands of their former masters and mistresses charged across the sand.

Many picked up weapons of their choice, while others continued forward barehanded.

Cries and shrieks filling the air, the execution unfolded. Blood poured into the sands.

Rayden took no pleasure in the savage frenzy, but she bore witness without pity, knowing that the Teveren high-born had meted out far more suffering to their victims than anything they could incur now.

The young woman who had clawed the face of her former master resumed her grisly effort, tearing his face to ribbons and leaving it unrecognizable when she finally ceased. The woman left the dying man trembling in agony on the sands behind her, and the look on her face told Rayden that a few of her inner burdens had been set free.

Though in a crude and brutal manner, she had held her violator to account.

Yet not all burdens had been lifted. The woman would carry many unseen scars throughout her life, long after her tormentor's death brought his momentary suffering on the sands to an end.

Nearby, a man pummeled a former noble to death, raining blow after blow into his face, even when it stood clear that life had fled the condemned man's body.

Screaming and held down by three men, Sulpinnio Onnidaccus received the experience of being skinned alive. Shuddering with each slow, methodical passage of the sharp blades applied to his skin, he was made to endure the excruciating suffering that he had meted out to so many of his own slaves.

Rayden held no sympathy for him either. She had been sickened to learn at the trial of how many victims he had skinned alive for the amusement and pleasure of his guests.

The monster deserved every single moment of the ongoing punishment.

Not even death intervened to give him the mercy of an early end to his suffering. Sulpinnio Onnidaccus lasted a long time before he took his final breath.

No cheers arose from those watching the mass execution. Solemn in mood, the tribal warriors looked on in a hushed silence.

At long last, the executions drew to an end. One by one, the former slaves walked away. Spattered in the blood of the dead patricians, they said nothing.

A deep silence permeated the arena. A tendril of wind whistled in Rayden's ears, like the whisper of a ghostly voice within a sepulcher.

Those among the former slaves with weapons discarded the gore-coated implements close to where the Teveren speaker continued to stand. Grave in expression, Eddarinias acknowledged each of them with a nod.

Rayden and the other warriors departed the sands in the wake of the Teverens, leaving behind a bountiful feast to fill the gullets of carrion birds.

CHAPTER 16

A few of the tribes did not tarry long before setting out for the north, beginning their journey home laden with abundant spoils from the sacking of the Imperial City.

The Gessa and a few of the other tribes chose to remain behind for a little while longer.

It would be some time before the other Teveren legions still in place elsewhere within the former empire could be recalled or shifted to a new location.

Having lost several entire legions in the recent fighting, the Teverens would no longer be able to keep their hold on several lands. A withdrawal loomed in many places, including the territory across the sea taken from the Kartajenians.

In the meantime, a new force had been assembled. About half the strength of a legion, it had been formed to safeguard the city and help maintain order.

Survivors of the legions that had been destroyed, a group of older men who had been former soldiers, and a small number of others with legion training comprised the city's new guard.

The city would have some time to recuperate. The Kartajenians might chafe at the desire to take the city for themselves, but they had incurred a devastating loss of their own in the storm that had reduced an entire fleet to wreckage.

By the time the Kartajenians could rebuild a large fleet, so could the Teverens, in addition to recalling some of their far-flung naval forces.

Over the ensuing days, fishing boats began heading into the river in greater numbers. Not long after, the first merchant vessels in quite some time started to appear along the wharves and quays near the riverside.

The Teveren city would once more be ruled over by a true council. Several men had been nominated by popular acclaim to fill the places on the council for the interim, until a proper process could determine its members.

All of the men coming from lower levels in Teveren society, the new council members would be guided by a far different mindset than the one that had led them to ruin.

"It shall be called the Eternal City again," the elderly man in white ceremonial robes stated to Alcedan, Rayden, and other leaders standing with them.

The declaration gladdened Rayden, confirming what she had heard from Stramma.

"We look forward to Teveren merchants coming into our lands," Alcedan replied. "They will be given safe passage and will benefit in new trade."

"We look forward to that as well," the elderly man stated, nodding to Alcedan. "Mutual benefit, and sincere friendship."

"Let not the fires of war sweep across Teveren and tribal lands again," Alcedan said.

"Agreed," the Teveren elder replied, giving a bow of his head to the Gessa chieftain.

Rayden found the look of the men culled to form the temporary council encouraging. None had a trace of the pompous conceit so prevalent among the higher born in the Imperator's society.

A few her own peers, and others even older than the elder

speaking for the council, the men had a stoic, determined air about them. Rayden knew that the people of the city would enjoy a rare kind of leadership for a time, the kind where values governed, rather than an accumulation of valuables, power, and influence.

At long last, the assemblage drew to an end, and the tribal leaders dispersed to get ready for the long-awaited departure.

Walking over to them, Rayden grinned at Ammanus, Doros, Annocrates, and Hamilcar. All had been standing nearby, waiting in patience for the gathering with the city's new leaders to conclude.

"A good day to begin our return!" Rayden declared.

"It will be wonderful to return home!" Annocrates exclaimed. "I have a building to finish and land to clear."

"I will be there to help," Hamilcar stated, smiling at Annocrates.

"I am counting on it," Annocrates replied, laughing and ruffling the boy's curly locks.

"Such work will be good for growing your muscles," Rayden told Hamilcar, smiling at the boy. "You might get as big as Alcedan."

"Really?" the boy replied with an excited look in his eyes.

"You are going to be a strong lad," Annocrates declared, looking down at Hamilcar and tousling his hair again.

Rayden smiled at the fatherly pride reflected in the eyes of Annocrates.

"As strong as Annocrates?" the boy asked, looking from Annocrates to Rayden.

"You never know," she answered, giving him a wink.

"I will be going where you go," Doros then declared.

"As will I," Ammanus stated. "I do not want to lose track of you again after what happened in Kartajen."

"Who knows? I may not go anywhere for a while after

returning north," Rayden replied, grinning at them.

"Then we will enjoy the north together," Ammanus replied. Smiling, he continued, "I have no desire to find myself rowing war galleys, and I have long wished to see the lands that you came from."

"Just be careful that your tongue does not get you into trouble of the kind that I cannot save you from," Rayden replied, laughing. "The women of the north do not suffer foolishness as easily as these lands."

"Some may find my tongue more than welcome," Ammanus riposted, a lascivious twinkle in his eyes.

"I swear, Ammanus, you test my boundaries at all times," Rayden responded, laughing in a carefree manner.

"It is good to hear you like this."

The distinctive voice brought Rayden's attention around at once.

"Ingassa!" Rayden exclaimed, eyes widening a little in surprise.

A few paces away stood the tall woman that Rayden had last seen in the courtyard of the vast bath complex in the city.

Her black locks pulled back into a massed bunch higher on her head, Ingassa wore a simple tunic belted at the waist. She carried a larger hide pouch on her back and had the look of someone about to take a journey.

"I am glad you had not left yet," Ingassa replied. "It took me some time to find you."

"For my part, I am glad to see you unharmed," Rayden said, her face exuding a genuine look of relief.

"Those taking the city rolled right over the tenements and left us to ourselves," Ingassa said. "I have given thanks to the gods ever since."

"I give them thanks too," Rayden responded.

Ingassa seemed to be on the verge of saying something and

hesitated.

"What silences your tongue?" Rayden asked, sensing the other woman's reticence.

"I ... know it is not proper for a Teveren to make a request under the circumstances," Ingassa stated in a low voice, casting brief glances at Rayden's companions. "But I came to ask if I can go with you to the north."

"And leave your home?" Rayden asked, surprised.

"There is nothing for me here," Ingassa said, a look of deep sadness creeping into her eyes. "My father died during the fighting in the city. Nothing touched him, but something seized him, and he collapsed. I believe it was his fear of what your tribes might do."

"I am so sorry," Rayden told her in a low voice filled with empathy.

"It is not your fault," Ingassa replied, her voice choking with emotion. "It is just that now I seek a chance at a new life. I have no desire to remain here."

"There is a large settlement on the lands of the Tega, of many who had once been slaves," Annocrates interjected. "You will find many Teverens among our number. All of us are making a new life. It is not an easy path, but you will find a life there, with many to help you."

"It sounds wonderful," Ingassa responded, wiping a few tears from her eyes. She then looked back to Rayden. A hopeful, eager look swelled within her gaze. "Perhaps I can train at arms too and become the warrior that I always dreamed myself to be."

"You will find none to get in your way," Rayden told Ingassa, stepping forward and laying her right hand on the woman's left shoulder.

"I knew you were not of the Alettani," Ingassa said, her lips spreading into a smile.

"You are not the first to say so," Rayden replied, chuckling.

"When I heard word of the blonde-haired she-devil that felled over a thousand Teveren soldiers, I knew who they spoke of," Ingassa replied.

"A thousand?" Rayden asked, laughing. "Is that what they say?"

"It is what they say," Ingassa stated.

"Do I throw bolts of lightning in their tales?" Rayden queried, continuing to laugh.

Ingassa laughed heartily. "I did not hear such claims, but I am sure that I did not hear every tale now being told across this city."

"I am just a woman on a long journey home," Rayden replied in a softer tone.

Perhaps sensing that Rayden spoke of something deeper, Ingassa said, "I hope you reach your destination."

A little sadness mingled with joy as Rayden gently patted Ingassa on the shoulder. A journey to the north loomed, and the journey of a lifetime continued.

"Travel with us, Ingassa," Rayden invited after a quiet moment passed.

"Thank you, Rayden," Ingassa replied, the glisten of tears manifesting again in her eyes.

Rayden looked around at the others and a grin spread on her face. "It is time to set out for the north! Let us not waste a moment longer!"

Jubilant expressions met Rayden's declaration. All who would be going north began to gather up the things they would be taking with them.

***

Passing beneath the same Eagle Gate that she had worked to open under harrowing conditions, Rayden took her first steps on the return to the north.

Outside the city walls, many Teverens could be seen laboring in removing the earthen ramparts raised by the northerners. A few long sections of the wall had been taken down already, including the one directly in the path of the road leading from the Eagle Gate.

Inviting Rayden forward, the way now stood clear.

Rayden glanced over her shoulder and eyed the walls and large gateway behind, pondering whether she would ever return to the Eternal City. If she ever did, a part of her wondered whether it would have the same grandeur as that day she had first set her eyes upon the sprawling colossus.

Rayden had come when the city stood in thrall to a powerful, growing evil. Now, she departed a city in peace, leaving the population with a new chance to avoid the mistakes of the past.

It would be up to them to see that a new Imperator did not rise again to plunge the Teverens into bloodshed, war, and the deep night of dark sorcery.

Rayden carried no spoils of war along with her. Rather, she walked in the company of her rewards.

Ammanus, Doros, Annocrates, and Hamilcar had survived all of the trials and dangers. So had Polybius and Crassor, and even Oressius, the former slave that had given her bread to take with her on the journey to the Mist Vale.

Also returning to the north with Rayden was Dreaghen.

The sorcerer now rode in the back of an ox-pulled wagon trundling along the grooves shaped by countless others along the Teveren roadway. Lying in a pile of fabrics pillaged from the city, he had a little extra cushioning from all the bumps and jostles of the wagon.

Reclusive and living in the wilderness, Dreaghen and the other sorcerers taken captive in the north had been easy prey for the Teverens hunting them. Only a handful, those that Rayden and the faeries had freed from the cells beneath the temple, would return to their homelands.

Rayden turned and proceeded back to the wagon where Dreaghen lay.

"My bones are going to be rattled all the way to Gessa lands," Dreaghen told her with an edge of grumpiness.

Cleaned and healed further, he looked far better than when she had unlocked his cell. Not ready to undertake a long march, Dreaghen would have to ride in the wagon, but he would recover from his horrific ordeal in time.

"I will accept that as recompense for all the times I wished I could lay my hands on you, and teach you a lesson or two about invading others dreams, startling people, and being evasive in answers," Rayden told the sorcerer, a lighthearted grin coming to her lips.

"I imagine I am lucky that you accept that," Dreaghen replied, looking to Rayden. "Or I believe I would find myself shaken and slapped a lot."

"If you only knew what I wanted to do at times," Rayden said, thinking of the many times her blood had boiled in regard to the sorcerer's enigmatic ways.

"Yet you are here and so am I, after all that has happened," Dreaghen said, a smile coming to his own face.

"There is that," Rayden replied to him with a smirk. "I suppose that you think that pardons you for your cryptic ways."

"Of all the great warriors in his world, you are known to show mercy more than others," Dreaghen said. Laughing, he added, "I am counting upon it."

"I suppose that you are," Rayden said, unable to stifle her own bout of laughter.

The sorcerer's face then grew serious. "You did it, Rayden. No other that I could have called upon from the tribes in the north could have weathered the storm that you have. I owe you a debt that I can never hope to repay."

"You owe me no debt," Rayden told him. "You and I both had to undertake this burden, with a great many others, or see everything descend into darkness."

"Wickedness fell, and the promise of a new day was unveiled," Dreaghen said.

"When shadows fall, the dominion of light reigns," Rayden told the sorcerer. After a pause, she added, "If only for a time in this world."

"May it be that it lasts a very long time for the Teverens," Dreaghen said.

"May it be so," Rayden said, echoing the sorcerer's goodwill toward the masses dwelling within the great city.

***

Late in the afternoon, Ammanus' voice, brimming with excitement, drew Rayden's attention.

"Now there is a sight that I did not expect to see in the heart of Teveren lands," Ammanus exclaimed, gesturing up toward the summit of a hill to their right.

Rayden looked in the direction that Ammanus indicated and set her eyes upon a sight that could not be mistaken.

Atop the hill stood a lion, a particular creature that Rayden knew well.

Mane flowing in the winds buffeting the hill, the noble creature gazed down upon her.

Coming up from behind the lion and joining the majestic beast at the hill's crown, three lionesses padded into sight. Striding up to the lion, the lionesses rubbed their heads against his, and then the trio turned their gazes toward the humans far below them.

Seeing one that had a tattered ear, Rayden knew at once where the lionesses had come from. She had first seen them on the sands of a blood-soaked arena, where they had been survivors of a grisly, vile exhibition.

Later, Rayden had witnessed them racing toward the gates of the city, after mauling and biting their way through a horde of undead.

A pure joy flooding Rayden's heart, a radiant smile spread across her face. Taking the vision in and cherishing every moment, her spirit soared.

"No Ammanus," Rayden replied in a low voice. "That is not a sight that I expected to see in Teveren lands ... but it is one that surpassed my hopes and attained a wish held within my heart ... not a common experience in an uncertain world such as this."

Ammanus looked at Rayden for a moment. She expected him to make some sort of humorous retort, but his expression grew serious.

"No, it is a very rare thing to attain a wish," he replied, his tone filled with uncharacteristic sincerity. No spark of jest undermined the look in his eyes as his gaze met hers. "But if anyone in this world has earned the right to have a wish granted by the gods, it is you, Rayden."

"Then the god that granted my wish knows of the deep gratitude I have in my heart for this moment," Rayden stated.

"I am sure that one of them ... or perhaps more than one ... favored you," Ammanus replied.

The lion had been a part of her journey from the outset. She had first set her eyes upon the creature in the Mystic Kingdom, caged and offered for sale.

The next encounter had been in the tent of a Teveren commander, across the Great Sea and far to the north, close to the border of tribal lands.

The creature had saved her life more than once against foes that had origins not of the material world. Rayden had no doubt that Dreaghen had guided the creature to her, but she also knew that the sorcerer had not controlled the lion against its will.

The lion had carried out its own volition, and it had demonstrated genuine affection in the aftermath of its interventions, not just once, but twice.

Too distant to embrace the lion a third time, Rayden could only behold the creature and take the special moment into her heart.

"He will always have a place in your heart," Ammanus said in a reverent tone. "I also know any lion would find something familiar in your heart, for you have the heart of one."

Rayden kept her eyes toward the lions on the hilltop. The vision represented a triumph for so many; for the lions themselves, for her friends, for all the people of the northern tribes, and for those freed of the evil of slavery and bondage.

For her, the vision stood a symbol for her own triumph in the part of her life journey that began when Dreaghen had called for her to return to the lands where she had grown to adulthood.

His mane continuing to billow in the winds, the lion turned at last and strode away, followed by the trio of lionesses.

Rayden experienced a little pang in her heart as they disappeared from sight.

"It would not surprise me at all if you were to see him again," Ammanus told her in a consoling timbre, a few moments after the lions had departed.

Rayden looked to her friend and smiled. The melancholic ache inside ebbed.

"It is a good way to bring this part of our journeys to an end, Ammanus," she declared to him. "You and I set out for Kartajen with that lion trapped within a cage. Now, we are setting out for the tribal lands with him free and no longer alone."

A radiant smile spreading across her face, Rayden looked around at Doros, Annocrates, Hamilcar, and, a little farther back from them, and still riding in a wagon, Dreaghen. She returned her gaze back to Ammanus.

"We are also free and blessed with new companions," Rayden told him.

"Where will our journeys take us next?" Ammanus asked. "Will they be taken together?"

"You never really know where the journey may lead," Rayden told him. "It is why you should take joy in the present moment. We are heading north together. That is all I can tell you."

"It is something I am grateful for," Ammanus replied.

"I am as well," Rayden replied, giving her friend a warm smile.

A long march lay ahead, and new challenges would rise in time, but for the moment a sense of calm and serenity filled Rayden's heart.

In witnessing the fall of shadows, Rayden had gained a glimpse of the dominion of light. For her, that was a reward in itself, a harbinger of a greater possible reality yet ahead.

Looking ahead and eyeing the edge of the horizon where the sky met the land, Rayden knew that she needed only to keep to the path that she traveled.

Something deep within Rayden's heart whispered that the path would lead her to a place where the dominion of light reigned in unending glory.

Hearkening to that gentle, inner voice, Rayden strode forward in a state of confidence and peace, traveling a path leading onward and upward.